To

Mireya

My favorite

& historia 8

te ily

IT'S NEWS TO ME

Olga Campos Benz

To Kevin Benz, my husband and the real life photojournalist who kept me sane while writing this book and who kept the tequila stocked while we navigated the crazy world of television news and to our daughters, Corazon Marissa and Allegra Carissa, whose beauty and names are the only similarities to the twins in this book.

Introduction

From out of nowhere, a painfully bright ray of sunshine peeks through cheap plastic window blinds, forcing Marissa to wake up. An excruciating pain behind her eyeballs extends all the way down to the back of her head. Marissa's hair feels as heavy as the solid lead vest the dental assistant puts over a patient before taking x-rays. Speaking of which…the taste in her mouth reminds Marissa of a street gutter in Guadalajara the day after a *Dies y Seis* celebration, but she sure doesn't feel like celebrating. Instead, her body aches from head to toe and she has this sudden urge to vomit. She sits up, trying to locate the nearest toilet or trashcan. Bad idea. The fast movement only makes the room spin out of control. Marissa hasn't felt this hungover and disoriented since her college binge drinking days.

She lays back down, hoping to collect her bearings, only to discover the rumpled king size bed and boringly beige room are completely unknown to her. *Where am I?* she nearly asks out loud as she looks down to see she has nothing on but a man's t-shirt. A series of additional questions begins to fill her throbbing head. *How much did I drink? What happened last night? Whose bed is this?* She hears her mother's words echo in the back of her mind. *Esto no se mira bien, mijita.* This doesn't look good, my dear!

Then Ken, looking freshly showered and shaved, enters the bedroom. He's good-looking, grinning and unbelievably sober. All

1

the things she is not at this moment. She's envious of his calm composure. *How can he not be hungover? How is it he's not upset, although his solid reputation as a photojournalist was shattered just mere hours ago? Men!*

With a jolt back to reality, it suddenly occurs to Marissa that she is under orders to meet the station's general manager at eight a.m. *Ay Dios mio! Oh my God! That's in exactly twenty minutes!* She jumps out of bed, no longer caring that she's wearing only a t-shirt or that she feels like crap and may heave. She darts past Ken on her way to the bathroom and leaps into the shower where she turns the water on full blast. It's freezing! But she knows she must suck it up and withstand the torturous ice-cold water if she's going to wash away the alcohol-induced fog she's under.

Marissa hears Ken's voice through the shower curtain asking seductively, "You need help scrubbing your back? Or any other hard to reach places?"

"No, thanks. I'm fine, but I will need a clean towel, some aspirin and some very strong black coffee," she shouts back over the full-force shower spray.

He laughs and answers, "I already have it waiting for you on a tray. Clean towels are hanging on the rack on the wall. I've also made you my special foolproof hangover cure. Just ignore the smell and drink the whole thing." Before leaving the bathroom, he adds, "Oh, and if you throw-up, you'll feel better afterward. And in case that happens, I left a new toothbrush for you by the sink. Don't be in such a rush. It takes exactly six minutes to get to the station from my apartment. You've got plenty of time."

Marissa hears the door to the bathroom close behind him as he leaves. She breathes a small sigh of relief as she absorbs his words. The water starts to warm up as it washes down her back, rinsing some of her anxieties down the drain with it. She scurries out of the shower, downs the aspirin and swallows Ken's special concoction and the black coffee in quick succession. *Ugh, swamp water,* she cringes. Wrapped in a towel, she heads to the bedroom on a mission to find her clothes.

How ironic that the "special outfit" she chose to impress the All Access News Network talent recruiter is going to be the same outfit she'll wear when learning her fate. She wonders if she should credit the dress for bringing her good luck or blame it for delivering bad news. One thing is for sure, getting dressed goes a lot faster than it took her to take her clothes off just a few hours ago...as best as she can remember.

As quickly as possible, she wipes away the caked mascara and liner smudged beneath her eyes and touches up her face using products from the small bag of cosmetics she carries with her at all times. Every anchor and reporter (especially the preening male species), carries a makeup bag to be sure they look their best before any live shot. That's not easy to do under a blazing Texas sun and 100-plus degree temperatures.

But Marissa would take wilting weather to this hungover state any day! Come to think of it, this is the first time she's reached into her bag of cosmetic tricks after a night of wild abandonment since... she can't remember when. No time to try to recall what happened last night. Also, no spare time to go home and change or apply fresh make-up until after this crucial meeting that starts in...TEN MINUTES! OMG! What the hell was she thinking?

Marissa grabs her purse and car keys off the coffee table next to an empty bottle of tequila as she rushes for the front door, only to have Ken scoop her up, crushing her attempt to move past him. He pulls her close to him and envelops her in a luscious kiss. Her body tingles from head to toe. Hazy images from the night before slowly start to seep into her head. She wishes she could linger on the oh-so-enjoyable moments and the sensuous activity in between, but she can't. Unfortunately, she doesn't have time for anything more than a two-second kiss. She pulls

3

herself away and dashes out the door to her car with barely a wave goodbye.

Ken is correct. It takes only six minutes to make it to the station's parking lot from his apartment. What he didn't mention is that you have to catch all the traffic lights, while going slightly faster than the posted speed limit, to make it there in record-breaking time. It's a miracle Marissa wasn't pulled over by cops running radar or that she didn't kill someone, or herself, on the road. Note to self: in the future avoid driving while hungover. It's just as bad—if not worse—than driving while intoxicated. It's sad to think that getting to the station on time might be her biggest accomplishment of the day but at this rate, she'll savor any small victory.

She forces herself to walk casually through the front door of the television station and head straight to the office of Patrick Stone, General Manager. As she makes her way down the hallway, she passes a few coworkers who blatantly go out of their way not to make eye contact or talk to her. *WTF? Do I have a contagious disease?* And then it hits her. After the fiasco that happened during yesterday's five o'clock newscast, she is now an outcast to be shunned by her colleagues. Here she is being summoned to the general manager's office and the pounding in her head is growing louder. It's a blaring symphony of nerves, adrenaline and last night's tequila shots all coming back to haunt her.

Trying to shake off the physical pain, she knows her professional fate and her future at KATX are waiting for her. Behind. That. Door.

The general manager's assistant sees Marissa, looks down at her watch and then picks up the phone saying, "Miss Cavelo just arrived… Okay. I will." She turns to Marissa and says in a steely, monotone voice, "Go right in." The assistant pushes a button on her desk and the door to Mr. Stone's office opens automatically. Marissa walks in with her shoulders back and her head held high, bracing herself for the worst and wondering if this is how an inmate feels as he moves toward his executioner.

No doubt, more than a few heads have rolled in this office. Patrick Stone sits behind his imposing desk, looking pompous and cold. Seated across from him is Executive Producer, Jan Ruther, who has a folder in her lap. Her look is stern and very focused, but Marissa can detect a slight hint of delight under her facade of authority. It's no secret that Ruther derives a sick pleasure from the discomfort of others. In this case, Marissa is surprised her discomfort doesn't have Jan up on Stone's desk, dancing her ass off!

Mr. Stone motions for her to sit down and is the first to speak. "Marissa, when we hired you, it was with certain…" he pauses and looks down at his neatly manicured nails, as if searching for the right words among the trimmed cuticles, "expectations…that you had the skills and talent to be a productive member of the KATX news team. It's a team that is known for its high standard of journalism, which has earned the trust of our viewers." He then asks, "Do you know why you have been summoned here this morning?"

With the throb of her hangover about to make her head explode, Marissa gets the eerie sense that the firing squad she is now facing is about to pull the trigger. With the way she's feeling at this very moment in her life, a bullet to the forehead would be a welcome relief.

One

Three Days Earlier

At 2:00 a.m., the first of three alarms that Marissa set, just a few hours earlier, blares in her ear. She stretches an arm to the bedside table and hits the button. Ten minutes later, the second alarm also goes off. This clock is on top of the dresser on the other side of her bedroom. Sleepwalking, she gets out of bed, walks over to the source of the offensive noise, slams her hand down on top of it and then glides back to her bed. Exactly ten minutes later, the third and final alarm goes off. This noisemaker is strategically perched by the sink in her bathroom—a good twenty feet away from her bed. She knows if she doesn't hit the off button quickly the neighbor next door will call the landlord to complain. Again!

This morning ritual is a physical and mental struggle that pushes her endurance levels. It is one of many challenges she faces whenever she's assigned to fill in as the morning anchor at KATX. She looks in the bathroom mirror and asks her reflection, "Why am I waking up in the middle of the night when other people my age are just getting home from a night of partying and fun?" Marrisa sighs with gratitude that the station rarely calls her to be the substitute morning anchor.

In this 24/7 news world, the morning shift has its pros and cons.

On the positive side, there's no traffic while driving to work at three a.m. and the coffee is always on. On the negative side, she has to force herself to go to bed extremely early the night before. Sleep deprivation plagues her for days afterwards. It also means she'll be putting in an extra-long day; the early morning anchor duties are in addition to her usual ten-hour workday.

Before heading out, Marissa checks her phone to see what's on her calendar. She freezes as she realizes what day it is—the television industry's version of Friday the 13th. Today is the day before the start of ratings, which means that in each market the station with the highest percentage of viewers gets to charge the highest rates for commercial airtime. As Marissa sleepily drives to the station, she reflects on what she will endure in the month ahead.

In an attempt to attract as many viewers as possible during the ratings months of February, May, July and November, stations will air "special assignments." These are news reports aimed at scaring the hell out of you, such as, "What's in Your Refrigerator Could Kill You." Other gimmicks to boost ratings include: sending the sappy weather guy into a wind tunnel to see if he can withstand eighty-five-mile per hour gusts (the answer is yes, but not without seeing his cheeks flap around from the intense velocity, like that of a Category Four hurricane), and human interest stories that "check in" on famous quintuplets/sextuplets/fill-in-the-number-of-multiple births. The multiples in their matching shirts, socks and pacifiers are guaranteed to make viewers feel fortunate not to have as many kids as the pathetic parents featured in these news stories.

A recent favorite has been "Dumpster Diving." The tease promises, "You'll be shocked to see what personal information we found in the garbage!" The promo shows some poor schmuck reporter crawling around on his or her hands and knees in a trash dumpster, going through personal records the bank or pharmacy staff has tossed—papers that should have been shredded to prevent identity theft and to protect a person's privacy.

Some stations count on their anchors' medical maladies. Male anchors have been known to invite audiences to join them for their vasectomies, prostate exams or cardio fitness tests. Their female counterparts have shared their mammograms, liposuctions and pregnancy-related 3D ultrasound experiences. Marissa knows that anchors are always willing to share such personal journeys, but she is continually surprised by doctors who have no problem allowing cameras inside their medical facilities to film procedures.

Marissa remembers the time at the start of a six o'clock newscast when viewers were promised a sneak peek at the station's new "live" truck at the end of the newscast. The "live" unit consisted of a van with a microwave dish mounted to its roof. It had taken months to design and nearly a year for its customized construction. The state of the art equipment on top and inside of the van was the latest in broadcast technology at the time, giving the station the edge to deliver breaking news first over the competition.

A news crew was assigned to drive the "live" van to a designated spot in the station parking lot where it would be parked and ready to be featured in the final moments of the newscast. Parking it was all the crew was required to do but at the last minute, the reporter remembered she had a "special" outfit that she desperately needed to pick up from the dry cleaners that would be closing at six.

"Please, please, pretty please just swing by there before we park the truck. It's right around the corner and it'll just take two seconds," she pleaded with the photographer.

Everybody knew he had a crush on the young reporter and would've eaten shards of glass if she had asked. "Oh, all right," he agreed and without hesitation, he headed to the dry cleaners and pulled into the drive-thru service lane.

In a split-second, he realized his mistake, but it was too late to do anything about it. The top of the new van was jammed under the dry cleaner's concrete canopy. The reporter was shrieking and crying, and the poor photographer only made it worse by driving forward and then putting the van in reverse. Over and over, back and forth, he tried to free the vehicle. Each time, he caused more damage to the equipment until finally, the van broke free from the canopy's grip. Its mast was broken and the crushed microwave dish dangled by a few wires from the roof. The photographer was fired and that poor reporter never did claim her dress from the dry cleaners.

At 3:30 a.m., Marissa pulls into the KATX parking lot. She has worked for the station for almost three years, and at twenty-eight, is one of the youngest members of the news team.

She was initially hired to be a General Assignments reporter, but being a Latina with an engaging personality quickly landed her in the anchor chair to deliver the noon and the occasional morning newscast. Although Marissa would like to believe she earned the coveted spot through her journalism and reporting, she believes the station's true motivation is to build a loyal viewership among the area's fast-growing Hispanic demographic. Still, the high-profile position always makes her sit up a little taller, with shoulders back and head held high. It actually feels good to be the first Latina to be featured in a weekday newscast.

However, her co-anchor, Melinda Bale, has made it clear that she doesn't consider Marissa to be worthy of occupying the chair next to her. Marissa is savvy enough to know that they don't have to be friends. All they have to do is convince viewers of their positive chemistry and camaraderie from twelve noon until twelve fifty-nine Monday through Friday.

Marissa makes her way into the station's break room in search of coffee, but from the burnt smell she's pretty sure the black sludge has probably been sitting there untouched since last night's ten p.m. newscast. She's glad she always carries those tubes of freeze-dried instant in her purse. It tastes like crap, but if she pours two of them into her cup of boiled water, she'll get enough caffeine in her to clear her head. She can seek out some real coffee between broadcasts.

She goes to her desk to check for stories to include in the newscast. She checks the Associated Press wires, a couple of popular websites, some of the statewide political blogs and competitor sites. No one in the broadcast business likes to admit it, but the best sources for TV news stories are other stations and the newspaper. Everyone likes to think what the anchors are presenting is unique, but truth is, a lot of what is reported is reproduced.

By 4:00 a.m. Marissa is hurriedly rewriting scripts, correcting others' spelling and grammatical errors and pushing herself to finish so she can apply her makeup and put her hair up in hot rollers.

It makes her laugh when people ask her if she has a private hairdresser or makeup artist. There's no help provided for getting camera-ready and certainly none for putting together a wardrobe. Marissa developed her sense of style when she was a teenager growing up in Houston, working at an upscale women's store. She also skims the latest fashion magazines when she's online or at the grocery store. The real challenge is creating a Nordstrom's look on a Target budget. But somehow, with a few knock off pieces, she makes it work.

Guests invited for in-studio interviews are urged to apply makeup at home. The station's makeup room is no bigger than a bathroom stall with one electric outlet and haphazardly installed fluorescent lights.

She does her hair and makeup in record time and goes to meet with the producers to go over the order of the show. If there is any breaking news, if any guests are scheduled or if anyone has canceled, she'll find out now with the clock ticking until the live broadcast airs.

The next two and a half hours will be filled with morning headlines, weather and traffic. What viewers see at four-thirty will be repeated at five-thirty and at six-thirty since no one watches the entire newscast. They know from research that viewers tune in while they're getting ready for their day ahead, so the early newscast is nothing more than background noise as people go about their morning routines before heading out the door. There will be the usual minor hiccups of misspelled words, the occasional wrong video and even a couple of factual errors until they transition to the network's morning newscast.

◇◇◇

After the morning show, Marissa wishes there was a quiet, comfortable dark place she could sneak off to for a nap. She knows she's not the only sleep-deprived staff member. Anyone who's looking for the early morning weather guy knows to check the parking lot where he'll be sleeping in the backseat of his tinted-window Honda Accord. Instead of a nap, she heads out for some breakfast and some drinkable dark roast coffee; then she returns to the station to start the whole routine all over again in preparation for the noon newscast.

She rewrites a couple of stories and fact checks them. Then she sets up a couple of on-set interviews for the rest of the week before looking at the community calendar for items to spotlight. Time flies, and before she knows it, it's ten o'clock. Everyone is busy working, but one desk is empty—not surprisingly—the desk of her noon co-anchor, Melinda Bale. Her work day is scheduled to start at eight a.m., but she rarely arrives before nine-forty-five; and since she tends to make life miserable for others, almost everybody is relieved that Melinda is always late.

She finally walks in at ten after ten, looking like she just woke up. *Are those pajamas she's wearing?* Marissa wonders.

Melinda heads straight to the makeshift dressing room to get ready. It will take Bale the next two hours to get herself camera-ready.

Her female coworkers know not to disturb Melinda while she's fixing her hair and makeup. The last woman who walked into the restroom while Bale was getting ready ran out less than thirty seconds later looking like she'd just seen a witch! Luckily, there are other women's restrooms in the building to be used while Melinda completes her transformation.

The producer stops by Marissa's desk. In a nervous voice, she says, "We have major coverage on a story at the top of the hour with multiple live shots."

"Okay. Thanks for the heads up, but I've already looked at the rundown and I'm aware of what's planned. It looks solid. Plus, I've been writing a few notes on the subject...mostly background info to use as filler if necessary. Don't worry. Everything will be fine." Marissa studies her face. "You seem a little nervous. Is everything okay?"

The producer lets out a sigh before answering. "I'm not worried about you, Marissa. You're always prepared, but I can't say the same for one of the news crews out in the field. We haven't been able to communicate with them all morning. And if something happens with their live shot, I'm not confidant Melinda will be ready to roll. It's so nerve-wracking because it's the day before ratings start!"

"It'll be great," Marissa reassures her. "Don't worry about that silly pre-ratings curse. That's just a ridiculous superstition."

◇◇◇

The noon broadcast starts off as usual with Melinda Bale barely sliding into her seat just seconds before the red tally light signaled the start of the newscast.

"Good noontime to you. I'm Marissa Cavelo. Today is Monday, November 20, 2011."

"And I'm Melinda Bale. Thanks for joining us!" From Melinda's cheerful, upbeat tone it's obvious she's clueless that the top story is serious. She hadn't bothered to check the scripts or the rundown. If she had, she would know that the lead story is about the funeral services for a local man who is posthumously being hailed as a hero.

There's an awkward pause as the producer quickly explains to Melinda through her earpiece to cut the cheerfulness. "We're talking about someone's tragic death," the producer scolds.

Melinda adjusts her tone, "Thank you for joining us on this somber occasion. Our entire town is in mourning as funeral services are about to get underway for JR Brown. Let's go live to the Woodlawn Cemetery, in central Austin, where the graveside service is set to begin. A KATX crew is joining us now with the details."

There is an eerie, awkward silence in the studio as all eyes turn to the monitor where the live reporter should be seen. Instead, the monitor shows a wide view of the cemetery as hundreds of mourners stand around a tent as the burial is about to take place. The reporter on the scene is supposed to be explaining the scene to viewers. The shot appears to be of some kind of military honor guard and rows of giant floral arrangements. But there is no sign of the reporter.

Melinda tries again to conjure up the news crew saying, "And now let's check in with reporter, Nona Ryan. Hello, Nona. Are you there? Tell us what's going on at Woodlawn Cemetery."

Still no response.

"Nona, I know you are there somewhere…." Melinda sounds shrill bordering on frantic.

The producer tries her best to remain calm and professional through the earpiece. "Melinda," she instructs, "forget Nona, and start ad-libbing!"

In an attempt to help, the teleprompter operator rolls the scripts ahead looking for copy that will help Melinda fill-in the blanks left by the MIA reporter. Melinda begins to get flustered and reads the wrong copy while the producer communicates through her earpiece, trying to get her back on track to the right scripts. Melinda starts panting and sounds like she's about to hyperventilate. Suddenly, she lets out an audible cry of anguish. Then, with no warning, she pulls the ear piece out of her ear, yanks the microphone off her lapel and storms away from the anchor desk.

Without a second's hesitation, Marissa says, "Our coverage of JR Brown's funeral service will continue right after this short break."

The studio crew and the producer in the master control booth, down the hall, are stunned by the disaster they just witnessed.

As the commercials roll, the floor director nervously looks back and forth at Marissa and at the empty chair where co-anchor Melinda Bale should be sitting. He cups his hand over his headset microphone as he tries to prevent anyone else from hearing what he's saying to the producer. Everybody in the studio can hear him as he hisses into the mic, "How the hell do I know where the bitch is? She just stopped reading in the middle of a newscast, yanked off her microphone and stormed out of the studio!"

It's uncomfortably quiet in the studio as the seconds tick by on the wall clock. Less than twenty seconds remain in the three-minute commercial break. A decision has to be made *now* about what to do if Bale doesn't return to her anchor chair.

Marissa picks up the phone hidden below the anchor desk. The producer automatically picks up and can be heard yelling, "Not now, Cavelo, we have to figure out where Bale is and if she's coming back!"

The floor says, "We're back from break in ten seconds....9 ...8...7...."

"Let me fly this plane solo," Marissa says calmly to the producer. "If she comes back...fine. If not, I've got it." She hangs up the phone just as the red tally light goes on.

"Welcome back to the noon news. First, my apologies on behalf of my colleague, Melinda Bale, who has suddenly taken ill. Now, we return to the live coverage of the funeral service for an Austin man who was transformed by fate into a true hero. We know him as JR Brown, the Internal Revenue Service agent who died four days ago when a small plane crashed into his office building in south Austin." Marissa calmly keeps ad-libbing from the notes she compiled before the newscast. Her goal is to kill as much time as possible until she gets the signal that a news crew is ready to go live from the cemetery.

"Here is what we know about that fateful day. Investigators have confirmed that Mr. Brown died when a suicide pilot crashed his private plane into the Internal Revenue Service office building where Mr. Brown worked. Angry about an audit and the back taxes he owed, the pilot apparently plotted to go down in flames in a huge protest against the IRS. Reminiscent of 9-11, the smoke from the building could be seen for miles. Reports of a small plane slamming into a building sparked initial rumors of a copycat terrorist attack, but investigators quickly determined it was a taxpayer whose anger was misdirected, especially since JR Brown had a reputation for helping taxpayers work out payment plans and resolve their issues with the IRS."

There is still no sign that the news crew is ready to go live, so she continues, "Mr. Brown was a retired military member, a respected leader of his church, a beloved father and grandfather and an outstanding member of this community. His funeral service, which should be wrapping up at any moment now, is being attended by a host of local and state dignitaries, fellow IRS employees and a representative from the Washington D.C. office of the Internal Revenue Service. It is the largest funeral service held in recent Austin history."

What Marissa doesn't say is that the funeral is also expected to draw a record number of viewers to the noon newscast. *It figures that a somber event of great local significance is the one where Bale chooses to lose it*, she thinks.

Through her earpiece, the producer lets Marissa know that the crew is finally ready out in the field.

15

Marissa picks up the prompt. "Reporter Nona Ryan is standing by live at the cemetery where JR Brown is being laid to rest. Let's check in with her now. Nona, how is Mr. Brown being remembered today?"

As soon as the live shot begins there is a sigh of relief in the studio since the report will provide at least two-and-a-half minutes to regroup. Suddenly, the studio door swings open and in walks the constantly befuddled News Director, Hank Johnson. Marissa has observed that he never seems to have a clue about what's going on around him, and today's no different. He scratches his head and asks, "Did I miss something in here? Did Melinda Bale suddenly leave? Is she coming back?"

"We were having trouble getting the first live shot up. The crew was nowhere to be found, so that forced Melinda into an ad lib situation and she bombed," the floor director explains.

"Were the anchors aware of the problems with the live shot?" Johnson asks, puzzled.

"Marissa was because she was on the set ten minutes before the newscast started, but to be honest, Melinda barely slipped into her chair in time to clip on her microphone, which meant she had no idea she might have to ad lib."

There is a collective intake of air. Although the floor director tried to sound diplomatic, everyone at KATX dreads crossing Melinda Bale. Anyone who antagonizes her pays the price.

"I want both anchors in the studio as soon as the newscast is over."

Marissa hears Nona Ryan through her earpiece, finishing her live coverage. "...and I'll have a complete wrap-up of the funeral service for the man who's being hailed as a hometown hero today at five. Live from central Austin, I'm Nona Ryan, KATX News."

"Thanks, Nona, for that report," Marissa says. She did not hear a word the field reporter uttered. She anchors the rest of the newscast solo and is relieved when it is over.

16

Marissa dreads the post-newscast powwow with Hank. Melinda is a fixture at KATX and has been anchoring the noon broadcast there for most of her news career, but she's also a known diva and has become even more self-conscious of her looks since reaching her forties. She's quick to inform anyone who dares to challenge her that she's been in the news business for more than twenty years, which in turn challenges her claim to being younger than forty-five years old. She is still an attractive blonde, albeit softer and curvier with age. Unfortunately, her natural beauty has been impacted by her cynicism, which has given her a hard, pinched look (the Botox injections haven't helped in that regard).

"I can anchor the news with my eyes closed," she's been known to brag. The trouble is, she's actually been caught with her eyes closed—sleeping on the air. Of course, when she is awake on the set, she's busy scrolling through People.com or looking for bargains on Craigslist. It's a joke among the studio crew that Melinda has no clue what's happening during the newscast. She smiles and laughs at appropriate times and pauses when she's supposed to, but she's not really concentrating on what she's saying—hence her inability to ad lib.

The studio crew is busy turning off lights and putting equipment away when Melinda slinks back in and takes a seat. She has already changed clothes and removed her makeup. The news director walks in and picks up a headset that hangs on a hook while not in use.

"I've asked the director to re-cue the noon newscast so we can review what happened," Johnson says. Into the microphone, he instructs the director to roll the tape. He watches Melinda reading the wrong copy, struggling through awkward and tense pauses then ultimately storming off set.

Marissa who saw it all unravel live sees it now through the eyes of a viewer and can't believe her eyes.

Johnson instructs the director to pause the tape and then asks, "What happened next, Cavelo?"

Marissa clears her throat, "I tossed to a break and the producer inserted some commercials so we could figure out where Melinda went or if she was coming back. Right before the break ended there was still no Bale, so I did what I thought I should do. I stepped in and took over the newscast. I apologized for Bale by telling viewers she was sick. Fortunately, I was prepared enough to fill the empty time until the live shot crew was finally ready to go."

Melinda is seething with anger at Marissa's debrief. "Oh, Marissa! This is just like you, wanting everyone to think that you somehow saved the day with your quick response. You've got everyone fooled. The producer and even the floor director are always conspiring to come up with ways to make me look bad on purpose," she hisses.

"Don't try and put your screw-up on me," Marissa protests. What happened is a perfect example of why you need to be on-set at least ten minutes before the newscast starts. If you'd been in place on time, and if you'd bothered to be familiar with the subject matter, then this fiasco might not have happened."

"Hold on, ladies," Johnson breaks in before Melinda can respond. "A few viewers called the station and sent emails to complain about Melinda's "unprofessional behavior." He uses air quotes on the last two words. "From now on, we'll all be required to work out our differences and help each other through any future rough spots. We are—"

Before he can say 'family,' Melinda blurts out, "This was not my fault! You should be talking to your news crew to find out why they weren't in place at the top of the newscast. Oh, never mind. I'm too upset to talk about it. I'm leaving before I say anything I might regret." She stomps out of the studio for the second time in the past hour with Johnson close behind her.

Well, that was a waste of time, Marissa thinks.

A studio crew member walks back into the otherwise empty studio to retrieve his backpack stashed in a corner. "We're placing bets to see which excuse the news team uses to explain why they missed today's live shot," he says.

Marissa knows this isn't the first live shot they've missed and their explanations have included, "We got caught in traffic getting to the scene," and "The battery for the camera died at the last second," and even the more unbelievable, "The audio was accidentally turned down in the live truck."

It's common knowledge that Nona Ryan, a very perky reporter, and her he-man photographer are sexually heating up the live van every time it stops. This even happens at red lights. "When the engine turns off, Nona turns on," is the current joke. At least one live shot recently started with a disheveled Nona stumbling out of the van, trying to tuck in her form-fitting top. That resulted in an unstated warning for anyone approaching the news van—if the van is a-rocking, then don't come a-knocking.

"What do you think, Marissa? Which excuse will it be this time?"

"Sorry, I'm not into betting," she responds.

"DON'T BE LATE!" The preset text flashes across the screen of Marissa's cell phone. Even with the fifteen-minute warning, Marissa is the last one in the newsroom and does her best to slip discreetly into the nearest empty chair.

Executive Producer Jan Ruther spots her immediately and stops in mid-sentence to acknowledge her tardy arrival. In a voice that's worse than nails on a chalkboard, she screeches, "Marissa, is there a good reason you're late? Is there breaking news the rest of us are unaware of? Bring us up-to-date. Puhleeeez."

"No...no...reason," Marissa stammers. "After meeting with the news director in the studio, I was just checking my email and messages from sources." As soon as the word sources leaves her lips, she knows she's in trouble.

"Your sources?" Ruther spits. "Pray, do tell. Who? The police chief? The governor? The POTUS, perhaps?"

19

And right on cue everybody around the table laughs.

It's a big no-no not to laugh when Jan Ruther makes a joke, no matter how lame it might be. It's especially true when the joke is told at someone else's expense. This time Marissa is more than the punch-line—Jan wants to make her an example. Ruther believes that the only legitimate sources are people in power or close to power. She doesn't believe Marissa could possibly have that kind of access.

As a journalist, Marissa knows that a source can be anybody who's reliable and trustworthy. Her mailman once told her about up-coming cuts in delivery service; the clerk at the corner convenience store always alerts her just as prices at the gas pumps are about to jump, or take a dive and her neighbor, who's a high school teacher, once revealed how test scores were being manipulated at his school. All valid news sources, and the origins of several stories she's written.

"Did I say 'my sources?'" Marissa demurs. "I meant my mail. I was checking my mail. So sorry I'm late. It won't happen again." Marissa hates not standing up to her but knows nothing she says will erase Ruther's disdain.

"It had better not," Ruther grumbles and turns back to the reason for the daily meeting. This is when the previous noon newscast is critiqued and when stories for the next day are assigned.

Ruther continues in her sour mood. "So let's start with a review of the noon newscast. Anything positive worth mentioning?" Everybody at the table pretends they're looking at their notes, not daring to utter a positive comment.

Marissa clears her throat and Ruther immediately focuses on her like a high-beam laser. "Yes, Marissa? You have something to say?"

Before she loses her nerve, she responds, "I think the in-studio news team managed to quickly get back on track after the crew in the field wasn't ready to go live at the beginning of the newscast. And my response was prompt after my co-anchor suddenly walked off the set."

She takes a deep breath and braces herself for the verbal fireworks that are about to launch.

"Is that what you call a 'prompt' response? I hardly think two full minutes into the newscast is prompt. And your co-anchor, Melinda Bale, might not have walked off in exasperation if she didn't feel her on-air performance was being undermined."

Ruther releases her glare on Marissa, straightens up and surveys the rest of the staff before declaring, "Just so everybody at this table is clear, Melinda is an experienced journalist who's given her best, day in and day out, to help make this station number one in the ratings. Just yesterday, she came to my office to express concerns that someone was tampering with her scripts. She has proof that someone is intentionally scrambling the order of the scripts and is introducing destructive viruses to her computer. She has a strong suspicion that it's someone who would like to see her permanently vacate the anchor chair. I won't mention names, but I want everyone in this room to know these allegations are being investigated and I will fire the person responsible for intentionally disrupting our operation."

During her declaration, Ruther steals accusing looks at Marissa. Her temperament and physical appearance remind Marissa of the Wicked Witch of the West. Ruther is a tall, thin, craggy woman who acts like she's never experienced a happy moment in her life. While her keen news sense has resulted in award-winning newscasts, a couple of regional Emmys and top ratings, her cutthroat dictator-like qualities make her the most hated person in local news. She's been called many things, but her established nickname is "Ruthless Ruther."

The irony is, Ruther seems to take pride in being despised.

Ruther is almost fifty and has been in the news business since before most of the members of her news team were born. She has no patience or respect for young, inexperienced reporters who whine about having to work holidays, being on-call 24-7 or who complain about having to brave the elements in flash floods and snowstorms. "Today's reporters only think it's news if it's in a press release or if they see it on the *Daily Show*," she's been known to snarl. Ruther considers herself to be among the last of a dying breed of old-school journalists. She proved herself back when it was mostly a male-dominated profession. The photos on her desk and office walls are from her field days in the early 1990s when she covered all types of natural disasters, including hurricanes, tornadoes and earthquakes. She was fairly attractive when she was younger. Globe-trotting from disaster to disaster kept her physically fit with a freshly-scrubbed face that required little or no makeup. It's that natural look that today's reporters try hard and pay big bucks to recreate.

But over the years, too many cigarettes and too much alcohol have taken a toll on her looks and on her personal life. Now her hair is dull with so much gray that even Lady Clairol can't adequately cover it. Her face is a map of wrinkles and frown lines. Except for her two cats named Wallace and Walters (after Mike and Barbara), Ruther has no friends or family who are worth mentioning. Over the years, her obsession with news coverage, combined with her caustic personality have alienated anyone who ever meant anything to her. Sadly, even Wallace and Walters appear to be unhappy hostages who receive little attention or affection from Ruther.

"Enough with the critique. Let's get back to the news assignments for the day," Ruther bellows. "Marissa, we have another feature assignment for you. Check with the news director for details and try not to blow it."

Marissa knows better than to challenge Ruther over anything, especially another dreaded feature story assignment. It is the third time this week she's been assigned to cover what's known in the news biz as a "fluff" piece—features that are light in content. This usually means a review, a store opening or community festival. Marissa dislikes these pieces for their lack of journalistic acumen, and the ones she *has* done have been flops on more than one occasion.

It was one piece from late last August that caused her the most embarrassment. The city of Austin takes on a whole new energy with the start of the college football season. The first home game for the University of Texas Longhorns is like a local holiday. Marissa is a proud Texas Ex, having earned her journalism degree from UT. She was actually thrilled when she was assigned to cover an annual tradition—the first tailgate parties of the college football season. It's invigorating to see the parking lots near UT turn into a tent city filled with enthusiastic, tipsy fans watching giant flat screen TVs and playing drinking games. Sound systems are blasting music, barbecue grills are smoking and kegs of cold beer are flowing as large crowds of co-eds and alumni proudly flaunt their school colors while flashing the "Hook 'em Horns" hand sign.

The parties and drinking usually start the night before the Saturday game, which guarantees a wild crowd for the background of any live shot. Marissa was covering a raucous tailgate party and was interviewing a Longhorn fan who was about to explain what he was grilling on the barbecue pit. The crowd was "energized" from too many tequila shots. About four feet behind the grill, the camera zoomed in on a rowdy game of beer pong just as a fight broke out between fraternity members. All of a sudden, a few of the frat boys lost their footing and stumbled right into a porta potty. An occupant was locked inside as it went over, its putrid contents splattering everywhere. It took hours to clean up the accident and even longer to calm down the distraught sorority girl who was trapped inside the porta potty. She was unharmed but embarrassed and disgusted beyond belief. No one wanted to talk about grilling after that.

And then there was the nightmare that happened on Independence Day. It was supposed to be another easy fluff piece.

Like the tailgate party, it was practically the same story year after year but unfortunately for Marissa, this one didn't turn out to be predictable. Just as she was getting ready to go live from an annual Fourth of July neighborhood parade and picnic, some careless teenager set off a string of firecrackers which spooked a horse that was pulling a wagon carrying Uncle Sam and Betsy Ross. The wagon veered out of control. Parade onlookers scattered while the runaway wagon mowed down lawn chairs and crashed into a snow cone vendor as he was setting up. Fortunately, the horse-drawn wagon was brought under control and no one was hurt. But the endless stream of loud and colorful curse words coming out of Uncle Sam and Old Betsy couldn't be bleeped out. Nothing patriotic about that! These two embarrassing episodes drew thousands of views on the Internet and can still be found on YouTube. It took Marissa months after the football season was over to live down the nickname, "Porta Potty Reporter," leaving Marrissa with enough fluff pieces to last her a lifetime.

Marissa isn't sure Hank has calmed down from Melinda's meltdown and decides to give it some time before getting her assignment from him. Instead, she calls the one person who's always willing to let her unload, no matter what's bothering her or what time of day it is. She hits speed dial, and after two rings she hears the one voice in the world that's always a comfort, that of her identical twin sister, Carissa, who goes by the nickname, CC.

"Hey, how are you?" Marissa asks. "Do you have a minute to talk? Or better yet, do you have a minute to let *me* talk?"

CC laughs and says, "I knew you were going to call after I watched your co-anchor lose it during the noon newscast. It was like witnessing a car wreck and not being able to turn away. What the hell happened?"

Marissa tells her about the missing field reporters, Melinda's response and her second meltdown when they met with the news director. "It's so frustrating to try and cover for her every time she screws up on the air. Somehow I doubt viewers believed me when I said she left suddenly because she was sick."

"I can't believe they put up with her bullshit," CC says.

"I know! And now I have to go see the news director about another feature story. It would be so nice if I was allowed to chase some hard news. Instead, I'm stuck covering the same old light topics day after day. I'm desperate to sink my teeth into something solid."

"Maybe there isn't anything juicy right now."

"But there is. I'm desperate to cover a story about one of our local City Council members who might be taking bribes. My gut tells me that's why a certain construction company was recently awarded a lucrative contract with the city. Unfortunately, I never have time to comb through public copies of submitted bids."

"Tell me again what you want to cover," CC demands. Although she's heard it all before, she wants to be supportive and encouraging.

Marissa had wanted to be a journalist ever since she was a kid growing up in a rough barrio in Houston. She'd been a news junkie from an early age.

"It would be great to look into allegations of widespread cheating on state-mandated tests taken by public school students. I think there's something fishy about the unusually high test scores posted in at least one otherwise low-achieving school. One parent left me a phone message about her suspicions that a couple of greedy teachers practically took the tests for their students with the hopes of earning a bonus for high test scores. Also, if I only had just a couple more hours in a day, I could check into allegations of falsified overtime reports being submitted by county employees at the taxpayers' expense. These are the kind of hard-hitting situations most journalists want to cover."

"I don't know, sis. It sounds like you wanna catch criminals. Is that what you're into?"

25

"Well, when it comes to hard news, criminals are sometimes involved. Anyway, thanks for listening. I'll call you later, okay?"

"Just make the most out of your assignment, and don't let anyone get to you," CC advises.

Marissa tries to take that advice with her as she goes to find Hank Johnson for her assignment. When she can't find him, she returns to her desk to brood.

She looks at a faded, black and white photo that's among other personal items on her desk. It's a simple wooden frame that has a few scratches and is worn smooth in some spots from being held so often. The photo shows a young smiling couple, in clean, carefully pressed clothes, standing next to two little girls with their hair in braids. All are in their Sunday best.

The happy faces belong to her parents, Maria and Jesus Cavelo. She and her sister were just six years old when the picture was taken. Then, just days before their thirteenth birthday, the simple family life they enjoyed was gone in an instant. Marissa and CC became orphans when both of their parents were killed during a random home invasion. The picture is one of the only reminders Marissa has of their time together as a family.

Instead of depressing her, the photo inspires her. It represents family and heritage—the factors that have shaped who she is and have set the foundation for her life goals and aspirations.

Two

Marissa puts down the treasured picture and picks up her reporter's notebook. She heads to the break room to track down Hank for her assignment.

By title and tradition in any newsroom, the news director is a respected leader. He or she typically decides what topics are worthy of coverage and who's hired or fired. Most management decisions, including annual budgets, salaries, equipment purchases and upgrades in facilities and technology are all under the news director's leadership. In the most successful newsrooms, great news directors earn respect and their reputations for being visionaries who are willing to do whatever it takes to stay ahead of the competition. Sadly, KATX News Director Hank Johnson would not be described as a respected authority figure.

He's a short, middle-aged and average looking guy, and his only distinguishing feature is his full head of hair. Determined to hold onto his youth, he went on an extreme diet and dropped forty pounds in four months. The weight loss left him looking gaunt, but he didn't bother to buy new clothes or have the old ones tailored. Instead, they hang on him and make him look like a kid playing dress up in a grown-up's wardrobe. As if the drastic diet wasn't enough, Hank Johnson had eye surgery to remove extra skin on his upper lids. But no matter what Johnson does to improve his looks, it's not enough to make up for his lack of leadership skills or personality.

Any respect Marissa had for him vanished during today's impromptu meeting with her and Melinda. She knows he's nothing more than a figurehead—a puppet whose strings are pulled in two different directions by two much stronger individuals. On one side is the Executive Producer, Jan Ruther, who rules the newsroom by instilling fear and intimidation. On the other side is the station's general manager, Patrick Stone, a tall, slender imposing man with gray hair and a booming voice. Like the Great Wizard of Oz, Stone spews orders and decisions while remaining safely hidden behind his desk. His nickname is "Mr. Made-of," as in "made of stone," since he rarely displays empathy for what employees might be feeling. With Stone and Ruther calling the shots, Hank Johnson is left regurgitating commands almost verbatim.

The machinations of this threesome has led Marissa to believe there is a conspiracy against her. Although she has no real proof to back that up because her only evidence is casual comments she's overheard. One afternoon, Stone's executive assistant, Lila, didn't realize Marissa was in one of the bathroom stalls when she walked into the ladies' room talking on her cell phone.

"Yes, the Cavelo girl is the fluff puff. Viewers like to see her doing feature pieces. So, no matter how strongly Cavelo might want to get out and cover hard news, it's not gonna happen anytime soon." Not daring to flush the toilet, Marissa waited quietly until Stone's executive assistant finished her conversation.

So, Marissa thought, *there is an intentional effort to keep me away from hard news.*

Lila quickly changed the subject to whether getting a boob job would eventually pay off in a salary increase for her. The "Double D salary boost" debate ended before Marissa learned anything more about why she was being pigeonholed.

This memory is foremost in Marissa's mind as she finally catches Hank in his office.

"Okay, boss, what do you have for me today?" she says, trying to sound upbeat. "Something strong I hope."

"Marissa, every story is only as strong as the effort a reporter is willing to put into it. You should know that by now."

Marissa knows there is no point in arguing and nods silently.

"Today, we're sending you on an urban safari." His tone is that of a teacher speaking to a first grader. We want you to head to the grand opening of a national chain pet store, which will be the largest store of its kind in the nation. During your live shot in the five o'clock broadcast, I want to see cute fuzzy faces of puppies and kittens. Oh, and be sure you track down a couple of exotic pets like lizards or spider monkeys. We want to see plenty of interaction between you and these critters. Wrap a reptile around yourself. Perch that parrot on your shoulder. How about a little pirate-speak? Arrgh!"

Marissa wants to pummel him with curse words. Instead, she grabs the copy of the assignment details, turns on her heels and walks out of his office. She goes to the other end of the building to find a photographer who's available to head out with her immediately.

The photographer's lounge, where the photojournalists hang out while waiting for their next assignments, is an informal room with a well-worn couch and some sports-related posters on the walls. The posters aren't there to bolster team spirit, but rather to cover scuff marks and at least one hole in the wall caused by a flying fist planted there by a frustrated photographer. There are some mismatched chairs with torn upholstery and a couple of TV monitors, which are always tuned-in to some sporting event or an old sitcom—mindless background noise. On one side of the room, there's a row of lockers—one assigned to each photographer. There is also a desk with a couple of phones, a computer keyboard and a monitor. In one corner are shelves where miscellaneous equipment is kept including video tapes, camera batteries, extension cords, duct tape and just about anything else a news crew needs while working out in the field.

There he is. Her body shivers slightly every time she sets her sights on Ken Jordan—the best-looking guy she's ever worked with. Ken just turned thirty, is six foot two and well-built, with medium brown hair and piercing green eyes. He's a sports enthusiast who also happens to be well-read and intelligent. Those last two characteristics are rare qualities for most news photographers who are usually male since the cameras, tripods and other equipment are heavy and often have to be lugged for long distances. The term photojournalist is often misleading since most "photogs," as they're often called, are focused on what the video looks like. Photogs pay close attention to lighting, composition, and capturing the perfect images. The challenge is finding photographers who shoot great video and have an actual interest in and knowledge of the subject matter being videotaped.

Marissa cringes when she thinks about some of the photographers she's worked with who didn't have a clue about what the news assignment was about. A few didn't even know the location for the shoot or who was going to be interviewed. Some photographers believe that these annoying details may get in the way of capturing great video and sound. But not Ken. He always knows where they're headed, who they'll be talking to, and why the subject matter is newsworthy. He also comes up with insightful questions to ask as well as creative suggestions for how to make the story memorable. Marissa loves working with Ken for several reasons: he's a talented and smart guy, a consummate professional who also happens to be good-looking, well-mannered and even-tempered.

"Hey, are you busy?" she asks, trying to sound nonchalant.

"Not too busy to hear what you're working on today. What's up, Ms. Cavelo?" teases Ken, with a smile that lights up the entire room.

"Well, I wish we were rushing out the door to track down a real news story. Hell, I'd settle for a two-alarm fire; at least it would be visual, but I'm afraid I have another fluff piece to offer you."

"I'd happily tackle a fluff piece with you any day, Cavelo."

She responds to his obvious flirtation with a joke, "Great! Then pack your pith helmet and let's go stalk some wildlife. Are you game?" She tells Ken about the pet store grand opening and some of the lame ideas the news director wants included in the live shot.

"We'll make it worthy of an Emmy!" Ken assures her as he grabs his gear.

Marissa stands there, smitten, as she watches his muscles ripple under his basic black t-shirt. It's easy to see he's been working out, but what Marissa finds sexy about Ken is that he doesn't have that narcissistic swagger that so many good-looking guys seem to possess.

They leave the news station and jump into Ken's truck for the drive to the pet store in south Austin. Despite all that she has on her mind, it's hard for Marissa to concentrate on anything with Ken sitting just a few feet away in the driver's seat. She tries to force herself not to think about him except as a coworker. Although he's single and a super nice guy, she's never thought about being romantically involved with him or any other coworker. She knows that workplace romances can get messy fast.

She remembers one relationship that started with an innocent flirtation between a popular male anchor and a friendly female producer. Both were married with children, but that didn't stop them from engaging in illicit trysts in cheap motels and in the backseats of empty news units. Coworkers tried hard to ignore what was going on, but both of their spouses became suspicious when dinner breaks extended for hours. And then there was that out-of-town assignment to cover a hurricane that was tearing across the Gulf Coast and the anchor's wife couldn't reach him. The producer's husband also had no luck calling his wife's cell phone. The double dose of missed communication might have gone undetected except the news photographer who was the third member of the news team panicked when he couldn't find his colleagues. There was no answer and complete silence from the producer's motel room. Next door in the anchor's room, you could hear the loud volume of the television set, but no response to knocking or the constant ringing of the telephone. It was almost six a.m. and they were supposed to be heading to the Galveston Seawall to capture live coverage of the hurricane just as it was coming ashore. Concerned the anchor had experienced an accident, the photographer convinced the hotel clerk to use the passkey to check on him. Instead, they found the TV blaring on the porn channel while the couple was passed out following a crazy night of heavy drinking and much heavier sex.

The news crew failed to get any video of the hurricane coming ashore, but the anchor and producer felt the full brunt of the storm when they returned home to their fuming spouses. Months later, in a bitter divorce, the anchor agreed to give up custody of his child after the wife threatened to go public with the details of the affair and ruin his perfect public image and professional reputation. The producer resigned, and her husband also filed for divorce. She was stripped of all shared property and was ordered to pay him child support. But the biggest fallout came from the teenage kids of both adults who refused to forgive their wayward parents for breaking up their families.

Marissa finds it hard to believe anyone would risk everything for a fling. It helps that she is focused on advancing her career because she doesn't afford herself time for romance.

"There may be a way to get an angle on this pet store opening," she tells Ken and pulls out her cell phone to call the one person who knows more about animals than anyone else she's ever met.

Three

The screen flashes the familiar initials "MC" and a photo pops up that is a mirror image of CC. It barely rings once before she answers and hears a voice that sounds just like hers. It's not that unusual for her twin to call more than once in an hour. There have even been times when Marissa has called CC twice in two minutes.

Both CC and Marissa have flowing, dark brown hair, big brown eyes and a flawless olive complexion. They both have a slender, trim build and long legs. The biggest difference between them is how they dress. Marissa is almost always impeccably dressed in professional clothes—fitted suits or wrap dresses, paired with high heels and understated jewelry. Viewers admire how she's managed to develop her own signature look. Marissa is modest and prefers her clothes to be flattering without being too revealing, whether she's sitting behind the anchor desk or reporting from the field.

CC sports a casual, unstructured look. She's always been athletic and a bit of a tomboy always sporting workout clothes—shorts in the summer and yoga pants in the winter. The casual look works for her since she's the manager of a posh daycare for small dogs. Her duties involve grooming and exercising the type of pups that travel with their owners tucked safely away inside designer bags via limousines and private jets. Some of Austin's wealthiest residents wouldn't think of leaving their pedigree dogs anywhere except Royal Watchers Pet Care.

"Hey, sis, didn't I just talk to you?" CC says. "I know you miss me but two phone calls in less than an hour? *Estás loca?* Seriously, though, what's up?"

"I'm on my way to cover, of all things, the grand opening of a pet store. This is your area of expertise, CC. I've already been instructed to get video of cute cuddly puppies and kittens. The idiot boss also wants live shots of interaction with exotic animals. Do you have any suggestions about which animals are small enough for me to handle? And which ones are less likely to bite?"

CC laughs. "A pet store manager is not going to let you handle anything that's too dangerous. The last thing the store wants is for you to be bitten, especially while you're live on the news. It's not just a matter of liability, it would also be a PR nightmare! Can you imagine if the beautiful Marissa Cavelo was bitten by a lemur or clawed by a macaw?"

"You have a point."

"Tell them you want something docile and not too big." CC quickly changes the subject. "Tell me, what are you wearing? What shoes do you have on?"

"What? This isn't the time to talk about fashion, which I know you don't care about. I need solid advice on how to handle pets and which ones might be unpredictable. The Internet is filled with clips of reporters with birds pecking at their hair or monkeys pooping on their clothes. I can't be one of them"

"That's exactly why I want to know what you're wearing. Bright, wild patterns or large dangling jewelry can excite some small animals. Do yourself a favor and take off your jewelry and go with dark, solid clothes. Got it?"

"I'm taking off my jewelry right now. Any other suggestions?"

CC feels a twinge of annoyance. Marissa always turns to her for advice and then acts surprised when she's able to deliver. There is some jealousy at her sister's success, but as much as she gets a bit of pleasure when Marissa slips off her pedestal, she doesn't want her to get hurt. As usual, CC is torn between being envious of her twin and being protective.

"There is one more thing I want to warn you about," CC says. "Please be careful which exotic birds you handle."

"Why do I need to be careful about handling birds?"

"Some are extremely valuable and you don't want to be responsible for one getting hurt, or worse, flying away. I've seen your paycheck stub. You can't afford to pay for one of those babies. Other than that, my advice is to relax. Animals can sense when you're tense and that's when their claws come out. Have fun, and I'll be watching at five!"

"Okay, thanks for all your suggestions. I'll talk to you later."

As CC hangs up, her hands are shaking. She dreads the next phone call she must make because she knows it is going to get ugly.

Four

Ken has a slight smile as he peers straight ahead, eyes on the road. He overheard the entire phone call.

"What's so funny?" Marissa asks.

"Oh, it's just how you have such little confidence in yourself, even though you can tackle any story. You're the best, most focused, serious reporter I've ever had the pleasure to work with," Ken says. "You have no idea that you're as good as you are and that your skills will take your career as far as you want to go. Now, put away those doubts and let's go bag some big game."

His words of encouragement make her confidence soar. By the time they arrive at the pet store, Marissa is determined to get the best feature story ever.

It's about three o'clock and already there's a large crowd waiting to get inside the store, even though it will be another hour before the doors officially open. Advertised bargains, offers of free samples and drawings for door prizes have lured about two hundred people to the opening. Some people have their cats and dogs with them. Members of the news media are being allowed in early to shoot video before the grand opening madness begins. Ken and Marissa carry the gear from the live truck and move past the crowd to the store's front door. It makes a huge swoosh sound as it slides open and just as it does, out runs a Chihuahua. An employee with leash in-hand runs after it. Ken and Marissa stop and watch as the dog plays a game with the frantic worker. The dog stops, barks and then prances on its hind legs as if dancing and taunting the worker. Then it takes off again just as the employee is within inches of catching it. The crowd cheers as this little game of catch-me-if-you-can goes on for about five more minutes. Finally, the pooch is safely apprehended and returned to the store as the audience claps wildly.

The instant they step inside, they witness even more canine chaos. Dogs of all breeds and sizes are being placed into display cases. The animal noises are loud. A frazzled store manager is barking orders to his employees who are scurrying around putting pets in place and making sure products and merchandise are ready to sell. This store is huge—about the size of a big box store with wide aisles of pet food, beds, bowls, leashes, toys, grooming products and just about everything else needed to take care of all types of animals. Staff members pass back and forth through the rear service entrance, bringing in pallets filled with pet beds and carriers. In addition to the whirl of activity, the atmosphere is festive with balloons and special banners marking the store's grand opening, which will happen in about thirty minutes.

Ken starts videotaping some of the pets waiting to go home with new owners. In the meantime, Marissa browses the store, looking for the exotic animals per the news director's "urban safari" idea. She's not crazy about having a snake slither around her arm.

Maybe I can convince an employee to hold the snake for me while I interact with a slow-moving turtle, she thinks.

Ken finishes shooting tail-wagging puppies and mewing kitties, bunnies with their twitching noses and some colorful fish that seem content to swim around in their aquariums. Then, like a well-oiled machine, he goes and fires up the live truck, raises the mast, dials in a signal and feeds the video back to the station without breaking a sweat.

A great deal of work is required to beam back a live shot, and Ken gets it all done without a hitch.

Inside the store, Marissa arranges for a parrot in its cage to be taken out and placed on a display perch during the live shot. It's a talking parrot, but so far all it has said is, "Awwk! You're pretty pretty. You're pretty pretty."

Great. Another big flirt for me to put up with, Marissa thinks. She turns around to ask the store manager some questions about the company's background and why Austin was chosen as the location for this ginormous pet store, but he's gone. She heads to the back of the store, in search of him, and is soon past the restrooms and the employee break room. A sign posted on the door states: "Store Employees Only" but they're only minutes away from the crowd rushing through the front door, and she wants to capture all the action. She decides to ignore the sign.

As soon as Marissa makes her way inside the warehouse area, she hears angry voices. It's a mix of English and Spanish with some words too vulgar to translate. She is shocked by what she sees. Two imposing men have weapons pointed at employees and are ordering them to load large shipping crates into the back of a semi waiting at the loading dock. The frightened store employees are moving crates as fast as they can. One nervous employee, in his haste to get a crate in place, loses his footing while walking up the loading ramp. His misstep causes the crate to crash to the ground.

"*No seas idiota. Sabes cuanto cuesta ese pinche pajaro? Si le molestas una sola pluma, puedes pagar con tu vida!*" screams one of the armed men. "Don't be an idiot. Do you know how much that goddamn bird is worth? If even one feather is ruffled, you'll pay with your life."

Marissa freezes, afraid the sound of her pounding heart will alert the thieves to her presence. But the commotion caused by the broken crate creates a diversion, which allows her to slip unnoticed back inside the store while the thugs check the birds for any signs of damage. As soon as she is clear from the loading area, she dials 9-1-1.

"9-1-1. What is your emergency? Do you need police, fire or ambulance?" It's obvious the dispatcher has asked that same question hundreds of times.

Marissa tries to retain her composure. "I need police. NOW! I'm at the grand opening of a pet store on Stassney Lane, near MoPac. There are armed gunmen threatening workers in the loading dock area."

The dispatcher remains calm. "Police are on their way. Where exactly are you calling from, ma'am?"

"I was in the rear of the store by the loading dock, but I moved back inside after I saw guns drawn. Please hurry! These men are armed and dangerous." Her heart is about to jump out of her chest when she remembers some valuable information. "Officers need to know the doors of the store are about to open to let hundreds of customers inside in just a few minutes!"

As she's speaking with the dispatcher, she heads back to the center of the store. She hangs up and sees Ken waiting behind the camera for her to get in place for the live shot. She grabs the wireless microphone and yells, "Get your camera and come with me."

Fortunately, he's pulled enough length of cable to provide the leeway needed to extend all the way back to the "Employees Only Area." She explains to Ken that she's stumbled upon the theft of some very expensive birds.

He can hear the producer screaming at him in his earpiece saying, "What happened to the set up with the parrot and the puppies? I'm seeing a door in the preview monitor. What the hell's going on? We're thirty seconds away. Get back in place NOW!"

Ken tries to reassure the panicked producer. "Trust me. Live TV will never be the same." And then Ken cues Marissa to start her live shot.

"I'm Marissa Cavelo, coming to you live from the much-anticipated opening of one of the largest pet stores in the nation. But instead of grand opening excitement, we've stumbled upon a crime taking place right behind this door." Her voice is calm and steady. She pushes the door open and the camera zooms in on the frightened workers in the process of loading the last crate of expensive and exotic birds. The two gunmen are pointing their weapons directly at the frightened employees, threatening their lives. *"Pronto! O quieres morir?"*

Then, like a scene out of an action movie, more men armed with handguns and wearing the store's t-shirts emerge from behind stacks of large cardboard boxes, yelling, "Austin Police! Freeze! Drop your weapons and put your hands up! Now!"

Instantly, the two crooks drop their weapons. As they put their hands up in the air, officers rush in to put handcuffs on them. The officers then lead the gunmen to a patrol car that's pulled up next to the semi.

Ken has captured the entire scene and turns the camera back on Marissa.

"And there you have it, folks," she says. "This is an actual crime being revealed to you live, exclusively on KATX. What you've witnessed unfolding appears to be undercover police officers breaking up a suspected animal smuggling ring. While I can't confirm the breed of birds involved, I can tell you that those feathered creatures inside the shipping crates are worth thousands of dollars. Not a single shot was fired. Two men are in custody and the birds are safe, except for some slightly ruffled feathers. We'll talk to investigators and bring you all the details as soon as possible. Live in South Austin, I'm Marissa Cavelo, KATX news."

"We're clear," Ken calls, and then adds, "You kicked ass, Cavelo." He sets down his camera.

Marissa breaks into a spontaneous dance. "Oh my God! I can't believe our live shot was perfect. We did it!"

As Ken approaches Marissa for a congratulatory hug, something automatically clicks between them. They are physically pulled together in the adrenaline rush, and she has a strong urge to kiss him.

I'd do almost anything for one passionate, impromptu lip lock that would move us beyond being coworkers who harmlessly flirt with each other, she thinks.

She marvels at how in sync they were, as if busting a crime in progress is a daily occurrence. In one quick instant, it felt to her like they were truly partners and perhaps, soul mates who are destined to share great things together.

Five

Miles away, in a luxurious penthouse high above the Austin skyline, a giant flat screen is rebroadcasting the scene from the pet store bust that aired several hours earlier. The anchor tells viewers it's being called "Operation Feathered Friends" by the police chief during a hastily called news conference. The chief explains that officers had been working undercover, posing as store employees for months leading up to the store's grand opening. He credits excellent detective work for cracking the smuggling ring that targets expensive and exotic animals. He sums it up by saying, "Today's arrest is just the tip of the iceberg. More arrests are expected." And with that, the chief turns and walks away from the podium as reporters shout more questions that bounce off his back like boomerangs.

Marissa Cavelo is among the reporters covering the news conference. As he finishes speaking, Marissa turns to her camera. "To recap the chief, this pet store is the site of what was an elaborate undercover investigation into the smuggling of exotic and expensive birds. KATX was the only station to bring you exclusive live coverage of the police bust in progress. In addition to the arrests made today, officers are confident more suspects will be rounded up. We'll be following this story and will bring you the latest as it becomes available. Live in South Austin, I'm—"

But before Cavelo finishes her name, a masculine hand sporting expensive jewelry pushes the button on the remote and the screen immediately goes black. He picks up his cell phone and says slowly and eloquently with just a hint of anger, "I want that Cavelo girl stopped. And I want her stopped, now!"

The penthouse suite is filled with expensive artwork and high-end furnishings and occupies the top floor of the most exclusive high-rise building in downtown Austin. With three master bedrooms, a media room, a gourmet kitchen, a private gymnasium with an adjacent spa, and a huge balcony, the luxury dwelling recently sold for nearly three million dollars. The new owners paid cash, which raised a few eyebrows among the building's management, but no one dared question the new tenants who happen to be brothers. The two men have quickly built reputations as successful, wealthy investors who own several popular nightclubs in the city. All their clubs cater to the young, hip and wealthy crowd, and all the venues are located in the city's popular entertainment district.

The brothers are of Middle Eastern decent and in their early thirties. Both are of average height with thick, wavy long hair that hangs a tad over their shirt collars. The brothers are always impeccably dressed in the finest suits, silk shirts and custom Italian shoes. Both men are dripping in masculine jewelry, including heavy gold chains, expensive watches and each one sports a three-karat diamond stud earring. Both are physically fit, thanks to a personal trainer who provides private daily sessions. The two men have been known to call their trainer to come over at all hours of the day or night. A masseuse, a chef, a manicurist, a barber and a tailor are also on call twenty-four-seven. And of course, some professional women of pleasure are ready to perform at any moment if summoned. If you work for the brothers, you do what you're told whenever and wherever you're asked.

The older brother is the brains of the operation; he handles all of the investment issues. His younger sibling is the brawn and is in charge of all efforts to keep staff members in line while collecting any outstanding debts. He also makes sure unexpected problems are resolved, and isn't afraid to carry out a physical threat to ensure cooperation by all parties involved.

On this particular evening, the gigantic room, with its plush carpet and amazing artwork, is as silent as a tomb. The older brother is seated facing a bank of windows that take in a panoramic view of the city. In one smooth move, he swivels around in his chair to finish a conversation that was interrupted by the KATX "Live at Five" broadcast that featured the undercover bust of the exotic bird smuggling operation.

"Who the hell does she think she is?" he asks his younger sibling. Anger simmers under his cool exterior.

"Those birds should have been on their way to California by now. My men would've taken down those undercover cops and driven off with those birds in a flash. They're equipped and trained to do that in a heartbeat. But with that news bitch and her camera rolling, it would've been too risky. Now the video from the live shot has been replayed a thousand times, making it impossible to revive the operation. We'll have to cut our losses and silence those who might lead investigators back to us."

"It means a huge deficit that I won't tolerate. We need to teach that bitch a lesson she will never forget. She wants to be a media star? Over her dead body!"

◇◇◇

At the KATX newsroom, it's like the entire news team won the lottery. There's a contagious atmosphere of excitement and victory following Marissa's unbelievable live shot. A standing ovation greets her and Ken as they enter the newsroom. Even the usually cynical and sarcastic studio crew members are cheering the two.

But not everybody at the station is celebrating. Hank Johnson is sitting in his office at his desk running his hands through his hair. It's a nervous habit he resorts to whenever he's worried. Johnson has no explanation for what happened during today's five o'clock news.

How did Marissa manage to take a simple store grand opening and turn it into the top news story of the week? he wonders.

The exotic animal smuggling ring is not a big deal, but the live shot, capturing police in action, that's an MTVM (memorable TV moment). The entire two-minute clip is drawing thousands of hits on the Internet, making it the kind of coverage that no one will soon forget.

Exclusive coverage of an action-packed scene is exactly what TV stations want. KATX managers just don't want Marissa Cavelo in the starring role. Not when their audience research shows viewers like her best in light-hearted, feature pieces. When promos air, alerting viewers that Marissa will be covering a pie-eating contest or that she'll be judging a children's artwork competition, there's always a spike in viewership. Management has long-range plans for keeping Cavelo as a feature reporter.

Johnson runs his hands through his hair again as he worries that future plans will unravel if Cavelo begins to believe she has a knack for real journalism. *I have to figure out how to put an end to her dream of being a hard news journalist.* His phone rings, breaking his concentration. The caller ID reads: "Patrick Stone." The news can't be good if the general manager is calling. Johnson reluctantly picks up.

Abruptly, without any greeting, Stone asks, "What the hell happened? Your instructions are to send her on feature stories only. All of a sudden, I look up and see her busting in on a crime scene in progress."

"I don't know what happened, sir, but I'm investigating the situation. I'm trying to figure out how it happened and who to hold responsible," Johnson replies nervously.

"Don't bother with an investigation. I am holding you completely responsible for this fiasco and for any possible changes that might occur with our plans for Ms. Cavelo. Do I make myself clear?"

Before Johnson can answer, the line goes dead.

◇◇◇

Stone is not the only one who is irate. Jan Ruther is fuming and Melinda Bale is as mad as a rooster in a cockfight! Both women have their own agendas for not wanting Marissa to succeed. The two women are huddled in a corner of the break room, talking in hushed tones so as not to be overheard by anyone who might walk into the room.

"Who the hell told her she could bust into a police operation on the air? I hold you responsible for this, Jan!"

"Me?" Ruther shoots back. "You know the news director assigned her to cover the grand opening of a stupid pet store. It was just supposed to be another fluff piece. Don't you dare blame me!" Ruther takes a big gulp from her coffee cup that's inscribed with the phrase, *Life's a Bitch* before sneering, "I think you're still upset with yourself for that obvious on-air meltdown on the noon newscast. Or do you blame me for that, too?"

"I'm going to pretend you didn't just say that," Melinda whines. "It's just that my confidence is so fragile. You have no idea what it's like to be forty-three years old and constantly feeling upstaged by a co-anchor fifteen years my junior. I know my career peaked a long time ago. I don't need you or anybody else to remind me of that."

Ruther knows it's best to keep quiet when Bale is feeling sorry for herself.

Melinda continues, "At my age, it's hard to conceal wrinkles and imperfections, especially under those unforgiving high-definition cameras you insisted on installing in the studio. When we're sitting side-by-side, I look tired and old while Marissa looks radiant and energetic. It's not fair."

Jan Ruther nods her head in sympathy and bites her lip to prevent saying anything about how the HD cameras also make it hard for Melinda to conceal her thinning, graying hair and her expanding hips, thighs and mid-section. *It's bad enough being an old news manager,* Jan

46

thinks, *but it must be hell to be an aging anchor, especially since viewers are such tough critics.*

Melinda continues her wallowing. "Not a day goes by that I don't get an email or phone call from someone who's critical of my hair, my clothes, my makeup…even my jewelry. It's been years since I felt confident enough about my looks to leave my house without wearing full makeup or with my hair not perfectly styled. The last time I tried to slip into the grocery store au natural, an unflattering picture of me was posted on the Internet."

"What can I do to improve the situation?"

Without hesitation, Melinda growls, "I want her to fail. You know that's what I've been hoping would happen for months. I've been plotting and planning all kinds of different ways to undermine Marissa's success. I've tried everything. I even slipped the wrong shade of liquid foundation into her drawer so she'd use it in her airbrush applicator. I was hoping my trick would result in an embarrassingly dark shade of makeup for that little Mexican."

Ruther must keep from laughing at Melinda Bales' racist comments, which occasionally surface like stink on a big ugly bug. The irony is that the makeup provided Marissa with a bronze, sun-kissed look. Female viewers even called the station asking for the brand name of the makeup she was using.

"My other attempts also failed. I tried to scramble the words in Marissa's scripts so she would stumble while reading on the air. But the jumbled words didn't even faze her. I also tried hiding items of clothing. But every time Marissa was able to pull together a polished look. How was I to know she keeps back-up items stashed in her car?"

Ruther knew Melinda was desperate, but she was unaware of the lengths Melinda was willing to go.

"I slipped a heavy dose of laxative into Marissa's container of soup while it was being heated in the microwave. I timed it so that the laxative dose would hit her while we were on the air. I was waiting for her to suddenly bolt from the anchor desk on her way to the ladies' room. When Marissa walked to her desk empty-handed without her bowl of soup I asked her about it. I couldn't believe it when she told me that a studio guy asked to borrow some money because he was hungry and she gave him her soup!"

The irony of that failure was the guy who got the doctored soup was assigned to work Melinda's camera. The laxative caused him to keep sprinting out of the studio to the bathroom, which often left Melinda out of focus, or worse, completely cut out of the shot.

Melinda gets up to leave the break room. "I hate her and all that she has accomplished!" she fumes before going out the door.

Jan returns to her own office. She takes out her phone and dials a familiar extension. *I need to stop Cavelo in her tracks. We'll have to work fast before her head swells and, more importantly, before she receives an offer to become a serious broadcast journalist at another station—or another market.*

She says into her phone, "I have an idea that I guarantee will improve your mood. Come to my office now. You won't be disappointed."

Jan Ruther hangs up the phone and sits back in her desk chair waiting for all hell to break loose. Just the thought of shaking things up brings a smile to her face.

Six

It's almost six-thirty in the evening before Ken and Marissa finally get back to the station. She's exhausted, but still running on adrenaline.

As she reviews her notes from the police chief's briefing, Norman Baker stops by her desk. Norman is the nicest guy at the station and has worked at KATX for more than thirty years. He's part of the building's operational staff and his duties include delivering the mail, re-stocking office supplies and occasionally making minor repairs. On a typical day, he keeps busy changing light bulbs and replacing air filters. He's low-key and quiet and is always around, which is why hardly anyone notices him.

Unlike most of her colleagues who ignore Norman, because they have no use for him, Marissa enjoys talking to him because he has a subtle, yet keen insight into the internal workings at the station. "Hi, Norman. How are you?" she asks.

"I'm doing pretty good, although I'm surprised to see you here." He stands by her desk, sorting through the day's mail, looking for items addressed to her.

"Why's that? Where did you think I would be?"

"After what Jan Ruther has planned, I thought you would have told her to take a hike."

"What plans are you talking about?"

"From what I understand, she and Bale have been busy figuring out ways to keep you in your place. You're supposed to be covering

49

ribbon-cuttings, not exposing exotic bird heists. Or didn't you know that?" he asks with a chuckle, although it's clear this is no joke. "Those two cackling hens were in Ruther's office earlier."

"Talking about me? How do you know?"

"I was next door, working on the air vent. The new meteorologist swears a mouse is back in there. Anyway, Jan admits it isn't going to be easy because viewers are always calling the station to tell management how much they like you…." He pauses before continuing, "Just remember, you have a lot of fans among viewers and they'd be very upset if they learned you were being disciplined for doing your job." As he's about to walk away, Norman turns to tell Marissa, "Be prepared for her to threaten you during your annual performance evaluation." He walks away to finish delivering the mail.

There isn't much that Jan Ruther enjoys, but job evaluations are an exception. She savors the opportunity to penalize anyone who's crossed her. She seems to enjoy citing news department policies that employees have broken. She's been known to make up policies on the spot.

Just as Marissa is trying not to think about Norman's warning, her desk phone rings. *Oh, no! This can't be good.* It's Jan Ruther. "Hi, Jan. I was just about to head into an editing room. Is there something you need?"

"Come to my office, now." It's an order, not a request.

Marissa heads to Jan's office and knocks on the door. Jan calls her in and then instructs her to close the door and take a seat. "That was a pretty amazing live shot you and Ken managed to pull off at the pet store today. There you were right in the middle of all the action as bullets and feathers were about to start flying." She smiles before suddenly becoming very stern. "Don't get any ideas about trying anything as daring as that again. Do you hear me? Failure to follow directions is grounds for dismissal…and that includes veering from your assignment without authorization. So, I strongly suggest you leave the police busts to news reporters."

Marissa cannot believe what she is hearing. It doesn't make any sense for a reporter to be told not to go after hard news as it's unfolding. "I understand what my assignment was…but any real journalist would've done exactly what I did."

"That may be true, but I'm not talking to any other journalist. I'm talking to you. Let me remind you of two very important factors: A—your contract is up for renewal, and B—it's almost time for your annual performance evaluation. As the executive producer, it's my responsibility to review your work from the past year. In your case, your actions today will be cited in your review since you failed to follow directions. You were supposed to provide a light, feature story not a breaking news event…. And, there's also the more serious matter of placing other people in danger by your actions, including store employees and customers. The outcome could have been tragic and it would have been your fault."

"I'm sorry. Ken and I never meant to place anyone in danger." She cringes, imagining what could have happened had undercover police not stepped in when they did.

"You should know that the station is facing a possible lawsuit by one store employee who is threatening to sue for emotional damages because of the dangerous situation you single-handedly created."

"That's awful. I feel terrible. Tell me, is there anything I can do to make this right?"

"Well…since you seem dead set on proving yourself as a serious journalist, I'm willing to assign you to cover a hard news story," Jan says matter-of-factly. "You can thank Melinda Bale for this idea since she stumbled upon it by chance the other day. A woman stopped her at the neighborhood grocery store and asked Melinda to help make her fifteen-year-old daughter's wish come true. At first Melinda thought, like so many other strangers, this woman just wanted an autograph or a signed photo. But it turns out this woman is raising money so her daughter can fly to Hollywood for a dance audition. Can you believe that?"

Marissa wonders about the accuracy of what Jan is telling her. She is having a hard time picturing any stranger brave enough to approach Melinda Bale. Just picturing Melinda in a grocery store is also a stretch. "Why would the woman's daughter need to pay for a tryout? Who's holding the audition?" Marissa asks.

"It's an audition arranged by the Regency Dance Studio. You've heard of them, haven't you? They have locations worldwide. Anyway, it turns out the school reps told the woman her daughter has the rare qualities that guarantee fame and fortune in live theater productions, TV commercials and even in movies with the current dance craze in entertainment. All the woman has to do is pay the school five thousand dollars for the audition. This woman told Bale her family has already spent hundreds of dollars so the daughter can attend classes at the dance school. Personally, I wonder, what's another 5k down the drain?" Jan asks sarcastically.

"Well, coming from a family with limited resources, I can tell you that five thousand dollars is a major investment," Marissa says. "It would be next to impossible to raise that kind of money in a short period of time."

"I'm not interested in your family's struggles. I want you to put on that investigative hat you've been so anxious to wear and find out if this audition is legitimate. Talk to the girl and her family and see if they're just throwing money away. I have the name and number of the mom. It'll be up to you to find out if the five thousand covers travel expenses and hotel room or if it is simply for the opportunity to meet with a talent scout. Certainly nothing illegal on the surface, but it's worth a closer look. Your time is limited to check into this. This story will air Thursday at six p.m. Are we clear?"

Although she only has days, Marissa is not about to let a tight schedule stop her from accepting the challenge. "Thursday at six. It'll be ready to air!"

Ruther shoves a piece of paper with a name, phone number and address scribbled on it. "This is the contact info for the woman whose daughter is enrolled at the Regency Dance Studio. Now, go on. Get out of my office. I have work to do."

As Marissa turns to leave Ruther's office, she catches a quick glimpse of what appears to be a smile on Ruther's face. *What did I do to generate that smile? Whatever it was, it's not good.*

Seven

t's too late to start working on the story so Marissa decides to go home and get a fresh start tomorrow morning. She stops by her desk to get her purse and the stack of mail Norman left on her desk earlier. As she stuffs it into her computer bag to go through at home, an envelope falls to the floor. As she bends over to pick it up, it only takes a split-second to recognize the return address. Anyone in the news business knows the familiar logo and address of Marcus Feldman, the top talent recruiter for AAN—All Access News. It's the number one 24/7 news network not only in the U.S. but around the world. Feldman has the power to propel any anchor at any station into stardom with just one phone call. Her hands are shaking as she rips open the envelope.

For a moment, she imagines what it would be like to be invited to audition for a network anchor position. Getting a job with AAN would mean living in an exciting, vibrant city like Washington, D.C., Los Angeles or even New York and hobnobbing with celebrities, high-ranking government officials and foreign royalty. She'd lead an exciting social life dressed in haute couture and travel to cover assignments in exotic locations. Not to mention the salary.

She allows herself to daydream, *I'd be assigned an assistant who'd coordinate my wardrobe. I might never wear the same outfit more than once. My hair and makeup would be taken care of, and I'd have access to a private car and driver to take me wherever I need to go.*

Then reality slaps her in the face as she realizes such a promotion would also involve a great deal of hard work and would bring intense pressure. A new, high-profile anchor position would also mean saying goodbye to her sister and friends in Austin. *But, hey, I can make new friends, right? And I'd be able to fly back and forth. The truth is, adjusting to a new position and a new city would be easy. So why are my hands shaking?*

Marissa hasn't read a piece of mail so quickly since receiving the letter from the Admission's Office of the University of Texas.

Dear Ms. Cavelo,

Thank you for your interest in All Access News. We welcome correspondence from up-and-coming journalists such as yourself. As you know, AAN is a global news operation with stations and bureaus around the world. However, the opportunities to become a member of our award-winning team are limited. Currently, there are no openings for general assignment reporters or anchors. However, you're encouraged to continue reviewing job postings on our website since new positions do become available from time to time. We don't keep applications on file, so job candidates are required to re-submit applications and updated resume tapes when applying for a new position. Again, thank you for contacting us and best of luck in your career as a journalist.

Sincerely,

Marcus Feldman

Short and sweet. Most rejection letters are just that. Except this one has a handwritten note added at the bottom of the letter just below the signature line. It reads: "I'll be in Austin for the annual AAN convention. Stop by the booth. I'll be meeting with other journalists and prospective applicants. Hope to see you there. M."

In all of the excitement from the pet store bust, Marissa lost track of what else was going on in the world. The AAN convention kicked off two days ago, but she had no reason to attend. Now wild horses couldn't keep her away. *And I'll have an updated resume tape to show Mr. Feldman that includes the pet store bust. It's proof I can handle breaking news and that I'm capable of much more than fluff pieces,* she thinks with newborn confidence.

She grabs her notebook and makes a list of everything needed in advance of meeting with Marcus Feldman:

- Check the AAN convention schedule to see when he's holding one-on-one meetings with potential applicants.
- Edit my resume tape to include live coverage of the pet store bust.
- Print resume with updated headshot photo attached.
- Stop by dry cleaners to pick up my "knock 'em dead" outfit.

The next item on her list is going to be the toughest to tackle. She'll have to find time to get away from work in order to stop by the convention center. It won't be easy since the station is in ratings, which means no one is allowed time off for any reason. Not even if you're sick as a dog and need to see a doctor. Even death is inexcusable during ratings.

Jan would be furious if she found out Marissa was going to meet with a talent recruiter. She'd consider it an act of treason. *I'll just have to work extremely fast to complete my work so that I can slip away unnoticed.*

She closes her notebook and tucks it in her purse for safekeeping.

Eight

Marissa wakes up the next morning, wondering if the past twenty-four hours has been a dream. She's filled with a mixture of relief and pride knowing she's finally proven to the world she's a serious journalist.

The pet store bust unfolded before my eyes, but more importantly it unfolded right before Ken's camera! Ken. Just his name brings a smile to her face. *I wonder what it'd be like waking up next to him? What the hell am I thinking? Was that rush of sexual tension that we felt yesterday real? Or a fluke?*

As Marissa jumps out of bed, a feeling of dread washes over her. *What if I see him at work and he pretends nothing happened between us and we go back to being just coworkers who flirt? Nah…that's crazy. There's something there all right. I don't know what it is or how it happened, but I know it's real and I know I can't wait to see him again.*

Marissa would forever be appreciative of Ken's professionalism yesterday. Immediately after they went off the air, Ken kept his camera rolling and managed to capture exclusive footage of the suspects being placed in a patrol car. Plus, he snagged video of the exotic birds being unloaded from the semi. They also got great sound from the people in the crowd who came for the store's grand opening and had no idea a smuggling ring had been busted. They thought the cop cars that pulled around back were somehow part of the grand opening festivities.

It was the top story at six p.m. and again at ten. The personal triumph for Marissa came at the end of the police chief's news conference. Members of a rival television station asked for video or photographs and the police chief looked at her and said, "Sorry, but you'll have to talk to Miss Cavelo about video, since she's the only news reporter who was on the scene and the only one who can help you with that."

She loved every single exclusive moment of it. And it felt like vindication since until now, she'd felt like some of the other reporters from competing stations were looking down their noses at her. She wasn't just being super sensitive; she'd heard the catty whispers intentionally spoken loud enough for her to hear, "features only"… "a *muñeca*," a doll with a pretty face and no brains. But not anymore. She's proven she's a serious journalist.

Since Marissa is back to her regular shift, she can focus on her new assignment—the Regency Dance Studio and its expensive audition policy.

Before leaving her apartment, she checks her cell phone. There are two new voicemail messages—both are from CC. Her immediate instinct is to return CC's call, but just as she picks up the phone to call her, CC texts her, "Meet me at our place before you head to work."

Marissa replies, "On my way now."

She hops into her car for the quick drive a couple of blocks away through her north central Austin neighborhood. "Our place" is a small, quiet park that's halfway between both of their apartments, which makes it a perfect meeting place for the both of them. It's well maintained with huge shady oak trees and a path where people are often seen walking their dogs, jogging or pushing children in strollers. After they both graduated from the University of Texas, CC and Marissa made it a point to spend time together at "our place" on a regular basis. At first, it was daily. Sometimes they'd meet in the late afternoon after getting off work. But then things got busier with their separate careers and, as expected, their scheduled time together became less and less often.

Now they're more likely to head to "our place" alone. Marissa takes a book and a thermos of coffee in the morning when it's quiet. CC often brings one of the dogs entrusted to her care to the park. They both hate that their lives have sent them in separate directions, leaving less time for each other than ever before.

Although lately, Marissa can't put her finger on it, something in Carissa's demeanor and mood has changed. If she didn't know better, she'd think her twin is hiding something from her. They've never had secrets from each other. Never. CC has always been her closest friend and confidant—just the two of them against the world. The trauma of losing their parents at an early age made them inseparable. That's the main reason they both applied to the University of Texas so that they could move to Austin together. They were roommates throughout college where CC received a business degree and Marissa received a degree in broadcast journalism. By their junior year, they'd began developing their own friends and areas of interest. Carissa got a job working as a dog groomer. She really loves the dogs and customers really love her. So, it wasn't surprising to anyone that her goal was to open her own dog care center.

Carissa knows Marissa's desire to be a serious journalist started when they were growing up in Houston, watching the news and reading the newspaper to their parents as a way of helping them learn English. CC encouraged Marissa to take her first job in the small town of Victoria, about 130 miles south of Austin. She worked there for less than a year before being hired by KATX. It felt like the longest year of her life because it was the first time they'd been apart. They were both excited when Marissa landed a job in Austin, so they could be in the same city again.

Having shared the pitfalls and frustrations and the roller-coaster ride of her TV career, Marissa can't wait to share her excitement over the pet store bust with her sister and her plans to impress the AAN talent recruiter. *And then there's the subject of Ken!* Neither of them has ever seriously dated, so talking about a guy will be a totally new topic of conversation for them.

Marissa sees Carissa getting out of her car in the parking lot. She looks like she's scowling and her lower lip is swollen. Marissa parks, gets out of her car and before she even reaches her sister Carissa is yelling, "Are you crazy? You could have gotten yourself killed! What the hell is the matter with you busting in on such an obviously dangerous operation?"

Marissa loves her sister and how alike they are in so many ways and how different they are in others. Growing up, Carissa was always the one who was taking risks—skateboarding without a helmet, driving without a license, swimming when and where signs warn you not to. And then there were the dangers she faced when she decided to travel alone to Europe after college graduation. Her choices in guys to date and places to live have also proved her fearlessness.

"Why, CC! I'm glad to know you care and that you were watching," Marissa jokes.

"Of course I was watching! I wanted to see what the inside of that giant pet store looked like. Instead, all I saw was a crazy view of the loading dock area. I cannot believe you pulled off that live shot. How did you know what was happening? Do you have an inside source? Who's been tipping you off?" she asks. Marissa cannot understand why CC is so angry.

"Whoa. Slow down a minute. Where are all these questions coming from? You sound like a detective. Honestly, I stumbled upon what was happening in the loading dock area when I went looking for the store manager."

"The store manager? Did he tell you what was about to go down? What's his name?"

"As far as I know the store manager didn't have a clue about what was going on. Why are you asking so many questions?"

"No reason. I was just wondering… and believe it or not, I was worried about you. The anger has turned to exasperation. "You walked right into a danger zone where bullets were about to start flying. We've already lost our parents. I don't want to lose you, too."

"I'm touched by your concern, CC, but to be honest, I wasn't thinking about any possible danger. I was just following my instincts. I've been trying so hard to prove myself as a serious journalist. This was my best shot at doing that, and I wasn't going to let anything stop me."

"Not even flying bullets?"

"Nope, not even the risk of flying bullets."

"Okay. The important thing is you're safe. And you've got your big news scoop. So now what? Are you going back to being a feature reporter where you're not in any danger?"

"I hope not, because feature reporting is the last thing I want to do. So far all I've experienced are near disasters anytime the words 'feature' or 'fluff' are even mentioned. You know that."

CC finally laughs.

"The pet store bust seems to have convinced the executive producer to give me more hard news assignments. She gave me one yesterday as a matter of fact, but, enough about the pet store bust. Tell me what happened to your lower lip? It looks like you busted it."

"Oh, this?" she asks as she gently touches the cut that's poorly camouflaged with a bandage. "I was trying to put a squirmy dog back in its cage when he wriggled loose and slammed the back of his head into my lip. I was ready to strangle his furry neck." She starts laughing. "I busted my lip wide open, but all I can think about is dripping my blood on to his expensive bedding. Can you believe it?"

"Are you sure you don't need stitches?"

"No, don't be silly. I'm fine."

"Well, if you're sure you're okay…. I've got more exciting news to share with you."

She seems relieved at the change of subject. "Really? What is it? You bought one of the exotic birds those crooks were trying to smuggle out of the country, didn't you? I warned you to stay away from them. They're expensive."

"No, I didn't buy a bird. But I am going to use that entire episode to grab the attention of an AAN recruiter who's in Austin this week. Isn't that great?"

"What do you mean 'grab his attention?'" CC asks, warily.

"My goal is to get him to notice me and to consider me for an anchor/reporting job at the network level. Wouldn't that be exciting?"

"Of course it would be exciting, but where would you live?"

"AAN has bureaus in New York and Los Angeles, and their main headquarters is in Miami."

"But that's so far away. Are you sure you could handle moving away from me and Austin?"

"It's too early to worry about that. It's a long shot, so let's not talk about it now. Besides, I have some other exciting news to share." Marissa's voice is giddy with excitement, but before CC can ask what her news is about or try to guess Marissa blurts out, "I've met a special guy!"

"What? Who is he?"

Marissa tells CC about Ken, and how they "clicked" while facing the unknown dangers of the pet store assignment. "I'm not sure where our relationship is headed, but I've never felt more physically and emotionally attracted to someone in my life."

CC's reaction is not what Marissa had expected. She thought her sister would be happy for her, and anxious to meet Ken, but instead she drops back as if the wind's been knocked out of her. And although she tries to sound cheerful it's hard for her to hide her disappointment.

"I'm happy for you. I can't wait to meet him," she says in a forced manner.

"You will. I promise. You are, and always will be, the most important person in my life so, of course, you'll meet him. I just don't want to rush into anything. I mean, even though we've been working together for months, we're just coworkers who sometimes engage in harmless flirting. Nothing more. That is until this last assignment. I don't know. Maybe it was the excitement of the live shot. Anyway, I'm glad you took time out to see me this morning. I don't know about you, but it feels like we never have enough time together anymore. I miss you. I miss our long talks. I want to hear more about what's going on in your life. We've been so busy talking about me, but I want you to know that your life is important, too."

Marissa starts firing questions at CC so fast there's no way she can answer, "How are you? How's work? Are you making any progress securing the loan to open your own pet care center?"

"Thanks for asking," CC says. "But I have nothing new to share. In fact, I gotta head to work, too, before clients stop by to drop off their dogs for the day. Running a doggie day care for the super-rich means you have to work hard to keep everybody happy. I'm hoping to get loan approval soon, which means I'll be looking around for a location to open up my own place. I'm going to call it, 'CC's Pet Palace.' What do you think?"

"Are you serious? That's awesome news! Hey, that would be a feature story I'd be happy to cover...the grand opening of my twin sister's own pet palace." Marissa gives her sister a hug and as she releases her from the embrace, she feels a pang of sadness. "I miss you, sis. Do you wanna grab something to eat later today? Or tell me when you can come over and I'll make one of Mami's *comidas especial...* just for us."

"You? Cook?" she quips and bursts out laughing. "Seriously, I'd hate for you to butcher one of the few sweet memories we have of Mami by messing up her recipes. We'd end up making a mess of your *cocina* and ordering pizza, which would be fine." She sighs. "Unfortunately, I have no idea when we might be able to get together. Your schedule is crazy and I've picked up extra hours at work, too."

"I understand." Marissa tries not to sound too dejected. "Maybe we'll play it safe. No cooking. Just drinks. Anyway, let's promise to start making time for each other and not let our crazy lives keep us apart, okay?"

"Okay," she says. And with that, they hug and kiss before Marissa turns around to leave, neither one really knowing when they'll see each other again.

Nine

CC decides to stay put and finish her coffee as she watches Marissa drive off. She thinks about all the times the two have shared at this park. As she thinks, she realizes that the gap between them began a long time ago. CC does not want to accept this truth. It's hard for her to wrap her brain around it because of how inseparable they used to be. Besides looking and sounding alike, they used to think alike and they could sense how the other felt. Most people think being a twin is the best thing in the world and in many ways it is, but there's also a downside that only a twin understands.

CC remembers all the two experienced together—from the discomfort of the chicken pox and the loss of a first tooth to the fear of the first day of school and the times they were both teased by mean girls. They never faced any childhood or teenage experience alone. They were always there for each other.

But Marissa began to blossom as a young adult before CC. *I've always taken a back seat to her,* CC thinks. *She's older, but only by five minutes. She's more outgoing and has always had an easier time meeting people and getting what she wants.* Resentment begins to build in CC. *She wanted to attend the University of Texas, so I applied, too. After graduation, she accepted her first job in Victoria, but I knew she wanted to get back to Austin as soon as possible. So, I stayed put. It felt like I was holding her place in line, waiting for her to return.*

Thinking back on it, the years Marissa was gone were amazing for CC, like a quiet rebellion. In her mind, it was the first time she alone decided which movie to rent, where to eat, how to dress without being criticized and whether or not she wanted to stay up late without anybody chastising her for the dark circles under her eyes the next morning. She could party whenever and with whomever she wanted to. It was no big deal for her to sleep with a guy she never planned to see again. It was during this time that she believed she was able to define her own interests and to recognize her self-worth. It was liberating. And she slowly came to realize that she didn't need Marissa to be complete.

CC feels conflicted as she does anytime she starts to feel confident about herself. When Marissa moved back to Austin, CC felt that she expected them to automatically return to the inseparable life that they'd shared before, as if nothing had changed. But Marissa returned as a television reporter—a big shot celebrity wherever she goes, while CC washes dogs.

Marissa seems unaware of the attention, but CC notices it whenever they go into a store or restaurant and how people stare at Marissa as she walks by. CC hears them whisper as they try to figure out why they recognize her. And sometimes there's the subtle victory when they figure it out, 'Oh, she's that girl on the news!' CC became the girl who looks like the girl on the news. At first, it was kind of funny and then it became downright annoying to be mistaken for Marissa. CC even thought about cutting her hair and dying it a different color, but then thought, *No. This is my life and I shouldn't have to change a thing.* She vowed to continue to be her own person, even if it put her at odds with her sister.

A litany of complaints runs through her mind: *I'm tired of feeling like Marissa Cavelo's shadow and sidekick. I put my dreams and career on hold so hers could take priority, but not anymore!* With a renewed sense of defiance, she gets into her car and heads to work, determined to put herself first from now on.

I can't believe my life has boiled down to this, she thinks, an hour later as she shovels poop out of a custom-made canine crate and into a disposable bag. Running an upscale daycare and boutique for dogs and their super-rich owners is tedious work. Shoveling shit is not even her least favorite duty. Sometimes she feels like a robot that automatically performs menial tasks without a second thought. To break the monotony her mind wanders to what she'd rather be doing. CC dreams of cruising the Mediterranean Sea aboard a luxury liner, sitting at a high-stakes roulette table in Monte Carlo, or sipping on a cocktail under a palapa on the beaches of Cabo San Lucas. These aren't unattainable fantasies for CC. These are all-weekend excursions she's experienced recently with a special guy. Just brief flashbacks of these adventures can make any dumb doggie-related duty go by faster.

CC remembers the day, nine months ago, when he first walked into the shop. It was early on a Saturday morning, in February, and it was one of those rare winter days in Austin when the temperature hovers right around freezing. He walked in with an expensive customized Louis Vuitton pet carrier. He put the carrier down on the counter and up popped the cutest face of a tiny purebred that had obviously been enjoying a pampered life. The toy Yorkshire Terrier was sporting an expensive custom-made collar with Bulgari crystals.

CC's first thoughts were, *What's this good-looking, manly man doing with such a girly dog?* And then she imagined how much better that expensive dog collar would look strapped around her wrist. The dog was sitting in a mink fur-lined carrier and wore an unbelievably soft cashmere sweater. None of this surprised CC considering she was used to dealing with over-indulged dogs and their over-indulging owners.

The boutique she manages bills itself as a "Four Star Resort" for discriminating pet lovers. Personal assistants, maids and occasional limo drivers drop off the canines of wealthy owners. It's rare for her to deal with any of the owners, most of whom think they're too good to speak directly to someone as subservient as a dog caretaker and groomer.

This was only one of the reasons why this particular dog owner made such a powerful first impression on her. The main draw was his sheer sexuality! He was handsome in a rugged, macho way with brown, wavy hair. He had a dark, exotic look to him and a very serious demeanor. His jeans and leather jacket hugged his body perfectly. His boots, watch and sunglasses, like the rest of his outfit, were obviously very expensive. All of this prompted her to quickly glance at his ring finger. *Nothing there.* She tried to be discreet as she looked outside the front window to see his car—a shiny, red, one-hundred-thousand-dollar Maserati waited curbside. This was CC's version of "love at first sight."

She replayed that initial meeting in her mind: "Welcome to Regal Pets. I'm Carissa. Who have we got here today?"

For an instant, he stared at her, as if he was trying to place where he'd seen her before. CC is familiar with that 'I-know-you-from-somewhere-but-I-can't-remember-where' look. Once, while partying with friends in a downtown club, a guy asked that same tired question and she was drunk enough to have a little harmless fun with him. She answered, "Yes! I'm the girl on the news. Why are you asking? Would you like an autograph?" She pulled a pen out of her purse and scribbled on a napkin. She could tell he was extremely happy to meet who he thought was TV anchor Marissa Cavelo until she told him, "That'll be fifty bucks…and I don't take credit cards." The fan was stunned and disappointed until she started laughing. "I'm kidding," CC told him, and he'd bought her drinks all night. They ended up sleeping together. CC never told him the truth and he probably still thinks that he slept with a real TV anchor.

The man told CC, "This is my dog, Ace. I've been called out of town suddenly and need to board him for the weekend."

"Well, that shouldn't be a problem," she responded cheerfully. "We have a form to fill out that asks a couple of basic questions. And we'll also need your veterinarian to email a copy of Ace's vaccination records."

His forceful gaze made her slightly uncomfortable and she had trouble maintaining a businesslike attitude as she stood a few feet in front of him. "Does Ace have any special dietary requirements?" she asked while handing him a clipboard.

Suddenly, he grabbed her arm with a little too much force. Then, just as quickly, his touch became gentle as he released his hold. "I'm sorry if I startled you," he said. "It's just that I'm in a hurry. I'm on my way to the airport and I doubt I'll be able to contact my vet on such short notice. This is an unplanned trip." He continued to hold CC in his gaze and then added, "Will this help in lieu of the vet's records?" He slipped a one-hundred-dollar bill into her hand.

CC liked two things about this man: his smile and his money. "Sure, no problem," she answered without hesitation and discreetly slipped the bill into her pocket.

He hurriedly filled out the form, gave Ace a pat on his little furry head and then flashed CC that unforgettable smile. In a wink, he was out the door, and before CC could look up from the completed form, his red Maserati was gone. Ace began to whimper with the realization that his owner, H.N., left him behind. H.N. was all that served as his signature on the Client Agreement form. CC peered into Ace's little brown eyes and wondered how such a macho, slightly sinister mystery man could own such a yappy little dog? Realizing that Ace would require personal, round-the-clock attention, CC smuggled him out of Regal Pets and took him home with her, knowing it was a violation of the facility's policy and could get her fired.

When H.N. came to retrieve Ace two days later, CC made sure she was the only person on duty. She wore something sexy rather than her usual sweatshirt and jeans. He appeared more relaxed and seemed genuinely happy to see CC. They flirted, and she told him about providing Ace with her undivided attention.

One thing led to another. First, they met for coffee. He seemed attentive and asked her about her family and how she got started in the pet care business. She told him about her love of animals, how she started volunteering at animal shelters years ago and described her special bond with cats and dogs abandoned by their owners. She told him, "I know it's probably related to feeling abandoned at an early age when my parents were suddenly taken away from me and my sister."

"What do mean 'taken away?'" he asked.

This is the first time a guy had taken a genuine interest in CC and she found herself sharing the details of the day her life fell apart. "My sister, Marissa, and I were walking together on our way home from middle school. When we turned the corner to the street where we lived, we saw crime scene tape draped across our house. Police officers and other crime scene technicians were moving about like busy ants. I remember my sister and I both dropped our backpacks and started running to our house. As soon as we reached the front yard, some cops grabbed us and held us back. I know they meant well, but we were so upset not to be able to go inside to see our parents. It was awful, and so bewildering, not knowing what had happened to them. We were placed in the backseat of a waiting sedan and driven away by a case-worker with Child Protective Services. We didn't find out until hours later when a special Victims Assistant counselor informed us that our parents had been found murdered!"

"What else did they tell you about what happened that day?" he asked her.

"The house was pretty much undisturbed except where my dad had put up a fight. Robbery didn't make any sense because there wasn't anything of value in our house. All our furnishings and clothes were second-hand. My mother took care our items were clean, but just about everything we owned was some kind of hand-me-down."

H.N. listed to her with empathy. He asked her where they had lived in Houston, what her parents did for a living and whether or not their case was ever solved. It was a relief to answer his questions. For the first time in her life, somebody cared enough to ask and she didn't hesitate to answer. She told him about the low-income neighborhood where they grew up and more about her family and about that night. "My dad was a night watchman; we didn't find out more about the senseless crime until years later and only because the lead detective is a close friend of ours. In fact, Detective Hector Garcia eventually took on the role as our protector and guardian. We even call him Tío Hector. That means 'uncle.' He told us that when he arrived on the scene, the first responding officer pulled him aside to tell him that a suspect had been in the process of ransacking the house, when my mom and dad came home and startled him. The kid was tying up our mother when our father tried to stop him. He had a knife, though, and ended up stabbing my parents to death. By the time officers arrived, the suspect, who was in his early twenties, was picked-up a few blocks away. He was walking around in a daze with blood on his clothes, but with nothing taken from our house. Tío Hector knew we didn't own anything of value, which prompted the police to question why our home was targeted by a burglar. To this day, we've never known if there was another motive behind the break-in."

H.N. sat there and listened attentively. He told her that he'd be happy to help her forget the painful past if she would let him.

CC thought he was just being nice, but the next day, he stopped by Regal Pets as she was closing up for the day and asked if she wanted to get something to eat. She assumed they were going to a nearby restaurant. She was stunned when she learned he had arranged for a four-star restaurant to close for the evening so that the chef and staff could provide them with uninterrupted service.

From that moment on, her life was never the same.

Now it's a whirlwind of living the good life filled with exclusive clubs, a private jet, the best restaurants, shopping sprees and gifts—expensive gifts. CC spends unlimited amounts of money on whatever she wants, with only a few caveats. H.N. insists that she not be 'flashy' with his wealth. He prefers discretion about everything including where they go and what they do. He's also very discreet about himself. Since they started seeing each other, he's revealed very little about his personal background or his professional life.

CC likes it this way—having a secret sugar daddy. In exchange, all she has to do is look good and be available whenever he calls. Sex is always something he wants from her. And she obliges. There's little kissing or foreplay and any intimacy between them ends as soon as H.N. climaxes. Her sexual satisfaction isn't important to him, and there is no post-coital cuddling. Once finished, H.N. jumps out of bed, gets on his cell phone and leaves CC to pleasure herself. CC doesn't mind. She can easily satisfy herself before falling right to sleep—alone.

They rarely go out in Austin, but when they travel to other cities, they go out in style. CC is leading a double life. She's the girlfriend of a wealthy man who indulges in travel and shopping in other cities. But she's also his secret intimate companion who lives a simple life. CC doesn't really care where their relationship is headed and is relieved that he has not made any promises about the future. There are few demands as long as she remains available and discreet. What CC likes most is that she's managed to sock away a nice little chunk of change from the money he regularly gives her—what she calls her "girlfriend allowance." *I've earned every penny!* She's waiting for the right time to ask him for a small loan to start her own dog care and grooming business. She just needs to convince him he'll get a return on his investment.

Her ultimate goal is to be her own boss and to operate a chain of elite full-service dog care centers. Most importantly, she wants to create a distinct identity that's separate her from her sister's. She longs for the day when someone asks Marissa if she's related to that successful, independent businesswoman, Carissa Cavelo!

CC goes back to scooping poop and refilling water bowls. She thinks about her chat with Marissa earlier. Marissa, flying high on her big "scoop" at the pet store, has no idea how many problems that stunt caused for CC. H.N. blames her for Marissa's actions. She touches her swollen lip, the biggest reminder of everything that's gone wrong in the past twenty-four hours.

All of the drama that has unfolded makes her even more determined to work her ass off to launch her own business—the sooner the better. *I just have to be patient and play my cards right.*

CC goes to the cupboard and locates the two-hundred-dollar bottle of designer dog shampoo infused with Moroccan oil. She laughs to herself at how easy it is to fill the fancy glass bottle with cheap puppy shampoo from the grocery store. It's also easy to get customers to pay the invoice and pocket the markup. She can't help but smirk when she thinks about how dumb and gullible some rich people can be. *What they don't know won't hurt them, but it will help me…a whole helluva lot!*

Ten

Marissa is thinking about her visit with her sister. *Fifteen minutes is not enough time for two people, let alone two sisters, to bring each other up-to-date on their lives,* she thinks. A twinge of sadness fills her during the short drive to work. She understands that changes in her life also mean changes in her relationships, especially with CC. If her career takes off and she becomes an anchor in a major market, then she and CC will be living in different cities again. The time she spent in Victoria was hard on both of them. She worries how potential changes in her life will impact their relationship.

She puts the future aside. Right now she needs to focus on the dance studio story. She knows that people have very short memories, especially when it comes to television segments. An outstanding live shot one day is forgotten as soon as the next live shot begins. So, when she enters the studio she is not surprised when coworkers walk right past her, ignoring her just like they did the day before yesterday.

Her thoughts are interrupted by Hank Johnson who is looking at his watch and yelling, "Cavelo, you're late. What's the problem? Did you get sidetracked signing autographs?"

A few people nearby manage to laugh at his lame joke. They always do, which only encourages him to tell another one. "Or did you have to solve another crime on your way in?" he asks. "Ha, ha, ha,'" he chuckles, not realizing he's the only one laughing this time.

Marissa chooses to ignore him and heads to her desk to start reviewing scripts. She hopes there's a message there for her from the man who's a close and trusted relative, Austin Police Department Detective Hector Garcia. He's left two messages asking her to call him. The second one is marked "Urgent."

Marissa has known Hector Garcia for as long as she can remember. Her family watched him grow up when they all lived in Houston's rough Eastside. Back then, he was a young officer who was just starting out on the force. Officer Garcia always managed to drive through their neighborhood and would stop to see how they were doing. He would ask for her father's advice on various matters, although it was evident Hector Garcia didn't really need an answer. Instead, he knew it made her father feel good to be asked his opinion. Her mother always offered him a cool drink of homemade lemonade. It was like he was the older son her parents wanted but didn't have. In the evening, or at church when they said their prayers, her mother always prayed for Officer Garcia's safety.

Marissa could not have predicted that he'd be the one, a few years later, to take her and CC under his protective wing. He was the only familiar face on that gruesome day. She believes that Hector would have taken them into his home if he could have, but that wasn't possible back then. The Department of Family and Protective Services, which oversees children in crisis, would have turned down a request for custody from a non-relative single man with his own hectic work schedule. Instead, on his own, Hector managed to stay involved in their lives in many other ways. Over the years, he became a surrogate uncle. She often wondered if planning and strategy landed him on the police force in Austin about the same time she and CC started attending the University of Texas. She doubted it was a coincidence because he was too serious and focused not to shape his own destiny, especially with how much their care and wellbeing meant to him.

IT'S NEWS TO ME

Marissa is happy that he now has his own family. He is married to a wonderful woman who loves him and who recognizes the special relationship he has with the twins. CC and Marissa are always included in their family functions and holiday gatherings. The Garcias know no one will ever replace their parents, but for the twins, it's nice to be part of someone else's circle of closeness.

Marissa dials his direct line and is happy to hear his stern, but kind voice saying, "Hello, Marissa. I was hoping you'd call. Have you recuperated from the excitement of your latest adventure?"

"If you're referring to yesterday's live shot and brief encounter with some of your fellow law enforcement colleagues, then yes, I have. This is also my first chance to call you back. What's up?"

"It's not something I want to discuss over the phone. Do you have time to stop by my office after you finish the noon newscast? It won't take long. All I need is about a half an hour of your time." There is no sense of urgency like his messages conveyed.

"For you, Tío, I'll always make time. But wait, is everything alright? Your message was marked urgent. Are you and the family okay? Do I need to see if CC can join us?"

"Yes, everyone is fine. No, it doesn't involve family, and no, you don't need to bother CC. But it would be nice if you could bring along the news photographer who worked with you on that pet store assignment. I assume it's someone you know well and trust?"

"Yes, he is, and actually it's someone I was hoping you'd be meeting soon anyway." There's a hint of nervousness in her voice since introducing a man with whom she's secretly in lust with is not something she's ever done before.

"Great. I'll share details with you both when you stop by...let's say one-thirty?"

"You've piqued my curiosity. We'll see you at one-thirty, if not a little earlier."

Marissa is still trying to figure out why Tío H is being so secretive as she sends Ken a text to see if he's available at one o'clock. Fortunately, his response is prompt and positive. "I'm available any time. I'll be waiting at one."

She realizes Ken has no way of knowing this is a professional meeting and not a personal rendezvous that would allow them to take up the bliss where they left off yesterday. She wonders what his reaction will be when he finds out they've been summoned to APD headquarters.

Marissa makes notes for her busy day. First up is the newscast at noon. If she manages her time right, she hopes she can call the dance studio mom and try to squeeze in an interview with her and her daughter later in the day. She dials the number on the piece of paper that Jan gave her, but a recording says the number's been disconnected, which means they'll have to stop by the address to see what they can find out. They'll do that after their meeting at APD.

Knowing that Marissa will be working side-by-side with Ken gives her a boost of confidence. With her schedule set, she turns her attention to the noon newscast. Suddenly, the alarm clock on her phone goes off, letting her know she has ten minutes to get on the set and another ten minutes before the newscast starts.

She heads into the restroom before taking her place behind the anchor desk in the studio. While she's in the bathroom stall, the exterior door opens and someone enters the restroom. From the fumes and the vigorous sound of aerosol hairspray, she realizes it must be Melinda, touching up her hair before the newscast.

She hears the door open again and worries about the poor female who's about to get chewed out since Melinda doesn't like to share limited counter space with anyone. Her cosmetics usually take up every inch of space.

"I thought I might find you in here. Applying that last layer of plaster, are you?"

Marissa cannot believe that Jan Ruther is making fun of Melinda. She peeks through the crack in the stall door to watch the fallout.

"I guess you have no choice but to go with the heavy-duty stuff in order to look good on the air for as long as it's physically possible." Her tone finally softens a little. "Female anchors are under such pressure to beat back the aging process while men are allowed to have wrinkles, gray hair and even a paunch. Guys command respect right up until the moment they fall out of their anchor chairs from old age. But women are forced to resort to facelifts and Botox to stay in their seats." Jan's sarcasm returns, "I'll bet your co-anchor won't have to worry about wrinkles for years to come."

"Why do you have to bring her up? You know how much it irritates me when you do," Melinda says through gritted teeth.

"I know you don't like her. It's obvious the way you refuse to even acknowledge her existence while you're sitting inches away from her on the air. So, come on, be honest with me. What's your beef? Why do you dislike her so much?"

"I don't dislike her. I downright hate her... And I told you before it's because she makes me look and feel old."

Jan responds with laughter and points her crooked finger inches from Melinda's slightly wrinkled face. "I've got news for you. You are no spring chicken. At your ripe age, you're lucky to still be on the air. You know that. It's the nature of the news business. There's only one Barbara Walters and one Diane Sawyer. All other on-air female anchors are subject to replacement by a younger version of themselves after hitting their prime at thirty-five. And honey, you are past your prime." Jan moves closer to the mirror. "By the way, you might want to consider scheduling a little cosmetic help, while you still can."

"I had an eye lift two years ago and I get Botox injections every few months, thank you for noticing. And what would you know about what it takes to retain good looks?"

"Hey, I'm just trying to be helpful. Don't get your panties in a wad." Jan says as she lets out a playful laugh before turning to walk out of the restroom.

Once the door closes behind Jan, Melinda says, "You are one bitter bitch."

Marissa flushes the toilet, adjusts her skirt, opens the stall door, and walks straight to the sink to wash her hands. She catches the stunned look on Melinda's face. Before she opens the door to leave, she says, "By the way, I think your eye-lift is a huge improvement."

An hour later the studio crew chief announces, "...and we're clear!" Marissa senses that something's different. It takes her a few seconds to figure it out, but then it hits her like a sledgehammer. The noon newscast is over and for the first time since she's been anchoring, there are no technical errors to note in the daily discrepancy report. She types in, "Clean newscast!"

Even Melinda notices the positive difference and says, "That was a solid newscast if I do say so myself."

Several unflattering thoughts come to mind for Marissa, but she decides to take the high road. "Let's hope we're on a positive roll that'll continue through the ratings period."

"It would help if we had more exclusive hard news stories, like your pet smuggling bust. Got any other similar crime rings hidden up your sleeve?" she sneers.

Is she implying that I knew those thieves? Or is it just another one of her poorly phrased questions? Marissa wonders. She decides to give her the benefit of the doubt. "Well, I'm working on what might turn out to be a pretty good story, but it's too early to talk about. In fact, I'm headed out the door now to see what I can track down." And with that, she tosses her scripts in the recycling bin, stops at her desk to grab her purse and reporter notebook and goes to find Ken in the photographer's lounge.

She' thrilled to see he's there by the entrance, smiling and waiting for her.

She feels a sense of camaraderie, like they've been working side-by-side together for years. *Maybe it's just a daydream that won't last much longer, but I'm going to enjoy every moment of it, for now,* she thinks. She feels bold, "Hi there, handsome! If you're ready to go we've got two stops to make. I'll be happy to fill you in about both."

"I can't wait for you to share the details, but if it's okay with you, I wouldn't mind skipping more undercover police work at least for today. Is that a deal?" he asks, laughing.

"Fine by me, but we are headed to the Austin Police Department. I don't know if you've ever heard of or if you've ever met Detective Hector Garcia. He's in charge of the Organized Crime Unit. He called me earlier and asked me to stop by. Full disclosure here: Detective Garcia is also a longtime family friend. He's like an uncle to me and my sister. We even call him Tío. Anyway, I'm not sure why he asked me to stop by, but I'm glad to have the chance to introduce you to each other. He might seem like a tough law and order guy, but he's really a softie. You'll like him. You want to hear something funny?"

"Sure. I love a good punch line."

"Tío Hector asked if I would bring you with me. Actually, he asked me to bring the photographer who was with me on yesterday's live shot. He assumed it was someone I trusted and I said yes I would bring you and yes you are someone I absolutely trust. So, let's go. I don't want to keep my uncle waiting. And on the drive to the police station, I'll fill you in on our next news assignment so we can get started on it right after we leave police headquarters."

In the truck, Ken asks, "Is it another feature story? Or is it a feature story that turns into a crime scene? So far, those are my favorite."

"Very funny. Believe it or not, it's a real news story involving a locally owned national franchise. The franchise owner is suspected of ripping off customers." She tells Ken what Jan has shared with her thus far.

"So the school told her that the audition is her chance to make it big in Hollywood?" Ken asks.

"Yes, exactly. I've got to see if there are any documents with disclaimers about the fame and fortune part. Or if there were actual promises made about the outcome of the auditions. The problem is the phone number for the mom has been disconnected, so our best shot of talking to her is to stop by the address I was given. Oh, and there is one other slight problem…"

"What are you leaving out?" Ken asks.

"We only have until Friday to put this story together, so while you drive to police headquarters, I'm going to make some phone calls."

While Ken drives to the police station, Marissa calls the Complaint Department of the State's Consumer Affairs office. She also checks with the Texas Entertainment Industry Commission for a list of reputable talent agents who are known for organizing auditions that have resulted in the placement of actors, dancers and models in TV commercials, print ads and in films. Various genres of entertainment are constantly being produced in the state of Texas. The very best talent agents are licensed by the Texas Entertainment Industry Commission, although it means being put on hold and being transferred several times. When she finally makes it to the right people within the TEIC, she knows she's hit the journalism jackpot. "Okay, thanks for the information," she says. "I'll send in my official request for more details by email. You've been very helpful!"

Marissa has been so engrossed in her phone conversation that she didn't realize the news unit was already parked at police headquarters. Ken is sitting behind the wheel, patiently waiting for her to finish her phone call. When she does, he says, "I can tell by the excitement in your eyes that you uncovered something juicy."

"Oh, you have me all figured out, do you?" she teases.

"As a matter of fact, I'm starting to read you pretty well. I can tell when you're excited about something, like you are about this story. You're like a lioness that is ready to pounce on its prey. I can also tell when it's something you can't figure out, like when you were talking to your sister on the phone yesterday about which animals to stay away from."

Ken turns in the driver's seat to look directly at Marissa. He slowly picks up her left hand and holds it in both of his. "...And, I can definitely tell when you want something. For instance, I can tell you really want to kiss me right now. Right here while we're parked in front of the police station with cops walking by. I can tell you want to kiss me even though it's way too obvious that we're members of the news media sitting in this news unit with the station logo plastered on the side panels that clearly identifies where we work. I nailed it, right?"

"You are dead right about me wanting to kiss you." She leans in closer to him. "And you are dead right about all your observations, which is why it won't be happening while we are sitting here in broad daylight in a news unit that says we work for KATX, in front of the police station under surveillance by my Tío Hector!" She laughs, slaps his hands away, and says, "So let's just put what you think I want aside, go upstairs and get this little meeting over with. Okay?"

She hops out of the news unit and walks briskly into the station; Ken follows. They clear security at the front desk and get on the elevator that delivers them to the third floor, Organized Crime Unit. The receptionist gives them a quick once over before buzzing Detective Garcia to let him know they've arrived.

They are in his office with the door closed. Garcia says, "I must say I was surprised to look up at the bank of TV monitors in the lobby and watch as the pet smuggling ring started unfolding on television. That was a dangerous undercover operation that was supposed to be carried out in top secret. Were you aware of that, Marissa?" His tone is stern as he turns his attention to Ken. "Are you the photographer who was working with her in such a dangerous situation?"

"Yes, sir, I am. My name is Ken Jordan." The two men, unsure of each other, shake hands, awkwardly.

"You didn't give me a chance to introduce Ken properly. He is my friend and trusted colleague," Marissa protests.

"I would say it's nice to meet you, but I'm not sure that's true under the circumstances," Garcia says to Ken, ignoring Marissa's comment.

Marissa will not be ignored. "Tío, I…I mean…we… had no idea the situation at the pet store was covert or dangerous. We didn't stop to think about the possible consequences. We just automatically followed our instincts. What happened was simple. I stumbled onto a crime in progress. I alerted Ken to the drama and instinctively he went into action to capture the event as it was unfolding so that we could share it live with the public. We just happened to be lucky that undercover officers announced themselves when they did and that the crooks were outnumbered."

"I would say you were very lucky and completely oblivious to the reality of what was going on right in front of you!" Garcia rarely raises his voice. He takes a breath, looks at them and says, "It was an undercover operation that we've been working on for almost a year. The officers in organized crime have been tracking elaborate plans to smuggle about a hundred of the rarest and exotic birds from here in Austin to the West Coast where they fetch two to three times their market value on the black market. In the broadcast, you revealed to the world the identities of some of the small-time players in this smuggling ring. Those two thugs who were holding store employees at gunpoint aren't very high up in the chain of command. But when their faces were splattered on the big screen, they became even less important to those in charge. Our goal was to have them leave with the expensive cargo and follow them to their destination. We have a pretty good idea that the birds would've been unloaded at a warehouse just south of town where they would have been kept until the search for the birds had cooled off. Then, as is true with most other stolen or smuggled goods, the exotic birds would have been transferred to pickup trucks or other vehicles which are much easier to move to hub cities," Hector explains.

"So in the news briefing, when the police chief said more arrests are likely, is that what you're counting on?" Marissa asks.

"That won't be so easy anymore. Our goal was to allow the men to finish loading their precious cargo and then track them to their next destination, but the surprise presence of you and your TV camera ruined that plan!"

Marissa knows Garcia is trying hard to contain his simmering anger. He adds slowly, "Our undercover men had no choice but to stop the operation in order to prevent anyone from being shot at the warehouse. I don't think you realize the negative impact your actions have had on our investigation. And it doesn't end there. You jeopardized your own safety, Marissa, as well as that of your colleague, Ken. Not to mention the lives of our undercover officers. Now the ones who are really in danger are the two men in custody. Because of you, their faces were on television and their names have been revealed in court documents following their arrest. Now their crime bosses will be looking to silence them in order to take the heat off the rest of the crime ring and themselves. The two men are now in protective custody while they're locked up in the county jail. But when they're transferred to state prison facilities, orders will no doubt be issued to carry out their murders. Those orders will come from outside prison walls. No matter what kind of prison security is provided, it's just a matter of time before the two men are killed. It might look like an accident, but it will be an ordered hit. If this case drags on unresolved much longer, it's going to be hard to keep them alive and even harder to get to the real leaders of this animal smuggling ring."

Garcia pauses and says with a dead serious tone, "Smuggling birds, even expensive ones, is nothing for the criminal masterminds who we suspect are in charge. The ringleaders are undoubtedly ruthless men who also deal in drugs and weapons. We also suspect their involvement in other types of stolen goods, including jewelry, artwork and electronic equipment. It's possible this crime ring has expanded into human trafficking of young girls who are forced into prostitution. Girls as young as twelve and thirteen years old." He sits back in his chair and lets out a long sigh.

Marissa can't believe what she's hearing. She glances over at Ken and sees he's also shocked.

"I had no idea, Tío! I'm sorry. I feel so ignorant." Tears well up in Marissa's eyes as she imagines the potential fallout from yesterday's live coverage. As she thinks about the implications of what Garcia has just told her she asks, "Tío, am I in any danger?"

"Well, to be honest, if the crime leaders think you intentionally exposed their operation, you'd be targeted by them. However, it's likely they realize you stumbled upon the heist." He sighs. "It wasn't all your fault. In reviewing the sequence of events of the operation, investigators realized there were serious flaws in how it was carried out. For one, Operation Feathered Friend was supposed to go down the day before the store's grand opening. Unfortunately, there was an unavoidable delay in the delivery of the birds to the store.

"The second mistake on our part was APD's failure to prevent your accidental involvement. No civilians should have been allowed anywhere near that Employees Only loading dock area. While the illegal cargo was being loaded, there should have been officers stationed outside the area to prevent anyone from entering what was a potentially dangerous area. What if a citizen had wandered back there in search of a water fountain or bathroom? Since no one was hurt, we managed to dodge a whole bunch of bullets."

Garcia lets out another long sigh and shakes his head as he imagines everything else that could have gone wrong.

After a brief but awkward silence, Ken speaks up. "Detective, sir, we cannot express our regret enough for exposing so many people to possible danger. In no way did we realize we were taking such risks. We just instinctively reacted as journalists. We jumped into action to capture the crime as it unfolded. We don't have much in the way to offer, but if there is any way we can make it up to the department, please, sir, just let us know."

Detective Garcia gets up from his desk and begins pacing behind the chairs where Ken and Marissa are seated. "As for restitution, yours is an honorable offer, but no, there's nothing the two of you can do to make amends for what happened. However, there is something I want to put on the table. It's the reason why I called you to my office," he says. He returns to the chair behind his desk and sits down.

On the desk is an envelope that he slides across the desk toward them. "Here are photographs of the two men we suspect are the masterminds behind the extensive web of criminal activity. The two of you are private citizens who have become entangled in this police investigation. Neither of you have formal police training. Marissa, unless you have been keeping it a secret, I assume that you do not own nor are licensed to handle a weapon?"

"No. No weapons, Tío."

"Very well, then. It's for your protection that you study the photographs and be aware of the men. These are the suspected crime leaders. And, while you probably don't recognize either one, you should know what they look like since there is a possibility that they may be after you. Both of you," he says sternly.

Ken and Marissa sit in complete silence. She's stunned by the reality that her life might be in danger. As she reaches for the envelope, she knows that the photographs of the two men might rock her whole world.

Eleven

As they leave Garcia's office, Marissa turns to Ken who, like her, is walking at a fast pace down the halls of the police department. Nerves move them quickly out of the building. They finally get to the parked news unit and as soon as they're inside and the doors are closed, she asks, "Now what do we do? Do we back down? Or do we keep on with our lives as if nothing's wrong? I mean…we don't have any law enforcement training. How would we know if someone is targeting us? You heard how close the pet store situation came to ending in gunfire. What if someone had gotten shot? Or worse, killed?"

The panic in her voice intensifies. "Look at my hand. It's shaking."

Without hesitation, he reaches over and grabs her trembling hand. In a soothing tone, he says, "Your uncle just wants to make us aware of the scope of the investigation. He didn't intend to scare us. He wants us to be on our toes about all possible dangers. Believe me, he strikes me as the kind of man who would have ordered armed security for you if he thought it was necessary."

"You're right. He wanted to alert us, not alarm us. There's a huge difference."

Ken starts the engine but doesn't attempt to move the car. Then, as he's hit with a second thought, he turns the engine off and looks directly at Marissa. "We've just been warned that we might be in danger and that our live coverage had a major impact on a huge undercover criminal operation. But don't forget there was a positive impact, too. Your uncle says the video was seen by more people than they ever could have imagined and that members of the Organized Crime Unit have been busy fielding tips from people who've been calling in."

"You're right. Tío said every thug and criminal in the nation must've been watching KATX like it was *America's Most Wanted*. Crooks are always the first to offer up information leading to the arrest of their rivals in exchange for reward money."

"The ringleaders are ruthless bastards who wouldn't think twice about ordering hits on the two men arrested. It's not like a video game where you take aim and mow down the bad guys and no one actually gets hurt. This is a very serious and dangerous situation. Still, I have to believe your uncle would never leave you unprotected," Ken's words convey genuine concern. Marissa has never had a coworker express such interest in her wellbeing. After all that Garcia has done for her family—for her and her sister—she trusts him. And now, Ken has earned her trust as well.

Ken is still holding her hand. "I think the best way to ease our nerves would be for us to focus on work. Why don't we get started on this Regency Dance Studio assignment and go after another bad guy?" he asks.

She nods and he starts the car again. This time they head to the address scribbled on the piece of paper Jan gave her. As they drive, she tells Ken about her calls. "My first call was to the the Texas Consumer Affairs Division Complaint Department. The Public Information officer ran a check on Regency Dance Studio franchises and found seven complaints. One customer claimed tuition rates were excessive, two people filed complaints demanding a tuition refund after classes were suddenly canceled, and listen to this, four people called claiming the school engaged in false advertising about career and job opportunities for students who completed the courses. There's definitely a pattern of dissatisfaction among students. Also, the PIO says three of the franchise schools closed suddenly in the middle of the night. That's serious stuff for a school, especially if it continues taking tuition right up until the doors are slammed shut."

Ken is quiet while digesting the information. Then he says, "It sounds like several students pinned their hopes on making it big as professional dancers."

"Yeah, but the challenge will be proving that those promises were made either in writing or verbally. Let's hope the mom we're trying to track down can show us some valid paperwork. As for my other call to the Texas Entertainment Commission, they gave me a list of reputable talent agents who book all kinds of entertainers, including dancers for appearances in TV commercials, movies, magazines and billboard ads. I left messages with a couple of them before our meeting with my uncle. One of the agents left a message. Let me play it on speaker phone so we can both listen."

A very agitated voice comes on stating, "This is Sherry West of Westbound Talent Agency. I want to make it clear we have no affiliation with the Regency School of Dance. Nor do we know anything about their so-called audition process. But I can tell you this, no reputable talent agent or agency charges potential clients to take part in an audition. Also, we've already filed our own complaint with the American Association of Talent Agents, an independent affiliation that governs those who claim to be talent agents. This school is not in good standing within the Texas entertainment industry. If you'd like further information, you're welcome to call back. You have my direct number." And with a click the message ends.

"Wow! Ms. West doesn't hide her feelings does she?" Marissa says as she dials the number.

Sherry West answers on the first ring in a curt, businesslike manner, "Sherry West of Westbound Talent Agency. How may I help you?"

"This is Marissa Cavelo with KATX News calling back. I received your message and would like to interview you about what's involved in a legitimate audition call. It would also be helpful to hear from you what aspiring dancers need to know if they hope to make it within any aspect of the entertainment industry."

"What's your purpose? Why do you want to talk to me?"

"We have a complaint from a mother who says her daughter completed the course work she paid for at the Regency School of Dance. Now organizers are asking her to pay five thousand dollars to attend an audition session in Hollywood."

The laughter by Ms. West is so loud, Marissa has to pull the receiver away from her ear. Finally, she composes herself and asks, "When can you stop by? Our office is about five minutes east of downtown."

"We are just pulling up to the family's home. I would like to talk to the woman and daughter now so that we can hear their allegations against the school first. If they agree to talk to us, it shouldn't take more than about an hour, which means we would arrive at your office by four-thirty at the latest. Will that work?"

"Sure. I'll be here, but I could save you the time by telling you exactly what the mom and daughter were promised. It was something along the lines of… 'she has a natural, raw talent—the kind all producers are looking for…blah…blah…blah.' Then the school official will add, 'oh, but this is a once in a lifetime opportunity that will never be available again. Every year you wait is a year wasted since the prime age for the best dancers is between fourteen and fifteen years old,'" West says in a falsetto voice, mimicking the person she's quoting. "Mark my words. That's exactly what that mother and daughter were told. It's an old high-pressure sales tactic that works on the very gullible. Are you at the family home now?" she asks.

"Yes, we just pulled up. Why?"

"Because I would bet the house is in a modest to low-income neighborhood and the family is very likely a hard-working minority family whose members only want a better life for themselves and their children."

I look around at the house and front yard and say, "You're right about the house and neighborhood, but we haven't met the family yet."

"You will, and when you do, I'll be proven right. I'll see you at our office at around four-thirty p.m." And with that, she hangs up.

Marissa turns to Ken, who's grinning after overhearing the entire exchange with Ms. West. "It sounds like you have the beginning of an interesting story featuring at least one colorful interview with Ms. West," he says.

The insight provided by Sherry West is motivation to dig deeper into what the dance studio and staff promises its students. They walk up to the modest home, which reminds Marissa of the simple house where she grew up in Houston. The neighborhood is rundown but quiet. There's nothing fancy around here. It's definitely a place where working families live and raise their children. Marissa knocks on the door and a small dog starts barking. It's the kind of four-legged security alarm system many families depend on. It doesn't take long for an attractive teenage girl to answer the door. "Hello," Marissa asks, "is this the Lopez residence?"

Before she can introduce herself, the teenager breaks into a huge smile and excitedly says, "I know who you are! You're Marissa Cavelo, from the news, aren't you?"

Marissa is always surprised when teenagers and other people who she doubts ever watch the news recognize her. Once, a young man told her that he never watches the news, but that he *did* recognize her from the TV promos and the ads on billboards and on the sides of buses. She smiles at the girl who has answered the door and says, "Why, yes I am. And what's your name?"

"I'm Julia, but what are you doing here?" she asks as she takes in the sight of Ken standing slightly behind her, holding a video camera.

"We're here to talk to you and your mom about the Regency Dance Studio. Julia, are you enrolled there?"

"Yeah, I just finished the classes last week. Why?"

"I tell you what. Before I answer your questions and you answer any of mine, let me ask if your mother is home so she can be part of this conversation?"

"She just got home from work. Wait here. I'll go get her." Julia leaves them standing by the front door and they can hear her yelling, "Mama! The lady from the TV station is here and she wants to talk to you. Hurry!"

It doesn't take long for the mother and daughter to return to the front door. Mrs. Lopez is wiping her hands on a dishtowel and trying to fix her hair when she invites them in saying, "Please, come in."

"Thank you, Mrs. Lopez. My name is Marissa Cavelo and this is my coworker and photographer, Ken Jordan," she says by way of brief introduction. "We've already met your daughter, Julia. She's lovely," she adds with a smile.

As they move into the small, simple home, Mrs. Lopez offers them seats on a worn but clean couch. In an instant, the smells coming from the kitchen remind her of the aromas from her mother's *cocina*. A wave of homesickness hits her hard and she finds herself fighting back feelings of sadness. "Mrs. Lopez we are here to talk to you about the Regency Dance Studio. Julia just told us that she recently finished the classes. Is that right?"

She hesitates before answering, "We had to take out a loan to pay for the classes, but Julia loved it. Her instructor said she was a natural. Her teacher described her as a dancer just like professional choreographers are looking for, especially those in Hollywood," says Mrs. Lopez in a quiet voice.

"Mrs. Lopez, is it all right if Ken sets up his camera so we can videotape our discussion? Are you okay with that? We'd like to talk to you and your daughter, with your permission," Marissa asks and then waits for her answer.

Mrs. Lopez doesn't hesitate. "Oh sure, sure, although I don't understand why you want to talk to us. Is this about Julia's future as a dancer?"

And that question from this obviously dedicated mother is hard to answer, but Marissa gives it her best shot while Ken quickly sets the camera on a tripod and puts a microphone on the collar of Mrs. Lopez's house dress. "Mrs. Lopez, we understand you're trying to raise money for Julia to attend an audition in California. Is that correct?" she asks.

"Yes. It's what we told the other lady who works with you on the news…what's her name? Melinda? When we ran into her the other day, we told her that we're trying to raise five-thousand dollars, but we've only been able to collect a thousand."

Marissa can see the disappointment in Mrs. Lopez's face and proceeds cautiously. "Tell us what the Regency Dance Studio officials told you about the audition. What did they say would happen to Julia if she went to California?"

The camera is rolling as Mrs. Lopez responds. Slowly, she begins to describe how the instructor called her and her daughter into a private meeting right after the last dance class was held. According to the instructor, the head of the school stopped by the meeting to say Julia was a special girl. 'A real stand-out' was how her daughter was described. Mrs. Lopez recalls the meeting being long, with delays and interruptions right when she should have been home fixing dinner for Julia and the rest of the family.

As Marissa listens, she is reminded of the forced wait tactics that some car sales people create for potential buyers. The buyers are held hostage as a salesman tries to force them into signing on the bottom line.

Mrs. Lopez remembers being told that the cost of sending Julia to the audition should be considered, 'an investment in her future,' and that the audition is a 'once-in-a-lifetime opportunity,' to put Julia's face in front of entertainment agents, movie directors and agents who book dancers for music videos and live performances. And then, this woman, who looks older and more tired than her true age, starts weeping quietly as she explains how hard it's been to try to raise the money and to know that her lovely, sweet Julia might be missing out on the chance to succeed in life. She wipes away her tears and works to compose herself.

Marissa asks, "Mrs. Lopez, did you sign any type of agreement or were any promises made to you in writing?"

She shakes her head. "No. We cannot finalize the agreement until we pay the balance. But I do have the pamphlets that give details about the audition next month in Hollywood. Do you want to see them?" she asks. She turns to her daughter and instructs her, "*Mija*, go to your room and bring Ms. Cavelo the flyer with the info about the trip to California."

Julia races out of the living room and quickly returns with a slick pamphlet that features flashy photos of attractive young girls with dazzling smiles lined up to perform high kicks. The description of the audition is very generic with phrases like 'opportunity of a lifetime,' and 'well-known directors and choreographers will be attending.' In bold letters, it states: '*COMMERCIALS, MUSIC VIDEOS, FILMS, AND PHOTO SPREADS ARE IN YOUR FUTURE!*' The words promise employment opportunities for those who participate in the audition. The next phrase that catches Marissa's eye is the price tag—five thousand dollars.

On her direction, Ken turns the camera to capture Julia. "Julia, what did the instructor tell you during that meeting?" Marissa asks.

Julia looks at her mother as her eyes seek permission before speaking. Her mother nods her head slightly, which prompts the nervous girl to begin answering in a shaky voice. "She told me I was a natural dancer. She said I had raw talent that would get even better with time and experience. She said my Latina features are what all the music video directors are looking for."

Marissa recognizes what the instructor told Mrs. Lopez and her daughter as some of the same phrases that Sherry West predicted would be used to convince prospective dancers. *Damnit!* Marissa feels anger rising in her as it becomes apparent that this poor woman and her daughter have been tricked. She composes herself and asks, "Were any promises made about the results of the audition? About what would happen if you were to pay the money to participate in the audition?"

In a timid voice, Julia whispers, "She said there'd be scouts for movies and live dance performances who'd be there ready to sign girls like me on the spot. She said at sixteen I'm the perfect age to start a career as a professional dancer, but if I wait any longer I'd soon be past my prime."

Then comes her toughest question for the nervous teenager, "Julia, what do you want? Why is this so important to you?"

"I want to try to raise the money to go on this audition because I want to earn money to help my family. My mother has to work two jobs. My dad works out-of-state on construction sites and my younger sister's been sick—very sick. It's hard for everyone. I want to drop out of school to find a job, but my mom won't let me. I've been trying to find work as a babysitter to help raise the audition money, but it's no use. We won't have enough for next week's deadline. Can you help us, Ms. Cavelo?"

"Just a moment, Julia," she says, "I promise to answer your questions and those of your mother, but first let's stop the interview and take the microphone off the two of you."

She turns to Ken who's quietly working behind her, videotaping every painful word. "Let's stop the interview for now. Instead would you please take shots of the pamphlet? Be sure you get close-ups of the key phrases on the front and the back, okay?"

Ken nods in understanding and quickly and quietly begins collecting more video evidence from the printed brochures.

Marissa turns back to Julia and her mother and braces herself to deliver the information she knows will be painful for them to hear. "First, let me explain why I'm here. Unfortunately, I'm not here to help you raise the audition fee. I've been assigned to find out if the Regency Dance Studio is legitimate in its business operations or if the school charges unnecessarily high fees in exchange for empty promises of fame. Phone calls to check the school's background and reputation reveal complaints against the dance school franchises from former students. Several parents have filed complaints with the State's Consumer Affairs Division, claiming the school's ads are misleading. Some even used the word 'false' to describe the ads. I haven't seen the complaints. I only have preliminary info provided to me over the phone."

Julia starts crying so softly that Marissa can hardly hear her. Her mother is sitting there shaking her head in disbelief. "Ms. Cavelo, what happens now?" she asks.

"I can't tell you what will happen next. I also can't tell you what would happen if you are able to raise the rest of the money and Julie goes to the audition, but I do suggest that you and your daughter go online and do your own research. Check out other dance schools. Learn how auditions are held and what fees, if any, are standard. I'd also advise you to learn as much as possible about what it takes to become a professional dancer before you spend another penny on this audition or before you enroll Julia in any more dance classes.

"After we leave here, we're set to interview a reputable talent agent. She's going to tell us more about the audition process and what it takes to launch a successful career in the entertainment industry. I'd be glad to let you know if she has any information that might help you and Julia decide what to do in the future, especially if she still wants to become a dancer."

Marissa turns to Julia who has her face buried in her two hands and is whimpering softly. Marissa gently puts her hand on Julia's back and tells her, "Julia, you're young and beautiful and you have your whole life ahead of you. Please don't let this experience—or anyone—stop you from going after your dreams. I was a teenager, just like you, growing up in a house in Houston, not too different from yours, with a close and supportive family like yours. And despite hardships, I managed to succeed. You can, too, *mija*. You will survive this setback, as long as you learn from it and move forward. More than anything, have faith in yourself!"

Marissa knows her words will do little to ease the pain these two women are feeling after hearing that Julia's dream of becoming a professional dancer are all part of a suspected money-making scheme. Julia slowly lifts her tear-stained face from her hands and shows a faint smile as she looks up at Marissa.

"I do have one more bit of advice for you, Julia. And that is you should stay in school. Your parents are right not to let you drop out since your education will be extremely useful no matter what career path you chose."

She nods in agreement.

"Now, Mrs. Lopez, what's your phone number so I can call you with an update on this story?" She was dabbing the corner of her eyes with a dishtowel. Like her own mother, Marissa suspects Mrs. Lopez always has a clean dishtowel in easy reach whether or not she's in the kitchen cooking.

She bows her head in another display of embarrassment and says, "We don't have a phone anymore. The service was disconnected because we couldn't pay the bills."

Marissa suspects this isn't the only bill that hasn't been paid while trying to send Julia on this expensive audition. She knows from the Regency Dance Studio website that classes aren't cheap, which makes her even more determined to uncover the truth about the school operators. She will publicly expose them to prevent other families from falling into the same trap.

Ken, who has been working quietly this entire time, speaks up, "We'll be happy to stop back by and personally share with you what we find out. And Julia, if you have some photos of yourself, like some headshots, will you please share a couple of your favorites with me?"

"Sure, I'll go get them. The dance studio brought in a photographer to take professional pictures for us to build our portfolio," she says before leaving the room to get the photos.

Marissa is tempted to ask how much that service cost, but bites her tongue, knowing the answer will just add to the family's distress. She makes a quick note to herself to check the cost of photography sessions later.

Julia returns with an envelope and hands it to Ken who promises to bring it back when he stops by with an update from the talent agent. Marissa and Ken are about to say their goodbyes and leave when suddenly, Mrs. Lopez hugs her and says, "I feel so foolish for believing the instructor and the school officials. I wish there was more that we could do. Thank you for taking an interest in my family and in my daughter."

Marissa assures her, "Mrs. Lopez, you are providing a very valuable service by talking to us and by sharing your experience. Hopefully, when this is on the news, it'll serve as a warning to other families, whose children might also have dreams of becoming performers not to fall for false promises."

As they start to drive away, Marissa looks back and sees Mrs. Lopez and Julia standing on the front porch of their modest home. The two women are holding hands while waving goodbye and for a split-second, she spots her own mother in her simple house dress holding a dish towel in one hand. She's also waving goodbye and saying, *"Adios, mija! Ten cuidado y que Dios te bendiga."* Goodbye, my dear. Take care and may God bless you. Just as quickly as she appears, her mother is gone.

Twelve

Ken and Marissa head to the office of Sherry West, of the Westbound Talent Agency. While en route, they discuss their strategy.

"The promotional material sure makes it sound like the dance school students who do participate in an audition will reap awesome career opportunities," Ken says. "If I were hoping to break into music videos as a backup dancer for J-Lo or appear in a movie scene like the big dance numbers in *Moulin Rouge* or *Step It Up*, I wouldn't think anything of spending five thousand dollars on a shot at fame and fortune. What do you think?"

"I agree. That's a pretty slick brochure; it makes it all sound so glamorous. What makes me angry is hearing Mrs. Lopez repeat to us, almost word-for-word, what Sherry West already said potential performers are told. And worse than that is the fact that the Lopez family is so vulnerable, not just emotionally, but financially. They can't possibly raise the money in time. They've already taken a big hit just trying. Their phone service has been disconnected and no telling what other bills or expenses they've let slide while trying to come up with the funds to send Julia to Hollywood."

"Okay. Let's not jump to any conclusions about what the school promised or about what Mrs. Lopez and Julia have sacrificed. Let's just talk to Sherry West and hear what has she to say."

"To be fair, we need to allow the school owner and operator time to respond to these allegations of false advertising." Marissa dials her phone, knowing this call is going to be tougher than reaching out to Sherry West.

Someone answers the phone. "Regency Dance Studio. How may I help you?" says the cheerful voice on the other end of the line.

"This is Marissa Cavelo, of KATX News here in Austin. I'd like to speak to the owner of the school, please. Mrs. Gloria Linden. Is she in?"

"One moment, please." a pre-recorded message plays in Marissa's ear. "Do you have what it takes to make it in the rigorous, exciting world of dance? We're always looking for fresh faces and smooth moves. So are entertainment executives. Don't miss your chance to be the next top dancer, like those seen on *Dancing With the Stars* and *So You Think You Can Dance*. If you have what it takes, the Regency Dance Studio will help you reach your goals! Thank you for holding. Someone will be with you shortly." And just as the message starts to repeat, a woman's voice, sweet and dripping with slow Southern charm, comes on the line. "Ms. Cavelo? This is Gloria Linden. How nice to hear from you. I watch your noon newscast just about every day. How may I assist you today?"

"Ms. Linden, thanks for taking my call. I'm working on a story about dance studios and I'd like to talk to you in person about your school, your students and about an upcoming audition that aspiring dancers have been invited to attend. Are you available for an on-camera interview?"

Suddenly the free-flowing Southern charm detected in Linden's voice comes to an abrupt end. Her response to an interview request is businesses-like and to the point. "Who contacted you and what are you trying to prove?"

"Well, you know how popular dance competitions are, especially the ones on network TV? This whole trend fueled by *So You Think You Can Dance* is really heating up among aspiring dancers. And we understand there's an upcoming audition in Hollywood. We want to ask you about the audition process and what the requirements are for those who want to attend. If you're available, the interview will only take about fifteen to thirty minutes of your time. That's all. How about tomorrow morning at nine a.m.?"

There's a brief pause before Linden says in a more positive tone, "Any questions first need to be submitted in writing to my attorney. He must also be present during the interview. If there are any questions we feel are unacceptable, we'll let you know." Ms. Linden sounds like she's automatically stating a standing legal policy for the one-hundredth time.

"Well, to be honest, I've never heard of such imposed restrictions from someone I've asked to interview, but I don't see any problem with submitting the questions to you in advance. They're pretty straightforward. As for your attorney being present, you can have anyone you want in the room with you. However, *you* are the only person we'll be interviewing. What about the suggested time? Will nine a.m. at the Regency Dance Studio work for you?" Marissa hopes to nail her down to a definite commitment before she changes her mind.

"Nine will work just fine here at the school. Your questions must be received by five o'clock *today.* Any later than five and the interview is automatically canceled. Is that understood, Ms. Cavelo?"

"Yes, Ms. Linden. I'll get these questions to you as soon as possible. I look forward to meeting you. See you at nine tomorrow morning." She barely finishes speaking before Linden hangs up the phone. "Wow! That was weird."

Ken pulls into the parking lot at the Westbound Talent Agency. "So, from listening in on your end of the conversation, it sounds like she agreed to an interview."

"Yes, but with a couple of major restrictions. As soon as we finish this next interview I need to draft and send my questions to Linden.

They must be sent by five p.m. so that her attorney can review them. And she wants him to be there during the interview. Does that sound like she's ready for a legal fight or what?"

"Sounds like she's being defensive about something."

The two carry the camera and gear up the steps to the front door of the Westbound Talent Agency. As Marissa steps inside the front door, she notices the lobby is filled with sleek, modern furniture. The decor is very hip. On the walls are huge portraits of good-looking men and women of all ages and ethnicities. A hallway off the lobby area is covered in various plaques and awards as well as the logos of some major companies and institutions. Techno music is playing and the young, thin receptionist looks like she's headed to a nightclub. Marissa and Ken take in the entire scene, which feels more like a club than a business lobby. Then the hip receptionist says, "You must be the news crew Ms. West is expecting. Please sign in and I'll tell her you're here." They comply and she escorts them to a huge conference room that's set up with all the latest media gadgets, including a giant flat screen.

Ken wastes no time setting up the tripod, camera and lights. As Marissa watches him, it's hard for her to imagine anyone walking through that door who wouldn't look stunning even under the harsh lights. Right on cue, a knockout beauty in her late forties with a dramatic, short haircut walks in. She's wearing a long, flowing top over slimming slacks. Her right hand is extended in greeting. "Hello. I'm Sherry West. You must be Marissa Cavelo."

Marissa notices her tasteful jewelry. Not too flashy. She wears beautiful designer bracelets on both wrists. "Yes, I'm Marissa and this is my friend and photographer Ken Jordan."

She looks right past Marissa to Ken and says without hesitation, "You are a gorgeous man. Great coloring and physique. Have you ever considered modeling?"

Ken blushes and says, "You mean walking a runway?"

Sherry laughs and says, "No, big guy. Modeling is also about being the subject for photography. Or with your chiseled face, perhaps even posing for a painting or sculpture. You look exactly like a nude statuette I recently admired in Milan, that I now regret not buying," Sherry looks Ken up and down in one fluid glance. The same behavior by a man toward a woman would be perceived as being sexist, but this is, after all, a talent agency. Sherry says abruptly, "If you're interested, leave your card with the receptionist and I'll get back to you." And just like that, her interest in Ken is over.

She turns to Marissa with a big, mischievous smile and a twinkle in her eyes and says, "Ms. Cavelo, this is your lucky day! After our phone conversation, I talked to some colleagues in the business who've had dealings with Gloria Linden and the Regency Dance Studio. I've asked two of them to join us later. But first, let's sit and visit. I want to be sure you understand how talent agents work, how auditions are conducted and who benefits from both. How does that sound?" she asks pleasantly.

"It sounds like the reason we're here," Marissa jumps into the interview. "How did you become a talent agent?" she asks.

"When I was in my twenties, I was the type of girl fashion designers and photographers were looking for. I was tall, thin, no curves, and no experience doing anything else. That was more than twenty-five years ago and it didn't take long for me, as a model, to be past my prime. But by then, I'd picked up all aspects of the modeling business and more importantly, the entertainment industry. When one photographer asked me to help him find new faces for his next shoot, I knew recruiting talent was something I could do. It started with a couple of gals and one or two guys who were great in front of a camera. Slowly, my reputation grew and I started getting calls from movie directors and advertising agencies who were all looking for various types of models. Not long after that, I added singers and dancers to my stable of talent. It's not just stunning individuals like your photographer here. Depending on the product or service being sold, advertisers are also looking for average folks. They want a grandmother with a full head of silver hair; a young Asian male or female with a perfect smile; a Hispanic pre-teen with braces; a five-year-old with freckles and a missing front tooth; an elderly African American couple...the list goes on and on. Whoever the clients are, they come up with what types they're trying to cast and I take it from there. In my twenty years in the business, I've always been able to fill roles. And that's great for my clients, which include advertisers, film producers and so on. It's also great for the prospective talent. I'm here to promote models, dancers and occasionally singers and actors." Sherry smiles and points to a wall that features a photo gallery of her beautiful clients.

Marissa has Ken scan the wall with his camera and then turns it back on Sherry who continues her explanation of the entertainment business. "Now here's what may surprise you. I receive a finder's fee, which is a standard percentage. The talent, whether it be a dancer, a model or an actor, is paid when the work is completed, although they often receive an advance. Of course, better known, recognizable dancers and models command higher salaries and have their own legal representatives draft contracts for them. Most newcomers to the business have only minimal previous dance, modeling or acting skills. Only a few, if any, have ever enrolled in any type of formal school or training. It's just not necessary. Nor do they pay to attend auditions. That's because auditions are held in the cities where the projects are being shot or cast. In other words, a film being made in New Orleans holds its auditions in the New Orleans area. The only auditions held in California are for projects being shot in California. It makes no sense for aspiring talent to pay thousands of dollars to attend an audition in a distant location. That's why many hopefuls move to New York or Los Angeles to be where films and commercials are being shot. And it's only a lucky few who land parts. It would make more sense for an aspiring actor to attend drama school than it would for a model to go to modeling school or a dancer to a dance studio. The only initial legitimate expense is a portfolio of photographs. But honestly, expensive doesn't necessarily mean better. All the gorgeous faces in the photographs on my walls—many of those actors, models and dancers landed their first jobs with simple headshots taken with inexpensive digital cameras."

Marissa is fascinated by Ms. West's clear cut explanation of the entertainment industry and how aspiring performers break into the business. She looks over her notes and asks, "So if a modeling or dance school is offering its students an audition opportunity in California that costs five thousand dollars to attend, what would you think of that?"

"I think it's a wonderful money-making opportunity. Not for the aspiring actors and dancers, but for the organizers who are hosting the audition," she answers with a knowing laugh.

"How would you advise the individuals who are considering actually paying the five-thousand-dollar fee?"

"I'd tell them to take the money and plant it in the ground and wait for it to grow because that's going to be as productive as paying good money to attend a rigged audition," she says, sarcastically.

Then her tone becomes serious. "This is *not* the first or the last school or studio that charges students an outrageous amount to attend an out-of-town audition. My experience is that those who can *least* afford it are the ones who fall for the empty promises of fame. And that's a shame. It may not be illegal, but it *is* immoral," she shakes her head in disapproval.

She talks some more about the movies and commercials her clients have been featured in, and she tells Marissa how she'd like Texas lawmakers to better regulate so-called 'performance' schools so that the public knows that they are not about learning how to model or dance.

"These kids would be better off attending schools that teach poise, confidence, proper etiquette and even fashion and makeup tips. These are the essential skills many young girls and boys could benefit from without empty promises of becoming a star."

Marissa and West are about to wrap up the interview when there's a knock on the conference room door. Two staff members enter. Sherry West invites them to sit down and introduces them. Alice Harrell is an attractive redhead with a quiet personality and Hanz Moore is a dark-haired, anxious type who looks like he's uncomfortable being in the same room with them.

West explains, "Alice and Hanz have agreed to be interviewed but prefer to do so together. They're willing to talk about their experience with the Regency Dance Studio."

Ken adjusts the chairs and the lights and places microphones on both Harrell and Moore. Meanwhile, Sherry excuses herself. "I have to meet with a client. Please stop by the front desk when you're finished so that I can say goodbye before you leave."

Once Marissa, Alice and Hanz are settled in place, Ken gives the signal.

Marissa asks the first question, "Please state your name and tell me about your experience with the Regency Dance Studio."

And that's when the information floodgates open up.

Thirteen

At seven that evening, it hits Carissa that she's been working nonstop all day without bothering to take a break to stretch her legs, step outside to clear her head or eat. Her stomach is growling so loudly that the little Pekinese dog she's brushing cocks its head when it hears the rumbling coming from her belly.

"Settle down, Sadie, it's just hunger pangs. Don't worry, I promise not to eat you. Although…that expensive dog food your owner has flown in from Germany is starting to look pretty good right now. What am I saying? How disgusting. I have to get out of here before I go crazy."

She finishes the grooming duties and puts the pooch, whose full name is Sadie Louise Whitfield, back in its kennel. Most of the groomed, fed dogs have already been picked up by chauffeurs or caretakers.

While she busies herself putting away supplies and prepping food bowls for the next morning, she replays the visit with her sister earlier that morning. *She looks good. Real good. That bitch!* She loves Marissa, but at the same time has a growing dislike for what she's becoming. Marissa's confidence about what she wants for the future frustrates Carissa. It makes her stomach churn that Marissa is so focused on not only clinching a network anchor job but seems eager to move to another city. *Marissa has all these grandiose plans while I don't even know if I'll be able to scrape up the money to pay my monthly bills,* she grouses.

Even her sister's love life seems better as Carissa thinks about the guy at work Marissa told her about. He's probably boring, and like her sister, he probably doesn't like the club scene. *Their idea of a fun date is probably watching the evening news. Or if it's a special occasion, splurging by going to see an old black and white documentary.* Her sister's pathetically unexciting life is the only thing that makes Carissa feel better.

Carissa craves excitement. She enjoys going to new places and meeting new people. She has convinced herself that she is not cut out to be someone's traditional, demure girlfriend or wife, which is why her relationship with H.N. suits her just fine. She loves it when he calls or shows up with spur of the moment plans. His private jet is always fueled and ready to fly. They can be in Vegas for dinner, take part in some high-stakes gambling, catch a sold-out show and be back in Austin before morning.

She thinks about their latest adventure. Last week, he pulled up in his latest sports car and made her wear a blindfold because their destination was a surprise. They hadn't driven very far when he pulled the car over. She took off her blindfold and saw an amusement park with twinkling lights, carnival music and all kinds of rides and attractions— all in full motion! There was a House of Mirrors, a Ferris wheel and even a roller coaster. It was fully operational with crew members waiting to take their tickets—except there were *no* tickets! The two of them were the only customers. They had the entire amusement park to themselves. He remembered her telling him that she'd never been to one as a child, so he created the whole experience just for her. There was even a food trailer that offered pink swirls of delicious cotton candy and all the tasty kettle corn she could eat! It was like a child's fantasy come true.

The week before that, he surprised her with a different blindfolded ride to an unknown destination. He kept dropping confusing clues along the way until finally, he stopped and pulled her out of his car. He told her to hold out her hands, palms up. Just as he removed the blindfold she opened her eyes and was shocked when he placed a cold steel Magnum 57 in her hands. Her first instinct was fear since she'd never in her life held a weapon before. She couldn't believe the rush of adrenaline that came from aiming a gun at a target. And it was even more of a rush when she pulled the trigger. H.N. had arranged for private lessons at a shooting range before giving the gun to her as a gift.

Those over-the-top gestures are what keep their relationship so exciting.

But there is a downside to being with him that she'd never admit to anyone, especially not to Marissa. Carissa doesn't like it when he takes off and she doesn't hear from him for days or weeks at a time. During these absences, she doesn't know where he is, what he's doing or who he is with. The word "love" has never been uttered by either of them. Carissa doesn't think the word is even in his vocabulary. There is no talk of a future. They don't even discuss plans for the next day, let alone life plans. She has no reason to demand or to expect him to be faithful to her. And while he shouldn't expect fidelity from her either, she has seen flashes of jealousy when other men pay even the slightest bit of attention to her.

But even the jealousy is short lived and Carissa senses that he really doesn't care that much about her. She can't figure out if he's sad, disappointed, enjoying himself or bored. It's as if any expression of feelings is seen as a sign of weakness. Yet weakness is definitely one word that is *not* used to describe him or his brother. The two men have an uncanny knack of silent communication compounded by the fact that they often speak to each other in Farsi, which is a language she doesn't understand.

She can sense there is a special bond between the two men. Something beyond brotherhood that ties them closer than any two siblings. Not being privy to their communication leaves Carissa feeling shut out. She also feels uncomfortable when she senses, but can't confirm, that the two brothers are talking about her. When it comes to her boyfriend, all Carissa knows is that she's supposed to look beautiful, be flexible with her time, be ready to go anywhere at a moment's notice and most importantly, she is not allowed to ask any questions—ever.

There is, however, one emotion that he and his brother are quick to display—anger. Pure unleashed rage by the two men is frightening to observe. She once watched as a restaurant chef was reduced to a mass of quivering flesh after screwing up a dinner order. The fury was released verbally, but the threat of physical violence was also present. It left her cowering in her seat, afraid to look up for fear she'd witness a beating.

It wasn't long after that incident that H.N. first turned his rage on Carissa. She was flipping through a magazine while relaxing in his penthouse when he walked into the room and asked her to fix him a drink—well not ask, but commanded. She wanted to finish the article she was reading before putting the magazine down and didn't respond quickly enough to his order. In one sudden motion, he grabbed the magazine out of her hand and threw it across the room before yanking her to her feet and pushing her toward the bar area of the living room. He yelled, "When I command you to do something, I expect you to do it immediately!"

It was the first time he roughed her up, but there have been other incidents. One time he grabbed her arm so hard that he left bruises where his fingers pressed into her flesh after. The assault was because she laughed at him for something as ridiculous as buttoning his shirt wrong.

Then there was the time he got angry after his dog soiled the carpet. He yelled at her to clean it up and pushed her to the floor, threatening to rub her face in the mess if there was even a trace of a stain on his expensive rug.

Carissa pulls a compact mirror from her purse and checks to see if the swelling has gone down on her lip. It has subsided a little, but the slightest touch still causes a sharp pain to shoot through her. Her busted bottom lip is from his most recent loss of temper. It happened a day earlier in the parking lot of that pet store. She wishes she'd never mentioned that Marissa had called to ask her what she thought were silly questions about animals. Carissa thought it was funny that her sister had been assigned to a store grand opening, which was like a free advertisement for the store. She thought he would find it amusing, too.

Instead, he slapped her across the face, grabbed her, pushed her to the car and ordered his brother to drive them to the store's location. Carissa had no idea what had pissed him off because she couldn't understand what the two brothers were saying to each other.

Because of the busted lip, the attack earned her two hundred dollars, which always makes the pain more bearable. After every violent incident, he's somewhat remorseful and usually slips Carissa a few hundred dollar bills to make up for his nasty behavior. While his temper makes her nervous, he always seems to push his anger right to the edge of the cliff. Lately though, she's seen him fly out of control at others, and she fears that he's headed for a violent free-fall straight off that cliff.

After the first time he lost his temper, he promised he'd make it up to her. In addition to a one-hundred-dollar bill, it was the first time he surprised her by placing a hit of Ecstasy on the table in front of her. Carissa has always been a party girl who could slam down tequila and other liquor with no problems. And she has smoked pot, but that's about as far as her involvement in illegal drugs has gone…until H.N.

Ecstasy opened up entirely new experiences for her. One little pill not only provides a wonderful rush, but it also leaves her tripping. She's heard that it's better than LSD. All she knows is that it gives her unbelievable energy while putting her in the mood to party and to have sex—lots of it. She calls it the "love drug." H.N. only gets high with her occasionally because he wants to remain in control at all times. But lately, he's been indulging in the drugs right along with her. There's no doubt he enjoys how the drug morphs Carissa into an uninhibited woman with a voracious sexual appetite. The problem is that she needs more and more of the same drugs to reach the same high, and he's willing to provide her with all she needs.

Carissa finishes her work. She's starving but has to wait for one last dog to be picked up. Once the dog is on its way home, she can order food to be delivered to her place. She figures if she times it just right, she can lock up the business, head home, change and fix a strong drink all before her dinner arrives.

Just as she's about to look over the menu of her favorite Chinese restaurant, a bell rings signaling the door to the shop has opened. But it's not the dog's owner—it's H.N. At first glance, she can see he's angry.

"You have exactly two minutes to get your things and clear out of here. Don't ask any questions. In fact, don't waste anytime talking," he says. His fury is palpable.

At first, Carissa freezes. She is all too familiar with the depths of his anger and the physical dangers that confront her if she says the wrong thing, so she chooses her words carefully. "But…the owner for this last dog will be here any moment. Surely…we can wait just a few minutes for her to arrive?"

He becomes a raving lunatic—an agitated monster that has suddenly broken free from its cage. In one fluid motion, he moves in and slaps her so hard across her cheek that she crumples to the ground in pain. She screams and curls her body in an attempt to avoid another forceful blow. Crying, she can barely speak. "What have I done to make you so angry?"

He leans down until she can feel his hot breath on her neck. He reeks of alcohol and his shirt is uncharacteristically wrinkled. Sweat stains start spreading underneath his arms. He whispers through clenched teeth, "Unless you want to experience more physical pain than you could ever imagine, you'll get up, get your purse and leave with me. NOW!"

"But…"

"Leave a note for the dog's owner, saying you didn't feel well and that you left the door unlocked so the dog could be retrieved. Tell her a coworker will stop by to lock up the store later."

Carissa tries not to cry as she tries to get up. She has no idea what just happened or why. Out of fear, she does what she is told and scribbles a note to the dog's owner. As she does, she prays at any second someone—anyone—will open the door, walk in and interrupt the crazy turn her world has just taken. But no such luck.

He begins to pace, planning his next move. His cell phone rings and for a brief second, he turns his full attention away from her. As he's speaking in hushed tones, Carissa looks for tape to stick the note to the dog's owner on the counter. While he's distracted by the phone call, she scribbles a cryptic plea for help and stashes it in a secret spot behind the base of the cash register. It's been a long time since she's attended church and even longer since she's prayed but in desperation, she pleads, *"Por favor, Dios mio. Ayudame!"* She hopes a higher power will lead her sister to this spot since she's the only person who will know where to look for her note.

At that moment, H.N. hangs up his cell phone, moves towards Carissa, and pulls her out the door. She reaches for her purse that's tucked away in a drawer below the front counter and at the same time discreetly presses the silent alarm hidden underneath the cash register. Tío Hector insisted that the alarm be installed in case of an emergency. The device, like the kind used in banks, alerts police of a possible break-in or some other emergency. Her heart is beating fast as H.N. pushes her outside and into the idling sports car parked curbside.

As they speed off, Carissa wonders how long it will be before officers arrive and more importantly how long will it take for anyone to figure out that she didn't leave willingly.

Fourteen

"**Y**ou think you're so smart, don't you?" H.N. growls at Carissa as they speed through the city streets. Carissa winces. She is worried his reckless driving will cause an accident, but she knows better than to ask him to slow down...or to ask where they are going. She knows a single word could trigger another backhand to her already battered face.

Finally, he begins to talk. "You're smart enough not to ask questions about my brother and me...about our business investments or about our family history. But you think nothing of enjoying the lavish lifestyle that I have provided you. Thanks to me, you get to wear expensive clothes, eat in the finest restaurants and travel to exciting cities aboard my private jet."

He turns a corner a little too sharply, which causes the sports car to feel like it's slightly lifting off the road. His daredevil driving is only adding to her nervousness and fears about where they're going.

His rant continues, "And from you, I ask for very little in return. You're expected to look attractive when you're with me. But look at you! You look awful in those baggy sweatpants and I can smell dog feces in your hair." He wraps his hand in her ponytail and tightly tugs on it, causing her to lean her head towards him.

He finally releases his painful hold on her hair, only because he's pulling into the underground parking garage that has a private elevator that will take them directly to his high-rise condo. He turns off the engine and looks at her with his angry dark brown eyes. It's a look she's seen directed at others before, but this time his hate is focused on her.

"Your role in my life is minimal. I expect you to be discreet in your spending and to be available for companionship and sex whenever I want. That's certainly made easier thanks to those little blue pills you seem to enjoy so much," he sneers. "Let me remind you that you're never to make demands on me at any time. You'll have no expectations about where this relationship is going because there is no relationship. You're no more than a possession, like this car or a painting. You have no say in what happens. Your opinions and feelings don't matter to me. If I pass you anywhere in Austin, you're not to show any sign of recognition. It's all part of the discretion I require from you for which you're well compensated."

She tries not to react to his angry description of her "duties." Her body tenses as she anticipates another physical blow that could come at any second.

He continues to seethe, "Don't think I don't know about the hefty portion of my money you've managed to pocket for yourself. If there's one thing I am good at it's tracking the money that I work so hard to earn."

She flinches at this revelation. The last she checked, she had almost fifty thousand dollars stashed in an account from money she thought she'd discreetly helped herself to from H.N. She was always careful to pocket only small amounts—a hundred here…a thousand there. *What's five or ten thousand dollars from someone who thinks nothing of dropping a hundred thousand during one night out?* she justified.

"Yes, I know all about the money you've been stealing to fund your future business venture…." He pauses before saying, "I know you better than you know yourself. I know you're determined to open your own business even if it means hoarding every nickel and penny you find underneath sofa cushions for the rest of your life!" He continues to demean her by saying, "There aren't enough sofa cushions in the world for you to dig through. So instead, I've made it easier by providing a lucrative way for you to prostitute yourself and do it while enjoying a luxurious lifestyle."

Carissa feels trapped within the confines of his sports car. It's not just the cramped physical space. It's also the realization that his comments are dead-on accurate. He knows she's been stealing from him and that her future aspirations are being built on his earnings.

"I know you also hate to be mistaken for your sister, Marissa. I can see it drives you crazy when some stranger approaches you because they think you're *the* Marissa Cavelo from TV. It's even worse for you when you see the disappointment on their faces when you tell them the truth. Even your voices sound the same. You thought you knew what I was thinking. You thought I was trying to figure out why you looked so familiar to me. Well, you were wrong. I knew exactly who you were, although I made it a point not to ask you about your sister."

His words are sharp jabs that stick straight into the open wounds that have been festering inside her for so long. These are wounds that, lately, have become hard to deal with and impossible to heal.

As he opens the door to get out of his car, he takes a parting shot, "I don't have to ask anything about you, your sister or your sad, dead parents because I know all there is to know."

From the glove box, he pulls out an all too familiar item—a prescription pill bottle. He grabs her left hand that's been clenched in her lap and shakes out three pills into her palm. "Here, bitch! Take these and get ready to earn your money."

Carissa doesn't have the strength to resist. Without resistance, she pops the pills into her mouth and braces herself for what she knows will follow. He'll insult her and push her around a little too hard. She'll drink heavily before they have rough sex. Then she'll make herself up in expensive makeup and clothes to do as he demands—another possession he owns, to do with as he pleases.

◊◊◊

Carissa has no idea how much time has passed—an hour—days? All she knows is that her brain is under a fog whenever she takes hits of E and slams down a couple of drinks. Although she doesn't remember it, she's pretty sure the sex was aggressive and physically exhausting—as always. There is no hint to how much time has passed since all sunlight is completely shut out by the heavy drapes. She tries not to move as she listens for any sign that H.N. is still in bed with her. It's hard to tell if he's there since the bed is custom-built and almost twice the size of any commercial king size bed. It's big enough to sleep four adults comfortably without ever coming into contact with each other.

Slowly, she senses there's no one next to her. Instead, H.N. is sitting on the edge of the bed, smoking a hookah pipe and mumbling to himself. She tries to keep her breathing quiet so she can hear what he is saying.

"Father, what happened?" he seems to be crying out to a ghost in the dark bedroom. "Is this what you wanted for our family when you left your life as a successful merchant in Iran to hide in Houston? Was life so bad in the 80s that it was worth leaving the wealth you'd built to come to this foreign country?"

She hears him sob quietly before he continues speaking to himself. "I can't imagine why you—a wealthy person—would end your allegiance to one of the greatest leaders the world has ever known, the Shah of Iran. You should have had the courage to withstand the Islamic Revolution. Instead you, the Shah, and many other followers, including your brothers and families were forced to flee the country. I curse you for bringing us here to Texas." The anger in his voice rises as he throws a glass into the fireplace across the room.

The shattering glass startles her and she quickly grabs the sheet to cover herself as he turns on the bed and inches towards her. She is resting on her side with her back toward him. She thinks, *If I stay perfectly still, maybe he'll think I'm still passed out from the drugs and drinking.*

But he continues to speak, and she realizes that he is talking to her. "Did I ever tell you that I was only a toddler when my family left suddenly in the middle of the night? We had no choice but to leave behind all our possessions, including artwork, jewelry, Persian rugs and furnishings. The few pictures that we were able to take with us are the only reminders I have from our early family life." He continues to crawl across the gigantic expanse of the bed and reaches to stroke her back. Again, she shudders at his touch. Carissa used to crave the sensation of his fingers on her body. Now it fills her with fear. She can tell he's unaware that she's afraid. *I doubt if he even cares whether or not I'm conscious.*

He continues to ramble. "Someday I'll show you the photos that are the only reminders of a life that no longer exists. Carissa, our home looked like a palace filled with servants and rich furnishings, the likes of which few people will ever see or experience."

He falls back on the pile of pillows and continues, "Then, in a firestorm of political turmoil…it was all gone. My mother cried incessantly as she was packing to make our getaway. Newly installed into power, the Islamic extremists would've recognized any of my father's expensive automobiles, so instead, we took an old station wagon that belonged to a loyal staff member. If we hadn't escaped when we did, the incoming regime would have thrown my father in jail. As it was, two of my uncles were incarcerated and executed after being brought before a tribunal."

He pauses for a few minutes and Carissa wonders if he's fallen asleep. Then she hears a sound she's never heard coming from this rich

119

and powerful man—cries of grief as he recalls more of his childhood trauma. "The wreckage of our lives broke my mother's spirit and destroyed my father's faith. When we arrived in the United States, we were told that Houston was home to a fast-growing population of Iranians and other Middle Eastern nationalities, so that's where we headed. What we found was a huge urban wasteland where we were unwelcome. The affluent Anglos didn't, and still don't, take kindly to foreigners. To some, we were no better than African-Americans or Latinos. We were lumped together as non-citizens along with the Koreans and the Vietnamese who also flocked to Houston to try to make a living after surviving political unrest in their countries."

If Carissa wasn't so afraid of him, she might actually feel sorry for this broken man.

"From the photos and stories, it's easy to see my mother was once an Iranian beauty with a flawless, complexion and dark, raven eyes and hair. Not much different from you, Carissa." He pauses and strokes her back. "But in Houston, my mother always felt like an outsider. She had a difficult time adapting to a new and very different environment. Imagine living in your homeland in a mansion and then in an instant, you're forced to live in a decaying, cramped, two-bedroom apartment in a complex where no one speaks your language and everyone dislikes you. To make matters worse, the associates who promised my father a job when he relocated to Houston failed to deliver."

Once again, the tide of anger rises within him as he talks about the injustices his family endured. "Once a respected, prominent man who helped rule his homeland, my father found himself living the life of a pauper who couldn't provide for his family. It didn't take long for him and other displaced Persians to band together to survive." And then his anger turns to pride as he says, "My father's survival was soon built on the destruction of others." A wicked laugh from him is a sign he takes pleasure from the pain his father inflicted on others.

Carissa turns over in bed so that she's facing him. She's intrigued by his words since he's never revealed anything about his family or his childhood before. She reaches over to stroke his hand, hoping that her touch will calm him. She remains silent.

H.N.'s flow of emotions continues. "My younger brother and I went to school and tried our best to fit in. We found ourselves working all kinds of odd jobs, including delivering newspapers and hauling trash. We performed whatever dirty, insignificant task other people didn't want to do themselves but were willing to pay someone else to do. While we were busy performing cheap grunt labor as teenagers, my brother and I slowly came to understand the illegal business my father was conducting.

"He'd fallen in with a couple of Middle Eastern con men who'd established a lucrative black market specializing in acquiring and selling 'hot' commodities. Anything easily stolen from warehouses in the various industrial areas of Houston brought a nice profit when peddled to residents in low-income neighborhoods. Those goods included television sets and electronics, home furnishings and even meat and exotic spices. Soon, my father and his business associates were importing cheap items from China, Korea and Mexico. Those goods were mostly knock-offs of expensive items that only experts could detect as being fake. Customers who didn't know better believed they were getting a real Rolex watch or Gucci purse. Customs officials working at the Port of Houston were paid to look the other way. No one suspected a thing. Almost overnight, my family was able to move into a modest house that was completely furnished in stolen or knock-off goods."

"It sounds like your father was a successful businessman," Carissa says, tentatively. "How long did the good fortune continue?"

"Good fortune? I'm still living the good fortune…and so are you for that matter. By the time my brother and I were old enough to drive, my father brought us into the business and we helped build the 'good fortune.' Of course, we had to prove ourselves. First, we were assigned simple tasks, like unloading and delivering the goods to various street corner vendors. Slowly, we took on other duties. We learned how to serve as lookouts while warehouses and delivery trucks were being burglarized. We collected past due bills, which meant occasionally roughing up a few customers who were late making payments. Then, as the revenue stream began to steadily increase, my brother and I entered the semi-legitimate business world. I earned a business degree and quickly began to make deals in the real estate market. Houston was a fast-growing city where commercial property in blighted, forgotten areas could be bought cheaply and renovated quickly. The real estate market proved to be lucrative for my brother and me.

"We bought up property after property. Abandoned buildings, empty lots, foreclosed homes, businesses that were moving or operations that were going-out-of-business. It all added to our real estate portfolio. And we didn't have to sit long on the property for the investment to pay off. Within the growing Middle Eastern community, we began to be known as real estate specialists who were willing to finance the purchase of property. We lured customers in by offering low-interest rates as an incentive. Unfortunately for them, and fortunately for us, many of the buyers were too trusting and failed to read the fine print that called for an extreme interest rate hike if a payment was late. Almost as quickly as we sold the property, we turned around and repossessed it after only one or two missed payments. And within the tight Persian community, there was no law enforcement recourse. Not that it would have made any difference. Our actions may have been unethical and immoral, but they weren't illegal."

Carissa wondered what prompted H.N.'s emotional floodgates to open up, forcing all these memories to come out in such detail. He seemed anxious to relive everything. She wanted to ask questions but knew it'd be best to just let him continue at his own pace.

"While my brother and I were expanding our real estate holdings, my father maintained his front for stolen goods. We told him many times that police investigators would start to notice patterns in large-scale thefts, but he would just scoff at our warnings. He was following business practices, like those carried out in Persia. There, everyone knows who accepts bribes, who pays bribes and the consequences of interfering with either. But this was not Persia. This was America, so it was only a matter of time before my father's crimes caught up with him."

H.N. moved back to the foot of the bed to take another hit from the Hookah pipe. Lulled by the soothing sound of the intake and release of his breath Carissa asked him, "What happened then?"

His tone turns sinister. "I'll tell you exactly what happened. My father's team of brazen, low-level thugs was riding around the vacant streets near the Houston Ship Channel where large, international cargo ships are docked. You know the area I'm talking about. It's a very desolate location occupied by giant warehouses and a few seedy bars and *cantinas* where dock workers regularly stop to grab a beer after their shifts are over. It's a rundown, blue-collar part of town. The men were crammed into a pickup truck and had been drinking. On a dare, they were trying to see which member of the group could figure out the warehouse where the most valuable goods were stored. The men accidentally tripped two silent alarms before stumbling across a cache of Japanese-made electronic gadgets in a warehouse on a dead-end, fenced-off street."

Something about the scenario he is describing sounds familiar to Carissa. It's almost like a scene from a movie she's watched, although she can't place the title or the actors.

Slowly, his voice fills with anger and sarcasm. "The men were whooping and hollering at the newly discovered treasure, unaware that a harmless, middle-aged night watchman was witnessing their every move. The security guard alerted police and led officers to the scene of the crime as members of my father's inept burglary gang were loading their pickup truck with stolen electronics. The band of drunken thieves was completely caught off guard by the officers who surrounded the building and they were caught red-handed. Literally, they were red-handed because a special device attached to the crates emitted a red-colored dye that appeared on the palms of their hands about fifteen minutes later." He takes another hit off the pipe and then continues, "The night watchman was considered a hero by members of the Houston Port Commission, which has jurisdiction over the Ship Channel and by the FBI and Houston Police Department, who'd been working together to try to bust the theft ring. As a sign of their gratitude for helping put an end to one of the longest running theft operations that anyone could remember, the night watchman was given a hefty reward."

Carissa freezes when he utters the words, "night watchman" *Could it be?* She wills herself to be perfectly still as he continues.

"The video of the bust and the interview with the night watchmen made the front page of every Houston newspaper as well as coverage on all of the radio and TV stations. The entire incident might have quickly been forgotten by the public…except for one small detail. Members of the burglary ring were still unwaveringly loyal to my father. All the men had followed my father's orders and would rather die than betray him. They didn't have to. The police detectives already knew about my father's involvement in the crime ring. There was enough evidence to go after him on numerous criminal charges, but the prosecutors chose to hit him with organized crime, tax evasion and possession of stolen property charges.

"Among the men arrested that night, one was threatened with deportation if he failed to cooperate with officers. He was the only sellout, proving that there is *not* always honor among thieves. Without hesitation, he agreed to testify against my father and was crucial in the prosecution's case.

"The media coverage of my father's arrest and his conviction a year later were both big news stories and were again covered by all of the Houston news media outlets, including the Spanish-language stations. Then, just as quickly as it unfolded in court, it was forgotten by the public. The photos taken during the trial captured my father as the dignified, intelligent man that he was. He insisted on having a Persian translator present throughout the trial, even though those close to him knew he understood and spoke English perfectly. When it was all over and the evidence was presented to the jury, my dad was sentenced to fifteen years in prison.

"I've heard of American-born businessmen being convicted on similar charges who served little or no time at all. Leaders of the tightly-knit Middle Eastern community were outraged, calling it a bias based on ethnicity, but no one seemed to care or to listen."

Carissa feels her body tense as the details of his story take on a gritty reality that she has tried for years to forget.

He turns to her and his venomous words spew slowly from his mouth. "Days after the trial ended, the night watchman, Jesus Cavelo and his wife, Maria, were found dead in their home. Nothing of value was taken. There was no motive to explain the double killing, but my brother and I knew it was a revenge slaying in retaliation for the fate of our father."

Instantly his voice rises in anger as he says in slow, measured words to her, "Your...father...was...responsible...for the...death... of...*my* father." His face falls into his cupped hands. He raises his head and his voice shakes with vengeance, "I hold your father responsible for all that's wrong in my life. One of my father's loyal followers was arrested and charged with the slaying of your parents. He was only a teenager and he felt his actions were justified. It was simple retaliation—an eye-for-an-eye. Even *you* can understand that concept. No one, other than my father's closest followers, was aware of why the killings were carried out. It baffled both the Houston Police Department and the District Attorney's office. Somehow, before his trial, the young man fled back to Iran where he still lives and is considered a martyr and a hero."

Carissa has no words in response to what he's just confessed.

"While the slaying of your parents was tragic for you and your sister, my father never mentioned it. The time he spent behind bars took its toll on his health and his mind. He died after serving only three years. As for my mother, she never recovered from her grief. She became a recluse who rarely left her house. A once beautiful and refined woman and the wife of a prominent businessman, she quickly became a shadow of her former self. My beloved mother slowly allowed sorrow to eat away at her life. She died just two days after my father's death. We take comfort in believing they are reunited in the afterlife."

He looks away as he says, "And soon…I'll take comfort in seeking revenge again. This time against you and your know-it-all sister!"

It's frightening to observe his sadness give way to anger. She knows there's no use trying to reason with him, especially since the drinking, smoking and drugs have clouded his thinking. The safe move is for her to lie quietly while he talks.

"Ever since our mother died of a broken heart, my brother and I were left on our own. We moved our operations to Austin where we wanted to build a new start. But no matter where we live or what business venture we are involved in, my brother and I have vowed to avenge our father's death so that he'll not be remembered as a broken man who died in prison. We're also determined to do whatever's necessary so that our mother can be at peace in the afterlife. I refuse to allow my dear mother to be remembered as a once beautiful woman who slowly went insane."

There is no emotion in his voice as he addresses her. "Carissa, you are stupid to think our meeting was a coincidence. I didn't just happen to walk into that damn place where you work. And it's exactly why I dragged you out of there today. Let me remind you of what I told you in the parking lot of that ridiculous pet store bust. Your sister won't interfere in the business that my brother and I have worked so hard to build. You will do exactly as I order to ensure that her reporting days are over."

Carissa's attempts to shield herself from his fists are useless. His blows come hard until she is knocked unconscious.

Fifteen

Hanz and Alice have a lot to say about their time at the Regency Dance Studio. Marissa plays the role of confessor to these two eager to confess their sins. She asks Alice, "Take us back to the beginning. How did you get involved in the dance entertainment industry?"

Alice is an attractive woman in her late thirties. She clears her throat before saying, "It might be hard to believe, but I used to be a professional dancer myself. I danced in high school and college and for a brief time, I considered a career as a showgirl in Las Vegas."

"What were your duties as an employee of the Regency Dance Studio?"

"I was a substitute instructor and a part-time recruiter."

"When you say recruiter, did you recruit performers for parts in television commercials and movies?"

She laughs. "No. At the Regency Dance Studio the position 'recruiter' takes on a whole new meaning. It has nothing to do with helping to place dancers in the entertainment industry or launching the careers of deserving individuals. At the Regency, a recruiter 're-cruits' students, their parents and more importantly, their money. It's all about making money." Alice no longer sounds nervous. Her voice fills with anger. "The school is nothing but a huge rip-off! We were instructed to tell students, 'you have a natural ability,' or, 'you have a unique look and style.' The line I hated most was, 'you are just what directors and choreographers are looking for.' In other words, it was my responsibility to convince students to keep enrolling in dance classes and to keep their parents paying the crazy tuition rates."

"What if parents were concerned about the fees? Marissa asks.

"If there was any hesitation about paying for lessons or paying the huge fees to attend auditions, that's when we were instructed to say, 'This is a once-in-a-lifetime chance that won't come around again. You'll regret your child missing this opportunity for the rest of your life.' Guilt and remorse were our tools if they even hesitated to hand over their hard-earned money."

"Those phrases you just shared with us...the ones you shared with the students and parents...were those statements ever true?"

"No. Never."

"Do you have any knowledge of families borrowing money or taking on heavy debt to pay the fees for these so-called, 'once in a life-time opportunities?'"

"Yes," she whispers. "And that's why I finally quit. I couldn't take the guilt anymore of pushing gullible, trusting families into accepting more than they could financially handle, especially knowing that their children would never have enough true talent to succeed in the enter-tainment world."

Marissa gives Alice a few minutes to compose herself. She and Ken turn their attention to Hanz who's been fidgeting while his col-league was speaking. Hanz is tall, with gray, thinning hair. He's wearing glasses and has a gentle manner about him. His German accent is easy to detect, but he speaks in clear, precise sentences that sound genuine.

"So," Marissa asks, "tell us about the work you're doing now."

"I am still photographer and I also shoot videos from time to time—mostly rough cuts of commercials that advertisers are trying to pitch to clients."

"What about your previous work?"

"I was hired by the Regency Dance Studio to take photos before performances. You know...recitals? It was simple work. The dance students would pose in their costumes before taking the stage. Of course, parents and grandparents can always be counted on to order multiple copies of every pose. Nothing is more adorable than youngsters who are in costumes ready to perform."

Marissa understands what he is saying. She is also aware that the cuteness ends for most youngsters when they hit that awkward pre-teen stage. That's when most kids need braces and glasses. Also, baby fat turns into not-so-cute extra pounds, which costumes can't camouflage.

He tips his head in Alice's direction and says, "As my colleague has already explained, very few dancers have natural ability... so the owners of the Regency Dance Studio came up with another way to keep students and more importantly, their money, invested in the school." He sighs and then continues, "Instructors like Alice are responsible for convincing families that their students would benefit by enrolling in more classes. Then, the students are encouraged to attend auditions, which are almost always held out-of-state. The cost usually runs between twenty-five hundred and five thousand dollars. Of course, each student is convinced they need an expensive portfolio of staged photos and even a video clip to show to potential talent scouts during the auditions. And that is where my services came in." He sits up a little straighter and says with conviction, "I'm ashamed to admit how many hours I spent taking head shots and various dance poses for their students. An assistant would package the photos in professional-looking folders...along with a DVD." His voice fills with sadness and remorse.

"Hanz, do you know what happened to those photos and videos that were purchased by parents for their youngsters to take along to the auditions?"

"Most of the photos and the DVDs were dropped into a trash bin after each audition." He bows his head, shaking it in shame.

"If you could deliver a message to the families of those students who were eager to be dancers, what would you tell them?"

"I'd be honest and tell them their children should pursue dance, but *only* if they love to dance. I'd also level with them and explain there are few, if any, opportunities for a career in the competitive world of professional dancing." He looks over at Alice, who's nodding her head in agreement.

"And I'd let the parents know that *any* legitimate audition doesn't require a fancy portfolio. A good photo taken with any digital camera will do. They also don't need an expensive audition tape. In fact, most producers and talent recruiters will hire a videographer to record auditions for their own review. It may sound like I'm trying to put myself and other photographers out of business, but that's how real decisions about dancers are made...not by someone who spends thousands of dollars to fly somewhere to be part of a mass audition."

Marissa shows Hanz a photo of Julia Lopez and asks, "Do you recognize this young woman?"

He turns the photo over and looks at the faint print on the back and says, "That's definitely a photograph I took. I can tell by the backdrop used and the photo paper it's printed on. However, I don't recognize the young lady. I took hundreds, maybe even thousands, of similar photos while I was the staff photographer at Regency Dance Studio."

Marissa turns to Alice and asks, "Are you familiar with the girl in the photo, Julia Lopez or her family?"

"No. I'm sorry, but I don't recall Julia or her family. Sadly, there were so many families who were pressured into making similar financial commitments," she says.

The interview concludes. Both Hanz and Alice express relief after talking about their experience and tell Marissa that they wish they had done so earlier. Before wrapping up, she asks each of them how their working relationships ended with the Regency Dance Studio.

Alice answers, "I quit and went back to teaching at a reputable dance school. Lucky for me, the popularity of the hit television show *Dancing with the Stars* reignited interest in ballroom and couples' dancing."

Hanz says, "I resigned as a school staff member. Besides the sizzle reels I produce for ad agencies, I'm now focusing on building a photography business that specializes in photos for high school seniors. I enjoy the niche I've managed to create, which keeps me very busy in the spring." He adds, "I'm also grateful to Sherry West for sending various clients my way. For those aspiring actors, I do my best to keep my fees reasonable."

"Thank you for your honesty and willingness to talk to us," Marissa says as Ken is packing up the gear. "I'm not sure how your interviews will be used until after we interview Gloria Linden. Regardless of what she says, I'm sure your words will give viewers something to think about before enrolling their children into any kind of instructional program that promises success in the entertainment world.

Ken and Marissa shake hands with Hanz and Alice before they leave the conference room. Marissa fumes just thinking about the Lopez family and how hard they tried to raise the money for Julia to attend the audition. In her heart, she knows that's exactly what her parents would have done for her sister or her if they had expressed dreams of being professional dancers. Thinking about her parents and all their sacrifices triggers a flood of emotions she hasn't allowed to surface in a while. It makes her determined to put this story on the air no matter how long it takes or how hard she must work to expose the scam. It's not just an assignment, it's personal—a way to honor her hardworking parents and others like them who'd do anything to improve the lives of their children. Marissa sees the value that comes from being an investigative reporter, and it's exactly the type of journalism she wants to pursue. She knows it isn't as glamorous as being an anchor, and it's extremely hard work, but if she can alert people about dangers, pitfalls and fraud, then it's a career move she's ready to make.

As they're getting ready to leave, Ken says to her, "This is probably the biggest story you'll tackle for a while. Are you sure you want to take this on?"

"I'm determined to see this story through. Why do you ask? What do you think I should be considering?"

"First off…consider the confrontation you'll be facing when you take on the dance studio owner. Sounds like she has a legal team standing by and they're not going to be thrilled that some attractive, smart television reporter is about to expose their lucrative money-making operation."

"People like Gloria Linden will keep doing exactly what they're doing until they're exposed to the public," she fires back. "I'm not worried about Linden's reaction…. I'm more concerned about families like the Lopezes who are misled into believing their children's talents are a sure path to fame. And now that we've interviewed Hanz Moore and Alice Harrell, we have additional proof that this is all a well-thought-out business operation. I'm *not* about to back down now. I know it won't be easy, but I also know it's absolutely the right thing to do,"

"I'm with you all the way," Ken reassures her.

Ken heads out to load the equipment into the news unit while Marissa stops at the receptionist's desk to let her know they've finished with the interviews. The receptionist asks her to wait until Sherry West can step out of her meeting to say goodbye.

Ms. West appears, talking on a cell phone while an assistant follows behind her taking notes. West interrupts her phone conversation and says, "I want to personally thank you for taking an interest in the talent recruitment business. There are some great kiddos out there who are enormously talented and if they're willing to work hard, their skills—whether it's dancing, acting, singing, or modeling—and their outstanding personalities will take them far. They don't need scam artists preying on them. Gloria Linden needs to be stopped. She's a negative reflection on those of us who are working to advance the careers of individuals with real talent. If you need any further help exposing her, just call me and I'll see what I can do."

"Thank you, I will. With the interviews we've conducted so far and with the complaints that have been submitted to the Texas' Consumer Affairs Division, we're building a pretty tight case. The toughest challenge is still ahead. We still need to talk to Gloria Linden, so wish us luck!" Marissa extends her hand to West.

"You don't need luck. You've got the truth on your side, so use it wisely. And remind your photographer to send me pictures if he's interested in some modeling gigs!" She laughs and then turns to her assistant and gets back on her cell phone.

As she gets into the passenger side of the news unit, Ken's on the phone and from the tone of his voice, she can tell the conversation is serious. Before hanging up he says, "Okay. I'll talk to her and call you back."

"What was that about?"

He lets out an exasperated sigh before answering, "That was the station. Ms. Linden's been calling and asking about your questions. She says you aren't providing her with enough time to review them before she responds."

"Well, there's still a couple of hours before Linden's five p.m. deadline. Why don't we head back to the station for more tapes and batteries? I can email the questions while you upload the interview tapes into the system. I'll also start drafting my story. Is that okay?"

"I have a better idea," says Ken. "Why don't we take a lunch break and decompress for half an hour? There's a great little deli right around the corner from here. My treat."

"Thank you, sir. I accept your invitation to lunch."

They go to the nearby deli where the sign outside reads: "Manwich Sandwich." It's a funky place with an eclectic mix of tables and chairs, colorful artwork and a small outdoor stage. A musician is singing and playing a guitar. Marissa appreciates that only in Austin, the Live Music Capital of the World, will one find a singer-songwriter performing for a lunch crowd on a weekday at a sandwich shop.

They take their food from the counter and head to a corner table on the shop's outside deck. It's a comfortable day with the noon sun taking the chill out of the November air. Their conversation is easy-going and she realizes how comfortable it feels talking to this good-looking guy. It feels like they've known each other forever. They talk about where they grew up and how they both ended up in Austin. She tells him how much she misses her parents and the sound of their Spanish-speaking voices coming through the thin walls of their Houston home.

"You would've liked my parents. They were like so many of the Latino families that we hear about these days. Honest, hardworking immigrants who risked their lives to come to Texas from Mexico in search of a better life for our family. When my sister and I were born, our parents vowed to do everything possible to become legal U.S. citizens. The first and most important requirement was to learn the language. So, every evening, I'd stay up late to greet my dad when he came home after working two jobs. His day would start at six a.m. at a factory then afterward he would go straight to his job as a security guard. While my mother was warming up his meal, I'd read the daily newspaper to them in English and then test them both on current events. On my dad's days off, which were rare, we'd sit together and watch the evening news. In unison, he and I would repeat, word-for-word, what the distinguished news anchor was saying. And then it was my responsibility to translate the meaning to Papi during commercial breaks. Papi…that's what we used to call him." She smiles at the memory of her father. "Of course, my sister, Carissa, was less interested in the news or taking part in the English lessons with our parents. She was happy to chime in but only when the topic turned to entertainment happenings or celebrity gossip."

Just the thought of Carissa's lighthearted personality makes her laugh. "My sister always managed to provide an upbeat balance to the often grim tone of the evening news. Honestly, if she wasn't so interested in building her own business, I'd pick her to be an entertainer!"

"So, did your parents meet their language and citizenship goals?" Ken asks.

"Yes. It took years, but eventually they mastered the language and culture. It was a proud moment for all of us when we attended their naturalization ceremony." She sighs. "Racism somehow always managed to dog them. Usually, the negative treatment came from ignorant individuals who somehow felt my mother and father had no business being in Texas or in America. But I was so proud of them because not once did it ever dampen their spirits. Or, at least they never let us see that. They were always positive. Our parents instilled values of hard work and determination in both my sister and me. They also believed in the importance of education as the key to success in life. After taking on extra hours and extra jobs, our parents managed to save enough money for an education fund. I'd give anything if they had lived long enough to know that their hard work paid for most of the costs that our academic scholarships didn't cover. They would have been proud to know that my sister and I received college degrees. I would give anything if they had been able to see us graduate, but it wasn't meant to be."

Ken takes Marissa's hand and they sit there for a moment in silence. Sometimes words aren't needed. After a while he asks, "What about the neighborhood where you grew up? What was it like? Is it similar to the Eastside here in Austin?"

"There are some similarities...the hardworking people...the strong sense of family and culture.... But I don't know.... Houston's a much larger, urban city where Latinos seem to struggle more with poverty and crime. Growing up in a rough barrio in Houston did provide me with my first exposure to life in a raw and brutal way. It's where I witnessed teen gangs roaming the hood, selling drugs and committing petty crimes. Old people were forced to live as prisoners locked inside their own homes with burglar bars covering the doors and windows. At night, you could hear sirens wailing and police helicopters flying overhead with their search lights scanning the ground for suspects."

"You managed to survive," Ken observes.

"Well, sure.... Lots of good people not only survive but thrive. Then again, many lives are lost. Even for law-abiding, hardworking people life can change in one quick instant. Our lives were shattered by senseless violence just like that," she says as she snaps her fingers. "Sometimes I wish I could remember the final moments I shared with my parents. I've wracked my brain trying to recall exactly what happened that morning while I was getting ready to leave the house to go to school. I can't remember what my mother was wearing or if my dad was reading the paper or tinkering with his tools, trying to fix something since items always needed repair or replacement in our house. I know one thing without a doubt. Our conversation that morning ended like it always did with my mom, my sister and I saying to each other: *Hasta luego. Que Dios te cuide.* See you later. May God protect you.*

Marissa looks off into the distance, staring at nothing in particular as her mind wanders back to that awful morning. "It was also the last time my sister and I ever saw the inside of our house. It's where we learned to read and write, where we were fed, clothed and loved by our parents." She pauses and then shakes the sadness from her mind and puts both hands on the table where the remnants of their lunch is scattered. "Enough about me and my family. What about you? I'd love to hear about your childhood."

Ken laughs at the sudden change in the direction of the conversation. "I'm one of six kids from a typical and very boring family from the Midwest. My mother's a teacher who'll be retiring soon and my dad has worked for the same company for nearly thirty years. I'm the oldest of the children. All my siblings still live in the area not far from my parents. As for me, they really doubted my career choice to become a photographer. I try to get back to visit at least once a year, but I hate the winters with the snow and ice. At least here in Austin, the chilly temperatures don't last long. For instance, look at today. Here it is November and we're sitting outside for lunch!" Ken's description of his family makes her smile as she pictures him wrestling with his younger brothers and sisters and taking part in other childhood activities.

"What about what you're doing now? Do you see yourself being a news photographer indefinitely? What are your career aspirations? Do you want to work in a larger market someday?"

"Always asking the 'big' questions, aren't you?" he says with a laugh. "Actually, someday I'd like to work on documentaries. An idea for one about homeless children came to me a few months ago after I came across some youngsters in the empty parking lot of a warehouse at night. The kids, ages two and eight, were sleeping in an abandoned car while their mom waited in line for the food pantry to open."

"That's terrible. What happened? Did you call anybody?"

"No, I didn't call authorities. I just couldn't bring myself to do that after the older child, a boy, asked me not to. He said his mother was worried the state would take them away. I couldn't just leave them there alone. So instead, I waited for the mother to return and then I took them to a shelter that takes in families." Ken smiles. "I still keep in touch with them and hope to share their experience with the public someday. There are so many families who are struggling, but the children…they really tug at your heartstrings. They're so resilient and so optimistic. That's what I'd love to be able to convey in a documentary…or even a short film."

Without thinking, Marissa reaches up to move an unruly curl that's fallen into his eye. Just brushing the wisp of hair behind his ear sends a faint electrical current from the tips of her fingers straight to her heart. Ken slowly takes her hand and places the palm side next to his cheek. His lips gently kiss her fingertips. Marissa wishes they could escape into seclusion to explore each other's souls and bodies.

Ken's cell phone rings, and just like that the spell of potential love comes to an abrupt end.

Marissa looks at her watch and sees this brief lunch has stretched into nearly an hour. Ken hangs up his phone and they resume a professional mode.

As they walk to the car, Ken says, "I told you this is a great little deli."

"A good place to talk. It's a heart-to-heart chat I'd like to continue very soon if you'd like. Next time I'll pick the place and I'll pick up the tab, okay?" she asks.

As they pull out of the parking lot, Ken jokes, "Ms. Cavelo, you have a deal. Next time it's your choice and your treat."

Back at the news station, Ken heads straight to an editing room to upload the tapes into the computer system so anyone can access them later. That'll make it easier for Marissa to pull the interview up on her computer so she can listen to the videotaped conversations and pick the best sound bites. Her first priority is to email questions to Gloria Linden and confirm she receives them. She types the following questions: How do you justify charging students fees for attending auditions? What types of professional employment opportunities exist for students who attend auditions? What's your response to complaints filed against you and your studio with the Texas Entertainment Commission? What's your response to allegations made by former staff members who say families and students are provided with unrealistic evaluations of their talents and abilities? How do you respond to complaints that the auditions you organize and the classes you offer are part of a money-making operation? What's your response to claims by former employees that they were pressured to secure financial commitments from students and their families? How do you respond to allegations that services such as photography and video recordings were unnecessary and were only offered to bring in more revenue?"

There is no rule—written or unwritten—that requires a reporter to submit questions in advance, but Marissa extends this professional courtesy to Linden. She has no idea how or if she'll respond, but it's a relief to Marissa to send the questions to her before the imposed five o'clock deadline. If Linden refuses to answer the questions, she'll have proof they were received by her and she can state, *"Gloria Linden refused to answer questions that she confirmed were submitted to her."*

After Marissa hits *send,* she checks her emails for a reply from the Consumer Affairs Division. Under the State's Open Records Act, she requested a summary of complaints filed by consumers against the Regency Dance Studio. The response from the state agency is waiting in her inbox. The number and types of complaints will be turned into a full-screen graphic. If Linden refuses to answer her questions, Marissa figures that the complaints on file will speak for themselves. Her next step is to listen to the interviews and pick the most powerful sound bites from each person. Before selecting the best ones, she checks her email to see if Linden has received the questions. As she scrolls through, she notices an email from a sender she doesn't recognize. Instead of a name, it's a jumble of letters and numbers. The subject line reads: "WARNING." She hesitates opening the email. It could be a link to a virus that will spread, causing damage to the entire computer system...or even worse...causing the system to crash. She decides to take a chance and open the email. The wording is cryptic. It reads: "If you value your life *stop* what you're doing. Now!" Then somehow, the typed message dissolves into the image of a human skull with deep, red blood dripping from its empty eye sockets.

Is this a joke or a real threat? Is this related to what Tío mentioned might be prompted by the exotic bird heist? she wonders.

Just then, her cell phone rings and the Caller ID reads: "Blocked." She is rattled but tries to sound professional. "Hello. This is Marissa Cavelo."

A gruff voice spits out vile words. "Shut the fuck up, bitch, and listen to me. Get the hell out of the news business. Now!" The caller suddenly hangs up. She is too stunned to react. No one has ever spoken to her in such a hate-filled tone. It doesn't sound like a practical joke. She's shocked but somehow manages to jot down the time and the exact words spoken. She takes a deep breath and considers finding Ken to tell him about the threatening phone call.

Then she thinks, *No. I should contact Tío Hector. As a veteran police detective, he'll know what to do.* Just as she's about to dial her uncle's number, she realizes Jan Ruther is standing behind her, looking at her computer screen. Instinctively, she clicks off the email and turns to face her.

Ruther is scowling. The words she scanned on Marissa's computer are the rough draft of her news story. Marissa keeps her tone light, "Hi, Jan. I didn't realize you were standing there. Is there something I can help you with?"

"I was just checking on your progress. I came to tell you that the decision's been made to air this story tomorrow instead of Friday." She seems amused by the change.

"That's cutting it close." Marissa tries to keep the panic out of her voice. "I still haven't interviewed the owner of the dance school. We're scheduled to talk to her tomorrow morning at nine. I can pull it together if you'll allow me to take time off from the anchor desk. Is it possible for Melinda to solo anchor?"

"No. Absolutely out of the question. You must be on the set. Have you forgotten that we are in November ratings? You should have plenty of time to get to your interview at nine and get back here in time for the noon newscast. You can finish writing the story after that. Just remember, the script must be approved by either myself or by the news director before it airs. Be sure it gets to one of us ASAP in case there are any corrections or changes that need to be made. Am I clear?"

She walks off before Marissa can respond. It's become an annoying habit of Jan's. She asks, 'Am I clear?' but it's not a question. Nor does she want an answer. She's just informing whomever it is she is talking to that the conversation is over.

Facing an earlier deadline causes a small sense of panic to gnaw at Marissa as she calculates how long it'll take to finish her story. She's almost done with a rough draft, but it won't be finished until after the interview with the studio owner tomorrow morning, which should take about an hour. Then she'll need to select Linden's sound bites. She'll anchor the noon newscast, and the minute it's over, she'll finish the script and get it to the executive producer for approval by two p.m. If she gets it back in thirty minutes or less, then she can get it to Ken to edit and will make the deadline to air on the six o'clock news.

Marissa calculates, *If everything goes as scheduled, I'll even have time to change clothes, touch up my makeup, and stop by the AAN convention and introduce myself to Marcus Feldman.* Marissa gathers her notes and starts to shut down her computer so she can head home to finish writing her rough draft without distractions. It will also give her a chance to stop by the dry cleaners to pick up the outfit she wants to wear to her meeting with the talent recruiter. A good first impression is so important. As she heads for the parking lot, she remembers the eerie email and threatening phone call. The coincidence of getting both within seconds of each other is unnerving, but she can't let an unsubstantiated threat stop her from her mission. She makes a mental note to call Tío Hector as soon as she gets into her car.

On her way out of the building, she pops her head into the editing room to tell Ken she's leaving. He's got the video from the interview with the Lopez family playing on a monitor. It looks crisp and clear in HD, conveying the raw emotion on Mrs. Lopez's face.

Marissa decides not to tell Ken about the weird email and phone call and instead says, "The video looks fantastic. You have a special skill for making people feel comfortable while sharing their most private feelings. They didn't even realize the camera was rolling." Then she thinks about Linden. "Let's hope Linden feels comfortable enough to open up about her questionable business operations. To be honest, getting her to be truthful will be as easy as pulling an abscessed tooth from a two-hundred-pound gorilla! I hope you're up for a good fight."

Ken answers with a smile, "She doesn't scare me and she shouldn't scare you…not with the ammo we have against her." He puts his hands on her shoulders, turns her around and gently nudges her out the door. "Don't worry about me," he says. "Go home and get some rest. I'll see you in the morning. I'll be here bright and early, ready to roll. It's going to be a memorable story."

Sixteen

As she drives home, Marissa decides that the creepy message is just a prank. She doesn't give in readily to fear, which is amazing, considering what happened to her parents. She's covered a few crime stories, but she has never worried about her own safety, maybe because she grew up in a crime-plagued neighborhood. *It's hard to take these phone or computer messages too seriously. Other on-air personalities have been the targets of nasty emails and phone calls,* she reasons. In a warped way, some egotistical anchors consider such messages from viewers to be a sign of their career success. *Only a narcissist boasts about being harassed by an angry viewer,* she thinks. She decides not to worry about it...at least not until after she discusses the details with Tío Hector. However, she knows her uncle will provide plenty of valid reasons for her to be cautious, if not fearful. She decides to put it out of her mind, at least for the next twenty-four hours.

Marissa's apartment is her safe haven from the crazy world of television news. This is where she either unwinds or is able to work without interruption. After slipping into some comfortable clothes, she pours a glass of wine and heats up some leftovers. She turns off her cell phone and computer, determined to ignore any emails or text messages that could distract her. She puts in her earbuds and starts listening to the interviews. She types not only what's said but also descriptions of facial expressions, background setting, etc. This transcribing session lasts much longer than usual for the five different interviews: Mrs. Lopez and her daughter, the two former employees of the Regency Dance Studio and Sherry West. When she finally takes out the ear buds and emerges from her self-induced cocoon, she's exhausted but satisfied; she knows viewers are going to be shocked and angry when the exposé hits the airwaves.

She gets up from her desk and takes a few minutes to stretch her legs and back before heading to the bathroom to get ready for bed. She stares at her image in the mirror and laughs. *I look like I'm posing for a horrible mug shot!* She's determined to get a good night's sleep and take time with her makeup in the morning before she goes to meet Feldman.

As she sets the alarm on her phone, she sees she's missed a call from Tío Hector. It's almost midnight. *I'll call him back in the morning,* she thinks as she crawls into bed.

She starts her day with a two-mile jog. Her increased energy prepares her for the day's challenges. The forecast calls for a sunny, cool day with low humidity. For a news anchor, that means it's a perfect hair day. By the time she leaves her apartment, she's confident she'll make a great first impression when she meets with the AAN talent recruiter later.

When she sees Ken at the station her first thought is, *How is it possible for him to look even better than he did yesterday?* He's packed and ready to head out the door so that they won't be late for their interview with Gloria Linden. As they drive to the Regency Dance Studio, she shares her research on Linden. "Listen to what I found in an old issue of *Austin Monthly* magazine. It says here she's very competitive. She entered the *Miss Texas* pageant three times. All three times she lost. The photos of her in her early twenties show an attractive young woman. Fast forward to a current profile that describes her as, 'a well-known socialite, whose claim to fame is based on her attempts to launch a career as a professional dancer.'" She scans the article before continuing, "'Once again, the third time is *not* the charm for Ms. Linden after she auditioned for the famous Radio City Rockettes twice and the Dallas Cowboys Cheerleaders once. Finally, Linden put her professional aspirations aside and married into a local wealthy family.' Her husband is barely mentioned in the article except to say he prefers to stay out of the limelight that his wife seems to crave. The couple doesn't have any children. Several years ago, Linden decided to open her own franchise—the highly successful Regency Dance Studio." Then she tells Ken, "Here's a quote from her where she says, 'I wanted to help aspiring boys and girls fulfill their dreams of becoming a dancer like I did.'" Marissa turns to Ken and asks, "How do you help aspiring boys and girls become dancers by selling them false promises of fame?"

Ken shrugs his shoulders and shakes his head.

"It seems to me that if you want to be a professional dancer or a performer, it'd be more appealing to take lessons from and be guided by someone who's achieved success, *not* from someone who failed to reach her own goals."

The news unit pulls up and parks outside the Regency Dance Studio. It's a clean, modern building. Large shady oak trees surround the facility and dot the parking lot that's big enough to accommodate at least fifty cars.

Inside the massive metal and glass front door, they're greeted by a receptionist who leads them to a large conference room where they're told the interview will be conducted. The neutral colored walls are covered by beautiful reproductions of artwork capturing dancers in pose and in motion. The receptionist leaves them alone to set-up their equipment. As they prepare, Marissa has an eerie feeling they're being monitored. Marissa writes in her notebook and turns the page to Ken: **Be careful what you say. We're being watched!**

Ken nods his understanding.

The room is furnished with an expensive area rug and a very cushy couch. A huge mirror hangs in the center of the wall amid the framed portraits and photos of dancers, but a closer look confirms her suspicions of being watched. The reflection is the surface of a two-way mirror similar to those used by police in interrogation rooms. Tío Hector taught her how to spot a two-way mirror a long time ago. Such mirrors provide officers with the opportunity to watch and listen while seated in a separate observation room as suspects are questioned. In this case, the two-way mirror is set in an ornate gold-plated frame that matches the rest of the decor. It's hard to detect by a non-suspecting person.

Why would a dance school need a two-way mirror? she wonders and thinks back to the interview with Alice who mentioned the pressure she felt if she failed to convince students and their families to sign up for more classes. Marissa realizes that the recruiters and instructors were under surveillance. *Who wouldn't cave under that type of pressure?*

While Marissa ponders the mirror, Linden walks in. She reminds Marissa of a modern version of Cruella de Vil from Disney's *101 Dalmatians*. She's not wearing a dog-spotted fur coat nor is she carrying an old-fashioned, bejeweled cigarette holder. However, Gloria Linden *does* sport a dramatic white streak in her otherwise raven-black hair and heavy eye makeup; and her fingers, wrists and earlobes are dripping in jewels. Linden reaches up with her hand to fluff her over-ly-sprayed hairdo as she stages a grand entrance into the conference room. One thing that *is* noticeably different is her breast size. Gone are the average-sized breasts seen in the photos from her days as a Miss Texas contestant. They've been replaced with bountiful double Ds.

Marissa can't help but think that Linden's inflated chest is so prominent there should be a flashing neon sign with the name of the plastic surgeon responsible for the enhancement. The collagen-injected lips and taught skin around her eyes and mouth complete the look of

147

someone determined to hold on to their fleeting youth at any cost. *A lot of little boys and girls had to take dance lessons to pay for that extreme makeover,* she thinks.

Marissa extends her right hand as she approaches Linden and says, "Ms. Linden. Thanks for agreeing to talk to us. I assume you received my email with the questions, so this interview shouldn't take long at all."

"Ms. Cavelo. How nice to meet you. Yes, I received your questions before five p.m. If I hadn't, you wouldn't be here," she sneers. "About your questions…I must say, the focus of a few of your inquiries doesn't make much sense. I still can't figure out why the media would be interested in a dance school. But I'm sure you'll explain your reason for being here during the interview. I'll be happy to answer your questions, just as soon as my attorney arrives."

"Yes, you mentioned wanting your legal counsel to be here. It's certainly your choice to have whomever you want present, and our news story will include the fact that your attorney is in the room. As long as it's understood that we're here to interview you and only you," Marissa says as firmly, but politely as possible.

Just then, a shifty-looking guy wearing a cheap suit, a cowboy hat and boots wanders into the conference room. Without waiting for an introduction, he blurts out in a loud, obnoxious voice, "Howdy! I see the news crew is saddled up and ready to ride. I'm Doug Diamond and you must be Ms. Cavelo. Nice to meet 'cha." His exaggerated Western drawl precedes his handshake. It'd be hard *not* to recognize Doug Diamond. He has a reputation for being a less-than-ethical attorney, and he's famous for his cheesy TV commercials that feature him riding to the legal rescue on a white stallion while wearing his signature cowboy hat and boots. Usually, he's coming to the aid of some damsel in distress—one with big boobs and a lot of makeup—just like Gloria Linden.

Marissa shakes his hand. "Yes, I'm Marissa Cavelo." She turns to Ken. "And this is my colleague, Ken Jordan."

Ken and Diamond shake hands. Then the slick attorney turns his attention to Linden.

She's standing, smiling adoringly at him and waiting to greet him with a warm hug and a kiss on each cheek. It appears to Marissa to be more than the average client-attorney relationship. Diamond turns to Marissa and says in his exaggerated Texas twang, "So...you want to ask my client the same questions you sent her by email? Well, let me just set some ground rules here for you, little lady. If you veer off the pre-approved topics, I'll order you to stop taping. If I'm not happy with my client's answers, or if she's uncomfortable in any way, you'll be ordered to stop taping. Are you following me?" he asks with a snide smile.

"Mr. Diamond, your requests are beyond reason. I get the feeling your client isn't allowed to answer questions without legal counsel... and there can only be one reason for that. So, my question to both of you is...what is she guilty of?" The strong conviction in her voice even surprises Marissa.

Behind the camera, Ken has discreetly been videotaping the entire exchange. He nods in approval and flashes a thumbs-up sign that only Marissa can see because Linden and Diamond are focused on each other in disbelief. Linden's smirk vanishes from her overdone, taut face.

"So Ms. Linden." Marissa presses, "It's your call. It's also *your* dance school and *your* reputation. Are you willing to respond to the questions submitted by me or not? Because this story will air with or without your answers. It'll also air without Mr. Diamond calling the shots about how this interview will be conducted." A strong surge of confidence fills her.

Gloria Linden doesn't have a chance to respond because Diamond starts talking in an obviously agitated voice. He's so visibly angry it looks like steam will start pouring out from underneath his cowboy hat, which he hasn't bothered to remove. "Ms. Cavelo, you're out of line! How dare you attempt to limit my client from legal counsel? You and your photographer can just pack up your ponies and get the heck outta here now before I call in a posse to have you escorted off the property!" he bellows.

Marissa turns to Linden and asks, "Ms. Linden, is that your choice? Are you opting *not* to be interviewed? And are you asking us to leave? Again, I remind you that this story will air with or without your recorded response."

Linden seems at a loss for words, like a puppet waiting for the puppet master to pull her strings. She turns to Diamond with her eyes pleading for permission to speak. He simply shakes his head vigorously. *Permission denied.* Linden says, "You heard Mr. Diamond. This interview is over. Please leave the property at once."

"All right then. If that's your decision. You can call me no later than noon today if you change your mind," Marissa advises.

Discreetly, Ken is rolling the camera as Diamond tells them they are not welcome and that they haven't heard the last of him. What he doesn't know is that he's providing the two with great TV moments. Anytime you have some puffed-up, self-righteous, pompous, bag-of-wind dueling with a TV camera it's a ratings grabber! Nine times out of ten, the person yelling obscenities, using their hands to block the camera or trying to knock away the microphone is guilty of something. Of course, an important rule of journalism is to keep it lawful. You always leave private property as soon as you're asked, but there's no rule about letting the camera roll. And that's exactly what Ken is doing as Diamond starts cussing.

In dramatic style, Gloria Linden, overcome with emotion, collapses into a chair all the while crying over and over, "Oh dear, oh dear, oh dear...."

The drama plays out as Marissa and Ken walk out the front door. Once outside, Ken hands her the keys to the news unit and tells her to move the vehicle out of the school's private parking lot and park it along the curb, which is public property. While she's moving the car, he heads to the front of the school to get exterior shots of the campus. He's careful not to step on private property since that would be trespassing. They faintly hear Diamond yelling something about calling the police from behind the school's closed front door.

Marissa has never felt so exhilarated in her life! She moves over to the passenger seat, pulls out her laptop and starts rewriting her story. The words fly from her fingers as they head back to the station. As soon as she can get in front of a monitor, she'll be able to pick the best video of the confrontation between them and Diamond and Linden. She has just one minor fact to check when she gets back to the station. Once that's done, her story will be ready to hit the air.

Seventeen

Back at her newsroom desk, Marissa dials the number for the Westbound Talent Agency and asks to speak to Alice Harrell. When she comes on the line, Marissa says, "Hi, Alice. It's Marissa Cavelo. I interviewed you yesterday. If you have a moment, I'd like to ask you a follow-up question. Is that okay?"

"Sure. I have a few minutes. How can I help you?"

"We were setting up for our interview earlier today in a conference room at the Regency Dance Studio. I couldn't help but notice some very ornate mirrors. So I have to ask…are those two-way mirrors?"

"Yes," she answers, "the mirrors in the conference room and in the two smaller interview rooms are two-way. How did you know? The owner was sure no one could detect them."

"My uncle's a police detective, so I've seen both sides of two-way mirrors in some interrogation rooms. I know officers use them when they want to observe suspects or witnesses while they're being questioned. But what I don't understand is why Linden would install two-way mirrors at a dance school."

Alice lets out a long sigh before answering. "It's all part of the elaborate attempt by Linden to control what happens to students and their parents. She uses the mirrors to monitor what we were saying. She and her management team wanted to know if we strayed from the approved script or if we failed to push hard enough to close a deal with parents. It's another reason I needed to get out of there. It was sheer psychological torture. No one should be forced to work under such conditions."

"Okay, Alice. That's what I thought. Thanks for taking my call and for answering this question. As I told you yesterday, you and Hanz have been a huge help. I think you'll both feel vindicated about the school's shady practices when this news story airs."

"I hope so. If that happens, then I'll be glad to have shed some light on this whole situation. Call me anytime," she says before saying goodbye.

Marissa hangs up, knowing she has a great story. She's so engrossed watching the video and writing that she loses track of time. Luckily, she is faithful about setting the alarm on her cell phone. At eleven-thirty a.m., the beeping sound forces her to stop working on the dance school story. There's just enough time to head into the dressing room so she can touch up her hair and makeup. Fifteen minutes later, she's ready to take her place at the anchor desk to scan scripts before the noon newscast begins. Studio crew members have already set the cameras and lights and have checked to be sure her microphone is working.

The same can't be said for Melinda Bale who's *not* on the set, although they're just minutes away from the start of the newscast. With seconds to spare and just as the floor manager is about to have a heart attack wondering where she is, Melinda manages to slide into place and clip on her mic as the opening music begins. Fortunately, it's a fairly routine news day so the newscast flows smoothly, although Melinda is more intent on cruising the internet and shopping on her favorite websites than she is on concentrating on news content.

The meteorologist is sharing some entertaining photos viewers have sent in of pumpkins, turkeys, children and puppies. Any combination of those images is always pleasing to viewers. Marissa rolls her eyes and thinks, *Who cares if the forecast is wrong? What difference does it make if the weather guy predicts a seventy-five percent chance of rain and not a single drop falls? It doesn't matter as long as he accepts invitations to speak at elementary schools and is willing to lead Boy Scout tours through the station. You gotta love him!*

Another highlight of today's newscast is the weekly feature called "Bob's Favorites." It features a self-appointed food critic who reviews his favorite places to eat. It's a joke since Bob is an obese, slovenly guy who never entered a restaurant that *wasn't* a favorite of his. The staff jokingly calls it, "Blob's Favorites." The studio crew's glad when the segments air, which are five to seven minutes long…plenty of time to lock down the camera, get a cup of coffee, make a quick phone call or run to the restroom. The ugly truth is that the restaurant reviews are suspect since eatery owners pay Bob to be featured as one of his "favorites." So technically, the segments are commercials—long, bad commercials. In no way do the reviews qualify as unbiased news but at least occasionally, the staff gets to pig out on the food the restaurants lay out for the video segments.

The hour-long newscast feels like an eternity to Marissa who is anxious to get off the set and finish work on her dance school piece. Finally, the floor manager yells, "We're clear!" She scurries to her desk to finish writing. She has about an hour before she has to submit the story to Jan for approval. Then, she'll record the audio track, leaving blank spaces where sound bites will be dropped in during the editing process. She knows that not only is Ken a great photographer, he's also an excellent editor. Before heading to Jan's office, she double-checks the facts and checks for errors. She is confident it is a strong piece that's fair and objective. It lays out the facts so viewers can draw their own conclusions.

Jan's office door is open and Marissa can hear her yelling at someone on the phone. "I said no excuses! Get the story and get it by deadline." She abruptly hangs up. Marissa takes advantage of the hastily terminated phone call to speak. "Excuse me, Jan, I need you to approve my script on the Regency Dance Studio so it can be turned over to Ken to be edited in time for today's six o'clock news."

"Fine. Just leave it on my desk. I'll get to it as soon as I can," she says nonchalantly.

"But…because of possible legal issues, this investigative story needs to be a priority."

Jan jumps up and lunges at Marissa. Her face, which is turning bright red, stops just inches from Marissa's and she spews, "I don't need you to instruct me on the importance of reviewing it on legal grounds. Now, get the hell out of my office, go back to your desk and wait there until I tell you to retrieve this script!" She grabs the script, returns to her desk and shouts, "And close the door on your way out!"

Wow! What a bitch, Marissa thinks as she heads back to her desk to wait for script approval. It's a nerve-wracking situation. Every minute that passes is one less minute Ken will have to finish working on their story. She doesn't dare start working on another news assignment since Jan might walk out of her office at any minute and hand over the approved script.

To pass the time, she decides to take another look at the photos in the envelope her Tío Hector gave Ken and her. The pictures are grainy, enlarged images of the two men believed to be the masterminds behind the attempted pet store heist. There's something familiar about them, but she can't put her finger on it. The two men are of medium height with long, thick wavy brown hair. There's nothing outstanding or unique about either.

Wait! What's this? She recognizes where the photo was taken. It's a trendy bar in downtown Austin called the Moroccan Hideaway…a club where CC has been trying to get her to go with her for the past few months. A couple of weekends ago she finally agreed to meet her sister and some of her girlfriends there. One of CC's friends was celebrating her birthday. There was a lot of drinking and some dancing, and Marissa remembered taking a video with her smart phone when the waiter brought out a flaming drink for the birthday girl. *Note to self: take a closer look at that video.*

Marissa goes online to the Texas Alcoholic Beverage Commission website to check the club owner's name and to see if there are past liquor license violations. After typing in the name of the club and the address, it takes a few seconds before the results appear. Up pops the names H. Nassine and N. Nassine, co-owners. The violations are lengthy but nothing out of the ordinary: serving underage minors, a late renewal of the club's liquor license, and an audit due to non-payment of the liquor tax. To check how the violations compare with those of other similar establishments, she pulls up the addresses of four other bars near the Moroccan Hideaway. Some of the same violations are also listed. And then something else catches her attention. The owners of the other four bars are also H. Nassine and N. Nassine! *Imagine that?* The same guys own some of the hippest bars in a three-block area. It's not illegal, but it *does* raise some interesting questions. Marissa smells another possible investigative story since the owners of multiple clubs could fix drink prices and cover charge fees. They could also unfairly be limiting who enters these clubs where there's always a long line waiting to get in. Marissa writes down a few notes and questions to check out later.

The clock is ticking...still no response from Jan.

To distract herself, Marissa decides to go through the stack of papers on her desk and clear items she doesn't need any more. While cleaning out a drawer, she looks up and sees Norman Baker. Today he's not delivering mail. He is instead wearing his "Mr. Fix It" hat. Norman enjoys tinkering with anything that doesn't work, including changing out a light fixture. He's setting up a stepladder near her desk as she drops sheets she no longer needs into a recycling bin. He's so unassuming that it's easy not to notice him until he says, "Waiting for script approval is like watching paint dry, isn't it, Marissa?"

She laughs and looks up from the papers she's sifting through. "This paint is drying very slowly. And I feel like I've already applied a dozen coats!"

"Well, this paint may not have a chance to dry at all," he says. "Not since Ruther is determined to block your every effort to finish what you started." He pulls a screwdriver out of his tool kit to work on the light fixture on the wall near her desk. "At least that's the conversation I overheard just moments ago in Jan's office right after you stepped out. I happened to be touching up the paint on the baseboards just outside her door, so it was easy to hear her on the phone. It's strange how she can be loud without even trying."

He pauses while taking a slow sip from his insulated coffee mug. "Now, I don't know who was on the other line, but judging from the syrupy sweetness in her voice, I would guess it was her sweetheart."

Sweetheart? Marissa can't imagine anyone being romantically interested in Jan Ruther. Just the thought makes her queasy. She stops sifting through old scripts and asks Norman, "What did Jan say to make you think she's sabotaging my work?"

"Jan asked the other person to guess what she had in her, 'hot little hands.' And then she said she had the document that was going to knock you right off your high horse. She said the document would have you groveling to keep your job. There was some exaggerated laughter exchanged between the two before Jan confirmed she had a copy of your script for the Regency Dance Studio story. Is that the script you are waiting for her to approve?" Norman asks.

Too stunned by what he's telling her to speak, she nods her head in response.

"That's what I thought you were working on. It's a big break judging from the way I overheard Jan describe it. She was scanning the script, telling the other person that you managed to interview a teenager who had hoped to raise the money to attend an audition. Ruther said it sounded like the teen's mother provided you with a real tearjerker moment as she described being unable to pay the family's bills and working two jobs to try and raise the dough.

"Ruther even read parts of the script out loud. She couldn't believe you were able to get not one, but two former Regency school employees to rat out the owner. She said something like, 'Wait 'til you hear this. There's a confrontation between Marissa and the owner and the owner's attorney.' Then Jan started laughing saying, 'The attorney is that Diamond guy who rides a white horse in his TV commercials!' Jan thought that part was hilarious as she described from the script how you and Ken were asked to leave the office without getting an interview."

Norman shakes his head. "I overhear a lot of conversations around this news station, but it's not every day you hear about a heated confrontation getting snagged on tape! I thought as the executive producer Jan would be thrilled to hear you managed to capture that, but instead, she said she couldn't wait to rip the script apart. She even said it was going to be fun! It's almost like she was having a tough time trying to contain her giddiness."

Norman steps down off his ladder before adding, "And then Jan cleared her throat and started speaking in a very matter-of-fact tone, like she was practicing some kind of performance. He begins to mimic her stern tone, 'As the executive producer, I feel it's my duty to review this script thoroughly. Of course, it's not *my fault* that it contains so many errors and legal landmines. It doesn't take a lawyer to see the possible court challenges that we'll face if this story airs *as is*. It'll be impossible to correct all the mistakes in this script in time for it to be edited and aired during today's six o'clock newscast.'"

Norman takes a seat on the edge of her desk, "Marissa, if I hadn't seen you walk out of her office with my own eyes, I would have sworn you were still in there because I heard her say, 'I can't tell you how disappointed I am, Marissa Cavelo, that you failed to live up to the simple task that was assigned to you. It just goes to show—without question—that you are not ready to handle hard news stories.'"

Marissa slams her fist down on her desk. She knows that Ruther was practicing the comments she plans to deliver to the news director or to the general manager to kill her story—a story that the public has a right to see. Ruther knows the bumbling boss won't have a clue about the details of the story. *He's so spineless he'll just agree to kill it,* Marissa thinks. *This is a blatant case of premeditated murder of a great news story. My story!*

Norman says, "Marissa, I'm not telling you this to hurt you. I'm sharing with you what I heard so you can be prepared for what's about to happen. The same explanation I overheard Jan reciting over the phone is the same one she'll present to the general manager before she tells him that you're being pulled from the anchor desk and from future hard news assignments. He's not going to be happy to hear that because he knows and Jan knows and *you* should know that you're very popular among viewers. Maybe you're too popular for your own good."

"What do you mean, I'm too popular for my own good?" Marissa asks. "That doesn't make any sense. The goal for any anchor is to be as popular among viewers as possible, isn't it?"

"Let me fill you in on a little protection policy around here," Norman says with a little laugh. "Ruther and the GM are ecstatic to exert some control over you. Their goal is to keep you in your place at least for the near future. The last thing the station wants is a smart, attractive Latina news anchor who understands just how popular she is with the public. That would give you the upper hand when it comes to salary and contract negotiations. Keeping you in the dark is always the best policy as far as the station is concerned."

Norman slowly starts packing up his tool kit. "And to the mystery person on the phone, I heard Ruther say, 'Now that I've come up with a plan of action, all I have to do is sit here and wait for the clock to keep ticking. Every minute that passes is another minute Cavelo's story won't make deadline. It's already approaching three o'clock. Less than an hour to go. We'll have reason to celebrate. So, let's plan something special tonight, okay?' And that's when I finished my painting. I figured it was as good a time as any to replace a light fixture by your desk. So here I am. While you and I are waiting for paint to dry, Jan has nothing better to do than watch the clock tick away behind that locked office door of hers." Norman takes another sip from his coffee cup and discreetly walks away in search of something else to fix around the station.

Marissa is fuming. She can't believe what Norman has just told her, but she has no reason *not* to believe him. *How is it that arrogant people are in a position of power and are allowed to get away with treating coworkers with obvious disrespect and contempt?* Marissa has learned not to take such treatment personally—until now. A few years ago, the head of corporate Human Resources launched an investigation into complaints that Ruther was discriminating against male members of the newsroom staff. A few people, including Marissa, were interviewed behind closed doors. The Human Resources Director asked if she'd ever overheard Jan speak condescendingly to male coworkers. He asked her if Ruther had ever made lewd comments to male colleagues. Her answer was simple: "Yes, I've overheard her speak rudely to male coworkers, but I've also heard her make rude comments to other subordinates—males, females, Blacks, Hispanics, young, old. It doesn't matter to Jan Ruther. She's an equal opportunity offender." Not surprisingly, the HR's case against Jan was dropped with no action taken.

Marissa checks the clock again—fifteen minutes after three. Only forty-five minutes until deadline. Every minute that passes seems to prove Norm Baker was right. Waiting around for script approval is all a ploy by Jan Ruther. She decides to go back to Jan's office and demand script approval. She knocks but there's no answer. She opens the door and finds an empty office. She goes to the newsroom and asks others, but no one's seen her or knows where she is. Marissa takes a deep breath and goes to find Ken to tell him what Norman overheard about the script and that she cannot find Jan.

Ken's not inside the photographers' lounge waiting for her to deliver a script as she suspected he'd be. She walks down the hall and peeks inside the glass window of a soundproof editing room. There he is. She looks at the monitor on the workstation in front of him and to her surprise, he's already working on their story. She opens the door, slips into the room and asks, "Is that what I think it is?" She points to the images on the screen, but he barely breaks his concentration from what he's doing to answer her.

"I hope you don't mind," he says. "I helped myself to a copy of the script so I could get started since it's getting late. I'm prepared to change whatever Ruther dictates when she hands over final approval." Then he adds, "Do me a favor and record the audio track so I can add your voice to this story."

"That's a brilliant and a somewhat daring move to start working on this package without securing approval, don't you think?"

"I've done it before a few times when there's reason to think getting script approval will be slow or delayed. So far, it's saved my ass every time."

"Okay, that's reassuring to know. But before I go knock out the audio, I have to tell you that approval might not be coming."

"What do you mean this story might not get approved?"

"I have good reason to believe Jan is intentionally withholding the script. And now she's nowhere to be found."

"Listen to me, Marissa, this story it too important to give up without a fight. And we have no time to waste waiting for Jan to do the right thing. So, do me a favor...." He stops and shakes his head and says, "No. Do yourself and the viewers a big favor and go cut the audio track and leave Jan's bullshit delays to me."

Ken kisses her and then puts both hands on her shoulders and turns her around before gently pushing her out the door. "Now, go cut the audio!"

Marissa knows she has nothing to lose and everything to gain, so she heads to the soundproof booth where audio tracks are recorded. She rereads the script and thinks about the power of words combined with video and how this story has the potential for impacting so many lives. It only takes her about ten minutes to record the script. She pushes *send* to electronically deliver it to Ken in the editing room. Then she heads back down the hall to check with him to be sure he received it.

He smiles when she opens the door. "Good news!" Ken says. "While you were cutting the audio track, Jan came here looking for you. She was smiling and upbeat. She definitely didn't look like somebody about to kill a story. And she didn't say anything about not approving the script. In fact, I asked her if our story was in jeopardy and she said, 'No. What makes you say that?' Then she started laughing and left the editing room."

"Oh my gosh, Ken! That's great news. What a relief!"

Ken turns back to the monitor before saying, "Now go on and get out of here. I know you have plans to go to the AAN Convention to meet with the talent recruiter."

She gives him a quick hug and says, "You're right! If I leave now, I can still make my scheduled interview with Marcus Feldman."

"Sure. Run off to find your fame and fortune in a large market and leave me here to get this story on the air. I'm starting to feel a little taken for granted."

Marissa steps closer to the back of the chair where he's sitting and put her arms around him, which causes him to abruptly stop editing. He looks over his shoulder at her as she tells him, "I'll never be able to thank you for all that you've done for me, starting with the pet store fiasco and listening to my woes about my sister. You've been so supportive of my career dreams, and you didn't even flinch during or after our meeting with my uncle. Now this investigative piece....I have a feeling this is going to be a game-changing story. And I have you to thank for being my partner in all this."

She starts to kiss him on the cheek, but he's faster. He uses his strong hands to pull her around and down, closer to him for a long, passionate kiss. Fortunately, editing rooms are small and dark and offer a little privacy within the always busy news department. It doesn't take much for his amazing physical appeal to draw her in. She has no intention of fighting the gravitational pull. She finally pulls away from his lips and tells him, "Don't let me keep you from your work. I'll check back with you in just a little bit."

He laughs as she leaves the editing suite while she can still control herself. She's flushed from the rush of emotions and body heat. She heads to the restroom to splash some cool water on her neck and face and touch up her hair and makeup. She wants to be calm and collected when she makes her way to the AAN convention site.

She's feeling confident about her work that will air at six. *I guess what Norman overheard was not true at all!* She concludes. *Or if it was true, something caused Jan to change her mind. Maybe the general manager vetoed her decision.* She doesn't know and doesn't care. For her, if just one family or one perspective dancer sees the news story and decides *not* to believe the bullshit of Gloria Linden and her team, then it'll be worth it. She makes sure she looks okay and heads down the hallway.

Just as she's headed to the parking lot to leave, she looks at the official newsroom clock and sees it's already four p.m. She has just enough time to get to the convention center. More importantly, Ken has just enough time to finish editing the package. She grabs her purse and sunglasses. As she's heading out the door, a colleague calls out from down the hallway, "Marissa, Jan Ruther was just looking for you. She says it's important."

"Thanks!" She hopes that Jan wants to tell her that the script's been approved. As she's about to knock on Ruther's door, Jan pulls it open with such force it startles Marissa.

"Cavelo. I was looking for you. Follow me. We're headed to the GM's office."

She doesn't even stop to see if Marissa is keeping pace behind her. It's a quick walk to the general manager's office. When they step inside, it's obvious he's expecting them. Ruther walks in first and Marissa is right behind her.

Patrick Stone presses a button that automatically closes the door behind her. "Sit down," Stone instructs. He pauses until he's sure he has her undivided attention before saying, "Do you know why you've been called to my office?"

Oh hell! I must be in trouble, she thinks because that's the only reason anyone is ever called into this office.

The person who sits calmly behind the desk is staring at her with steel gray eyes. He is legendary for making grown men and women cry or storm out of the room, cussing in response to some disciplinary action handed out.

"No, I don't know, but I assume it might be to answer questions about the special assignment that's getting ready to air. We're on a tight deadline to get it edited for the six o'clock news, but Ken's already working on it. I'm happy to answer any questions about it," she says, although questions are rarely asked *after* a script's been approved.

That's when Jan Ruther butts in and says with delight, "Marissa, as the executive producer, it's my duty to review this script thoroughly. In doing so, I detected numerous errors that would leave us vulnerable to serious legal challenges. There's no way the mistakes can be corrected in time for the editing to be completed for the story to air during today's six o'clock newscast. I can't tell you how disappointed I am that you failed to live up to the simple task that was assigned to you. I gave you a deadline and you missed it." She pauses before adding, "It just goes to show what I've been saying for a while now—without question—Marissa, you are not ready to handle hard news stories."

Marissa's stunned. It's exactly what Norman said he overheard Jan saying to someone over the phone! Jan's words cut like a knife and they leave Marissa shaking in anger. She starts to stand, ignores Ruther, and turns to plead her case to the general manager. She looks him straight in the eyes before saying, "This is a solid example of investigative journalism that was completed in a minimum amount of time with great attention to detail. This story blows the lid off a scam that the Regency Dance Studio owner has been pulling on innocent students and their families for years. I'm proud of the work and I stand by the details. The allegations have been proven. Just as importantly, a good faith effort has been made to provide Linden an opportunity to respond to the accusations against her." Marissa takes a deep breath before turning to Jan to make one more important point. "And Jan, you knew exactly what elements this story involved and how challenging it would be for even the most experienced reporter to conduct all of the interviews, select the sound bites, verify the complaints and get it written, voiced and edited by the four p.m. deadline. Just moments ago, you stopped by the editing room and you didn't say a word to Ken that this story was in jeopardy. In fact, you led him to believe we had the green light on this one. If I didn't know better, I would say you intentionally set me up to fail!"

"What? *I* set you up to fail? That's absurd! I'm the one who assigned you the story so you could cover hard news like you've been begging to do." Indignantly she asks, "Is this what I get for trying to give you a chance to prove yourself? As for Ken, the news director is letting him know, as we speak, that your story has been shelved. I say you owe the general manager and me an apology for your behavior and your unsubstantiated accusations. And, if I were you, I'd take this script with some suggested changes to see if any of it can be salvaged because, in its current version, it'll never make air! Now get to it. As for your future assignments, we'll discuss those first thing in the morning." Her tone is filled with rage.

Marissa grabs the script from her hand and says, "I'll consider your suggestions, but only because I truly believe this story needs to air. The actions by the owners and instructors of the Regency Dance Studio need to be disclosed to the public!" And with that, she turns around and walks out of the office before she says something else she'll regret. Fueled by anger, she decides this is as good a time as any to head to the Austin Convention Center so that she can keep pushing forward with her career goals.

She focuses on that task. *If I leave now, I can be downtown in fifteen minutes.* It's just enough time to corner the recruiter and hand him her tape and updated resume. Just the thought of making the leap to another TV station in a bigger market gets her excited. She is determined to prove KATX management wrong about the dance school story. She walks out of the building and jumps into her car, eager to look the AAN talent recruiter in the eye and convince him she's the best person for the next open anchor position.

166

Eighteen

There's a buzz of excitement moving through the hallways and meeting rooms of the Austin Convention Center, which is located in the heart of the city's entertainment district. Television sets are on every wall. Huge, flat screens broadcast newscasts on a continuous loop. Of course, AAN national newscasts are always on, but at five and six p.m. the local news takes priority. It's a great way for TV stations in the host city to be seen by thousands of visitors in town for the convention.

Day three of the AAN gathering includes workshops focusing on topics that range from political coverage to how to combine old-fashioned reporter street smarts with new age digital technology. The convention center's main exhibit hall is filled with vendors. Marissa's head spins as she walks past displays of studio cameras, wind-resistant microphones for news crews out in the field and weather radar systems. She walks past vendors hawking super-deluxe satellite trucks and high-definition cameras. Some are offering the latest in "on air" makeup and wardrobe "must haves" for anchors.

In another area, talent agents have reserved conference space and are happy to review the resume tapes of reporters and aspiring anchors. The annual AAN conference is *the* place for up-and-coming broadcast journalists who want to be noticed by network executives and station managers who run AAN-affiliated stations. Attractive, intelligent and enthusiastic journalists are all trying to claw their way up the network ladder. This is where station general managers and news directors who can help make or break the careers of journalists come to scout new talent. It's like a huge mating game between the would-be hires and those in charge of the hiring—dangling the promise of a promotion or a job. Often, these promises are made after too many drinks and after eager applicants are willing to flash some skin or something even *more* revealing if it means getting their foot—or another part of their anatomy—in the door.

There are also many hard-working journalists who are counting on their accomplishments to pave their way to success. It's what Marissa is hoping for as she makes her way through the exhibition hall. She thinks about everything she's read about Marcus Feldman. He's known as one of the top talent recruiters in the nation. In a business filled with giant egos, Feldman is described as a modest man who's earned a reputation for picking winning anchors and reporters from thousands of tapes and video e-clips he receives. He's said he enjoys the face-to-face meetings that take place at gatherings like this and has compared his knack for picking true talent from the masses of applicants to that of *American Idol* judges, except he has a better success rate for selecting winners. Feldman wrote an article describing what he called "disturbing trends" among female anchor candidates. He wrote:

Most are young, attractive females who are poised and polished. However, I question the common sense of those who wear short skirts and high stiletto heels while trying to chase after the day's big news story. Equally disturbing is the growing number of female applicants who've competed in beauty contests. Contestants always want the same two things: world peace and to become news anchors. There have been a few outstanding applicants with strong reporting skills and great on-air presence. The women and men who make the cut are attractive but not necessarily stunning. However, those applicants are rare, so it's my job to keep searching for undiscovered talent.

Marissa now wonders if good looks will count against her or if her talents will shine through? She takes a deep breath and hopes for the latter.

Marcus Feldman is wrapping up a conversation with a nice, but geeky-looking guy who's sporting a bow tie. She keeps a polite distance as they talk. Mr. Bow Tie is nodding his head eagerly while vigorously shaking Feldman's hand. Her bet is that Mr. Bow Tie is a meteorologist who's also a classical musician, but whose parents are disappointed that he's not a molecular scientist. When the handshaking finally comes to a stop, Mr. Bow Tie says goodbye and bows formally before walking away. Marissa approaches Feldman before another aspiring journalist has a chance to jump in front of her. "Mr. Feldman. Hi, there. I'm Marissa Cavelo." She extends her hand in greeting.

"Yes, Marissa. Nice to meet you. I'm glad you could stop by for a brief chat," he says. "I've reviewed your resume and would like to ask you a few questions." He then politely offers her a chair tucked into the wooden table in the booth where he's been holding court. "Please sit down and let's talk." She takes the seat on the opposite side of the table from him. Once settled he asks, "First of all, where do you see yourself in five years? What are your professional and personal career goals?"

But before she can answer, she notices that an eerily familiar image is on the giant screens now broadcasting the KATX five p.m. newscast.

WTF? That wasn't supposed to air at all and here it is rolling on the five o'clock news, she thinks as she watches the start of the dance studio story. It's on multiple HD flat screens throughout the convention center. Someone nearby points to her and says, "Hey, that's the reporter who's up on the big screen." In that instant, the immediate area becomes quiet and she sees her larger-than-life image, looming like a distorted giant in every direction. She's also on the TV set that's at the end of the table where she and Feldman are seated. He quickly turns up the volume with the remote control and for a moment she feels like she's having an out-of-body experience because her voice is the only sound echoing through the cavernous exhibit hall.

There's the interview with Julia Lopez and her mom talking about her dreams to become a dancer and their efforts to raise money to attend the audition. The story cuts to photos of Julia in different dance costumes and then to Hanz Moore admitting he was following orders to sell expensive photo packages regardless of the students' ability to dance—or to pay. Hanz's admission is followed by the remorse-filled words of Alice who describes how she felt she had no choice but to quit rather than continue to browbeat families into paying hefty audition fees and class tuitions. She comes across as being full of regret and sincere in her confession of preying on people's career aspirations.

And then come the fireworks like only local news can deliver. It's Ms. Linden and her attorney refusing to respond to allegations from Hanz, Alice and the Lopez Family; refusing to respond to complaints filed with the State Consumer Affairs Department and ordering Marissa and Ken off the property. Viewers have no choice but to see them as being guilty of unethical business operations and shady sales practices. The opulence of the school, the unrealistic demands of the attorney and the use of their two-way mirrors to monitor the sales pitches all paint a portrait of Linden and Diamond as being nothing more than money-grubbing bullies who victimize students. Students who only want to dance!

Then comes Marissa's stand-up that was shot in front of the Regency Dance Studio, "Several complaints of false advertising have been filed with the State's Consumer Affairs Division. A few students have demanded a refund, but to date, no complaints have been resolved. While there's been no denial of wrongdoing, there's likewise been no criminal or civil charges filed and no admission of guilt. In fact, there are hundreds of students—boys and girls of all ages who love to dance and who possess all levels of talent. For those students, this school...." Marissa gestures behind her, "...might be a good environment for learning dance moves and techniques. But at least one experienced talent agent advises future dancers to be wary of auditions that require any kind of payment in advance."

The striking image of Sherry West fills the screen as she describes her success placing dancers, actors, singers and other individuals in films and commercials. West speaks with authority and sincerity. "I have helped arrange hundreds of auditions and I've directed clients to attend auditions. Not a single time was there a charge for attending an audition. Fees are paid only *after* a talent is signed." The videotape concludes with Marissa saying, "Whether it be art, dance or modeling, paid lessons for a child are just like any other major purchase. Consumers are encouraged to research the school and instructors before making a financial commitment. For KATX News, I'm Marissa Cavelo."

As the story ends, the studio camera cuts back to the anchor team on the set who both look surprised, like deer caught in headlights, which is a sure sign a producer is yelling in their ear via their earpieces. The co-anchors look at each other in confusion and then back to the camera to tell viewers, "Stay with us; we'll be right back after this break." TV insiders know this is code for, *Oh shit! What just happened?* It's an old standby trick for anchors to toss to a commercial break when they have no clue what the hell to do.

As she watches, Marissa knows the studio crew members and the news managers must be pulling their hair out asking, "How did that piece get on the air?" She imagines Jan Ruther is yelling her head off. "WHAT THE HELL HAPPENED? THAT WAS NOT SUPPOSED TO RUN!"

Just as the news story finishes, the volume in the convention hall resumes. Marissa sits there—speechless. She's pulled back to reality when Feldman says, "Wow! Ms. Cavelo that was a pretty solid story. It took a lot of guts for you to run the segment after being ordered to leave the property. And who the heck brings their attorney to an interview?" He chuckles and then says, "You definitely have the kind of spunk we're looking for in a general assignment reporter. I can tell you're someone who can dig for a story and who isn't afraid to challenge someone accused of possible wrongdoing. Your conclusion makes it clear no laws have been broken, but that the viewers—the moms and dads of aspiring dancers—should check out schools and instructors before handing over money."

Marissa thanks him without saying anything about what she had to go through while working on the story. She's sure as hell not going to admit that the story was not supposed to air. She'll find out from Ken what happened as soon as she gets back to the station.

Her cell phone vibrates with a text: CALL THE STATION... NOW.

She says to Feldman, "I have more samples of my work I'd like to share with you, but unfortunately I'm being called back to the station. Is there another time we can meet before you leave Austin?"

"Sorry, but this is my last appointment for the day. I've got a flight out in a couple of hours." Then he writes something on a business card before handing it to her. "Here's my contact info so we can continue this conversation at another time. Please give me a call. If I don't answer, leave a message and I'll call you back."

She takes the card as Feldman offers a handshake. "Thank you, Mr. Feldman, for making time to meet with me. I have been looking forward to this, and I'm sorry to have to cut our time short."

"Well, I'm not surprised there's follow-up work to do. That was a dynamite story."

"Oh, you have no idea," she says, thinking about the explosion she is about to face. "I'll be in touch, and thank you, again."

As soon as Marissa is far enough away not to be overheard, she checks her phone that's been vibrating ever since the story finished. There are four missed calls from Jan Ruther and two from Ken. She calls Ken first.

He picks up immediately. Without waiting for her to say hello he says, "It's now five-twenty p.m. and I'm drinking! Where are you?"

She wishes she were sitting beside him, slamming drinks. "I'm leaving the AAN Convention. I was meeting with the talent recruiter, but I cut the meeting short so I could call you to find out what the hell happened. How did that story make it on the air?" she asks. "When I left the station I was told our story wouldn't air."

"You know that old joke about news people being in the communication business but not knowing how to communicate? Well, that's exactly what happened. The general manager and Jan Ruther *may* have told you that the story wouldn't air at six, but they didn't bother to tell anybody else, including the five o'clock producer or the anchors. So, it was easy to slip the story in the rundown and as they say, the rest is history."

"*You* put the story on the air? Are you insane?" she screams. And then she realizes people around her are stopping in their tracks to stare at her, and a few are pointing with raised eyebrows as they try to figure out if they recognize her.

"Yes, I am insane. I'm crazy…about you." His words are slightly slurred, which makes her wonder how long he's been drinking.

She tries to ignore what he's saying about his feelings for her since it's probably the booze that's affecting his speech and his thinking. She keeps walking at a brisk pace, but the distance through the exhibit hall to her car seems endless. She thinks about taking off her heels and running through the convention center. "Shut up," she says, playfully. "You don't know what you're saying. You're drunk."

He laughs but doesn't argue with her, so she keeps talking. "This is incredible! Here I am meeting with the talent recruiter at the convention center when the newscast starts and all of a sudden, my story is on every single giant flat screen as far as the eye can see! Imagine my surprise. The story received rave reviews from the recruiter, which, of course, is great…but… what was Jan's reaction when she realized what you'd done?"

"I left as soon as I made sure the tape was inserted and ready to air at five. I wasn't there to see her reaction, but I heard she was madder than a rooting javelina in a china shop. I've seen her get angry and lose her temper before, but I have never seen her scream and throw things. And that's what one photographer said she did. He sent me a video clip. You gotta see it."

"Are you okay?" Marissa has finally made it to her car and switches to her Bluetooth.

Ken says, "I can say without a doubt that I'm feeling pretty damn good right now because I quit!"

"*YOU* QUIT? I don't believe you. What were you thinking?"

"I decided I don't want to work at a place that stifles investigations. I don't want to be part of an organization that doesn't support journalists who are working their asses off. Journalists like you deserve better than that. You and other reporters should be praised for trying to inform the public and for attempting to uncover corrupt, unethical people and business operations. The hell with TV news. I'm done, and I don't regret a damn thing about what I had to do to get your story on the air."

"It's not my story. It's our story…" Another call is coming in. It's the station. "I have another call. It's probably Jan, which means it's the fifth time she's called in twenty minutes. I gotta let you go. I'll call you back. Oh, and get ready to mix a drink for me, okay?"

She disconnects Ken's call and answers the call from the station. "Hello. This is Marissa."

The voice on the other line is direct and calm. Surprisingly, there's no trace of anger or hysteria as Jan Ruther says, "Marissa, this is Jan calling. In case you haven't heard, your story on the Regency Dance Studio just aired during the five p.m. newscast, despite the instructions you received *not* *to* air that story until some legal issues were resolved. Whether you had anything to do with the story airing is irrelevant. The fact is, it aired and the damage is done. As a result, you're being called into a meeting with the general manager tomorrow morning at eight o'clock sharp. I strongly suggest you do *not* discuss this situation with any outside parties since this is a personnel matter that will likely result in disciplinary action." Then without saying another word, Jan hangs up.

All Marissa can think about is Ken. She wants to call him and invite him out for a drink, but since he's been drinking she doesn't want him to drive. She thinks about bringing him a bottle but realizes that she doesn't know where he lives. She sends a text and gets a thumbs-up reply.

Nineteen

Marissa isn't sure if Ken really wants her to come over or if it's just the booze talking. Once he sobers up, she's pretty sure he won't ever want to see her again, and she won't hold it against him for any resentment he might feel. She reviews the text exchange:

Are you ok? U want some company?
I'm fine. Why? U bringing friends from AAN over?
No. Just me. Where do u live?
Close to the station, but I'll be moving soon. Haha.
Very funny
Sure, come on over, but don't come empty-handed.
Beer? Wine? Tequila? Whaddaya want?
You & whatever you're drinking.

The last text is so flirty, it leaves her feeling a little anxious. Thoughts race through her mind. *Is he ready to take this thing that's been brewing between us to the next level? Are we about to get serious? Or, is he so drunk I'll find him passed out when I get there?* She knows that anytime there's a text exchange that carries even the slightest hint of sexual innuendo it's easy for both parties to misinterpret the meaning. She decides to go with her favorite liquid courage— tequila.

After her liquor store run, she gets back into her car and realizes that she's more than ready for a sexual adventure. She's been so busy with her career that she hasn't dated anyone since she started working at KATX nearly three years ago. A couple of guys have asked her out to dinner or invited her to parties and concerts, but once they see how other people react to her in public, they get cold feet. Complete strangers who recognize her from the news aren't shy about approaching her. Some even ask for autographs or want to engage in long, involved conversations. Some guys can't handle being with a girl who is well known. They're often nervous and lack the self-confidence to be with a public figure. Or worse, they're egomaniacs who are jealous of someone who steals their spotlight.

She thinks, *Ken just might be that special guy who can hold his own.*

Instead of directions, Ken starts texting clues for her to follow to get to his place. It's like playing some wild scavenger hunt and locating his apartment is the prize. He provides a couple of key landmarks as clues: the original Taco Shack restaurant, the giant neon Armadillo Beer sign and a funky mural that some consider art, while others call an eyesore. He adds a few navigational directions, which eventually lead her to his apartment unit.

It isn't easy, but after driving around for half an hour she finally finds herself standing in her "knock 'em dead" interview outfit outside Ken's apartment. She pounds on the door as hard as she can, but she doubts he can hear her over the loud music that's blaring away inside. She knocks again until finally the door swings open and Ken pulls her inside with one forceful, yet very tender embrace. Instantly, her worries about whether or not he's angry or resentful melt away. She also has no doubt there is a strong sexual connection between them.

His lips are inviting and his kiss is luscious and deep. For the first time in a long time, she allows herself to be enveloped in the arms of someone who she trusts completely. What she feels is pure animal magnetism that's instantly unleashed from its restrictive cage.

She wonders if Ken's passion is being fueled by too much alcohol. Or maybe he's no longer hesitant about coming on to her now that they're no longer coworkers. Not getting involved with a coworker has always been one of Marissa's rules. But that status officially changed a few hours ago.

They slowly make their way to the couch—step-by-cautious step—without unlocking their lips and while their hands carefully roam over each other's bodies as they slowly attempt to undress. Their romantic embrace quickly becomes comical. She drops her purse to the ground but holds onto the bottle of tequila, which makes it awkward as her arm gets tangled in her blouse that Ken's trying to remove. As he leads her to the couch, he backs right into the coffee table, knocking over a bottle and a lit candle. Fortunately, the bottle's almost empty, but the tipped candle splatters hot wax all over the table. And instantly, the magic moment is replaced with laughter from the two as they flop down on the couch.

"So much for impressing you with my suave moves," he says as his laughter rattles the apartment.

She's laughing, too, and sighing with relief that this kiss and all the nervousness that comes with it is over. "You really know how to kill a magic moment, don't ya?" She asks, still giggling and trying to catch her breath, as she straightens her half-unbuttoned blouse. "I would ask for a do-over, but I think I'd like a drink first."

Ken jumps. "I'm happy to oblige by making you one of my special margaritas since I see you came prepared with a premium brand of tequila."

"I could use a good margarita. I don't want to pressure you, but your skills as a bartender are about to be put to the test since I have yet to meet anyone who can match my margarita-making ability."

"That sounds like a challenge, Ms. Cavelo," he says in a mockingly serious tone.

"Please, sir, just give it your best effort. That's all I ask."

The familiar sound of a martini shaker actually has a calming effect on her. If her father were still alive, he'd be sharing a sip of tequila and telling them in great detail how tequila is distilled and about its history. He loved sharing with his daughters any and everything related to Mexico—people, food, religion, soccer, music, all of it. And with great pride, he'd talk about traditions their family followed for generations. Marissa is surprised that it is her father who comes to mind. She misses him terribly. She wishes he were there to help guide her through the challenges now facing her at work and to boost her confidence before she sets foot in the general manager's office tomorrow morning. He'd tell her to put her shoulders back, hold her head high and believe in the person she's become. *Mija, tu eres la mejor y no se olvide nunca.* You are the best, my dear, and don't ever forget that.

Imagining what her father would say puts a smile on her face just as Ken walks in with what looks like a perfectly salted rim and her favorite beverage. The cool light green color swirling in the glass is like liquid magic. Then something floating in the drink suddenly catches her eye. "What's that in there? A piece of an olive?"

"No," he answers with a smile. "It's my secret ingredient that I want you to try before it's revealed to you."

She takes a slow and delicious sip and closes her eyes to savor this new taste. "Wow! Now that's a margarita with a little kick," She takes another sip.

"If you promise not to tell anyone else, I'll let you in on my secret ingredient," Ken says as he sits down next to her on the couch.

"You and your games. First, you run me through a scavenger hunt just to get here. And now you swear me to secrecy? This is crazy, but okay. I promise not to tell anyone what's in this drink." She laughs as she enjoys the margarita.

179

"It's a slice of Serrano pepper that gives it that spicy kick. But it took many drinks to get the amount just right. And, no, that's not an excuse to drink more margaritas. So, cheers! Here's to the perfect margarita!" he says triumphantly.

"*Salud!*" she responds in a mutual toast. "Ummm…You definitely know how to mix a good drink with just the right spice. Were you ever a bartender?"

Ken chuckles as he sips his drink. "I worked as a mixologist part-time while I was in college. It's a good thing I picked up some basic bartender skills since those might come in handy now that I'm unemployed." He's laughing, but he is not joking.

The light-hearted mood of the past few moments takes on a serious tone. "Oh my gosh, Ken. I haven't even told you how bad I feel that you got fired. Please tell me, what hap…."

"…Whoa, whoa now. Let's get a couple of things straight. I wasn't fired. I quit. I don't regret for one second doing exactly what I needed to do to get our story on the air. And just so you know, walking out of that news hellhole felt pretty damn good." He triumphantly raises his glass. "Here's to the best investigative story that viewers almost didn't see!"

"Cheers!"

"I can't believe Jan Ruther was so determined *not* to let that story air," he says.

Marissa tells him everything that transpired in the GM's office. Then she describes the eerie feeling of disbelief when she saw herself on the monitors at the convention center. "I've been ordered to appear before the great and powerful Oz at eight a.m. tomorrow morning."

"It's almost eight o'clock now, which means you have about twelve hours before you'll officially join me in the ranks of former KATX staff members. That's plenty of time for me to teach you how to mix the perfect margarita. Or at least let me numb the pain you must be feeling through this agonizing wait to learn your fate." And with that, they laugh as they down the last of their first drink together before mixing drink number two.

Ken leads Marissa to the second bedroom in his sparsely furnished bachelor pad—not as a move to get her into bed. He wants to show her his pride and joy. The bedroom has been converted into a professional editing suite only cleaner, neater and more organized than any suite at KATX. Over the years working as a top-notch photojournalist, Ken, has acquired professional equipment, which allows him to work at home. "Come have a seat. I have a video clip I want you to see."

It takes a few minutes for Ken to get the equipment fired up. Marissa makes herself comfortable in the chair he's pulled out for her. She looks at the monitor and can't believe what she sees. It's the video of stand-ups and extra footage Ken shot for her right after the exotic bird bust. It was just two days ago, but in her current confused and slightly-infused-with-tequila state, her memory is a little fuzzy. It seems like ages ago since they recorded this story. She recalls they were gathering extra b-roll of the crime scene—the loading dock area behind the pet store. "Pause that," she says. She goes into the living room and returns with the reporter's notebook she always carries in her purse. He hits play and she starts jotting down notes.

This video will come in handy since they will each need an audition tape for job hunting. What Ken has captured enhances the coverage that aired on Monday by providing a behind-the-scenes look at how the crime unfolded. The video shows police detectives gathering evidence into paper bags and placing them into a police van. There are people—perhaps customers—who are milling around trying to see what's going on even as yellow crime scene tape keeps everybody a safe distance away. The camera holds a long, steady shot that includes video of a man in the crowd who's walking away and getting into a Range Rover parked about fifty feet from the loading dock area.

About thirty more seconds into the video Ken and Marissa both notice what appears to be a fight breaking out between three people standing outside of the Range Rover. Just as quickly as the trio gets out of the car, they get back in and it makes a wild U-turn in the parking lot before screeching away.

"Wow! Did you see that?" Ken asks. "It looks like there was some other parking lot drama going on while I was videotaping."

"It's hard to tell since the camera was so far away, but were those men fighting?"

"I don't know for sure, but the driver was pissed judging by the way he took off in such a hurry. Let's take a closer look, shall we? Or would you rather keep screening the video?"

"Oh, I'm curious about what the heck that group was up to. Can we zoom in on the Range Rover gang?" Marissa's curiosity is the same reason why crowds are drawn to crime scenes. People love watching any kind of real life drama that unfolds before their eyes. It's one reason why reality TV shows are such big hits!

With a quick flick of his wrist, Ken turns a knob and the video on the screen magically zooms into images that would've otherwise gone unnoticed in the background of the pet store parking lot. Now the figures are suddenly in focus—front and center. Marissa zeros in on the expensive Range Rover with tinted windows that are so dark everything inside the vehicle is concealed. But in this case, the windows are rolled down as the man who was standing by the crowd, watching detectives at work, returns to the car and gets into the driver's seat. There is another person in the passenger seat but it's hard to tell if it's another man or a woman.

Then suddenly, the person in the passenger seat flings the car door open and jumps out. In the magnified video, you can tell from the profile that it's a woman dressed in yoga pants and a sports bra. Although they can't make out what she's saying, it's obvious she's yelling at the driver. Then she turns away from the car and is leaning against it, crying. *It must have been a helluva fight if it left the woman in tears,* Marissa thinks.

While the woman in the video stands by the car, sobbing, the male driver gets out and comes around to confront her. She stops crying long enough to yell and stomp her foot. At a slightly slower pace, another man gets out of the backseat of the car and with one quick movement, he slaps the woman hard across the face. Her hair, which is stuffed inside a baseball cap, comes loose and her sunglasses are knocked off her face. It's then that Marissa realizes the horrible truth: *CARISSA!*

She gasps and puts her hand over her mouth at the sudden rush of emotions—fear mixed with anger. Her mind races: *How dare anyone hurt CC? Who the hell are these men? What is she doing with them? And what are they doing parked outside the loading dock of the pet store?*

Ken pauses the video. "Oh my God. Marissa, is that your sister?" He looks like he's seen a ghost. "If I didn't know better, I'd think it was you in the video. Let me roll it again."

He hits rewind and plays the magnified video in slow motion. They both stare at the screen in disbelief.

"Did you know she was there that day?" he asks. "Who are those guys with her?"

"No, I didn't know she was there, and I sure as hell don't know who those two guys are!" Marissa is practically shrieking.

"Okay…. Calm down…. Let's think about this before we jump to the wrong conclusions…. You don't want to do that, do you?" Ken asks.

"You're right. We don't know anything about what was going on…but that…that is definitely my sister with two sinister-looking guys. One of them was angry enough to slap her." He tries to slow her breathing as she pleads with Ken, "We have to figure out what happened to her. Maybe we should report this to the police? ….Or…at least show this video to my Tío Hector?"

She starts to pick up her cell phone to dial her uncle's number when Ken grabs her arm. "Whoa there…there are some key questions you need to answer before you dial that number." He sits next to her and puts his arm around her. "How do you think your sister will feel when she finds out you reported a problem she seems to be having in her personal life before talking to her about it? Have you talked to her recently? Did you notice anything different or unusual about her? Do you have any idea who those two men are?"

Marissa's mind is racing to come up with the answers to his rapid-fire questions. "Let me think about this." She closes her eyes and tries to recall her conversations with CC. "I talked to her when we were driving to the pet store location. I was asking her about the nature of certain animals for the fluff story we were assigned."

"Yeah, I remember you making that call."

"So…that was Monday…around one o'clock, and I just assumed she was at work when I called."

"Did you talk to her after Monday?"

"Yes. The next morning, she sent me a text asking me to meet her at our special place."

"What special place?"

"Oh, it's a park where we used to hang out together and talk or just to reconnect. It was nice to have CC suggest that I meet her there, especially that morning. It was yesterday, the day after our big pet store bust. I couldn't wait to tell her all about it."

"So is that what ya'll talked about?"

"Yes…. But now that I think about it…I remember she was asking me some pretty tough questions."

"Like what?"

"She asked me, 'Who told you about the stolen animals?' 'Did someone tip you off?' Questions that had more to do with the illegal operation itself instead of my coverage of it."

"What about her mood? Did she seem agitated or worried?"

"I guess she sounded kinda worried. I thought she was expressing sisterly concern…but now that you mention it, maybe she was anxious about something else." Marissa puts her face in her hands and lets out an exhausted sigh. She wonders, *What the hell was she doing in the parking lot with two thugs? Or worse…is she dating one of them?*

"Oh my gosh, Ken, that's why her lip was busted! I asked her what happened and she said it was an accident at work…that a dog slammed its head into her lip as she was putting him in his cage. Now I know that's not what happened at all."

Ken gets up and goes over to the monitor. "Let's finish looking at the video just in case there are any more clues," he says.

The magnified video shows CC regaining her balance while the driver picks up her hat and sunglasses and hands them to her. He must have said something to her because she stops crying long enough to grab the items from him before getting into the back seat of the Range Rover. The guy who slapped her jumps into the front passenger seat. The driver gets back behind the wheel and the car makes a quick U-turn before exiting the parking lot.

Marissa can't watch anymore. She slumps in her chair—exhausted. She pulls out her phone and dials CC's number, but it goes straight to voice mail. "Hey, CC, it's me." Marissa tries hard not to sound worried or angry. She knows that if CC thinks Marissa is angry or upset with her she won't call her back. "I wanted to make good on our promise to spend more time together, so call me back, okay? Let's both take a break from work and go do something fun. Please…call me back." And then she says words she hasn't uttered to her sister in a while. *"Te amo mucho."* And with that, she hangs up the phone.

Ken senses her sadness. He goes over and gently pulls her out of her chair to a standing position. He holds her in a warm, comforting embrace. Her heart rate quickens as his strong arms hold her tight. He says reassuringly, "Hey, now. You've seen your sister since this parking lot incident happened, so you know she's okay. If she is anything at all like you—smart and strong—she has probably handled the problem in her own way. And I bet she'll tell you all about it when she calls you back. What do you think? Am I right?" He moves her chin up with his finger so that she has to look up into his eyes.

"Yeah. She's a fighter all right. Knowing Carissa, she probably evened the score with that goon before the car made it out of the parking lot." She laughs, trying to convince herself. "But I just hate the thought of anyone physically hurting her. That's just not right."

"No, it's not right, which may be the reason why she didn't mention the incident to you. Maybe she was afraid you'd judge her. Maybe there's another reason she hasn't told you about him. What if he's married? Or maybe the other guy is his gay lover? There are all kinds of explanations that will drive you crazy, speculating about it. Let's finish scanning the video like we talked about."

She agrees and they sit back down in front of the monitor. After the parking lot fight, there's little else on the tape. There's the final video of undercover officers carrying four birds that didn't survive the heist and then, the final images of the store's exterior and loading area.

Marissa takes a deep breath and says, "You have a point. When it comes to CC, she'll talk to me eventually, but only when she's good and ready. And yes, telling my Tío Hector about what we saw on the video before talking to her would only make her explode, which would probably drive her further away from me. I don't want to risk that happening, so I'll just have to wait for her to call me back. Hey, dub me a copy of the tape that shows CC fighting with the two men."

He hands her the copy and she slips it into her purse for safe keeping.

"Now why don't you relax, have another drink and allow me to take your mind off all the unbelievable incidents of the past twenty-four hours," Ken asks convincingly. He kisses her gently at first, then more passionately. His sensuous lips and his exploring tongue make all her worries melt away. He stops and says with a sly smile, "I have a great idea for turning your mood around. Let's play a little game."

"A game?"

He takes her hand and leads her back into the living room.

"I'm only willing to play a game if I am guaranteed to win and if it involves drinking," she says.

Marissa and Ken sit close together on his sofa as he explains the rules of this game. "It's my version of 'Truth or Dare' for consenting grownups. We start by asking each other silly questions like, 'What was your favorite band in high school?' If you believe the answer and it turns out to be true, the other person has to do a shot. If you suspect the answer is false and you're correct, then they have to do a shot and kiss you. The goal of the game is to get away with more false answers, forcing your opponent to do more shots. The kisses are just thrown in for fun."

"So whatever the question and whatever the answer somebody has to do a shot and either way a kiss is involved. Is that right?"

"That's right. Since you're new at this, I'll let you go first."

"Okay…." She tries to think of a question she wants to know the answer to but doesn't mind what his response will be. "Where did you lose your virginity?"

"Oh, that's an easy question to answer. Like the average American teenager, I lost my virginity in the backseat of a car. A friend's car. It was anything but romantic or even enjoyable. It was memorable because it was so awkward and so physically uncomfortable. I was way too tall for the cramped space—all legs. Plus, my date hit her head and wanted to go home."

Marissa laughs just imagining this sexy guy sitting next to her as a gangly, nerdy boy making his moves in the backseat of a car. "That's pretty funny, but I believe you. Is it true?"

Ken pours a little tequila into her glass and slides it across the coffee table in her direction. "Drink up 'cause it's not true. I lost my virginity in my college dorm room at a much later age than most teenage boys."

"Wait! I don't get to pour my own shot?"

"You get to pour mine and you get to kiss me."

Marissa downs the shot before Ken pulls her close for a kiss—a nice, warm kiss that lasts just long enough. The kissing-drinking game continues with more questions that provide a wild way for them to learn more about each other. Within minutes she finds out that if he could travel anywhere in the world, Ken would go to Bora Bora. He doesn't believe her when Marissa states that if she could switch careers without risk of failure she'd be a circus clown. That answer has them both laughing and slamming back a shot.

Every kiss fuels their mutual attraction as they slowly savor good tequila and each other. They share a passionate, steamy tongue-exploration when either of them really likes the other's answer and quick pecks on the cheek if one of them is not impressed.

As the night and the drinking progress, the questions start to get a little more personal about each other's past and about their feelings. And another rule is added to the crazy game. The person caught in a lie has to take off an article of clothing. Marissa is winning the game easily because she's an honest person by nature and loves tequila. Also to her advantage, she has on more clothes!

By one a.m., the room and everything in it starts spinning slowly no matter how hard Marissa tries to stay awake. She's sleepy. Their game has turned into strip Truth or Dare and she's down to her lace panties and bra. Sheer exhaustion and more than her share of tequila finally knock her out cold with a big smile on her face and the lingering taste of tequila and salt on her lips, mixed with just a hint of Ken.

Twenty

"**J**ose Cuervo is no longer a friend of mine," she says under her breath and she curses herself for agreeing to play that crazy drinking game with Ken last night. It was fun, but trying to get to the station in less than ten minutes hung over is not the best strategy for the early morning meeting with Stone and Ruther. It's straight up eight a.m. when she steps into the station and the phrase "firing squad" takes on a whole new meaning for her as she waits to learn her fate before them. Her head is so fuzzy she has a hard time comprehending what Stone is saying.

"Marissa, I don't think you're grasping the seriousness of what I'm telling you. Let me spell it out in a simple, direct way. You are suspended indefinitely. This station has an enormous reputation at stake and it is my duty to protect the integrity of the high standards of journalism we strive to achieve every day—at all costs. We will not tolerate efforts to undermine that by allowing unauthorized news stories to air without complete approval and legal review."

Marissa knows it's futile to try and change his mind, but she is determined to have her say. "Mr. Stone, I didn't know that was going to happen. Nor did I have anything to do with the story airing, although I can't say I'm sorry it did."

Stone is unmoved. "We have no proof you were directly involved in this subversive act, which is why you're being suspended and not fired. Your employment status is under review while our legal team advises us on the ramifications of the story airing. We're especially concerned about the projected cost that may be incurred as the station defends itself against a libel lawsuit already filed by the Regency Dance Studio owner."

Marissa can't believe it. "You're kidding me? They have filed a lawsuit already?" she yells.

"Ms. Cavelo, you'll kindly lower your voice and refrain from any further outbursts or other inappropriate behavior," Stone utters sternly. "I shouldn't have to warn you that your actions from this moment on are under close scrutiny," he threatens.

Marissa is furious. She knows that she's done nothing wrong, and more importantly, that it was a damn good story. She takes a deep breath and tells herself to take some time so she can think through the best course of action for herself. What's important at that moment is to get out of the general manager's office before she says something she'll regret or before she vomits.

Stone is talking to her again. "Jan Ruther will accompany you to your desk where you'll be allowed exactly three minutes to gather any personal items you wish to take with you during your suspension period. Then Jan will confiscate your security badge before escorting you out of the building and to your car. We'll notify you if and when a decision is made about your employment status. Since this is a personnel matter, you're strongly advised *not* to talk to anyone about the situation."

Marissa nods, turns around and walks out of the office. *I vow never to drink another drop of tequila again for as long as I live*, she promises. *Scratch that. I could use a Tequila Sunrise right now.*

Jan is following close behind, trying to keep up with her fast pace. She wants to get out of this building as fast as possible and hopes no one will see her at the lowest point of her professional career. What really embarrasses her is that she's wearing the same outfit she had on yesterday afternoon.

They make a quick stop at her desk, but there's only one item she wants to take with her. She quickly grabs the family photo off her desk and stuffs it into her purse. "Okay. I've got everything I need," she says with a forced smile on her face. She is not going to give Ruther the satisfaction of seeing her upset. "I'm ready to head to my car."

"I'll walk you to the parking lot."

The two walk through the newsroom and then past the station's front offices. As they go, Marissa realizes that the place is eerily silent. Everyone they pass along the way stops to watch them. Although personnel matters are supposed to be kept confidential, it's obvious from the stares that everyone knows she's been disciplined. She's walking the infamous "Hall of Shame." It seems to take forever to reach the front of the building where Marissa leaves Jan staring after her as she gets into her car. She turns and waves goodbye as she drives off.

As Marissa pulls into traffic, she realizes she has nowhere to go. She drives about a block away, just far enough to be sure she's out of Jan's sightline or any other inquisitive station employee who might be watching out the window. She pulls into a vacant parking lot to figure out what to do next. *Should I go back to Ken's place? No, I am not ready to face him again so soon after what happened last night. What did happen last night?* She knows she got hammered and woke up this morning with very little clothing on, but the rest is a blur. She's not sure if they fooled around last night but knows she wanted to and is pretty sure he wanted to. *Oh how awful. I can't even remember if I had sex with the sexiest guy ever. What a complete waste of mutual lust and expensive alcohol.*

Then she remembers the videotape they watched at his place and that awful scene of CC being slapped by a mystery man. *I have to find out the truth about what happened to my sister.* She reaches in her purse for her cell phone but the battery is dead. *What if she called and I missed it because my phone was dead?*

With no other options, she starts her car and heads home to recharge her phone. As she drives, unanswered questions about her sister, her night with Ken and her future as a television journalist keep swirling through her mind.

Twenty-One

At ten a.m., nearly two hours since Marissa's exit from the station, the KATX receptionist is so busy answering the phone that she doesn't have time to greet the two men carrying matching briefcases and wearing identical sour looks on their faces as they enter the lobby. She just waves them through, knowing the legal duo is on their way to the general manager's office. Since the switchboard opened an hour earlier at nine, the phones have been ringing nonstop. Actually, the telephone calls started flooding the switchboard right after the dance school story aired on the five o'clock news yesterday. The steady stream of callers leaves the receptionist feeling helpless. Local media critics, bloggers and news junkies are all abuzz about the exposé and the reporter, Marissa Cavelo.

Within minutes after the story aired, people began calling to share how the Regency Dance Studio also duped them. The amounts of money some clients spent on these shattered dreams of success are breathtaking. A few callers offered allegations of new scams that the Regency Dance Studio referred them to makeup artists, hairstylists and costume designers. One caller started crying while describing the hundreds of dollars spent on a hypnotist who specialized in weight loss treatment for a dancer with a few pounds to lose.

After watching Marissa's exclusive story, each person now believes it was all part of the dance studio's organized effort to wring every last dollar available from themselves or from loved ones who could least afford it. Sadly, of all the people who call with complaints, not one single dancer was ever hired to perform in a commercial, film or a professional production of any kind. The only show mentioned was an amateur talent competition held at a local community recreation center and even then, the audience reaction was lukewarm. The receptionist works feverishly to take down all the names and phone numbers of the people calling. In desperation, she calls the news department to see if anyone can help answer calls coming into the front desk. News Director Hank Johnson had no clue that the dance school story was blowing up big time and the switchboard was being bombarded not only with corroborating stories but new angles. Real journalists know that a high-interest story, like this one, has the potential to generate follow-up stories. But at KATX there is no one to pick up the ball and score more journalistic points.

The current front desk chaos goes unnoticed by the two attorneys as they walk through the lobby. There's no mention of it as they converse with GM Patrick Stone. At issue is what to do in response to the lawsuit filed by Gloria Linden and her attorney, Doug Diamond.

"I can't believe a lawsuit was filed so fast. And what the hell is Linden alleging?" Stone asks. His eyes nervously dart back and forth from one attorney to the other.

Almost in unison, they answer, "It's a case of libel."

Then the older attorney with less hair and a bigger belly explains further, "Ms. Linden is alleging her business and personal reputation have been ruined because of the KATX report. Of course, she claims it's false or at the very least, inaccurate. And knowing Diamond's reputation for being greedy for both money and time in the media spotlight, he'll be seeking a huge amount in damages. As for the speed of this legal action, it's a known fact that Diamond is quick on the legal draw. Hell, he has a reputation for carrying around blank legal briefs that only need names and dates filled in just in case he drives up on the scene of a car wreck, a slip-and-fall accident in a grocery store or any other kind of mishap where he can defend a so-called 'victim.'"

The other lawyer chimes in. "In this case, Diamond probably had an assistant down at the courthouse waiting to file the moment the clerk's office opened its doors this morning. He's one sleazy, but effective, attorney."

Stone lets out a huge sigh, jumps up from behind his desk and begins to pace. "So what's the best strategy? Do we offer Marissa Cavelo as a token sacrifice and blame it on her inexperience? Or do we fight the allegations in court?"

The younger attorney speaks up, "We've had the opportunity to carefully review the script and it's our legal conclusion that it's a well-documented news story that will stand up to any legal challenge. Ms. Cavelo did an excellent job of presenting a balanced story based on facts that are supported by strong testimony by credible individuals." He pauses, chuckles and adds, "Of course, it doesn't hurt that huckster Dan Diamond and his client pitched a hissy fit before the interview even began. That said, we strongly advise you call their bluff by not backing down. Stand firm in your support of Cavelo and her work. Describe her reputation as impeccable. Feature her in some slick promos and get her name out in front of the public. The more fans she has, the better it is for the station and its defense strategy. That way, if this libel suit goes to trial, it'll be hard to find one single person to sit on the jury who'd find Marissa Cavelo guilty of any wrongdoing."

Then the older lawyer adds, "While you're putting her up on a pedestal, you might want to assign her another investigative story. This underscores the station's strong support of Cavelo and her ability to uncover scams. You know, make her out to be the 'Defender of the People.'"

Stone plops down in his chair. He looks defeated and somewhat vulnerable. "There's just one problem with that plan," he whispers and sighs again. "Earlier this morning, Marissa was placed on indefinite suspension for violating station policy."

"What?" the two lawyers blurt out in unison.

The older one says with a snarky smile, "You better have a plan for returning her to the anchor desk as soon as possible. If not, you might want to brush up on your dishwashing skills, because that's about the only job you'll be able to get once the word gets out. You'll be put out to pasture for punishing an extremely popular reporter who was uncovering corruption and defending innocent victims from being scammed by a money-hungry monster."

His cohort adds, "Marissa Cavelo is the hero in all this. And you should be doing everything you can to keep her happy, and more importantly, on the air!"

And with that, the lawyers get up and extend their hands, but Stone looks too weak to utter a single word of thanks, let alone return a handshake.

Twenty-Two

Marissa unlocks the door to her apartment and steps inside the cool darkness of the empty living room. Her first order of business is plugging in her cell phone.

She needs to get rid of her hangover so she can think straight. She kicks off her heels, heads straight to the bathroom and swallows a couple of aspirin. Then she pulls on her favorite pair of sweats. Immediately, the feel of the material relaxes her. It makes her smile because it's CC's favorite way to dress.

The reality of her situation hits her again. For the first time in years, she has no deadlines, no stories to research and no one to answer to. It's a surreal feeling that provides an unexpected pause from her usually hectic schedule. It's also her first unscheduled day, other than the rare vacation day. It feels strange to be home on a weekday when normally she'd be getting ready to anchor the noon newscast. She considers turning on her TV to watch the newscast but realizes that would make her stress over what's happening, which is totally out of her control.

Instead, she decides to let everything go. She turns off her phone while it charges and steps away from her computer, the Internet and the world in general. She considers her options. *Maybe I'll go back to bed... or read some of that popular soft-porn book CC gave me for my birthday. Maybe I'll channel surf through mindless daytime TV.* She remembers watching *telenovelas* with Mami when she was home sick from school as a little girl. Without fail, the over-the-top dramas in Español always had her mother crying, then laughing, which had a strange way of comforting her.

Maybe I'll go outside. It's too cold to sit by the pool, but if the sun stays out I can go for a run, which will help clear my head. The hangover still has a tight grip on her brain. She finally decides the first activity of her non-active life is to eat...and drink. After all, everyone knows it takes a little hair of the dog that bit you to feel better. She looks around her pantry and pulls out the ingredients for a kick-ass Mexican *Sangre de Maria*. While sipping on the vodka-infused tomato juice with a slice of jalapeño, she mixes up her Mami's migas—scrambled eggs, onions, tomatoes, tortilla strips, more jalapeños and lots of queso. *Delicioso!* The food melts in her mouth and fills her with contentment and wonderful memories.

She thinks that this is exactly the late night breakfast her mother would make when she and her father and some of their friends would come home late from a family event such as a wedding. Although she and her sister were supposed to be asleep, they'd always sneak a peek at the adults having fun. The house was filled with laughter, music and happiness. The memories bring a smile to her face and tears to her eyes. *What would their lives be like today?* she wonders. *Would they still be living in Houston? Would they be worried about CC and me? Or would they be confident in us and our ability to figure out our career paths on our own?* She has no doubt they'd still be in love and they would still be enjoying late-night *almuerzos* together.

She takes a piece of tortilla to scrape the last bit of queso off of her plate and into her mouth before placing the dishes in the sink. It takes real self-control not to wash them or clean the kitchen. In her new state of non-activity, she leaves the mess for later. Instead, she decides to take on another chore, one she's been putting off for years because she never had free time. *Now, I have nothing but free time!* she thinks.

She pulls out boxes from the hall closet that contain items that belonged to her parents. After their murders, their few personal belongings were placed into storage for safe keeping. Carissa and Marissa were too young to be responsible for the boxes, which were sealed and forgotten by everyone. It wasn't until after college graduation that uncle Hector told them about the boxes. He'd assumed responsibility for them and waited until the twins were adults before handing them over. CC didn't want to have anything to do with the boxes and Marissa wasn't going to let them be destroyed or forgotten, so she gladly accepted them from Tío Hector.

That was almost five years ago, and they've been untouched in her closet ever since. Until now. She understands why Carissa chose not to claim them. It's too sad to imagine how young their parents were when they were killed. What Marissa remembers most about them is that they were modest people who lived a simple life with few personal possessions. *What could possibly be in these boxes that is of any value?* She expects to find some photos, a few souvenirs and trinkets from their wedding or from her childhood but very little else. She sighs sadly as the reality settles in that maybe it's time to get rid of the items and let go of the painful past.

She recognizes the first box as a standard issue evidence box used by police departments. The beige cardboard has yellowed with age, but other than that, it's undisturbed. The sealing tape still holds strong and she reaches for a box cutter to slice it open. The various items inside provide a mini-journey through time. There are envelopes filled with family photographs from birthday parties, holidays and church events including the twins' First Holy Communion. There's a baby book in Spanish that their mother meticulously kept for her *hijas*. It includes the dates of so many "firsts." First smile, first bath, first laugh, first steps and on and on. The binder captures memories of their first year of life. There are even locks of hair from their first haircut. Marissa thinks that CC might want to see the book, so she sets it aside to show her later.

She finds a colorful floral print scarf which she remembers her mother wearing, along with two pairs of earrings—small gold loops and a pair of modest-sized pearls. Her father's watch is in the box wrapped in tissue paper, along with a money clip that he carried all the time although it often held nothing more than a few dollar bills and a religious medallion. Also in the box is her mother's lace *mantilla* veil, which she would place on her head before entering church along with her father's carefully folded *guayabera*, often referred to as a "Mexican wedding shirt." He always wore it on special occasions. Marissa thinks about how handsome he looked in it.

Digging deeper into the storage box, she comes across folders filled with important documents her father kept. He was meticulous about keeping records long before everything was electronically stored on hard drives. The folders are titled in her father's neat handwriting: Rent and Repairs, Car Maintenance, Girls' School Papers, Paycheck Stubs. It stirs a sense of pride to see how her father, with very little formal education, had his own system of preserving important documents. One folder's title is out of place. It's the only one with a typed label which reads: "News Reports." Marissa is puzzled. *News Reports? About what?* A look inside reveals newspaper clippings from the Houston daily newspapers that have yellowed over time. Tears fill her eyes as she scans the headline, "Night Watchman Praised as Hero," which is an article about her father's actions while he was on duty as a security guard in a warehouse area near the Houston Ship Channel. There's a photograph of him in his night watchman's uniform, shaking hands with an older gentleman who's wearing a suit and tie. The article describes how he was on patrol the night some men were caught attempting to steal crates of electronic goods from a warehouse. The thieves might have gotten away with their haul if her father hadn't called the police who stopped the men as they were loading the stolen goods into a pickup truck. The Houston Police Department and officials with the Houston Port Authority praised his actions. He received a proclamation from the city and his photo was taken with a Port of Houston Commissioner, who expressed his gratitude for his help busting a burglary ring.

Marissa's father was a humble man who felt he didn't deserve a reward since he was only doing the job he'd been hired to do. Finally though, he was convinced that the money could help pay for his daughters' future education. His wife and daughters were so proud of him. Any amount of money was simply icing on the cake as far as they were concerned. As a child who loved watching the evening news, the biggest thrill was seeing Papi on TV, being honored for his bravery. She honestly believes after those fifteen minutes of fame her father walked a little straighter with his chest expanded and his head held high. In this country where immigrants are often unwelcome, her father had earned respect among complete strangers. Sadly, there was little mention in the media when her father and mother were murdered a few weeks later. To the twins and their neighbors, it was a senseless crime since there were no items of value in their modest home, although the police concluded it was a home burglary that went bad.

Ironically, every item of value, albeit sentimental, is in these two boxes. They are trinkets of no material worth, but as the sole connection to her parents, the items—no matter how old and tattered—are priceless to her.

There's a second news article in the folder. Marissa recognizes the handwriting on the top of the yellowed paper as Tío Hector's. He must have clipped it and placed it there for safe keeping. It describes a young man who was arrested, charged and later convicted of the double homicide. The article says he was Persian—an immigrant. Back then, the news media didn't provide much coverage of crimes involving minority members and her parents' murder was no exception. Judging from the date of the article, Marissa knows that she and CC were in a foster home at the time. Their foster parents discouraged them from following news headlines and urged them to move on with their lives. The well-meaning couple thought the less the twins knew about the circumstances surrounding the death of their parents the better off they'd be.

Marissa sighs and smiles faintly, remembering the happier moments of her childhood. She puts the file back in the box, closes it and places it back into the closet where it will remain until the next time she has enough courage to revisit her family's past.

Twenty-Three

Looking through the box reminds Marissa that she needs to talk to CC. With her phone fully charged, she turns it on to check for missed calls or texts. There are no messages from Carissa, but four missed calls from Tío Hector and a text from Ken, which reads: Did you survive the firing squad? Or do I need to come claim your bullet-riddled body? Let me know if you wanna drown your sorrows. It's something I'm getting pretty good at.

She texts Ken back: Very funny, but I'm not laughing. I've been suspended. Indefinitely. I'll call you later with details. Don't drink all the tequila without me.

As much as Marissa wants to continue where they left off, she first needs to focus on the more serious situations in her life. She braces herself to return her uncle's call, knowing how tough it is going to be to tell him she's been suspended from work. He'll be pissed, but once she explains Stone's and Ruther's actions, his anger won't be directed at her.

Her cell phone rings. The caller ID says: "Blocked," like the threatening call she got Tuesday at the station. It keeps ringing. Something tells her this is one phone call she needs to pick up. "Hello, this is Marissa," she says, hesitantly.

Instantly, that same deep, hate-filled voice says, "Listen, bitch. I know all about you, including where you are at this very moment. This

is your last warning. Stop your stupid-ass investigation or else you…
and your sister…will be sorry." The line goes dead.

More than frightened, Marissa is pissed. Her heart is racing and
her fingers are shaking so hard she has trouble punching the numbers
on her phone. She tries several times before she manages to correctly
dial her uncle's direct line.

He picks up instantly. She can tell he's anxious and angry.
"Marissa where the hell have you been? I've been calling you since that
damn dance studio story aired. And where the hell is your sister? I
raised you girls better than this. I told you to be careful and to stay in
close contact with me until this police case is closed. You know we're
still trying to nab the ringleaders. There's a strong possibility those men
might come after you, *mija*. I was worried when I couldn't get a hold
of you last night and you didn't return my calls. What the hell were
you thinking?"

"Tío, please. Listen to me. I'm okay, but someone is calling and
threatening me." She swallows and composes herself. "Tío Hector,
I'm worried about CC. I think she's the one who's in real danger," she
pleads.

"Marissa, what are you talking about? What threatening phone
calls? When? What was the caller saying to you?"

"The first call came the other day while I was at work. It was a guy
who sounded angry and yelled at me to stop what I was doing. Then
I got this second call just a few minutes ago, right before I called you.
Both voices sounded the same, but the caller ID says "Blocked." There
was also a creepy email I received at work the other day. It said something like, 'If you value your life, stop what you're doing.' I thought it
was one of the guys in IT pulling a prank, but now I don't know." She
takes a deep breath. "Tío, there's more. There's another reason why I'm
scared for Carissa."

"What is it, Marissa?"

"I didn't want to say anything to you until after I've had a chance to talk to CC. You know Carissa, she'll be upset if I don't give her a chance to explain a situation first."

"What situation? What are you talking about? When's the last time you saw your sister?" His tone doesn't mask his growing concern.

"The last time I saw and talked to CC was Tuesday morning. She called and asked me to meet her at that little park where you used to take us for picnics. Remember? We still consider it our favorite place to meet or hang out and think. Our visit the other morning was brief because we both had to go to work. At first, she seemed like she was mad at me. Carissa was asking questions about the pet store bust like, 'How did you hear about it?' 'Did somebody tip you off?' questions like that. I told her that the timing happened to be luck of the news gods and that the photographer and I just rolled with our instincts. Then we talked about some of the crazy things going on in my life and she shared a little bit about her life, too. It was all the usual stuff as best as I can remember. Just before we said goodbye, we promised to spend more time together. That's the last time I talked to her, but that's not what's bothering me."

Marissa's heart is heavy because she knows she's about to break that close bond her twin and she have shared their entire lives. She sighs, "I didn't want to tell you this, but last night Ken and I were looking at videotape we shot right after the undercover officers busted that gang trying to steal those exotic birds."

Tío interrupts, exasperated. "What does any of this have to do with your sister?"

"I'm trying to explain it to you! Tío, *por favor*. Please, let me finish," she pleads.

"Okay, *mija*. Go ahead. Tell me."

Marissa tries to steady her voice as she recalls the images she saw. "The video was of the crime scene aftermath, mostly wide angle shots in the parking lot behind the loading dock where the semi-trailer truck was still parked. Ken was focusing on crime scene investigators who were gathering evidence. You know how it goes, Tío, at any crime scene there are always curious spectators standing around watching police work. Well, in the video we noticed one guy who walked away from the crowd and jumped into an SUV that was parked about thirty feet away in the parking lot. It was a little hard to tell at first, but it turns out there was another person sitting in the front passenger seat."

She feels a lump welling up in her throat as the image of her sister being slapped fills her mind. "From a distance you can see one person jump out of the passenger side. He turns around and yells something into the car window when suddenly, a third person gets out of the backseat, grabs the second person by the arm and slaps her across the face." She swallows again, "Ken managed to zoom in and during the playback we magnified the video. What we saw shocked us. The slap knocked off the person's cap and sunglasses…." She takes a deep breath, lets out a long sigh and says, "The person being slapped… it was…Carissa."

There's silence on the other end.

"Tío, are you there?"

She knows he must share the pain of her revelation. Marissa and CC are like daughters to Hector. He's been their self-appointed guardian angel since the day their parents were murdered.

Tío Hector lets out a long sigh of defeat before telling her, "Marissa, listen to me. I don't want you to panic, but you need to know that your sister may be missing. You met her in the park Tuesday morning. Well, later that day she left work suddenly. She did leave a note for a client stating that she didn't feel well. She also left the door of her business unlocked so that the client could pick up her dog. While it's a little unusual, it sounds like something your sister might do sort of spur of the moment. There was no evidence at the shop to indicate that CC didn't leave on her own. However, at about the same time, someone activated the silent alarm at the front desk of the business. I checked the report. It shows officers responded within five minutes and found nothing unusual or out of place. Maybe the alarm was triggered accidentally. CC's an adult who left a note saying she was leaving voluntarily, so there's no official reason to investigate," he says as if trying to convince himself. "But after what you saw on the video, it's very likely she's the one who triggered the alarm. We need to find her and talk to her. And I want to see that enhanced video as soon as possible."

"Okay," Marissa says.

"I'm sending an undercover unit to your place now, but I'm not sure how long it'll take them to get there. They'll be watching you from a discreet distance since it sounds like you're being followed. Here's what I need you to do: contact your photographer and ask him to bring a copy of that video here to the police station as soon as he can. Don't answer your phone unless it's a number you recognize. Especially don't answer any more blocked calls. And get out of your apartment as soon as possible. Before you leave your place, call someone on your cell phone. Anyone. It doesn't matter who. I don't care if you call to check the time and temperature. Do you hear me? The point is you need to at least *look* like you're talking to someone on your phone. If you're a possible target, you're less likely to be approached while talking on the phone to someone."

She listens intently to his somber instructions.

He finishes talking to her as a police officer and speaks in a soothing voice that's always been a comfort to her. "*Mija*, I'll do my best to protect you and your sister. I made that promise to God when your parents were killed. And I never break a promise. Now go on, do what I say and I'll see you and the photographer as soon as you can get here."

"Okay, Tío Hector. I'm on my way." She hangs up and calls Ken.

"Hello, Marissa. What took you so long to call? I thought you'd be back over here for round two of our favorite drinking game," he chuckles.

"Ken, listen to me. This is serious. I need your help. I just got off the phone with my uncle and he wants you to bring a copy of the video we shot in the parking lot. You know...the video that shows Carissa being slapped."

"Have you talked to your sister? Didn't you say you weren't going to tell your uncle about the video until after you talked to her?"

"All that's changed. I'm sorry, but I don't have time to go into all the new details right now. I will as soon as I catch up with you at the police department. If you get there first, my uncle can fill you in."

"Marissa. This is no Truth or Dare drinking game. What are you holding back?"

"It's something I wasn't sure about until just a few minutes ago when I was talking to Tío, but I've gotten a couple of threatening phone calls and one pretty nasty email. Before you freak out or anything, my uncle's sending an undercover officer and I've been instructed to pack a bag and get out of here until all of these questions are answered. We'll talk more when I see you at APD. In the meantime, I need to get a few things together and get out of here."

"Where are...?"

"I promise I'll call when I'm on my way to police headquarters."

She hangs up and looks around her apartment. It's her private oasis where she can curl up and read celebrity gossip rags, eat a pint of ice cream for dinner if she wants, watch her favorite movies over and over or just be by herself. This apartment is where she escapes the stress of work. Everything in it—the artwork, the pillows, the comforter and matching curtains in her bedroom—every single item was purchased for her ease and enjoyment. Now it all looks strange and foreign; she doesn't feel comfortable there at all. She no longer feels safe. It's the last place she wants to be as long as her sister's fate is unknown.

She throws some personal items in an overnight bag, including her computer and a few days' worth of clean clothes. Ironically, her suspension is advantageous since going to work is one less thing she has to worry about. Her professional life no longer seems important. All that matters is CC's wellbeing.

With her charged cell phone in hand so she can pretend she's talking to someone, she looks in her purse to ensure her family photo is still there. She locks the door behind her. *Hang on, CC. I'm on my way!*

Twenty-Four

Tío's words of caution are still ringing in Marissa's ears as she locks the apartment door behind her. She takes a visual sweep of the walkway down to the parking lot where her car is parked. She has her phone to her ear and occasionally nods and says, "uh-huh" as if responding to someone on the line. She crosses her fingers and recites the blessing that her mother used to say every time CC and she left the house, *"Que dios te cuide."* May God protect you. She prays for her sister and herself, hoping that somewhere out there an undercover officer, sent by Tío Hector, is on duty. She scans the area but doesn't see a single soul. It's the middle of the day, which means most residents are at work. The complex is eerily empty except for a cat peeking out from under a staircase and the mailman who's stuffing the day's delivery into individual mailboxes. She keeps up her end of the fake phone chat as she loads her bag in the backseat of her car, starts the ignition and makes her way to the Austin Police Station downtown.

Traffic is light since it's two in the afternoon, which means it'll only take her about fifteen minutes to get there and find a parking space. She looks in the rearview mirror and wonders if any of the cars behind her are being driven by an undercover officer? Or is the person behind the wheel someone who wants to hurt her? These two very different scenarios keep tugging at her as she tries to concentrate on where she's going. It's not just her own safety that has her worried. Her head is about to explode with concern and unanswered questions about her sister. *Where in the hell is she?*

Suddenly, she's filled with a strong hunch, like the ones she used to get when they were kids. She could practically read CC's mind and could always tell when she was sick or hurting. There was the time a sudden pain hit the lower right side of her body for no apparent reason. When she stepped outside their house to look for Carissa, she found her lying on the ground. She was barely able to prop herself up on her right elbow after falling while climbing a tree. Marissa knew she was hurt and felt her pain. It also wasn't unusual for them to know what the other was thinking even without words being exchanged between them.

At that moment, Marissa knows without a doubt that CC's in trouble. She has to follow her gut instinct. So instead of going to see Tío Hector, she heads to Royal Watchers Pet Care, the last place where CC was seen. Luckily, it's also downtown, not far from police headquarters. She decides not to call Tío Hector or Ken about her detour because she knows they'll try to talk her out of it. The drive there is short, but it gives her a chance to come up with a plan of action. After she stops at the pet care place, she'll go see Hector. Hopefully by then, Ken will be there so all three can look at the video together. She hopes that Tío Hector's police training will uncover hints that will help them figure out what's going on with Carissa.

Marissa remembers that she has a spare key to Carissa's apartment. After she finishes with Tío Hector, she'll stop by CC's apartment and look around for anything that might be out of place or that might provide insight into what's going on in her life. Carissa has become so protective of her privacy, but she hasn't always been that way. It wasn't that long ago when they used to share everything. All through college, they lived together and shared everything from class notes and homework to food and clothes.

One time, they even shared a boyfriend, although he didn't know it. He kept wondering how Marissa could possibly be so hungry all the time. She'd want to get something to eat less than an hour after they'd just finished a meal. Actually, she and CC were both seeing him, but he didn't know his one girlfriend was two people. The boyfriend-sharing arrangement ended when he dropped CC off after a fast food run and minutes later he ran into Marissa in the parking lot of their dormitory. She was wearing a different outfit than CC. After getting over the shock of seeing double, he was slightly pissed that he'd been fooled into dating—and feeding—two girlfriends. They sat him down and sweet-talked him out of his anger. Each planted a kiss on his cheek and sent him on his way with no lingering hard feelings. He got to brag to his fraternity brothers about dating a set of hot twins. And they got a couple of free meals out of the deal.

In those days, the two were inseparable and life was only as complicated as they made it. The complications began to increase after they both graduated from the University of Texas and started their professional careers. Marissa spent a couple of years working her first job as a television reporter in Victoria, Texas. CC, who'd earned an accounting degree, first tried working at a bakery and then at a jewelry store before finding her true passion, caring for small animals. Through her various jobs, she always showed a knack for business management and finances. For the first time in their lives, both women began enjoying newfound independence. When Marissa moved back to Austin, they were as close as ever, although they had their separate careers and apartments. They'd developed their own hobbies and interests and their own set of friends.

Marissa pulls her car into the Pampered Pets Only parking space outside Royal Watchers Pet Care. She knows the routine here. Most dogs are dropped off in the morning before their owners head off to work or some other destination. At the end of the day, owners return to take their pets home. That doesn't happen until much later in the afternoon, so it should be fairly quiet inside the shop right now. There's one specific area inside the business where she needs to check for a clue. She has figured out how to conduct a search without raising suspicions. Only CC would know what she's looking for and where it would be.

She opens the door and hears the familiar sound of the door alarm signaling her entrance. A guy in his early forties with a trim build and slightly graying hair is busy on the computer behind the front desk near the cash register. He hears the sound triggered by the opening door and without looking up starts to say automatically, "Welcome to Royal Pet Watchers. How may I...?" As he looks up and sees Marissa, his pleasant greeting gives way to an expression of shock that quickly turns to anger. "Where the hell have you been, Carissa? You have a lot of nerve showing your pretty little face around here. Or didn't you get my message telling you that you've been fired?"

"Mr. Welch, I'm not Carissa. I'm her sister, Marissa. I'm sorry if I confused you. I actually came here to ask you about her. What can you tell me about the last time you saw her?"

He stutters, "I..I..I can't believe you're not Carissa. You look and sound just like her. You really surprised me walking in here dressed just like her. Unfortunately, I don't have much to tell you about your sister." Welch walks over to the row of kennels and starts passing out treats to the row of waiting dogs. Most are barking and scratching at the kennel bars or wagging their tails with excitement. Welch keeps his attention on the dogs as he says, "Without receiving a valid explanation from your sister about why she suddenly left the shop, I had no choice but to fire her. Her departure without notice has really left me in the lurch. Already two high-profile customers have quit bringing their dogs here. Just look around for yourself...the conditions are a mess! It's awful, I tell you, and I blame your sister."

He pauses and turns to Marissa as he puts one hand on his hip. "So you tell me, Miss Cavelo, where is she?"

From what CC has told Marissa about Dan Welch, she knows he doesn't give a rat terrier's ass about her sister's whereabouts or her wellbeing. He's only interested in himself and how Carissa's departure has increased his workload and impacted his revenue stream. Marissa forces herself to stay calm. "Mr. Welch, I can't answer that question. You and I are both left wondering what happened to her. Maybe CC wasn't sick, which means she was forced to leave suddenly. There's a strong possibility police will be looking into her case. There's no conclusion yet about what triggered her to leave without first contacting anyone. That's why I came here…to find out if you've heard from her. Or if you know of any reason why she'd walk out of here so suddenly?"

He pauses to think for a few seconds and then shakes his head and says, "No, I can't think of any excuse that would explain your sister's actions."

"Well then, do you mind if I look around? Does she have an employee locker in the back where she kept her personal items?"

"After not hearing from your sister, I took the liberty of cleaning out her locker. I put the few items she had stashed away in a shopping bag to take to Goodwill. I was this close to writing her off for good." He walks to the back of the store to retrieve her items.

While he's gone, Marissa heads straight to the front desk and starts running her hand along the small space behind the cash register. She pulls out a paper clip…a couple of loose coins…some dog hair matted with dust balls and then…. *BINGO!* Her fingers come upon a folded piece of paper that was tucked away in a secret hiding place that CC designated for Marissa a long time ago. Only other twins would understand this communication system they devised. If in the event there was something they needed to convey to each other, but for whatever reason couldn't do so face-to-face, they promised to leave a handwritten note in one of two designated secret hiding places. The first secret place they've both used several times over the past few years: a small crevice along a rock wall in their park. The second secret place is there behind the cash register at CC's job. Marissa stuffs the note into her pocket and quickly moves back from behind the front counter just as Welch comes in from the back storage area carrying a bag containing her personal items. "There is not much here. And what is in this bag, I'm not sure even Goodwill would accept. You're more than welcome to it." He holds out the bag, like it's too disgusting for him to touch. His nose is scrunched up as if some horrible odor is coming from it.

"Thank you, Mr. Welch. I'm sure my sister will appreciate the return of these items." Her voice dripping with sarcasm she adds, "And I'll pass along to her your genuine concern about her whereabouts." With the bag in her hand and the note in her pocket, she turns around and walks out the door.

Marissa puts the bag in the back seat of her car before slipping into the driver's seat. Her hands are shaking as she pulls the piece of paper out of her pocket and unfolds it. The handwriting is scribbled, like it was written by a ten-year-old in a hurry. This isn't like CC who takes pride in her penmanship. It reads: "HELP! In trouble. Check out Nassine's. Now!"

Nassine—the name of the club owner. What kind of trouble is CC in?

A lump forms in her throat and her stomach churns. She says a silent prayer, *Please, let her be all right. Give me the strength and the intelligence to figure this out.* She starts her car and heads to the police station to deliver the note and her fears to Tío Hector. She knows that he and Ken must be wondering what the hell is taking her so long to get to get there.

215

Twenty-Five

What time is it? What day is it? Does anybody give a damn where I am or if I'm alive? The same rambling questions have been swirling in CC's head unanswered ever since H.N. went crazy on her. The nonstop booze and drugs have erased all sense of time. She feels like a prisoner being held against her will by a madman. She tries to open her eyes, but the effects of the drugs make it tough to shake off the drowsiness. At least the drugs dull the pain of being knocked around. Carissa wishes she had enough pills and booze to permanently take away the physical and emotional pain. She wills herself to stop the suicidal thoughts and instead concentrate on her surroundings. She listens for any sound or movement in the room, but all she hears is the steady whirr of the air conditioning system, which keeps this entire condo at sub-zero temperatures.

There is no sound of anyone breathing next to her, but just to be sure, she slowly sweeps her arm across the surface of the bed to her left where H.N. usually sleeps. The space is empty, but that's not unusual since he often jumps out of bed for all kinds of reasons. Sometimes he gets up suddenly and gets on his phone or on his personal computer that he always carries with him. Lately, she's noticed that he jumps out of bed right after they've had sex and gets in the shower. It's as if physical intimacy leaves him feeling dirty, which seems crazy since he always wants to have sex and she has no choice but to oblige.

She wills her brain to function and her eyes to open. She has to figure out a way to get herself out of this mess. These last few hours have revealed to her that his anger is directed at her family...and at Marissa.

Marissa! That bitch. She blames her sister and her high-profile life. *If it wasn't for her ambition, I would be safe instead of with a maniac with a deep-seated need to carry out a senseless revenge for something that happened in Houston ages ago.* CC's disappointed that Marissa has not made an effort to rescue her. *What a joke! I bet she didn't even bother to look for the note I left. She must be too busy digging up another exclusive news story. Damn her! H.N. is right, Marissa doesn't care what happens to me. And Tío Hector is no better. That silent alarm he had me install under the counter at work didn't get the police to respond. I have to face the facts that I'm on my own.*

Carissa has convinced herself that she is on her own and no one is coming to save her. She sits up in bed and looks at the clock on the bedside table: two o'clock p.m. She leans over the side of the bed and feels around on the carpet for her cell phone. She remembers putting it on silent so that ringtones or alerts wouldn't accidentally wake H.N. and send him into another rage.

The phone has almost no battery power, but she doesn't know who she would call anyway, having convinced herself that her twin and Tío Hector have written her off. Besides, what would she tell her sister? That she resents her and all that her public profile represents? That her crazy Persian boyfriend is holding her hostage? That she's fucked up on booze and pills? That she's addicted to his money and luxury lifestyle?

But...she has no one else. Her finger is shaking as it hits the preset button.

This is my one chance to save myself before terror walks through that bedroom door.

Twenty-Six

Just as she's pulling out of the parking space at the Royal Pet Watchers, Marissa's cell phone rings and she immediately recognizes her sister's ringtone. "CC! Is that you? Are you all right?"

All she hears is sobbing. CC is so hysterical Marissa can't understand what she's saying. "Slow down. Breathe. Carissa, please talk to me so that I can understand you. I need to know you're okay. Where are you? Have you been in an accident?" Marissa is relieved to hear CC's voice, but she sounds like an emotional wreck. "Are you at home? Because I can be there in five minutes. I can head that way now. Whatever it is—whatever's wrong—we'll figure it out together. We always have. We always will."

Carissa puts a few words together between her sobs. "Oh Marissa, I'm so sorry, but I had to call somebody…and…you're the only person I know who won't judge me."

Marissa turns onto a quiet neighborhood street and pulls over so she can concentrate on the call. There are a few parked cars. She looks up and down the street. She doesn't see anyone walking along the sidewalks in either direction and there are no moving vehicles.

"CC, it's okay. Of course, I won't judge you. Let me come get you and we can talk. You're my sister. I love you."

"I'm not at my apartment," she cries. "I'm at a…a…friend's… right now."

"What friend? Where? Listen, Tío Hector is worried about you. He's been trying to get in touch with you."

"Please, promise me, on our parents' graves, you will not tell Tío Hector anything."

"Okay," Marissa says. Her fingers are crossed so it's not really *una promesa de verdad*, a true promise she'll have to keep. Still, she won't break the promise unless it's absolutely necessary. She takes a chance and says, "CC, I found your note hidden behind the cash register at your job. I was there right before you called." Her response surprises Marissa.

"That note means nothing!" She laughs. Suddenly, the desperation in her voice is gone and she says, "Sorry, I can't talk now, after all. But thank you, anyway."

Marissa says in Spanish, "Is there someone close by so you can't talk?"

"Yes. That's correct. But I've changed my mind. I'm sorry I bothered you in the first place." She hangs up.

Marissa is even more confused by her sister's cryptic phone call. She knows that she is supposed to head to the police department but decides that she has to follow her gut instincts. She sends a group text to Tío Hector and Ken: **Hey, guys! Good news. CC called. She's fine and I'm headed to meet her. TTYL.**

She knows they'll both be angry that she's taken off on her own but hopes that they'll trust her. She then sends each one a separate text.

The one to Ken reads: **Let's do another round of your kick-ass margaritas later, okay?** Drinking is the last thing on her mind but hopefully, the message will make him think everything's fine and that there's no reason to worry.

The text to her uncle says: **Don't mean to make you mad or disrespect you. Trust me. Let me talk to Carissa alone first. I'm safe. Thanks for sending guardian officers to watch over me.**

She looks around, feeling hopeful, because at least for the moment, there are no signs of anyone following her. She decides to go to a place where no one will find her. A laid back coffee shop on Austin's Eastside will provide privacy, Internet access and most importantly, a strong cup of coffee. These are the three ingredients needed to dig for answers to the questions swirling around in her head. She pulls into the parking lot of *Casa de Cafe*. It's nearly empty as she steps inside the coffee house. Only one other customer, an elderly man in his mid-seventies, is at a table by the front door, reading the newspaper. A lone employee is wiping down the counter where fresh java is brewing. They exchange a simple greeting in Spanish as she fills a coffee mug and makes her way to a corner table where she opens her laptop.

She navigates her way around the Royal Pet Watchers website. She logs in using Carissa's username followed by her password, *BadDawg*, which, as Marissa knows, is also Carissa's email login. After a few seconds, a page opens, providing a portal for company employees only. She maneuvers her way past the week's posted work schedule, a checklist of daily duties and a calendar showing reservations booked by clients. She goes down the list, looking for names that sound familiar. CC never mentions the clients by names, just their dogs. Name after name. Address after address. *Who knew there were so many wealthy people in the Austin area willing to spend so much money on canine care?* She thinks. The names are not listed alphabetically. Instead, they are listed based on their frequency of appointments, which makes for a tedious search process. She scrolls past *Muffin, King Maker, Lucky* and *Alfonz, III*, before landing on *Ace*. Next to the dog's name is the description of the dog and instructions which read: **Purebred Yorkshire Terrier, no medications, has its own bed, blanket and food.** *Wow! Talk about pampered.* Ace's owner is named Hadid Nassine. According to the client's info, Nassine recently quit bringing Ace to Royal Pet Watchers, but no explanation was given.

Hadid Nassine, why does that name sound familiar? Marissa wonders. Then she remembers, it's also the name of the owner of the Moroccan Hideaway, which she discovered when she was checking the identities of the two men in the photos. The address on file for Nassine is in a high-rise, luxury condominium in downtown Austin. *Is that where CC was calling from? Was Nassine in the background listening so she couldn't talk to me? Did Nassine force her to leave work suddenly? Is he the guy in the parking lot video who slapped her?*

Marissa knows it's time to use her best investigative reporting skills. Not to break a big story but to figure out what the hell is happening to her sister.

Twenty-Seven

Marissa is desperate to find out everything she can about Hadid Nassine. It turns out Nassine is a popular name in Middle Eastern regions, much like Smith in the United States.

Using the *Positive Identity* website, she narrows the field of names by conducting a cross-reference search of nearby cities and zip codes. About a dozen people by that last name pop-up in Houston and a few in Austin. Most sites automatically notify you when the people you're searching for have been located and then the search effort completely stops until you pay the additional money for the search to continue. So-called, "search fees" cost anywhere from fifty to one hundred dollars, but since KATX has an account for reporters to use, she is able to log on and request additional information. She hopes her access hasn't been revoked because of her suspension. With fingers crossed, she types in the station's generic username and password. *Bingo!* She's allowed access to the site that holds all the info she needs about Hadid Nassine. She narrows her search to the Austin region.

The website lists the same downtown high-rise address that was listed on the Royal Pet Watcher's client list. She makes a note of the property address and realizes it's around the corner from CC's workplace. *How convenient.* Hadid Nassine has no spouse, has not been divorced, nor does he owe child support. He hasn't filed for bankruptcy, nor has he lost property to foreclosure proceedings. There are no current outstanding warrants. He's listed as the co-owner of six properties in a prime two-block area of downtown Austin, including the Moroccan Hideaway, which is also within easy walking distance of his condo. There's a link to the Travis County Appraisal District website that shows exactly where all the properties are located and the appraised value of each one. The real estate is expensive.

A slick, high-tech map provides a real-time view of the street. All six addresses are the locations of the hottest night spots in Austin. There is the Moroccan Hideaway where the photo was taken of the men Tío Hector wanted her to see. But of more significance to Marissa is that it's where she and CC recently went to celebrate a friend's birthday. The other hot spots include Tiger Eyes, The Cool Room, The Hip-Hop Shop, Ex-Rays and The Shark Tank. The clubs are always jammed and long lines of partiers are outside hoping to get past the bouncers. It's not unusual to see local celebrities and wealthy customers pull up in expensive sports cars. Drivers toss their keys to the valets and breeze through the front door. All the clubs cater to the extremely rich. Once inside, it's a sea of beautiful, barely clothed bodies sensually moving around the dance floor, super loud techno music and a never-ending supply of liquor.

Besides the time with CC at the Moroccan Hideaway, Marissa has been inside two of the other clubs with coworkers—once for a bachelorette party and another time for a birthday. Each of her three visits, Marissa walked out broke from the expensive drinks and sweat-soaked from her time on the dance floor. The atmosphere was that of an upscale private party, except it was anything but private. Marissa remembers covering the grand opening of the Shark Tank. She was sent there because it featured an unusual amenity—the largest dance floor ever built on top of a floor level, fully-stocked aquarium.

She makes notes about the Nassine-owned clubs. The website for each features a gimmick or unusual theme to justify the outrageous drink prices and exorbitant cover charges, although attractive women always manage to get in free. She concludes that the pricing strategy seems to be that for each beautiful girl who is allowed into the club at least two wealthy, high-tech nerds or one occasional visiting Saudi prince will follow. And of course, their platinum credit cards and ample dollar bills are not far behind!

The decors at two of the clubs, the Moroccan Hideaway and Tiger Eyes, are greatly influenced by the deserts and palaces of the Middle East, á la *Lawrence of Arabia* and *Aladdin* with luxurious tents that provide privacy for VIP members. Servers are dressed like harem girls who offer private table service and unbelievable belly dancing skills. One dancer was rumored to be able to flip a row of quarters with her abdominal muscles without missing a beat! Such skills prompt wealthy patrons to reward her by slipping hundred dollar bills into the waistband of her harem pants.

At the Tiger Eyes, a real-life Bengal tiger roams the premises every hour. A very buff and well-built handler holds onto the tiger's chain as he walks the regal animal through the crowd. The handler is tipped quite well by club patrons who have their picture taken with the tiger. Through her research on the club Marissa learns that the tiger, Simba, was de-clawed as a cub and has the personality of an overgrown cuddly kitten. But the patrons enjoy pretending that Simba is a ferocious feline ready to attack.

Each of the clubs has an elaborate security system with video cameras and a high-tech monitoring station. Three of the clubs, including the Moroccan Hideaway are connected by a corridor that runs parallel to the back alley. There are two things that Marissa wants to do, one is to scope out these clubs to determine if CC is being held by Nassine in one of them. Then she wants to check with Tío Hector to see if the police department may have installed security video cameras that might provide a good vantage point of the entrances to the clubs.

She remains in her car and continues surfing the web to find out as much as she can about Nassine and his associates. There are two more people with the same last name in the Austin area. One is described as a professor at the University of Texas who teaches classes in Middle Eastern History and Antiquities. Marissa writes down his contact info in case she needs it later. There's a third person with the same last name whose first name is Nassour. His birth date shows he's two years younger than Hadid. His profile info lists the same clean legal history as Hadid. Both of the Nassines are listed as co-owners of the six nightclubs.

Her next step is to dig deeper into what she can find on social media. Facebook shows no personal pages for either of the Nassine brothers, although photos of both are posted on various pages. Each of the clubs has an established Facebook page, but most of the pictures are of celebrities and the info is about upcoming events. She slowly scrolls through the posts. She sees a photo of a group of attractive women and realizes that one of them is CC! Off to the side, a good-looking man is looking at her. He has a scowl on his face. *Is this one of the Nassines?* She wonders. She reaches for the police file Tío Hector gave her that contains the enlarged photo. She compares it with the screenshot on her computer. She gasps. The scowling faces are the same. Her heart sinks at the realization that somehow these men who are criminally linked to the pet store heist also hold the key to her sister's safety and her location. Possibly even her life!

Marissa keeps digging, not wanting to believe what she has seen. She switches from Facebook to Google. It's usually easy to find images of any photo or advertisement that's been published or printed, but there are no photos of either brother. The only thing even close is a picture of Professor Nassine taken while attending a conference hosted by the United Nations years earlier. The lack of photos convinces her that these brothers don't like to have their pictures taken. There is one more website she wants to check, *A-ZArchives*, which in the past has always revealed useful information to her, even if it's just a simple one-line birth announcement or death notice.

It's an unbelievably thorough compilation of newspaper archives, and her favorite site to check when she's trying to dig up interesting background info that might otherwise go unnoticed. This is a treasure trove for compulsive fact checkers like Marissa. Only registered journalists from certified news outlets are allowed to access it. Newspapers and other recognized publications agree to submit the digital version of their pages including the advertisements. In exchange, their reporters are granted unlimited access. Other news outlets—such as television and radio stations—pay an expensive subscriber fee. Marissa thinks it's worth every penny to have access to the digital versions of newspapers and some magazines. Some of the archived editions go back for decades. What she likes best is how simple it is to use. She types in the names as search words: Hadid and Nassour Nassine, and then enters the geographical area the publication serves. The *Austin Daily Informer* is the newspaper that serves the Austin metro area. She sits back and lets the website do its magic.

In about fifteen seconds, the first match pops up. It's an article that appeared in the *Austin Daily Informer* about three years ago that mentions the mysterious disappearance of a club owner in Austin named Enrique Sanchez, originally from Colombia, South America. Sanchez was suspected of laundering illegal drug money through his club. The article includes a quote from Hadid Nassine, who was among the last individuals to see Sanchez before he disappeared. The quote states, "He [Sanchez] mentioned family problems back home in Bogota, Colombia, so I just assumed he left the country to head home to deal with those issues. We hope everything is okay and that he comes back to Austin soon." The article goes on to describe the reward Sanchez's wife is offering for tips leading to her husband's whereabouts. She says he never mentioned anything about returning to Colombia.

On a hunch, Marissa searches for more info on Enrique Sanchez. A few more articles from the *Austin Daily Informer* appear. One's an update on the missing club owner whose nickname turns out to be "Slick Rick." Sanchez has two prior drug-related charges and arrests that were later dropped after a witness disappeared and couldn't be found by prosecutors. A second, more recent article is less than a year old. It has details about the slow demise of Sanchez's club, *Eternity*, after his mysterious disappearance. His wife unsuccessfully tried to keep it open but was unable to pay the back property taxes and the tax on alcoholic beverage sales that were owed. Then the Texas Liquor Agency conducted a raid after issuing numerous violations for underage drinking. The article says there was also a huge inventory of alcoholic beverages that hadn't been legally paid for. Within a couple of months of the raid, the club closed and was sold at auction to the highest bidders. Hadid and Nassour Nassine were not only the winning bidders, they were the *only* bidders.

What happened to "Slick Rick" Sanchez? Did the Nassine's have anything to do with his disappearance? Marissa has no doubt that these are the men her uncle suspects are the masterminds behind the botched heist of expensive birds. But her thoughts return to her sister. *Why was CC with them lurking in the background of the pet store's grand opening in the first place? There has to be more to the two men and their current involvement in my sister's life.* Marissa assumes that CC met him because he brought his dog to Royal Pet Watchers. That, in itself, is not so unusual, but now she knows that he and his brother own all those clubs. What Marissa doesn't know is how much time CC might have spent with Nassine outside of the pet spa.

Marissa thinks about her sister's attributes: *She's beautiful. She's fearless. Or rather, she doesn't back down easily. She's a flirt who's always up for a good sexually-charged challenge.* Knowing that, it wouldn't be far-fetched to conclude that she and Hadid Nasssine developed more than a routine client relationship. What is unclear is his personal background. While his past legal records are clear, at least according to the Positive Identity website, there must be more about Hadid and Nassour's personal lives that isn't as obvious. Their last name is Middle Eastern, but that doesn't tell her their actual ethnicity. It's like knowing someone with the last name Garcia is Latino, but not knowing if they're from Mexico, Central America or Spain.

Marissa remembers the professor with the same last name and thinks that he might be able to shed some light on the background of the Nassines. She takes out her cell phone and dials his office number. He is listed as faculty in the Department of Middle Eastern Studies at the University of Texas. The phone rings four times before an answering machine instructs her to leave a message, as long as it's not about grades or a request for an extension for turning in a term paper. Marissa says, "Hello. I am not a UT student. This is Marissa Cavelo, a reporter with KATX news here in Austin. I have a couple of questions I was hoping to ask you. I understand you're an expert in Middle Eastern studies and topics." Just as she's about to leave her cell phone number, she hears a deep man's voice, "This is Professor Nassine. How may I help you?"

She's careful about how much information she reveals about her real reason for calling, while maintaining her ethical obligations as a journalist. She says she's researching the background of an individual who she plans to meet, which is true. Their conversation is amiable until she reveals the person's name.

The professor becomes very serious, "Are you calling about either Hadid or Nassour Nassine? Because if you are, I should warn you to be very careful...." He pauses before continuing. "I don't know, nor have I ever met either of the men, but I have mistakenly been contacted more than once by so-called associates of the Nassine brothers. I have no proof, of course, but these callers sounded like professional thugs."

"Well actually, I'm trying to pinpoint the nationality of the Nassine brothers. Do you happen to know?"

"Oh my dear, that's quite simple for me to answer since I, too, conducted some minor background research of my own after the first time I was contacted about the Nassines. For my own peace of mind and to satisfy my growing curiosity, I wanted to be sure I wasn't related to them, which I'm relieved to declare that I'm not. The Nassine brothers and their family are originally from Iran or what was formerly known as Persia. If you have a moment, Ms. Cavelo, I'll provide you with a brief history lesson."

"Yes, please," Marissa says.

"You see, the culturally-rich civilization of Persia quickly deteriorated as a result of the internal war raged by hardline religious leaders in the late 1970s. The American-backed Shah of Iran was forced out of his country and replaced with an Islamic extremist, the Ayatollah Khomeni. Many of those loyal to the Shah left behind personal wealth and pampered lives. They fled to the safety of the United States where they were forced to start different lives with few carryover luxuries from their former privileged lives. Most Persians struggled to survive and few were able to successfully rebuild their previous financial assets, but my research reveals the Nassine brothers have, in fact, managed to do quite well with their real estate investments. Their good fortune and business acumen started years earlier in Houston where they emigrated along with their parents."

Houston? The pieces are coming together. Marissa doesn't want to be rude, but she needs to end the call. "I'm sorry, Professor, I've got a call coming in from the station. Thank you so much for your time and information."

That the Nassine family spent time in Houston where her family lived is too much of a coincidence. She ends the call and picks up her laptop. She returns to the *A-ZArchives* website. She again types in the name "Nassine" but this time adds the geographic area of Houston and Harris County served by the *Houston Chronicle* and the now-defunct *Houston Post*. She searches from the start of 1975 through 1985. Since this more dated timeline search might take a few minutes, she decides to call Ken and Tío Hector. She wants to let both of them know what she has learned so far about the Nassines and their backgrounds.

She knows it is possible that Hector may already have this information, and if he does, he couldn't share with her because it's part of a police investigation. But if he doesn't, she hopes what the professor told her about the brothers and their family background, as well as what she learned online might ease her uncle's anger for disregarding his instructions.

The *A-ZArchives* screen refreshes and Marissa concentrates on the computer screen in front of her. *What the hell?* Her heart begins to race. Two of the newspaper articles are the same ones she was looking at earlier while going through the box of personal items that once belonged to her parents! She skims the lines of the news item that she already knows are about her father, a night watchman, who happened to help bust a burglary ring in the Houston Ship Channel area. Toward the end of the article, the suspects are named and identified as men who worked for a Persian businessman Hadid Al Nassine. *Is he related to this club owner here in Austin?*

Another newspaper article pops up on the screen that wasn't in the folder. This one pierces her heart. **Night Watchman Hero and Wife Murdered: Police check possible link to burglary suspects.** She reads it slowly, more than once, to be sure she's not misunderstanding any part of it. But it's very clear to her now; one of the burglary suspects that her father helped to apprehend carried out the murder of her parents as some type of revenge killing. The article mentions a strong sense of loyalty between the murder suspect and his boss, the Persian businessman Hadid Al Nassine.

Ay Dios mio! The Nassine brothers who live in Austin and who somehow know her sister are related to the elder Nassine who is indirectly responsible for her parents' death! *Is it possible Tío H knew about the Nassines' connection to the murder of my parents but didn't share it with me?* she wonders.

She dials Ken's cell phone number and is relieved when he answers quickly. "Ken, it's me." Before he can get a word in, she says, "Ken, I know who the two men are in the police photographs that my uncle gave us. I also have a good reason to believe that they're the same men who were harassing my sister in the pet store parking lot!"

"Whoa, whoa there! Slow down." Ken says. "Those are some serious allegations. Are you sure? Where are you?"

"I'm sorry. I know haven't been up front with either you or my uncle. I wasn't honest about where I was going because I had a hunch I needed to check out right away. It's complicated, but please don't be angry with me. I've got so much more to share with you and my uncle. I'll be at police headquarters momentarily. Can you meet me there? And bring a video camera." Before he can respond, she hangs up.

As she makes her way over to the police station, she worries that her uncle is going to be furious with her. *Wait a minute. If he did know about the Nassine brothers and didn't tell me then I'm the one who has a reason to be angry.* She dials his number.

"Hello, Marissa. Are you with your sister? Where are you?"

She takes a deep breath before answering. "No, Tío, I'm not with CC. To be honest, I haven't seen her." She takes another deep breath before admitting her deception. "The text I sent you earlier was an excuse so that I could dig for clues on my own."

"Dig for clues?! *Mija,* you have no business trying to solve a criminal case. You're only putting yourself in grave danger. It's a danger that I've already warned you about, and yet you failed to follow instructions to come to my office. Then you lied to me," he is clearly angry.

"Tío, I know it was wrong, but hear me out. I had to go see for myself if CC left any clues where she worked. And I'm glad I did because there was a message hidden behind the cash register that she must've stashed before she walked out the door. I'm the only one who knew where to look. I also think she didn't leave willingly, so it's very possible she was the one who triggered the silent alarm. Besides, I would've been honest with you if you'd been honest with me. You didn't tell me about the identity of the two men in the photos or what you knew about their background. You knew, didn't you?"

"I could only warn you about the two men since no charges have been filed against either of them," his tone is more conciliatory, "Investigators haven't been able to link them to any criminal activity." He becomes agitated again. "Do I have to remind you that our best shot at doing so was foiled by your pet store coverage?" He sighs and composes himself. "To reveal any additional information would only jeopardize your safety and this case. Now I know you mean well, and I know you're worried about your sister, but I'm ordering you to leave any additional detective work to my officers. Am I clear, Marissa?"

"But Tío, I have an idea how to get to CC," she pleads. "I'm not far from your office now. Ken is going to join me."

"No. Absolutely not. The last thing I need is for you to get further involved in this case. It's bad enough that there's reason to be concerned about your sister. I don't want to be worried about both of you. Do us both a favor and go to your friend Ken's place and stay put until Carissa's found. I'll contact you as soon as we track her down."

"Wait, Tío, please you haven't even heard my...."

"That's enough. Do as I say. Stay out of the way and allow my investigators to handle this case. Goodbye." He hangs up abruptly.

Marissa is beyond frustrated that he didn't give her a chance to tell him about what she has uncovered and that he didn't share with her what he already knew about the Nassine brothers.

She grabs her telephone and calls Ken again. "Stay put. I'm headed to your place instead."

When she arrives at Ken's it feels weird to think it was only hours earlier that she flew out of here hungover and half-crazed, not remembering much about the night before and not knowing what to expect in the day ahead.

His door opens and he pulls her into a warm embrace and a smooth kiss. His arm remains around her shoulder as they step inside the warmth of his apartment where she feels safe. He takes her jacket and places it over the back of the couch. They sit at the dining room table, which also doubles as a work space for him. There's a cardboard box haphazardly filled with videotapes, a chipped coffee mug and a few other items that he must have brought from the TV station when he walked off the job.

She tells him about CC's current situation as he gets her something to drink. She tells him about the silent alarm, the note CC left for her client, the stashed note she found.

"Is that true? Was she sick?" Ken asks as he walks back to the dining room table and sets down a glass of water.

"I doubt she was sick. She would never leave those dogs alone. I think CC was forced to leave, which is why I went by there to find out if her coworkers could tell me anything." Marissa goes on to explain where their clubs are located, about the mysterious disappearance of club owner Enrique Sanchez, the newspaper articles linking the Austin brothers with the elder Nassine from Houston who's probably their father or an uncle and her conversation with Professor Nassine.

"Wow, you got a lot of information in a short period of time."

"I tried to tell my uncle all this on the phone. I also wanted to ask him what he already knew about the Nassines, but I didn't get a chance to ask because he cut me off."

"You can't blame him for being worried about you."

"Ken, the Nassine brothers are dangerous, not just because of the pet store incident. I truly believe that they're somehow linked to my parents' murders. Tío Hector should have told me the truth! My sister's in serious trouble. She called me as I was leaving her job site and sounded really weird. I need to find her. I can't just sit here and do nothing! I'll go crazy."

"I know you, Marissa. There is nothing your uncle or I can say that will keep you from pursuing this."

"Now that you mention it, I do have a plan, but you have to promise to keep an open mind."

He nods and she begins her idea.

As she talks, Ken draws on a notepad. She knows he is listening to her but doesn't know if doodling is his way of relieving tension. When she's done talking, he turns the notepad around. It's a diagram of the three hundred block of East Sixth Street where at least three of the Nassine nightclubs are adjacent to each other. He says, "The three clubs are all located on the bottom floor of a building, which takes up an entire city block. A while back, when I was getting ready to set up a live shot nearby, I checked out the floor plan of the property to see if there was a way to run a cable through a door or window of the building. Anyway, I discovered there's a back hallway that runs the length of the building and connects all three clubs."

"I can't believe you already have a layout of the property! It's like you're a mind reader. So, there's a way to get into the clubs unnoticed."

"Yep, that back hallway connects all the clubs."

"That's where we need to be in order to keep an eye on who is coming and going."

Ken opens his computer and pulls up a street map of the same area of Sixth Street. He magnifies it for a closer look. On the map are several tiny blinking lights.

"Where did this map come from? It says 'Restricted Site.' Is this a police map?"

"I refuse to answer that question without first consulting my attorney."

"Ken, seriously. What are those blinking lights? Do those represent the location of security cameras installed by APD?" The answer is critical since at least one of the blinking lights is directly in front of the exit of the Moroccan Hideaway while two more lights are across from the entrance of the Moroccan Hideaway and Tiger Eyes.

Marissa is excited but cautious. *If Ken has accessed a restricted use website we could be breaking the law.*

"I am not revealing the origin of this site," Ken says. Just take a good look at it. Study it closely and let's come up with a plan to get in there and find your sister."

"Oh, don't worry. I have a foolproof plan." She takes a picture of the site with her phone and jots down some notes about distance and the location of some key landmarks. The detailed map Ken pulled up shows where a covered bus stop is located along with a massive concrete column that serves as a base for a giant outdoor sign. A little further down is a food trailer. All three are along the sidewalk across the street from the entrance to the clubs.

"What if I slip into the clubs looking and acting like CC?" Marissa asks. "I have a key to her apartment and can go and put together one of her 'party girl' outfits. I know what she wears, her perfume, even what she drinks. I know I can pull this off. I totally know my sister. Sometimes I know her better than she knows herself!" Her mind starts buzzing with ideas for how to fix her hair and makeup to look exactly like her.

"Wait a minute. If you're worried she's in danger what makes you think you won't be in danger, too?" he protests.

Marissa reaches over and puts her arms around his neck and pulls him close. "Because I won't be by myself," she purrs. "You'll be with me!" And then she kisses him softly. She holds the kiss just long enough to know she not only has his full attention but more importantly, his full cooperation.

Once she's convinced Ken of her plan to take on CC's identity, they get in his car and head to her sister's apartment.

Twenty-Eight

Ken drives along Sixth Street so they can scope out the scene before it gets lively. It's just after six o'clock and most workers who occupy downtown buildings and state offices are already gone for the day. A few bars are busy catering to after-work happy hours, but the real action won't take place for at least three more hours. That's when Austin's club scene will be hopping. And this is no any ordinary Thursday night in November. It also happens to be the weekend that the University of Texas Longhorns will be playing Oklahoma State for the number one spot in the Big Twelve in a nationally televised game.

The majority of students won't be in class tomorrow because they'll be partying hard tonight. As a reporter, Marissa has covered plenty of these crazy football weekends. When she was a student, she attended more than her share of pre-game blowouts. The local stations, along with ESPN's Longhorn Network, will have live trucks and crews set up along Sixth Street to capture the pre-game revelry. The keg parties that start in fraternity and sorority houses near campus will spill over into the Entertainment District. By nine o'clock, it'll be a huge impromptu parade of drunken college students as well as older alumni trying to recapture their glory days.

Marissa hates to admit it, but she's itching to be in the middle of the action, covering the antics. If she weren't under suspension, and her sister wasn't in trouble, she would have volunteered to work a double shift at the television station just to be part of tonight's news coverage, which is like covering New Year's Eve in New York City. She knows from experience that fights will break out, a couple of drunk guys will be arrested and a few intoxicated girls will try to get on TV by flashing their bare breasts in the background during an unsuspecting reporter's live shot. Instead, she'll be trying to blend into the crowd so that she can make her way inside the clubs dressed like her sister.

Ken and Marissa leave Sixth Street behind and a few minutes later pull into the parking lot of her sister's apartment complex. From the outside, the apartments all look the same. It's a large complex with more than ten different buildings, a pool and an activity center. Most of the residents, like CC, are single adults who like to party. CC says she enjoys the social life here, although she rarely invites Marissa to join her. At first, Marissa was hurt, but now she realizes it's important to CC to have her own friends and social life.

There's no one around in the courtyard, which makes it easy for Marissa and Ken to slip into CC's apartment unnoticed. Once inside, she looks around and sees that everything is just as expected—comfortable, but messy—at least by Marissa's standards. She resists the urge to fluff the pillows on her couch, fold the throw blanket that's tossed on one end of the sofa and straighten the books on the scuffed up coffee table. There is at least a week's worth of dirty dishes in the sink and the trashcan's overflowing.

Ken goes over to the combination bookcase and entertainment center where CC keeps her music collection, a sound system and her television. While he occupies himself looking at CC's CDs, Marissa slips into her sister's bedroom and starts going through her closet, looking for the perfect Sixth Street outfit—something tight-fitting and sexy. Marissa is stunned to see hanger after hanger of designer outfits—Prada, Gucci, Louis Vuitton, Chanel and Valentino. The expensive dresses, slacks, tops, shoes, purses and beautiful signature pieces of jewelry are enough to rival any fashion boutique. *How the hell did she get the money to buy all this? Scooping dog poop did not pay for this wardrobe!*

Marissa takes out her phone and consults the Facebook photo of CC taken at the Moroccan Hideaway. Then she gets to work transforming herself into CC. The clothes are easy since they're the exact same size. The exaggerated makeup is a little more of a challenge, but she finds everything she needs, including eyeliner and false eyelashes, in the vanity area of CC's bathroom. Marissa usually wears her hair down—a professional look that might even be considered boring by some fashion standards. It works for television news. CC's hair is a couple of inches longer than Marissa's and she usually wears it in a ponytail, especially while working around dogs. Marissa decides to put her hair up in a sleek, dramatic style that CC's sporting in the Facebook photo.

When she's finished dressing, she walks into the living room and asks Ken, "So? What do you think? Do I look like CC?"

He glances up from the book he's been reading and the look on his face tells her what she needs to know. He's so startled he almost drops the book but manages to recover from his shock in time to catch it before it falls to the ground. "Wow! Marissa, is that you?"

"Marissa? No, silly. Marissa is my boring, extremely professional twin sister. I'm Carissa. I'm the free spirit. The party girl!"

Ken laughs. "Is this what your sister looks like when she goes out on the town? I don't know anything about fashion, but you look like a runway model."

"Thanks. I'm glad this look impresses you…. I think…." Marissa walks across the room, slowly, trying to get used to the stiletto heels. "I hope I don't break an ankle walking in these! I looked for some flats in her closet but there aren't any. It was either these or running shoes." She sits down at the dining room table. "You wouldn't believe what I found in her closet."

"What? Weapons? Drugs? Dead bodies?"

"Okay. Ha-ha. I'm slowly getting used to your weird sense of humor. No, nothing illegal. At least I don't think it's illegal...unless they're stolen or knock-off items. My sister's closet is full of very expensive clothes. Get this. The items I'm wearing, including the shoes, the watch and the purse, are worth more than I make in a month. Can you believe it? Somehow my sister has become the proud owner of a complete wardrobe of designer clothes."

"Well, you look amazing. Here."

"What's this?"

"It's a little something I rigged for you to keep us in communication as you make your way into the club." He walks over to the table where she's seated. "Here, let me show you how all this works. Hand me the purse you'll be carrying."

She hands him the Prada bag that's about the size of a small lunch box. She finds it hard to believe that something so tiny is worth a couple of thousand dollars.

Ken opens the purse and places a tiny gadget that's smaller than a cell phone inside. "This is a state of the art camera. It'll be transmitting images back to me. I'm taping it in place so that the lens is always pointing through this opening on the side of the purse where the top of it folds over. As long as the bag's hanging off your shoulder, the camera will be focused straight ahead. It also has a very sensitive microphone that will pick up all nearby sounds. I'll be watching the images and tracking your movement on this." Ken pulls out a screen that is not much bigger than that of a large smart phone.

"I feel like an undercover cop. Hey, Ken, before we go any further you have to promise me that you'll contact my Tío Hector and let him know what we're doing. Only *after* I'm inside the club, okay?"

"So I get to take the heat when he explodes?"

"On second thought, maybe we should wait until we have some actual information to give him."

Marissa decides not to tell Ken about the weird feeling she's had all day that someone has been watching her. She has no way of knowing if it was undercover officers sent by her uncle or somebody the Nassine brothers sent to carry out those awful threats in those creepy phone calls and email. She's sure if she tells Ken he won't let her go through with the nightclub plan. She promises herself to come clean to Ken *and* Tío Hector as soon as CC is safe.

"I want you to practice with the camera," Ken says to her.

It doesn't take long for Marissa to get the hang of it. They also program his cell phone number into hers so that if anything happens she can hit one number and he'll respond immediately.

As they get ready to leave CC's apartment Marissa looks around one last time and tries to get into her sister's head to figure out where she is and what she's thinking. When they were kids, she used to feel a strong connection even when they were apart. As she locks the apartment door behind her, she hopes that twin bond is still strong.

She and Ken start walking to his car when a woman about her age passes them going the opposite direction. She's dressed in workout clothes and is carrying a bag of fast food and a to-go cup. She stops sipping on her straw long enough to say, "Oh hey, CC. You look smoking hot! Are you headed to the club?"

For a moment, Marissa forgets she's dressed like her sister, but she recovers instantly and says, "Thanks. I'm showing a friend around town, but yeah I'll probably end up there. Sorry. Can't chat, we're in a hurry. See ya later." She grabs Ken by the arm and they move along quickly.

Marissa throws her head back in an exaggerated gesture like her sister would and lets out a laugh that sounds like her. As soon as they get out of earshot from the woman, Marissa says to Ken, "Whoa! That was close. I wouldn't have been able to pull off a conversation with my sister's neighbor. But it's a positive omen that she thought I was CC. Don't you think?"

"I sure hope so. That was a good dress rehearsal, but the real test is still ahead," Ken says as he opens the passenger door of his car for her. Marissa finds it difficult to get into the car gracefully while wearing a tight, short dress and monster high heels. She can't help but wonder how it's possible to have so much fun in such an impractical outfit.

On the short ride downtown, they talk briefly about the layout of the club and how to get to the back hallway that connects the three venues.

"I'll hang back so you can get into the club by yourself first without raising any suspicions. Then I'll join you inside. Don't worry, I'll be monitoring your movements the entire time from the camera shots in your purse. Remember, you can alert me with a touch of a button on your cell phone."

The technology boosts her self-confidence, although she has no idea what's waiting for her on the other side of the club entrance.

They pull into a public parking lot that's a block away from the club, but before getting out of the car, Ken grabs Marissa's arm and pulls her to him so that her face and lips are inches from his. He says in a serious voice, "You're a special woman, Marissa, to care so deeply about your sister even without knowing what challenges or emotional issues she might be facing. Your loyalty and determination blow me away. I've never met anyone like you and I want you to know that whatever happens tonight, I'm here to see it through to the end."

An intense physical gravity pulls them together in a spark-filled, passionate kiss that makes the rest of the world melt away. For a few moments, nothing else matters. It feels amazing, and Marissa understands how a great love story begins. First, as friends or colleagues, working side-by-side and fueled by the desire to achieve a mutual goal before feelings evolve into a physical passion that burns for a lifetime.

Ken pulls away and she knows it's time for her to make her way inside the club. She gets out of the car and starts walking around the corner to the Moroccan Hideaway. Sixth Street is already packed with college coeds who are there to party. Most are wearing burnt orange—the school color of the University of Texas.

Marissa notices a KATX live truck parked along the curb right in the middle of the people parade and across from the entrance to the Moroccan Hideaway. She goes out of her way to avoid being spotted by her colleagues in the live truck. She is not too worried and assumes the reporter and photographer are inside the air-conditioned truck, taking it easy with the music turned up loud enough to drown out the noise of the Sixth Street crowd. She knows if it were her assignment, she'd be outside in the middle of the action where she could monitor the crowd in case anything out of the ordinary happened. You never know when a homeless person will sucker punch a drunk guy who refuses to hand over his pocket change or some stupid frat boy might decide to grope a passing female. The best journalists are always ready with the camera rolling. *The lazy crew tucked inside the live unit will be lucky if they get to watch the action on the competitor's newscast!* she thinks.

As soon as she passes the live truck without being detected, her cell phone rings.

It's Ken. "Walk around for a few more minutes before you approach the club entrance. Call me before you go inside."

"No problem. I can use the extra time to get used to walking in these heels!" Just as she's about to cross the street to watch a street performer who is juggling while riding a unicycle, she stops in her tracks. Two uniformed police officers on horseback are slowly making their way through the crowd in her direction. She turns to avoid being seen by them. It's the first time in her life that she can remember ever deliberately avoiding contact with police officers. If there's a patron saint of police, she seeks forgiveness for lying to her Tío. And for good measure, she asks for protection on her mission to find CC.

When she turns back around to make her way to the Moroccan Hideaway, she sees the cops on horseback have moved on. She heads over to the club, activates the camera in her purse, puts the earpiece in her right ear and calls Ken. "Is the camera working?" she asks.

"Everything looks good," he assures her.

She takes a deep breath and says, "Okay, CC. Here I come."

She steps up to the doorman standing outside the club. He's wearing loose fitting pants and a tiny vest over a bare, muscled chest and he has on a turban. With arms crossed in front of his chest, he looks like the genie in the Disney movie, *Aladdin*. She hopes he'll grant her wish and let her into the club.

In a booming voice, he says, "Well, if it isn't Miss CC. Welcome to the Moroccan Hideaway." Then, in a grand gesture, he bows at the waist slightly, causing the feathered plume sticking out of his turban to sweep down her chest. His movement makes Marissa laugh and she says in her best CC imitation, "Why thank you, sugar." She breezes past him, hoping the rest of her evening goes as smoothly.

Ken says in her ear, "Your first wish was just granted. Keep your purse cam steady so I can follow your movements. I'm walking up to the club now. There are two people in line ahead of me waiting to get into the club, but I'm not far behind you."

"I'll meet you at the bar. The first drink's on me. Non-alcoholic, of course, since we're on duty."

She hangs up and steps inside the club. The layout is just like Ken's diagram. There's a huge dance floor with flashing colored lights, pulsating music and people who are moving while trying to act non-chalant. Alongside the dance floor is a row of VIP booths where groups of four to six people are enjoying a close-up view of the dancers. Just past the dance floor, toward the very back of the room, is a bar that stretches the entire length of the room. On one side is the DJ booth. Just to the left of that is a hallway with three doors. The first two doors on the left are marked as restrooms. The third door on the right has a small window and a sign that reads: "Employees Only." She sees a security pad on the wall near the door handle that requires an access code before gaining entry.

This is going to be trickier than I thought. Just as she's about to turn around and head to the bar to wait for Ken, a woman comes out of the bathroom and practically bumps into her while Marissa is standing there, wondering how the hell she's going to get past the security system. Judging from her low-slung, navel-exposing harem pants and bare midriff, Marissa assumes she's a waitress. The woman looks up from adjusting her pants, smiles and says, "Oh hey, CC! Are you looking for Haddy?"

Haddy? A nickname for Hadid. "Uh, yeah. Have you seen him?" she stutters. "I wasn't sure if he's in the back." Marissa motions to the Employees Only door before saying, "I changed my personal code, and I can't remember it. Can you get me in?"

With a smile reserved for a woman who she believes is the club owner's girlfriend, she punches in a four-digit code and the red light quickly turns green. An electronic beep signals access. *How handy to have the purse cam pointed right at the security pad to see which digits the woman is entering,* she thinks.

"Hey, thanks for helping me out," Marissa says to the woman. "But, on second thought, I'd better slip into the powder room first." She puts her hand over her mouth and makes a slight gagging noise, like she's holding back a wave of nausea. She hopes the woman doesn't follow her into the restroom—she doesn't. At the mirror, two women are primping. Both are dressed like her. She slips into a stall and waits for them to leave before calling Ken.

As soon as she is sure she is alone, she calls Ken and asks, "Did you get the code that was entered?"

"Yes, I did. You were standing in just the right spot. Now come out here to the bar so we can plan our next move."

"I'm on my way."

She hopes the mystery to finding her sister is just on the other side of that door.

Twenty-Nine

The instant Marissa steps from the restroom into the hallway, a strong hand grabs her left arm and with one forceful move, she's whipped around and stands face-to-face with an obviously angry man. He's good-looking and extremely muscular with dark hair and an olive-colored complexion. She freezes in recognition of the face she's seen in photos. It's Nassour Nassine, the co-owner of the clubs and more importantly, the brother of Carissa's suspected boyfriend and torturer.

"Where do you think you're going, Marissa? Or would you prefer that I call you *Carissa* to match your outfit?" His voice is deep and seething with anger. She recognizes the voice immediately. It's the same voice who threatened her on the phone!

"Who are you?" she asks defiantly, hoping his answer will be captured by Ken's camera.

"Ah. Always the reporter—asking questions and snooping around for answers. Well, not this time, Marissa. You're coming with me, and if you're as smart as you are beautiful, then you'll do so quietly." Without saying another word, Nassour tightens his grasp on her arm and pulls her forward as he effortlessly uses his free hand to enter an access code to open the Employees Only door.

He pulls Marissa through a dimly lit hallway and she purposely stumbles on her high heels to slow him down. "Slow down! You're walking too fast. I can't keep up in these shoes."

Her pleas have no effect on him. She does her best to keep up with his fast pace while peppering him with questions. "Where are we going? Where is my sister? What have you done with Carissa?"

He glares at her before stopping outside of a double, highly-glossed wooden door. A gold-plated sign reads: "Private." Underneath is something written in foreign lettering. *Arabic, perhaps?*

Nassour knocks and an electronic buzz is heard. The door slowly swings open. He pushes Marissa forward into what looks like a waiting area. It's a beautifully decorated room with impressive artwork on the walls, an intricately tiled floor, plush chairs and a matching couch. An elaborate aquarium sits on top of a three-foot tall platform in the center of the room. The water-filled tank casts an iridescent glow in all directions. Beyond the waiting area, there's another door that's wide open. A voice from the room calls out in a sarcastic tone, "Marissa, don't just stand there looking like a prostitute who doesn't know where her next trick is coming from. Get in here. Now!"

Nassour nudges her in the middle of her back, a little more forcefully than is necessary to get her to move forward.

Ay Dios! She hopes Ken is monitoring what's happening. *Stay calm. Breathe. Don't panic*, she tells herself.

She walks into a luxurious office with expensive artwork on the walls and ornate furniture, like the kind you'd see on display in a museum. She walks across plush carpet until Nassour makes her come to an abrupt halt. Directly in front of her, sitting behind a polished steel and glass-topped desk, is a man who looks like Nassour. This man's also good-looking but is slightly older and has an angry and arrogant air about him. In the corner behind the desk on the left side of the room sits a metal crate, custom-made to match the desk. Inside is a small Yorkshire Terrier that hasn't stopped barking since she entered the room. *It must be Hadid's dog, Ace, that Carissa used to care for at Royal Pet Watchers. Damn dog! This is all your fault*, she thinks.

"That's a pretty mean watchdog you have on duty," she snipes.

Unfortunately, her attempt at humor is lost on the man seated in front of her. "Silence!" Fueled by anger, he jumps up from his chair, leans forward, places his hands on the desk and in a voice trembling with fury states, "I didn't bring you here so you can mock me. You'll not speak until I say so and you will answer all my questions!" He snaps his fingers, which prompts Nassour to place a chair directly in front of the desk. He then motions for Marissa to sit down. She manages to discreetly move the purse from her shoulder and hold it in her lap so that the camera lens is facing Hadid who's retaken his seat behind the desk. The dog finally quiets down, although she still hears a low growl coming from the crate.

Hadid lights a cigar. The obnoxious smell makes her crinkle her nose. She turns her head in an attempt to avoid the smoke he's exhaling in her direction.

"Ah…just like the other Cavelo bitch. She's also offended by my cigar smoke. Neither of you appreciates the rich tobacco that's used to make a fine cigar. Perhaps I should force you to smoke one and then you might become a connoisseur of rare commodities. It's taken a while, but your sister has learned to appreciate the best that money can buy." He stops talking, draws on his cigar and exhales slowly. "I see by your outfit you, too, have a taste for haute couture." Hadid swivels his chair so he can prop his feet on the desk while still puffing on his cigar.

Marissa can no longer contain herself. She stands. "What do you want from me?" She feels herself trembling with anger. Instinctively, her voice gets louder and more forceful, "Where the hell is my sister?"

Nassour pulls her back into the chair to restrain her. She sits back down, silently seething, waiting for answers.

In a voice dripping with sarcasm, Hadid says, "Let's see if I have this right. The reporter who's trying to land a main network anchor position is sitting before me dressed like an expensive whore and is asking questions about her twin sister?"

Marissa remains silent.

He laughs. "Are you surprised I know so much about you? You're here because you refuse to stop meddling in areas that don't concern you and because you ignored my repeated warnings to stay away from my business ventures." His anger increases. "You have no idea about the inconvenience and expense you caused by exposing my men who were about to smuggle rare birds out of this country, birds which are coveted commodities worth thousands of dollars each. You think storming into the loading dock area armed with a video camera somehow makes you important and invincible? Much like your meek and ignorant father mistakenly thought he was invincible so many years ago as he hid behind a cheap night watchman's uniform and badge!"

His words knock Marissa back into her chair with such force she feels as if she's been slapped. Just thinking about her parents revives the pain of losing both to violent criminals. It also brings into focus the image of CC being slapped by this same man just two days earlier.

Hadid continues, "I can tell by your facial expression that the truth is beginning to register." He takes another draw on his foul-smelling cigar and again exhales the smoke in her direction. "Your father interrupted my father's lucrative business—now my business." He recounts the details in an angrier tone as he speaks of the impact on his family. "One of the men arrested turned out to be the lowest form of human being ever to walk the earth. He's not worthy to wipe the shoes of any member of my family. He's an outcast among other Persians because he implicated my father and agreed to testify against him. The great Hassid was arrested and later convicted on trumped-up charges of organizing criminal activities and possessing stolen property. This happened because of the actions of a traitor. Such disloyalty is never tolerated in our culture. Never! That's why my father's conviction and fifteen-year prison sentence couldn't pass without retaliation against your father. I want you to understand your parents were killed in retaliation for the fate of my parents. My father, a disgraced and broken man, and my mother who went insane." He slumps back in his chair.

Marissa adjusts her body slightly to ensure the camera in her purse is getting a direct shot of Hadid as he confesses to the crimes of his father and his father's followers. It's not easy hearing the truth of what happened to her parents so many years ago. As she sits in the opulent office, it puzzles her that her father, an honest man, with a willingness to do the right thing is dead, while Nassine and his brother live the high life.

Hadid leans over the top of his desk and glares at her. "Now here we are so many years later, rebuilding our business and our family's legacy, then you walk into our lives and disrupt our operations. The Nassines have been cursed since the day the Cavelos entered our world! And now it's up to me to end this interference once and for all."

He snaps his fingers, and Nassour moves into action, grabbing Marissa from behind. Before he can put his hands on her, Marissa jumps up out of her chair and takes a bold stand directly in front of the evil man whose family is responsible for her parents' murders. She searches for the words that will buy her even a few seconds of time to turn the tables against Hadid. "Interference? You think I have intentionally interfered with you? You mean like you interfered with Enrique Sanchez's club operations?" She hopes the name of the club owner who disappeared will catch Hadid off guard.

She hears Nassour gasp with surprise from behind, which assures her that her question hit the mark.

Hadid pauses to respond, "And what do you know about the man? Do you know he owed me nearly half a million dollars? That he tried to trick my brother into signing over his half of the rights to the club properties? Sanchez was a liar and thief who deserved to be eliminated from the face of this earth. The way I see it, I performed a service to this community by getting rid of such a despicable character. It's pure coincidence that my brother and I happened to benefit from Sanchez's disappearance and the club he left behind."

"What about my sister? Did you make her disappear, too?" She's standing in front of the desk, trying to steady the camera. "Tell me where my sister is, you monster!"

With a full-bodied laugh, he replies, "What makes you think I've done something with your sister?"

Marissa is certain that he's manipulated her sister and is keeping her against her will. *She's probably tied up. Maybe she's somewhere in this very building!*

Before Marissa can say anything else Hadid says, "Why don't I let your sister answer your ridiculous questions for herself." He turns in his chair and reaches out to a security system control panel that's positioned on the corner of his massive desk. He pushes an intercom button and speaks into a microphone, "Come into my office."

Within seconds, a door hidden in the wall of the office glides open and Marissa sees her sister. Her hair and makeup, her short, trendy dress and even her platform shoes are a mirror image of Marissa and the way she's dressed. It's like looking into a three-dimensional mirror. She lets out a squeal of relief. "CC! Are you all right?" Marissa moves toward her and attempts to fling her arms around her in a reassuring hug.

"Don't. Touch. Me." She clearly does not want to see her twin.

Marissa is speechless. She watches in silence as Carissa walks around the desk so she can lean back on the front of it. "What? Were you expecting a tearful, 'Oh Marissa! Thank goodness you're here to rescue me?'" Marissa has never heard her sound so sarcastic. "The last thing I need is to be rescued by you—or anyone. I'm perfectly fine here. This…" she moves her hand in a sweeping motion around the room, "…is where I belong."

"So…you're here of your own freewill? No one's forcing you to be here? I don't understand." The video of her being slapped comes to mind. *That was real, wasn't it?* Then she thinks about the hidden note CC left pleading for help and instructing her to check out the Nassines. *That was also very real.* Then there was that mysterious phone call from her just hours earlier. Although it ended abruptly, in a way that didn't make sense, Marissa knows in her gut that CC was reaching out to her. But more than that, CC must know what these men did to their parents. *There's no way Carissa can be siding with the enemy!* She tries to reason with her sister. "CC, whatever you've been told, or promised, don't believe it. The Nassine brothers are not to be trusted. They're using you. These men and their associates killed Mami and Papi. I'm here because I love you and I want you to come with me. I'm your only surviving relative."

Carissa turns away from Marissa as if she is about to walk out of the room through the same door she entered. Marissa grabs her hand to stop her from leaving. "Wait. CC! "

She turns suddenly and Marissa is stunned by the fury in her eyes, "You may be my only living relative, but you don't care about me! You only care about advancing your career. You have no idea what it's like living in your shadow…to be mistaken for *you*, the popular television reporter. I'm sick of being asked about you and always feeling inadequate when anyone compares me to you. You've never approved of my friends, how I spend my free time, the clubs where I hang out or even my job. Well, I have news for you, *mi hermana*, I'm no longer stuck in your shadow, trying to live up to your expectations. I'm my own person and yes, I choose to stay exactly where I am. I don't need your approval and I don't want it."

Her words are like daggers to Marissa's heart.

Hadid, who's been quietly watching Carissa's tirade interjects, "Go ahead, Carissa, tell her why she's here."

CC walks around to stand directly behind the chair where Hadid is sitting. She places her hands squarely on his shoulders and says, "I lured you here on purpose, starting with that note I left behind the cash register. I knew your nosy reporter instincts would lead you to snoop around the clubs, but I never would have imagined you'd go through the trouble to dress like me. By the way, you look pretty hot. It's a big change from the squeaky clean image you portray on TV." She lets out a wicked laugh. "If you're nice, I might let you borrow more of my expensive wardrobe since you'll never be able to afford luxury items on your salary. On second thought, you won't really be needing much of a wardrobe from now on."

Her laughter is so familiar it sends chills through Marissa. She's crushed as she watches and listens to her sister's venom towards her. *Is she on drugs? Or has she been brainwashed?*

Hadid speaks up. "Just like your father, you've interfered with a very important Nassine family operation that cost me millions in potential profits. And now you come here asking questions about our sworn enemy, Enrique Sanchez. His whereabouts are none of your business. You leave me no choice but to seal your fate." He stops to flick the ashes from his cigar into a solid, onyx ashtray. "You've been lured here to do two things. First, you'll write a brief letter to your station manager explaining your decision to quit the business and start a new life elsewhere. You'll sign it and leave no forwarding address. With your current suspension—oh yes, we know all about your fall from grace—it's the perfect opportunity for you to take some personal time. Sort of like Enrique Sanchez did a while back. No one will be suspicious when you fail to return." His smile is pure evil. "And, your second reason for being here is to say goodbye to your sister and to let her reveal the truth about the life she's now leading." He reaches and pats CC's hand, which has been resting on his shoulder. It's a signal from Hadid that he's granting her permission to speak.

"Marissa, you blew it when you busted the pet smuggling efforts. You should have stuck to the fluff pieces you're so good at covering. How stupid of you to think that sticking your nose and camera where they don't belong would catapult you into the national spotlight. Ha!"

Marissa is stunned. Carissa seems evil in her giddiness as she takes verbal swipes at her. "Look at you sitting there in *my* expensive clothes, *my* makeup and sporting *my* hairstyle! I have to tell ya, sis, you have never looked so good. Seriously. Your work wardrobe is so boring. And your casual clothes are drab. But hey, even *my* clothes will only take you so far. Besides the dumb doorman, did you think you were going to fool anyone into thinking you were me?"

Marissa crosses her fingers, hoping the code caught on camera by Ken will gain him access to this back office. Suddenly a loud crash comes from the waiting room area causing Ace to start barking up a storm. Somehow the dog manages to push open the cage of his kennel and begins running around the office. Prompted by the chaos, Nassour reaches for a gun tucked in the back waistband of his pants, but before pulling the weapon out, Marissa elbows him as hard as she can right in his gut. The move throws him off balance. At that instant, Ace is underfoot, causing Nassour to stumble backward and fall. Marissa turns around and sees Carissa and Hadid slipping out through the wall panel door where CC entered the office just a few minutes earlier.

At that moment, officers with guns drawn enter from the waiting area and slam Nassour to the ground even as he tries to regain his footing. He's handcuffed before he knows what hit him. Marissa's heart stops as she looks behind the row of cops who've entered the office. She sees the one person she never doubted would walk through that door—Ken. He has a video camera rolling on the drama that's unfolding all around her.

Marissa has never been so relieved to see another human being in her life. She wants to throw her arms around him, kiss him, tell him how grateful she is to see him. But before she can say a word, he hands her a microphone. She takes it and immediately plunges into action. It's as natural as breathing. "I'm Marissa Cavelo, coming to you live from the back office of the Moroccan Hideaway, a popular Sixth Street night spot where Austin police are breaking up an alleged crime ring. The key suspects are two brothers…"

Right on cue, Ken focuses the camera on Nassour, who's lying face down on the ground with his wrists secured in handcuffs.

"One of the suspects is in custody here on the ground. He's been initially identified as Nassour Nassine."

The camera pans to the panel door where Carissa and Hadid slipped out moments earlier. There's slight hesitation in her delivery because the last thing she wants to do is identify her sister as a suspected criminal to a live television audience.

The panel door slides open and in walks Hadid with his hands handcuffed behind his back. Behind him with his gun drawn is Tío Hector! But there's no sign of CC.

Marissa continues her report. "Now entering this private office in police custody is the second suspect who's been identified as Hadid Nassine. If you're just joining us, I'm investigative reporter Marissa Cavelo. You probably won't recognize me…" she slowly steps into the view of the camera. "…since this is not my usual look. My outfit, makeup and hairstyle are all part of my attempt to gain access into the inner workings of a crime ring. The criminal activity that's been exposed in the past hour dates back for years and involves a long list of everything from stolen rare animals to a missing Austin nightclub owner." Her voice cracks just slightly with emotion. "Additionally, there's strong evidence collected in this office tonight that the suspects may also be responsible for a case that's of great personal interest to me—the murder of my parents more than fifteen years ago in Houston. Viewers can be sure that this is just the beginning of this investigative report. Live in downtown Austin, I'm Marissa Cavelo."

Although she is anxious to find CC, to greet Ken and to talk to her uncle, Marissa holds the microphone steady and keeps her gaze focused on the camera until she hears Ken yell, "We're clear!" Ken drops the camera from his shoulder and places it on the ground. In the meantime, four more officers enter the office. All are wearing SWAT team gear, which signals to Marissa that the officers were armed and ready for a possible confrontation. With both Nassine brothers in custody, the immediate danger is over and none of the officers have their weapons drawn, except for Tío Hector.

Marissa collapses back into her chair. The physical scare is over, but the emotional uncertainty of what happens next is still weighing heavy on her. She puts her head in her hands to think.

She looks up and sees Ken, grinning and walking toward her. He is carrying both the high-tech camera he installed in her purse, and the purse, which is slung over his shoulder. The sight of this good-looking guy carrying an expensive women's handbag makes her smile.

He kneels down in front of her, places the purse and the camera in her lap and says, "You kicked ass, Cavelo! That live shot was the best ever. Your timing was perfect and the info you shared with viewers was spot-on!" He stretches up to enfold her in a huge embrace and their lips meet in a perfect kiss. His arms are strong and yet his touch is so gentle. There's something so genuine about this man that's slowly pulling her closer and closer to the edge of falling in love with him.

When they release each other from their embrace, Ken continues talking excitedly, "I was just moments behind you when Nassour cornered you outside the women's restroom and hustled you into the hallway and office. I knew I needed backup before following you in here. While monitoring every move with the camera, I called your uncle to tell him what was happening. His men showed up in a matter of minutes. They were already standing by, waiting for orders to move in. You have your uncle to thank for the speedy response. I'll let you ask him about that when you get a chance."

Then he tenderly cups her face in his right hand and strokes her cheek with his thumb as he says, "I was so worried about you. I was seeing and hearing everything that Hadid and your sister were telling you. It must have been awful to hear the truth about what happened to your parents. But you were fearless! You didn't back down and...." He stops to pat the camera that's resting in her lap. "Guess what? We captured it all on camera. The last part of the drama was broadcast to viewers as part of a crime-fighting special report!"

Broadcast to viewers? "Wait. You quit and I'm suspended, so how the heck did you get the news nerds at KATX to agree to broadcast this?"

"That's the best part! It was *not* shown on KATX. In fact, it didn't air on *any* local TV station at all. It was streamed live on the Internet—completely independent of any news channel affiliation. I just got off the phone with some tech friends who helped me get this on the web. They're going crazy! Your undercover effort tonight was seen by a hundred thousand people! And that's just the number of hits while it was streaming. That doesn't count the number of times Internet users have pulled it up since the live coverage ended. It's out-of-control!"

Marissa can't believe what she's hearing. *A hundred thousand people is more than the number of viewers on the best night for the KATX ten o'clock news! A winning ratings night brings in sixty-five-thousand!* "How did you get so many people to watch on the Internet?"

"It's simple. When we decided we were going to rig a camera and go find your sister and get the dirt on the Nassine's, I let my tech friends know and they launched a widespread notice on social media. Periscope, Twitter and Facebook have never seen so much activity in such a short period of time. You don't realize it, but you garnered huge name recognition following the pet store bust and the dance school exposé! You've been trending high for the past two days. You're a cult hero and you didn't even know it!" He stands up laughing and beaming like someone who's just won a Powerball jackpot.

Marissa feels like she's riding an emotional rollercoaster. She can't help but be excited about the unbelievable number of Internet viewers that they've managed to attract. She's also thrilled to be part of the effort to bring down the notorious Nassine brothers. But her euphoria gives way to sadness as she thinks about CC. *How could the one person I love more than myself turn against me with such obvious hate and loathing? And where is she now?*

She stands up and kisses Ken on the cheek. "Please give me a few minutes alone with Tío Hector. I promise this won't take long."

He kisses her on the lips. "I'll be in the waiting area outside of the office." He takes his equipment and leaves the room.

Her attention turns back to the activity in the office where one of the cops has approached Tío Hector to relieve him of standing guard over Hadid. As the officer escorts the suspect out of the room, Hadid looks directly at Marissa and sneers, "Cavelo, I'm not done with you or your sister." The officer tells him to keep quiet and to keep moving.

Just as Hadid walks past Marissa, she looks him right in the eye and says, "Revenge to preserve your family's honor will only cause you more grief and earn you more time behind bars. I'm here with evidence to be sure of both! That's a promise I will keep on behalf of my parents and my sister!"

The officer nudges Hadid out of the room and out of her sight. She waits just a few seconds to be sure he's out of earshot before turning to Tío Hector who's holstered his gun and is wrapping up an exchange on his police radio. She grabs his arm and asks him the question that's been tugging at her heart: "Where's Carissa?"

"Let's get out of the way so these officers can finish doing their job and we can talk, *mija*," he says gently.

She can tell by the look in his eyes that he has bad news. She releases her hold on his arm as he guides her to a small sofa that's in a corner of the office. After they're seated, she notices crime scene officers have quietly moved in and are busy taking photos and securing evidence including the laptop and some folders that were on Hadid's desk. One officer manages to coax the dog, Ace, back into his crate where he's whimpering for attention. Marissa guesses that the poor pooch can sense his master and caregiver are both gone.

Tío Hector takes her hand. It's a gesture he uses when he has something serious to say. "Marissa, for the second time this week you've placed yourself in grave danger and you've interfered with an ongoing police investigation."

She braces herself for the expression of disappointment and frustration that she's about to hear from the man who's been like a father to her for the past fifteen years.

Tío Hector hunches his shoulders and hangs his head as he collects his thoughts. After a brief moment, he lifts his head and looks right at her. He speaks in a strong, steady voice, "I have never been so proud of you in all my life!"

WHAT? Did Tío Hector say he's proud of me? She can't believe what she is hearing. "You're not angry with me?"

"Now, I didn't say that I wasn't mad at you. Yes, I'm aggravated at your disregard for safety, but I'm very proud of you because you have the courage to go after what you believe in and you have the determination to dig for the truth!" He pauses and sighs before continuing, "I'm going to briefly put aside what could have gone wrong and instead focus on what is going right. First, you've helped to collect crucial evidence against two known criminals. And you've linked them to the murder of Enrique Sanchez. We've reason to believe Hadid's computer and those files will reveal details of extortion and racketeering involving hundreds of victims and millions of dollars in valuable property. While you were in this back office getting Hadid Nassine to reveal important information, my officers were simultaneously shutting down all six of the clubs. It's the single largest, multi-location raid ever conducted on a network of nightclubs in the history of Texas law enforcement."

Marissa is slowly absorbing what her uncle is telling her, but there's still one key question that hasn't been answered. "Tío, I'm relieved the police investigation has been successful, but where's CC? She all but told me she hates my guts and she was taking pleasure in seeing me suffer at the hands of her boyfriend and his brother. Those men are evil and as far as I'm concerned, their biggest crime is turning my sister against me."

Her uncle moves closer and puts his arm around her shoulder. "Carissa has been taken to police headquarters for questioning. Because of my relationship with her, I removed myself from her case. I don't want to be accused of saying or doing anything that would impact her status. Before she was taken away, I advised her not to answer any questions until she's able to have an attorney present."

It's not the answer Marissa wanted to hear. She didn't want the reality of her sister's involvement in a known crime ring to be confirmed. "When can I see her?"

"First, she'll be taken to jail and booked. She'll go before a judge and hear the charges against her and she'll be allowed to talk to an attorney. At the earliest, it will be twenty-four hours before she can place a call to a relative or friend. But remember, she may not want to see or talk to you." He sighs again and Marissa knows he's also emotionally drained by the revelation of Carissa's criminal involvement. He looks like he's aged five years in the past five minutes. He continues, "Judging by the charges the Nassine's face and their vast real estate holdings and assets, this is going to be a high-profile case.

Add that to the media frenzy stirred up by your undercover involvement and I bet the best defense teams in the nation will line up to take her case pro bono. That's the best we can hope for…for your sister's sake."

Marissa nods her understanding. "Tío, tell me how police were able to respond so quickly to the situation tonight?"

"When I instructed you to leave your apartment this morning, I told you plainclothes officers would be sent to follow you, didn't I?"

"Yeah, you did say that, but I never saw a cop. Not outside my apartment complex, not when I stopped by CC's old workplace or when I went to the coffee shop."

"Haven't you learned by now that I'm a man of my word? I swore on your parents' graves to do my best to protect you and your sister, and that's exactly what my men and I have been doing all day. We followed and anticipated your every move. When you left that message saying you had talked to Carissa, I knew you were being evasive and I anticipated you'd go looking for her. When you went to Ken's apartment, officers arrived before you did and watched you leave dressed like your sister. When Ken called to alert me that you had been forced into this private office, SWAT team members were already in place, waiting for the order to move in. Other officers were instructed to simultaneously shut down all six of the bars with as little disruption or notice by the public as possible."

"Thank you," she whispers.

Again he pauses before continuing, "I had hoped I was wrong about your sister, especially after the incident where she was slapped." He sighs and shakes his head. "What she said to you tonight, however, confirms she was willingly involved with the Nassine brothers and she may be fully aware of their criminal activity. I also strongly suspect from her erratic behavior that she's on drugs. Let's hope, for her sake, she retains an excellent attorney."

She looks at the man next to her; she knows he has to be gruff and tough to have made it this far in law enforcement, but she also knows his tenderness. "Tío, I know you're a good man who'd do anything to protect me and CC, but it must be hard to extend that protection to a loved one who you suddenly realize is living on the wrong side of the law."

"You're right, *mija*. CC's actions are hard to accept, but my pledge to love and protect both of you is a commitment I made a long time ago while I was a rookie cop patrolling your family's neighborhood." He remembers his time on the beat in Houston. "Some houses were in better shape than the others. In a few yards, there were carefully tended flowering plants. Some had a *Virgin de Guadalupe* keeping watch over the property. Barking dogs, gunshots and sirens were the most common sounds after dark. Yet, during the day, freshly scrubbed children walked to school. Adults went off to work, at one or often two or more jobs, and elderly people could be seen passing the time sitting on their porches or tending to plants in their yards. It's where I grew up and where I felt the most welcome. Most of the residents were friendly and respectful. They'd wave at me as I drove by in my patrol car. I could tell there was a certain pride among the citizens in seeing a brown-skinned officer who spoke Spanish and who didn't automatically suspect them of committing a crime."

"That's exactly how I remember you, *Tío*. You were always smiling and asking all the neighbors how they were doing. Everybody on our street trusted and respected you. Plus, you always had penny candy to hand out. You were like a piñata on wheels!" She laughs as the image of a young, friendly Officer Garcia comes to mind.

"Well, I don't have to remind you how fond I became of your parents. They worked hard to take care of you and your sweet sister. Even though I'd been assigned to patrol other areas of town, I always managed to drive through your neighborhood to check on the residents there, including your parents. So, it was like a bullet through my heart when I heard the dispatcher call for homicide to your address." Hector begins to wring his hands together as the memory of that fateful day becomes vivid. "I dreaded the moment the school bus would deposit you and your sister at the end of the street. A crowd had already gathered there. The yellow crime scene tape kept the area off limits so other officers and investigators could collect evidence. Just as I feared, you and CC came running up holding each other's hands. I'll never forget the look of pure fear in your eyes. You girls had seen enough crime in the neighborhood and on the news, so the scene was nothing new to you. Regardless, it was still gut-wrenching for me to watch a senseless, violent act completely rip apart innocent lives in a flash."

Marissa bows her head at her own memories of that fateful day.

"As an officer of the law, it was possible to check on you after you were placed in foster care. I appealed to the courts to keep the two of you together, although that wasn't easy to arrange as you moved between four different foster homes before your eighteenth birthday."

Marissa takes his hand and looks at him. "You were the one constant factor in our lives with all that moving around. And CC and I were so happy when you and Marianna got married, although we were afraid you'd drift away from us. But that didn't happen. You managed to stay close. You were there to teach us how to drive and to advise us about boys and dating, although no teenage guys wanted to take a girl out whose uncle is a cop! You might have scared the boys off, but you made up for it by guiding us through the teen years. You and Marianna were there when we graduated from high school and have been at every other major event since then."

They hug for a moment, and then Tío Hector reverts to the serious demeanor that's earned him unflinching respect within the department. "Marissa, I want you to know you and your sister are like my daughters and I'll never ever waiver from that promise I made to protect both of you, no matter what the circumstances are, including your sister's involvement with the Nassines. Together, you and I are going to find out what they've done to turn her into an accomplice. I'm heartbroken about CC, but don't worry. We'll be there for your sister." He hugs Marissa again and says, "I don't think we'll get the truth out of her anytime soon, but I'll let you know in the morning what her legal status is and if she wants to see either one of us."

He gets up from the sofa, pulls Marissa to her feet and steadies her since her legs are still wobbly in her sister's heels. "Now come on, Marissa. I believe there's a young man waiting to take you out of here. Just promise me you'll get some rest tonight. And try not to worry about your sister. There's nothing either one of us can do for her until after we know her status in the morning." He leads her into the waiting area before returning to the crime scene where APD members are still busy collecting evidence.

At first, she thinks Ken is gone because she doesn't hear or see anyone in the room. It takes a moment for her tired eyes to adjust to the glow from the aquarium. That's when she spots Ken who's fallen asleep on one of the plush couches. He's clutching her sister's handbag, the item that was her best weapon in this undercover operation. She smiles as she gently nudges him awake. "Hey, knight in shining armor, this damsel is no longer in distress and she's ready to go home."

He smiles and slowly gets up from the couch. He takes her by the arm and together they walk out. Instead of leaving through the club, they slip out the back door into the alley that runs behind the club properties owned by the Nassine brothers. Ken spots his parked car just as a police officer is about to leave a parking ticket on the windshield. Ken starts muttering under his breath, "What the…?"

Marissa holds him back by the arm just as the officer looks up and sees them. The cop says, "It's Marissa Cavelo! I'd recognize you anywhere—even in that uh…" he stammers.

"Outfit would be the right word, officer. My partner, Ken, and I were just leaving."

The officer smiles as he tears up the ticket and moves out of the way to let Ken and Marissa drive off.

Thirty

n all newsrooms, there's a constant overlap of workers from every
shift. When the ten p.m. newscast is ending, the early morning crew
is just beginning their workday. It's up to those leaving to share important information with those who are arriving, but somehow, important
information always fails to get passed on to crew members who are
coming on duty. It's like an ongoing relay race where the runners never
seem to be able to complete the baton pass.

At KATX, the baton gets dropped—a lot. And Friday morning
at five-forty-five a.m. is no exception.

The perpetually perky morning news duo has no clue what
they're describing as video from the night before hits the air. It shows
Austin SWAT team members escorting two suspects from a Sixth
Street nightclub into a waiting police van. The anchor team seems to
be following a popular rule of local TV news: *If you don't know what
you're talking about, just keep talking!*

The first anchor says, "Our overnight team was first on the scene
as two customers were escorted from the Moroccan Hideaway nightclub. No. Now I'm being told those aren't customers but rather, they're
brothers. No, wait. Here's another correction. The two men are the
owners who also happen to be brothers." The blonde female anchor
sounds excited at the prospect of getting at least one fact correct. A
piece of paper is slipped to her. "I've just been handed more confirmed

details about the video from last night. The police action involves a major prostitution and gambling bust at several Sixth Street locations."

Not to be outdone, her male co-anchor leans into the shot and makes a big deal of turning the piece of paper over in order to show that his partner's been incorrectly reading the wrong side. He adds, "The prostitution and gambling bust is old news." And then, as if he's whispering to the viewers at home to let them in on a private joke, he holds the back of his right hand to his left cheek and says, "I warned everyone in the newsroom this might happen when we started recycling old script pages. Yuk, yuk."

The screen shows side-by-side mugshots of the two Nassine brothers. The photos are followed by video from the undercover operation. It has the grainy look that comes from a hidden camera and shows Hadid Nassine seated behind his desk and Carissa standing behind him with her hands placed casually on his shoulders. The female anchor says, "This is video of one of the club owners. And directly behind him is KATX's very own Marissa Cavelo." Then she adds in her best ad-libbing attempt, "I just love her new hairstyle, don't you?"

Exasperated, the producer who's seated in the control room down the hallway yells at the anchor through her earpiece and tells her to quit talking.

Right on cue, the anchor says, "I've just been instructed to quit talking. I know what that means. You don't have to tell me twice to quit talking. I know that if I'm told to quit talking it means it's time for the chatter to cease so that we can turn it over to Lela Jones who has our traffic report. Right, Lela?"

Lela, an attractive redhead, is standing in front of a giant map of downtown Austin. When the studio camera zooms in on her, Lela is busy adjusting her bra strap and looks like a deer in the headlights because she's caught off guard. The producer is tossing to Lela, without warning, to move past the awkward on-air situation created by the anchor team. Lela quickly recovers and is ready to use a telestrator, the instrument sports commentators use to fill in the x's and o's of a football game. With just the touch of her finger, Lela uses the device to highlight the routes to avoid in the downtown area because of construction. She draws a line up a few blocks to the north, followed by an arc above the State Capitol and another line down a few blocks parallel to the south. Two circles at the bottom designate "men at work" zones. Men at work must have been on Lela's mind because the completed graph looks like a giant penis, which prompts the studio crew and the anchor team to double over in laughter. But poor Lela has no idea what's so funny about traffic tie-ups.

God! I'm a sucker for bad morning television, Marissa thinks. *Of course, it's easier to be a critic now that I'm not on the air.* She clicks off the remote and snuggles back under the luxurious covers where Ken's still sleeping. Just thinking about their sexually charged tumble in bed the night before brings a smile to her face as a hot, electric charge passes over her entire body. She knows this is how lovemaking and love are supposed to unfold. Their mutual attraction and a great working relationship morphed into…*into what?* Marissa realizes that she's not sure just what their relationship has become. *Are we crime-fighting partners? Are we a news duo? Lovers? I do like the sound, smell, and the feel of that!*

Just as she's about to drift back to sleep, Ken's cell phone rings and within seconds hers does, too. They prop themselves up in bed and answer the calls simultaneously.

"Hello. This is Marissa," she says in a professional tone, not sure who'd be calling so early in the morning. The caller identifies herself as an associate producer at KATX. Marissa can tell the woman has already had more than her share of strong coffee or Red Bull. Or maybe both. Her voice is high-pitched and animated, which makes it hard to understand what she's saying.

"Okay. Slow down!" Marissa says. "You're calling to ask questions about the video from last night? No, I wasn't on duty. What? No, Ken Jordan doesn't work there anymore. If you'd check your updated employee roster, you'd know he quit two days ago. As for me, it's no secret I'm suspended." She fights the urge to hang up but knows it's not the woman's fault that she doesn't know Marissa's status. Good internal communication is not something KATX management is known for.

She's finally able to convince the associate producer that she and Ken were freelancing last night and that news outlets are free to use the video off the Internet as long as she and Ken receive credit for producing it. She also tells her to correct the facts presented by the morning crew. "That's my twin sister, not me, standing behind the man seated in the desk chair." Satisfied with what she's been told, the associate producer promises to pass on the corrections. Marissa turns and sees Ken is still on the phone with his head propped against the pillows. The person on the other line is doing all the talking.

Marissa gets up, pulls the blanket around her naked body and makes her way to the bathroom. *Funny how this feels vaguely familiar. It's hard to believe it was yesterday morning when I was waking up, disoriented in Ken's apartment with no clue where I was...or what I was doing. Now, here I am standing in the shower—again—but this time I feel like I'm on top of the world.*

Warm water and pure joy wash over her as she recalls the events of the past twenty-four hours. The shower door slides open and Ken steps in behind her. His strong hands caress her from behind and they melt in the physical ecstasy that only seems to grow stronger with every passing moment.

Later, as they're getting dressed, she's amazed at how comfortable she feels in his presence. She's glad her overnight bag has a change of casual clothes since the last thing she wants to do is put on Carissa's clothes from the night before.

CC in police custody is the one sad thought that can't be ignored. She sits on the edge of the bed and holds her sister's dress, wondering how she's doing. As if reading her mind, Ken says, "She'll be all right. Your sister's very much like you. She's smart and beautiful. She also has no previous criminal record. And a top-notch defense attorney will be sure she spends little, if any, time behind bars."

"I still can't believe I had no clue about her drug use. It's also hard to accept her turning against me like she did. It's as if she's a complete stranger. And now I have to brace myself for this being one of those sensational crimes that just screams for continuing coverage."

Ken nods. "Have you thought about the very real possibility that the media will be asking you questions about your sister?"

"I've been thinking about little else ever since *Tío* told me she'd been taken into custody. It's just a matter of time before reporters start contacting me since I'm her next of kin. They'll want to know about her involvement in the Nassine crime ring, her relationship with Hadid and her relationship with me. I have to be ready to answer every single question that I'd be asking if I were covering the story. Some of this info will be included in the police report, but I may be forced to share some painful facts." She finishes putting her hair into a sleek, no-fuss ponytail as she lays out her strategy to Ken. "Here's what I'm planning to do. You and I both know it'd be wrong to ignore reporters and their questions. If I put them off, they'll just keep hounding me. So, the smart thing to do is to issue a statement listing the limited facts that can be confirmed. As soon as an attorney's hired to take her case, I can work with him or her to issue additional statements and handle any follow-up questions. With any luck, another more scintillating news story will break and the media will forget about this one. What do you think?"

"Put yourself in the place of other journalists. What questions would you be asking if you were working on the follow-up story? It's the most efficient way to figure out what questions will be asked of you. Share the fact that you love your sister very much but can't speak for her. And let the media know you've withdrawn yourself from all future news coverage of developments involving your sister." He sits down on the sofa and adds confidently, "You and I both know the media will be less interested in your sister if you provide some basic info about her."

"Of course, it's too late to do anything about her Facebook page. I imagine that's the first place reporters are checking for pics and information about CC. Detectives, too for that matter, probably pulled everything off her page." Marissa changes the subject. "Come on! Let's go grab some migas and fresh coffee. I know a great place on the Eastside. Remember our deal? Our next meal is at the restaurant of my choice. My treat!"

◇◇◇

Once seated and served at Joe's Bakery, Marissa feels herself relaxing for the first time in days. There's something soothing about warm, home-made tortillas and strong coffee that eases all her tension. She tells Ken about the crazy call from the associate producer and lets him know, tri-umphantly, that they will be credited for the video as freelancers. Then, since he hasn't offered any details, she asks, "Your phone rang pretty early, too. Anyone or anything interesting worth sharing?" She hopes she doesn't sound nosey but can't help wondering, *girlfriend?*

"Well, Marissa, I'm glad you asked because yes, there's some new information that is worth sharing." He gives her a sly grin. "I was talking to my buddy. You know the tech mastermind who helped pull off last night's internet coup? Anyway, he called to tell me the number of views of what's being called, 'Prada Cam' have surpassed one million since midnight! Plus, it's all over the newswire and it played on *Good Morning America* and AAN." He pauses to take a sip of coffee before saying, "Not bad for a suspended reporter and her unemployed photographer sidekick." He laughs and they raise their coffee cups in a victory toast.

Just as they're finishing breakfast, Marissa's cell phone rings. She recognizes the number. It's the station. "Hello. This is Marissa Cavelo."

"Marissa, this is Patrick Stone calling with good news. The station has decided to lift your suspension. That clears the way for you to return to work immediately. In fact, since it's nine a.m., why don't you get here by noon today?" It's a question, but he's not really asking. In true Stone-faced management style, he's issuing an order. "We'll pay you for a half a day. How does that sound? Oh, and please come see me as soon as you get here so we can take care of some paperwork. I have a copy of your contract to be renewed. It's very standard...no major changes. All right then. See you at noon." Stone hangs up without even waiting for a response.

"The nerve of that son-of-a-bitch. He hung up on me!" she tells Ken. "That was Stone, telling me my suspension has been lifted. He wants me to be in by noon. He acts like nothing happened. Like Jan Ruther didn't sabotage our dance school story! Like you didn't quit! And, more importantly, like *we* didn't break another major exclusive story on our own time! He sounded smug and so sure that I'll renew my contract 'with no major changes.' I have news for him. There *will* be big changes or else I won't be back."

Ken laughs. "I'm not surprised KATX wants you back. You're trending big time on all social media platforms. I'll tell you this, when you do walk into that station, own it!"

Marissa checks the time. She's in no rush to go anywhere. "I have plenty of time to go home, change and get to the station when I'm good and ready. What I need now is a java refill. How about you?" She pours two fresh cups with a splash of *leche fresca*. *Just like Mami used to serve. Fresh milk makes it delicious!* That puts another smile on her face. That along with the idea of walking into KATX to take her sweet revenge.

Thirty-One

Scotch sloshes out of a glass as it's poured from an expensive crystal decanter before being slammed back on the tray where it usually sits. All the other containers have been drained of whatever liquid they used to hold. An ashtray on the gleaming wooden surface of the table is overflowing with lipstick stained cigarette butts and ashes. The faint sound of a phone ringing can be heard from the other side of the closed door just out of earshot from where Gloria Linden is wallowing in self-pity.

"Give it a rest, people. I'm not going to talk to anybody anytime soon! I have nothing to say," she slurs. The woman has been locked in her office since Wednesday evening, doing her best to avoid complaints. She says to the empty chair in front of her, "Let me remind anyone who has any doubt, it's my dance school! I'm the one who's worked hard to build it...with my own blood, sweat and tears. I dare anybody to try to be as successful as I've been teaching children who can't dance worth a damn. I'll never understand how so many youngsters were born with two left feet. Thank goodness costumes, photography and auditions kept the dough rolling in or else the doors to this place would've slammed shut a long time ago."

In the three days since the story aired, the phones have been blowing up with irate callers demanding their money back, canceling their children's enrollment and threatening lawsuits. Two of her newest instructors had the nerve to quit in protest, telling her that they'd never have accepted the teaching positions knowing the 'unethical policies employees are expected to follow.' And, as if all that wasn't bad enough…rotten eggs and vulgar graffiti were splashed across the front of the building late Wednesday night.

The last straw for Linden came with the cancellation of the audition that was set to take place in Los Angeles next month. The story by Marissa Cavelo was picked up by *Entertainment Tonight* and *TMZ*. Their stories described Linden as being, "a ruthless, money-grubbing ex-dancer whose real talent is squeezing cash out of vulnerable victims."

Linden is desperate to figure out how to salvage what's left of her business and her reputation. Doug Diamond has quit taking her phone calls. He originally told her that a lawsuit against Cavelo and the station would be the best way to stop negative publicity generated by that damn story. But nothing could be further from the truth. "That reporter has ruined my life!" she screams.

There's a knock on her office door. "I said I don't want to be disturbed! What part of that don't you understand?"

The voice of her timid receptionist can be heard through the door. "I know Ms. Linden, but two officers from your bank are here and they say it's urgent. They need to speak with you now!"

The excitement in the newsroom is out of control. Everyone has heard about or seen the undercover video of the Nassine brothers being arrested in the private office of the Moroccan Hideaway. It's the kind of undercover work seen only in action movies. It's also the once in a lifetime story every local reporter and photographer hopes to snag.

So, it's not surprising that Marissa and Ken have become cult heroes to their news colleagues. In the photographer's lounge, someone has blown up a poster-size photo of Superman and replaced his head with Ken's head. Captions under the figure read: "Takes Down

Criminal Club Owners Faster Than a Speeding Bullet," "KATX's Man of Steel," and "Truth, Justice, and the American Way—featuring Marissa Cavelo as Lois Lane."

Meanwhile, at the front desk, the receptionist is busy fielding a flurry of phone calls. But this time it's not from viewers who have horror stories to share about the Regency Dance Studio. Those calls have been replaced by people wanting to know when Marissa Cavelo will return to the air. The receptionist has been instructed to answer: "Ms. Cavelo is due to return to work today after taking time off to assist in a very important police investigation. We hope you'll be watching tonight's six p.m. news for an exclusive update. Thank you for calling."

Down the hall, behind the closed door of her office, Jan Ruther is sitting with her elbows propped up on the desk as her fingers massage the temples on both sides of her head. *God! I could use a stiff drink! This has been the most stressful twenty-four hours of my entire career.* Jan was so sure that recommending Cavelo be suspended indefinitely would put an end to her aspirations of becoming a hard news reporter. She hoped it would give Melinda Bale a break from having to share the anchor desk with that bitch. But her plan to sabotage Marissa backfired. This morning she had to face the wrath of Stone who had just been told by the station's attorneys that suspending Cavelo was a huge mistake. Jan was sure Stone was going to fire her right there on the spot. Instead, the general manager has tasked her with figuring out how to make Cavelo feel grateful she's being allowed back into the noon anchor chair.

More than Stone, Jan is afraid that Melinda is going to be as angry as a wet rooster in an overheated hen house when she hears Marissa is returning. *How am I going to keep Bale happy and convince Cavelo she's lucky to still have a job?*

It's up to her to guarantee Marissa renews her contract. And she has less than an hour to make it happen!

Thirty-Two

The alarm on Marissa's cell phone goes off, alerting her it's straight up high noon. Right on time, she walks past the receptionist, waving a greeting to her and heads directly to the general manager's office. She doesn't bother waiting for Patrick Stone's secretary to buzz her into his private office.

"Marissa! So nice to see you," he says, trying to hide his surprise. "You're right on time. Are you ready to get back to work?" he asks. "I have your contract ready for you to renew. I've also instructed the news director that you are to join the main anchor team on the set during the six p.m. newscast so they can officially welcome you back. More importantly, it'll be an opportunity for a debrief."

"An on-set debrief? About what?" she asks, although she already knows the answer. It gives her pleasure to watch Stone squirm.

He fumbles for the right words before answering. "Well, we just assumed you'd want to share your experience from last night. That was certainly some adventure. It was quality drama that far exceeds any reality show on television. And I must say, your loyal fans are eager to hear all the exciting details about it from you."

"Mr. Stone, I'm surprised that you'd ask me to share the news coverage experience from last night, especially since it had nothing to do with the station. Ken and I were acting as independent freelancers with no ties or commitments to KATX. What you're not aware of and

277

what I'm not willing to disclose to anyone besides you in this private conversation is that last night's investigation is very personal to me. That's all of the details I'm willing to reveal at this time." She is calm and in control. "Now, I'd like to refresh *your* memory. The last time I was in your office you made it clear I was being suspended because of my suspected role in the airing of the Regency Dance Studio story. I stand by what I said then. I had no part in that news story being included in the newscast, but I also don't regret that it aired. We should have had the station's full support while working on that story, but that wasn't the case. Ken had to sneak it on the air and then he had no choice but to quit. As for me, I've spent the past two days uncertain about my future here at KATX. So, to be honest with you, Mr. Stone, I'm here to tell you—"

But before she can finish her sentence, the door to Stone's office suddenly opens and his receptionist rushes in saying in a very nervous voice, "Sorry to interrupt, Mr. Stone, but the news director says it's urgent. You have to come right now. There's an emergency in the newsroom."

Marissa and Stone follow the receptionist toward the newsroom. As they get closer they hear voices yelling.

"You bitch!" Melinda is screaming at the top of her lungs at Jan Ruther. The slightly heavyset Melinda still has her wireless microphone clipped on her jacket. It's obvious she's just stepped off the set of the noon newscast. The two women are in Ruther's office where the door is wide open. Activity in the newsroom has come to a standstill and all eyes are watching the two women go at each other. Jan is cowering behind her desk, using a handful of folders to deflect the items Melinda is throwing at her—pens, a stapler, a computer mouse. If it's not tied down on the desk, Melinda is using it as a projectile! "You promised me that she wouldn't be back on the anchor desk. You said I'd be named solo anchor of the noon newscast by the end of the year! You also said I wouldn't have to share anything with her... not even the counter space in the makeup room. Well, guess what, baby? You lied and if there's one thing I won't tolerate in my life, and certainly not in my bed, is a liar!"

What? Did she say 'not in my bed?'

Ruther responds, "Do you want the whole world to know about our relationship?" Jan doesn't realize that all news staff members have stopped what they're doing so they can listen to every word being hurled between the two women. Their relationship is no longer a secret.

Patrick Stone walks into Ruther's office and slams the door behind him. Through the closed door their raised voices can still be heard, but this time it's Stone yelling at Ruther and Bale.

"Shut the hell up!" he says, "Are you both out of your minds? Emotional outbursts like this will not be tolerated! Not on my watch. Marissa Cavelo's in the newsroom watching this catfight. She's here to assume her place on the noon anchor desk, so I suggest you pull yourselves together and warmly welcome her back as a valued member of the KATX news team. As for the personal dirty laundry that's being aired, I'll see you both in my office in exactly fifteen minutes. We're going to get to the bottom of just what was promised by whom...and while your sexual orientation is your personal business, we'll discuss inappropriate personal relationships between employees and supervisors. Am I clear?"

The door opens and Stone walks out with the two women following close behind him. Those gathered in the newsroom who've been absorbing all the juicy details of the spat between the lovers quickly look away as if they haven't been hanging on every word. The shocked looks on their faces reveal otherwise.

Patrick Stone says, "Marissa, I'm headed to my office. Please join me in ten minutes, after you've had a chance to check in with your colleagues. Oh, and Jan Ruther and Melinda Bale have something they want to say to you. Again, welcome back and see you in my office in a few minutes." He turns on his heels and heads back to his office.

Ruther and Bale look like wild dogs that have been temporarily beaten into submission. Anger is still obvious in their eyes and it's clearly directed at Marissa. Ruther says with fake sincerity, "Hey, Cavelo, glad to hear your suspension's been lifted. I can't wait to hear all about your undercover exploits."

Ruther uses her sharp, bony elbow to jab Melinda Bale in the side, which prompts her to say with full contempt, "Yes, I heard you and Ken are Internet sensations. Hope you'll share your tricks with me. I'd like to know how you managed to look so cheap while wearing such expensive clothes."

Bale's obvious dig at CC's wardrobe makes Marissa laugh. After the catfight she just witnessed, there's no way she can take insults from her seriously. Worried that another skirmish will erupt, Ruther pulls Bale away and guides her out of the newsroom. Marissa turns to walk to her desk and she's greeted by smiling coworkers who are eager to congratulate her. A couple of photographers ask her to pass along greetings and their congratulations to Ken. Most of them say they're glad to have her back.

As she approaches her desk, she is pleasantly surprised to see two flower arrangements. One's an extravagant bouquet from an upscale florist in trendy Westlake Hills. The card reads: "You kicked Linden's a _ _! And for that, we are eternally grateful." It's signed, "Sherry West and the staff of the Westbound Talent Agency." The second vase is a little worn with a small chip on the side. The flowers are understated, but beautiful. It only takes a few seconds to recognize them as having come from the Lopez' front yard. Marissa's mother lovingly tended the same kind of garden outside their Houston home years ago. It's one of those cherished childhood memories that gets harder to hold onto as time passes. Her eyes fill with tears as she reads the card: "Marissa, *muchisimas gracias por el reporte que vimos en las noticias. Tu eres muy preciosa. Que Dios te bendiga. Con cariño, Sra. Lopez y Julia.* Marissa, thank you for the story that we saw on the news. You are so precious. May God bless you. With affection, Mrs. Lopez and Julia."

Only fellow journalists know that euphoric feeling that comes with the completion of a story that changes people's lives for the better or that prevents people from making a grave or expensive mistake. In this case, Marissa knows the Regency Dance Studio story stopped the Lopez family from spending hard-earned money on empty promises for their daughter. If this is the last story of hers that airs on this station, she'll be satisfied with her efforts, knowing that she has established herself as a serious journalist. She smiles, knowing she won't ever be stuck in a rut covering fluff stories again.

A light is blinking on her desk phone, indicating new voice mail messages. The first few messages were all left on Wednesday afternoon right after the dance studio story aired. All the calls came in less than fifteen minutes and are from parents with their own complaints about the studio and Ms. Linden's policies. Another message was left early on Thursday afternoon from her uncle. He sounds angry as he reminds her that she might be in danger and he warns her not to try anything crazy. *Too late,* she thinks as she deletes the message before checking her watch.

She has less than two minutes before she's due back in the general manager's office to sign a new contract. *This is crazy! I haven't even decided if I even want to return to work. Maybe this is a good time for me to walk out the station door and never look back.* She usually wouldn't think of making a decision this major without first consulting her uncle. Besides, before she shares any additional information about last night's story, she needs to be sure the police investigation isn't jeopardized. She finally determines that she will only take part in an on-set debrief if Ken can join her.

She goes back to her voice mail. There are two messages from earlier this morning from rival station reporters leaving numbers and asking her to call back ASAP. She writes them down and makes a note to herself to draft a statement to release to the media as soon as she finishes with Stone.

The last call came in at ten a.m. this morning. The number's not familiar, but the area code is. It's 305, the area code for Miami, where AAN's headquarters is located. The voice is also familiar. "Marissa! Good morning to you. It's Marcus Feldman calling from AAN. We met briefly Wednesday just moments before your Regency Dance Studio exposé aired. I must say, it was the best example of local journalism I've seen in a long while…that is until today. Unequivocally the *best* sample of journalism is your undercover work from last night. And the intriguing part is the unlimited access to a potential audience of millions on the Internet. Congratulations. Call me at your earliest convenience so we can talk about what I believe is a future opportunity for you here at All Access News. My direct line is 305 …."

Her hand is shaking as she jots down Feldman's number in her reporter's notebook before stuffing it into her bag. She has everything she needs for her meeting with Patrick Stone. For the second time today, she breezes past Stone's secretary who doesn't even look up as Marissa walks by. She's engrossed in a personal phone conversation. Marissa overhears her say, "Who would've believed Melinda Bale swings the other way? No, I don't know how long they've been hot for each other, but from what the whole newsroom witnessed, they definitely fight like an old married couple." And then she bursts into uncontrollable laughter.

Marissa enters Stone's office and closes the door behind her. It feels like *déjà vu* with the general manager and the executive producer sitting in the same chairs they occupied twenty-four hours earlier. Except this time the smug looks on their faces have been replaced with worry. Jan is sitting with eyes downcast, waiting to be addressed. Having been on the receiving end of Melinda Bale's wrath, Marissa feels sorry for her as she imagines how uncomfortable Jan's love life is about to become.

"Ah, Marissa. We were just waiting for you so we can review the plan Jan has drawn up for your on-air return," Stone says as he attempts to assert control over Marissa's future. "As I mentioned, you'll join the main anchor team on set during the six p.m. newscast. We've drafted a script for you that focuses primarily on your undercover experience."

Did this man not hear a word I said to him earlier? "Mr. Stone, I don't mean to sound repetitive but as I explained earlier, the work performed last night was a team effort between myself and photographer, Ken Jordan. It has no connection to KATX. The final outcome was in cooperation and under the strict supervision of the Austin Police Department's Organized Crime Unit. Without permission from the lead investigator and without the consent of my freelance partner, Ken Jordan, there will be no on-set debrief."

Stone isn't used to being challenged. The veins in his neck start to bulge from underneath his tight shirt collar as his face turns a deep shade of red. "Let me remind you that you're still an employee of this station and a condition of your suspension being lifted is your willingness to do what's best for the station…." He pauses before saying, "And its ratings!"

"Ratings?" she yells. "Is that what all this boils down to? Mr. Stone, viewers care about story content and the value of the information we put on the air. Our news coverage should be relevant to their daily existence. It should be about saving lives, protecting people, uncovering waste in government and issuing warnings about potential dangers threatening the public. Those are some of the key issues that drive ratings. If the content is of exceptional quality and it's presented in a fair and balanced manner, then viewers will watch and appreciate it and the station will win the ratings war. But if you blow up sensational topics or air stories that are graphic or shocking in nature with no validity, then viewers will see right through it and they'll quit watching." She sighs. "Don't you see? That's why the dance studio exposé was well-received by the public. It's the type of story that I've proven I can do and that I insist on tackling in the future. Last night's undercover video was part of gritty, real police work; it's not something to sensationalize. Nor should it be put on the air simply to shock viewers."

"So what are you saying? Are you making demands before agreeing to return to work?" Stone asks as he and Jan Ruther exchange worried looks. It's obvious any plan to get Marissa to feel grateful that she still has a job is blowing up in their faces.

"Thank you for asking," Marissa says, confidently. "I wouldn't call these demands, but rather suggestions. I strongly suggest that Ken be reinstated. If he agrees to return as a photographer, I suggest that he be assigned to work exclusively with me on investigative assignments only. As for the script that Jan has drafted, I'll be happy to run it by police investigators. But I'm not making any promises it'll be approved or that I'll appear on set to share my experiences with viewers. If I do appear on set, I insist on Ken being part of the debrief. Now, if you'll excuse me, I've got to talk to Ken and to the officer in charge of the police investigation."

She turns to Jan and plucks the script out of her hand. "Oh, I almost forgot. I know you've described the contract as being standard with 'no major changes,' but I'll need more time to consider renewal. I have another pending job offer, which I'll be taking under consideration before making my final decision." She can almost hear their jaws dropping behind her as she turns and walks out of the office.

◇◇◇

Marissa, Ken and Tío Hector meet for a late lunch at El Sol y la Luna, just a few blocks from the Austin Police Department. The popular eatery is also close to the properties raided by officers late last night, just before the Nassine brothers and CC were taken into custody. Her uncle looks slightly older than she remembers with a few more gray hairs scattered around his temples. Yet, his face is still strong and his voice carries authority. Ken appears relaxed, although she knows, based on their time together, he hasn't slept much.

Tío puts down the script he's been reading and carefully takes off his reading glasses before saying with disdain, "This version is, pardon my Spanish, *puro caca*. There are so many factual errors and unsubstantiated conclusions it would not hold up in court!"

"It's not for court, Detective Garcia. It's for television news," explains Ken. "However, if it is incorrect, then it shouldn't air under any circumstances. Anything that goes on television or the Internet, especially when it involves evidence collected or charges pending against the Nassine brothers, should be based on police documents and attributed to investigative officers. If the information is proven to be false, then defense attorneys will level the station faster than a springtime flash flood."

"Then I advise you not to put anything else on the air until the investigation into the brothers' suspected criminal activity is complete. It could take several more days before officers finish combing through computer files. The confessions the two of you captured on video are going to be crucial as we verify the facts surrounding the disappearance of Enrique Sanchez."

"I told the general manager that I'd have to run the script by you and that if it didn't meet your approval it wouldn't air."

"Then this is my official response," he says as he crumples the script paper and tosses it on the table. His sarcasm brings a faint smile to Marissa's face, which quickly fades as she tells him, "Tío, I failed to mention to the GM that in addition to running the script by investigators, I can no longer be assigned to any news story involving CC. It would be impossible for me to be objective."

He sighs again. "That's a wise decision. It's best for Carissa if we both keep a professional distance from her case. That way we can focus our efforts on helping her get through all this." He takes her hand. "Now, here's the latest on your sister. She's been moved to the women's holding facility in east Travis County. A very high-powered defense attorney out of Houston has offered to take her case pro bono."

"I don't understand. Her identity and involvement have only been mentioned minimally in the news so far. How did a Houston attorney hear about CC's case?"

"Let's just say I have good friends from my rookie days in Houston and this particular guy owed me a favor. He's already arrived in town…" Tío pauses to check the time on his wristwatch before saying, "…and he's probably wrapping up his initial meeting with her right now. The sooner she goes before a judge, the sooner her case moves forward. I understand from the investigators who booked her that she's agreed to meet with the attorney. However, she's refusing to meet with you and offers no explanation. Maybe the attorney can get her to change her mind. Sorry, *mija*. We'll just have to be patient about all this."

While her sister's rejection is painful, she tells her tío that she understands and briefs him on her plans to issue a statement that will answer reporters' initial questions. Her uncle writes down the name and phone number of Carissa's attorney so he can review her statement and field future questions from reporters. Then he gets up to leave. "I have to get back to police headquarters. I'll check with you later to let you know if there's anything new with your sister's case or with the Nassines."

He shakes hands with Ken and kisses Marissa on the forehead, leaving the two seated side-by-side in the booth. She watches as Tío Hector walks out of the restaurant. Marissa gazes out the window and lets her mind wander back to a different time and place. Up until this past year she and CC were inseparable. Many times, they sat together in one of these same booths sharing queso and chips and sipping on margaritas. They knew each other's thoughts and shared their plans for the future. Now she can't help but wonder if during the pursuit of her professional goals, she somehow managed to erase Carissa's identity? Her spirit? Her dreams? Until her sister agrees to talk to her, she won't really know the answer to these questions.

Ken looks at his watch and says, "I don't mean to rush you, but it's almost two p.m. Are you going to head back to the station?"

"*Ay Dios mío!* I've been so wrapped up in talking to my uncle about CC and the criminal investigation that I haven't told you the latest developments. I'm in no rush to get back. There are things we need to talk about before I make any decisions."

"What do you mean? What things?" he asks.

She takes his hand and says, "I strongly suggested to Stone and Ruther that you be allowed to return to work. That is, if you decide you want to go back. And I strongly suggested you and I be allowed to work on hard news stories together. Exclusively."

"Hmm…" Ken says while rubbing his chin between his thumb and forefinger. "That exclusive partnership would be an interesting arrangement, but who knows if the station will agree to your recommendations?"

"Well, it just so happens I put something else on the bargaining table that might persuade them," she says with an air of confidence. "I informed them I have another job offer. I checked my voice mail messages before my meeting with Stone and there was a message from Marcus Feldman of AAN. He saw our undercover work and was blown away by it. He wants me to call him back to talk about what he described as, 'my future at the network!'"

Ken's smile fades and then quickly returns. He hugs her and says enthusiastically, "That's great news, Marissa! Wow! That's awesome! You have a shot at a network anchor position. It's what you wanted and worked so hard to achieve."

Her excitement gives way to doubts. *Is this really what I want? Am I ready to move to Miami or some other city?* It's all happening just as she's started a great working partnership and an amazing personal relationship with an awesome guy. *How can I leave all this?* And what about the criminal proceedings against the Nassines? It'll be hard to follow what happens if she's living in another city. But the most important question to consider is whether she could move away and leave unresolved issues between her and CC.

On the other hand, her ultimate career achievement is within reach! She closes her eyes and imagines sitting behind the news desk at the AAN studio surrounded by competent, professional staff members. There would be co-workers whose only job is to verify facts—producers with decades of experience who are passionate about crafting award-winning newscasts of relevant topics. No more misspelled supers. No more bad video or clipped microphones to keep viewers wondering what the hell is going on. She'd have access to unlimited resources and the opportunity to work on stories that are important to viewers. She'd be taken seriously as a journalist! The benefits of moving to a major market are endless. She wishes her parents were alive to witness her accomplishments. She realizes that there's no better time than the present to make a major career decision. She grabs her purse and takes the last few sips of her liquid courage—her margarita. As she starts to make her way out of the booth, she grabs Ken's face and gently pulls him toward her for a kiss.

He reaches over and squeezes her hand. It's a simple gesture of unconditional support. Just his touch gives her strength and the faith in herself that her decision will be the right one.

Thirty-Three

Three Months Later

On the monitor, three middle-aged women in handcuffs are removed from a police van before being escorted by officers into the entrance of the county jail. One looks like she could be someone's grandmother. She has short, wavy black hair with gray strands scattered throughout. She's wearing a worn housedress and thick-soled shoes. The other two women are slightly younger, but their tattoos, bad hair coloring and wrinkled faces make Marissa think these women are already familiar with life behind bars.

"The three suspects face charges of fraud after collecting thousands of dollars from the State's teen foster care program. Although there's no evidence that any teenagers ever lived in the group home run by the women. Coming up tonight at ten—part two of my investigation into the victimization of teens. It's exclusive undercover video you'll only see here. Thanks for tuning in at six. Have a great evening, everybody. See you back here tonight at ten." And with that the floor manager yells, "We're clear!" It's Marissa's signal that another great newscast is over. She turns to her co-anchor, Mario Martinez, who's already writing up the discrepancy report for the newscast. It's a task the two gladly take turns tackling. Neither of them minds since

289

there are rarely any technical errors to report during the six or the ten p.m. newscasts.

Martinez says, "Hey, Marissa, that was an awesome investigative report. You're killing it with your undercover work!"

"Thanks, Mario. Wait until you see how the trio of women tried to fool authorities into believing life-sized dummies were actually teenagers. It's crazy. The best shots were captured with a hidden camera after we were tipped off by a neighbor."

"Why doesn't that surprise me?" he asks with a laugh. "Okay. Can't wait to catch it later. See you in a little while and enjoy your dinner break." He grabs his scripts and walks out of the studio whistling a lighthearted tune as he leaves. Marissa smiles. It's so refreshing working with a co-anchor who enjoys working hard, is a complete professional and is pleasant to be around. He's everything Melinda Bale isn't!

The fact is that if Bale were still around, Marissa wouldn't be working for KATX. She refused to return to the same old daily grind of co-anchoring a newscast alongside the vile, unprofessional Bale. The revelation Melinda and Jan Ruther were lovers was captured on someone's cell phone and within fifteen minutes, it had been viewed a thousand times on the Internet. The station had no choice but to fire both women, citing unprofessional conduct and the inappropriate relationship between a manager and a subordinate employee.

No one's heard from Jan Ruther, although there are rumors she cashed out her life savings, bought a seaworthy sailboat and stocked it with cheap booze. She already had a reputation for being able to cuss like a drunken sailor. As for Melinda Bale, she wasn't able to land another anchor job in another television market. She also tried and failed to land a public relations job. Recently, someone saw her at a Dallas-area mall selling Acai berry-flavored water as a sure weight loss product. Unfortunately, Melinda's hefty weight makes it tough for her to convince anyone that the drink works.

It took almost a month for the station to resolve the status of Bale and Ruther, especially since both women threatened to cause more public scenes. Marissa wasn't willing to stick around to see if the female firecrackers would burn each other or fizzle out together. She didn't care. More importantly, she didn't want to witness the aftermath.

She sits back in her anchor chair and reflects at the events of the past three months. When a dirty house needs cleaning it's always good to start at the top. And that's exactly what happened at KATX. Patrick Stone was the first to get the ax after being held responsible for placing her on indefinite suspension. Stone and the rest of the news managers were completely caught off guard by the strong viewer reaction to the dance school story. Besides the few messages she received, Marissa later found out people flooded the switchboard, calling to report their own stories of being ripped off by Gloria Linden, but the news director dropped the ball. No one bothered to help the receptionist answer the phones or take messages after the story aired. Then, Hank Johnson failed to assign another reporter to work on the obvious follow-up stories. It's a major rule of news coverage: when you break an exclusive story you squeeze out as many related follow-up segments as possible. But in this case, no one had the contacts or the knowledge of Linden that Marissa had. When a KATX staff member finally did try to get moving on the story, it was too late. Mrs. Lopez and her daughter, Julia, refused to talk to anyone, saying they only person they trusted was Marissa. The lawsuit filed by Gloria Linden frightened Johnson so much he took no further action. And *that* proved to be a huge mistake. In the news biz, your competitors are like sharks. When they smell fear and hesitation, they're ready to pounce!

In this case, another television station and the local newspaper conducted their own follow-up investigations against the dance studio. Both news teams put together a couple of solid stories, exposing more allegations of scams. The media attention generated so much heat for Linden that her new attorney advised her to throw in the legal towel. She reluctantly agreed to drop the lawsuit against KATX. More importantly, she abruptly closed the dance studio. In order to avoid civil charges, State authorities convinced Linden to forfeit her license to operate a school and encouraged her to sell the business and use the proceeds to pay refunds to students.

The timing of Marissa's suspension also came back to haunt the general manager. Poor, Stone. With two blockbuster stories to Marissa's credit, he found himself in serious trouble when she flatly turned down another contract. The general manager had refused to budge on any of her suggested changes to her contract. While he claimed to agree with her request to work on investigative stories instead of features, he refused to put it in writing. He also refused to budge on allowing Ken to return to work, although Marissa wasn't sure Ken would have agreed to come back even if it was guaranteed the two would be allowed to work together exclusively.

Marissa's decision to resign resulted in the worst of consequences for Stone. Before being fired, he came up with a few flimsy excuses as to why she quit, but a savvy media blogger did a pretty good job of setting the record straight. Once Stone was gone, the rest of the news heads rolled easily. The news director who agreed with Stone on all points suddenly retired, although he was only fifty-one years old. Within weeks, a new general manager stepped in. He hired a new news director with solid leadership credentials who also happened to be a former photojournalist with a real understanding of what news crews face on a daily basis. Almost immediately, experienced news team members replaced those who had become lazy and/or jaded. The quality of on-air work improved dramatically. Morale and ratings both hit an all-time high. Marissa found it hard to believe it was the same environment where she'd felt so trapped just three months earlier.

The day she walked out of Patrick Stone's office she had no regrets. She went to her desk and banged out a resignation letter and a farewell message to her coworkers. She also drafted a personal statement providing brief facts about her sister, herself and their family history that she knew reporters would be eager to know. She also announced she would, for obvious reasons, be pulling herself from any further coverage of CC's case or that of the Nassine brothers. She sent the draft to Hector so he could look it over before forwarding it to Carissa's attorney for his review. Then it was distributed to the media.

Once she finished sending her final emails, she put the last of her personal possessions into a cardboard box and walked out the front door with her shoulders back and her head held high. She got into her car and drove to the nearest parking lot where she stopped the car. She sat there, feeling like a heavy weight had been lifted from her shoulders. Her mixed emotions of relief and sadness had her crying and laughing all at the same time. After a few minutes, she was able to pull herself together. The first thing she did was call Marcus Feldman who invited her to Miami for a tour of AAN. She thanked him for the invitation and promised to get back to him after she confirmed her travel plans.

Once that conversation was over, she headed to Ken's place. In such a short time, he'd become very important to her life and to her decisions. As her mother would say, "*Si, mija, es amor.* Yes, dear, this is love." Once she made herself comfortable at Ken's place, they spent hours talking about everything that was on their minds. They talked about their professional goals, their fears, their feelings for each other, and their hopes for the future. After all they shared that first evening, there was no one—not even her sister—who knew Marissa better than Ken.

Ken was her rock when it came to dealing with Carissa, who refused to see Marissa the entire time she was in the county jail. Marissa was forced to depend on CC's attorney for basic information about her sister's case. Not surprisingly, her attorney was more than happy to go before television cameras to answer questions as the case progressed. A plus for taking on the case pro bono is the media exposure it provided him. The attorney was also able to arrange a speedy hearing for CC, and he convinced the judge that Carissa was coerced into being an accomplice to the Nassines' criminal way of life. Drug tests confirmed what her uncle suspected. Carissa had been using drugs including Ecstasy, marijuana, cocaine and sleep-inducing drugs. She told the therapist who evaluated her that she'd become very good at functioning while high and that few people, including her coworkers or her sister, suspected a thing. That knowledge shattered all belief that Marissa had about knowing her sister so well. Fortunately, since Carissa had no prior convictions, the judge approved a plea bargain agreement that placed her on probation for five years. In exchange, she agreed to cooperate with investigators and to testify against the Nassine brothers.

Upon her release from the county jail, she also agreed to enter a drug rehabilitation facility in New Mexico. It's a location Tío Hector recommended. When the initial eight-week detox period ended, Marissa was able to visit, although she wasn't convinced CC was ready to see her. Before her visit, CC had written a brief letter to Marissa. It must have been part of an exercise all patients are required to complete—write a letter to your next of kin and let them know you're alive. Marissa believes this because that's about all the letter covered. It read: *Marissa, I'm in a rehabilitation facility in Las Cruces. My room is small, plain and padded. It's not a place worth writing home about, but it's what I am required to do. I've been told I'm making progress and that I'll be allowed to have visitors soon. Whether you visit is a choice I'll leave to you. Your sister, Carissa*

Marissa immediately called Tío Hector and read the letter to him so he could provide insight into Carissa's state of mind. Marissa wanted reassurance she hadn't missed some deeper meaning in the letter. He reassured Marissa that CC was just beginning to come out of the drug-induced fog that impaired her sense of reality. He encouraged her to visit Carissa as soon as she could but not to expect too much. He said she needed to be patient about getting answers to all her questions about what had happened to CC and about her feelings toward her twin. Whatever might be shared between them, Tío Hector assured her it'd be the first step in a very slow process of reconciliation.

◇◇◇

A week later, Marissa was sitting across from Carissa in the modestly furnished visiting area of the rehabilitation center. The decor had a distinct Southwestern influence with cacti and other succulents in terra cotta pots around the room. Paintings of sunsets and sunrises over mountain landscapes hung on the walls. The peaceful atmosphere helped to ease the uncertainty she felt as CC and she exchanged pleasantries about the weather and her flight. CC looked pale, slightly gaunt, even frail. It was not the physically fit CC who could hold her own against any athlete. This CC wore a drab gray jumper that swallowed her frame because it was at least two sizes too big for her. Her hair was cut short and she wasn't wearing any makeup or jewelry. Marissa squirmed uncomfortably in her seat as she struggled to find the right way to phrase her thoughts. It was not easy to ask about issues that had been gnawing away at her brain and heart almost nonstop for the past few months. These were the questions and doubts that caused sleepless nights since the last time she saw her sister in Hadid's office. As she struggled to find the right words, Carissa took her by surprise by wasting no time getting to the heart of the matter that hung between them.

"I guess you're wondering why I turned against you, aren't you?" She blinked, but showed no real emotion as she waited for Marissa to respond.

"Uh…uh…" Marissa tried to find her voice and willed her mind to come up with an answer that made sense. "Carissa, yes, I'm anxious to understand your actions and feelings. It's just one of the questions I have, but I also want to know if you're all right?" Suddenly there was no hesitation in her voice. "I want to know what happened to change your feelings toward me? What did I do? Or what didn't I do? Sure, I have a lot of questions, but I'm also here to answer your questions, too. Most importantly, though, I want you to know I love you and will do anything to get you back in my life." As Marissa talked, CC's head dropped to her chest and from where she sat Marissa could see a tear roll down one cheek. She reached across the table to take her hand, but her gesture prompted CC to flinch as she pulled both of her hands off the table and folded them together in her lap.

Marissa got up from her chair, and without hesitation, moved around the table and knelt down by CC. She put her arms around her and engulfed her in a strong, steady hug. At first she could feel CC's resistance, but she whispered in her ear, "CC, I'm here for you and I'm not leaving." Slowly the tension in CC's body eased and after a few seconds, Carissa returned the hug with all the strength she could muster. They stayed locked together for a few moments before releasing each other. Tears ran down both of their faces. Marissa got up and pulled her chair around next to her sister. After sitting down again, she took her hands in hers. This time she didn't pull away.

Marissa said, "I was so worried I'd lost you forever to a world of drugs and crime. But sitting here with you, looking into your eyes and holding your hands, I feel like I have you back in my life. I'm so grateful for that."

"Oh, Marissa, there's so much I'm just beginning to understand about myself and my actions. I was desperate to carve out my own life after years of constantly being mistaken for you and compared to you. I thought my relationship with Hadid would provide me with a way to build my own business. Where else would I ever have access to that kind of money? I'm talking about lots of money. I'd already managed to save nearly fifty thousand dollars to open up my own business and Hadid promised to loan me the rest. All I had to do was pledge my loyalty to him." She sighed and looked down at her hands and her short, clean fingernails. "Now I know why he was promising financial security and providing me with an endless supply of drugs. The money and drugs were used to turn me against you. Hadid convinced me you were holding me back on purpose. He said you wanted to control me so that you'd always have someone who stroked your ego. Slowly, I found myself believing him and doubting myself. He often lavished me with luxuries—the clothes, the travel, the whole lifestyle. He'd say things like, 'Your sister will never share her career successes with you. Not like I will.' I began to believe I was a failure if I remained close to you…and an even bigger failure if I didn't pledge my loyalty to him."

Carissa paused and looked out the window and off in the distance before continuing, "Numerous times I'd seen him getting angry at other people. Some simple act would push him over the edge. Then he began directing his anger at me anytime you were mentioned. It wasn't until I learned more about his 'business' operations that I figured out how he and his brother were dealing in stolen goods. The nightclubs were a front for money laundering. Just when I figured out was going on, he started making sure I had all the drugs I wanted. Pot, cocaine and Ecstasy in exchange for keeping quiet. Although it was more like being kept sedated. Then, when you and that camera guy showed up at the pet store and interrupted his plans to steal all those expensive birds, he came unhinged. He was ready to take you out. By that time, I didn't care what happened to you. I hate to admit it, but I was convinced that my world would be better without you in it.

Marissa gasped in horror at her sister's words. Her only surviving flesh and blood was admitting that she wished she wasn't alive! "But CC, after losing Mami and Papi it was just us. After all we've survived together, didn't that mean anything to you?"

"I told you he brainwashed me and made me believe you had no interest in my wellbeing. I didn't have any reason to care about you anymore. In fact, I hated you and how self-absorbed you'd become with your career. All the talk of pursuing a network anchor job just convinced me you were too busy worrying about yourself to give a damn about anybody else. As far as I could tell, there was no room in your world for me. I guess my survival instincts kicked in and I was willing to do whatever I needed to do to save myself, even if that meant giving you up." She sunk back into her chair having unloaded all her darkest thoughts and feelings. "Just before that night when you slipped into the club, I found out about the link between Hadid's father and ours. How Papi's job as a night watchman led to the arrest of Hadid's dad and to the undoing of his criminal empire. Taking you down was going to be the last act of revenge to vindicate the death of his father and what he said was the slow loss of his mother's sanity. In a way…I guess Hadid and I were both orphans."

There was an awkward silence between them before she continued, "Do you remember that hysterical phone call I made earlier that day before you came down to the club?"

Marissa nodded. "I knew you were in serious trouble and that you needed my help, but I didn't know where you were. Then suddenly your voice changed and I could only guess that your tormentor had walked into the room. CC, is that what happened?"

She looked up at Marissa. "That's exactly what happened. I had no choice but to pretend I was talking to a stranger, like a food delivery person. Anything not to let on that I'd been trying to call you to come help me. He would have beaten me to death and that's no exaggeration." CC shrugged. "Looking back, I realize death was the escape I was seeking. When Hadid walked back into the room, he was still high and emotionally unstable and angry. Very angry. He started all over again, convincing me that no one cared about me, telling me I was worthless and that he offered the only real life worth living." Her voice got quiet and Marissa could tell she was still coming to grips about the psychological control he held over her. "I didn't want to believe him, but sometimes he'd tell me I was beautiful and smart and that made it easier to swallow his lies…and his drugs. When you came into the club, I was so high I wasn't afraid to tell you that I didn't care about you. I'd come to believe it myself."

Marissa wasn't sure how to respond to her sister's confession. She'd had no idea CC had been living under the control of a monster who used her for his own evil purposes. "Carissa, I wasn't sure about coming to see you since I had no way of knowing what you were thinking or feeling. Now I'm glad to be here and to listen to what you've shared with me." Marissa hugged her again and softly kissed her cheek. "I still have a lot of questions about what was happening in your life over those few months, but we don't have to go over everything during this visit. We have the rest of our lives to make amends for the past and to build a stronger, more secure relationship for both of us. I promise you, I'm here for you and nothing, absolutely nothing, is more important to me than you."

The rest of their visit was quiet with neither of them revealing much more about their past or current feelings. Their limited time came to a close with Marissa promising CC that she'd be there for her when she was released from rehabilitation and allowed to return to Austin. She asked her if she'd consider staying with her when she did and she said she'd think about it. Of course, neither of them knew with any certainty about the legal hurdles CC still had to face, but Marissa let her know she'd be by her side every step of the way. They hugged goodbye. It was tough to say *adios*, but the twins finally ended their visit with Marissa saying, "We'll talk soon, and remember, no matter the miles between us, *estas en mi corazon siempre*. You're always in my heart."

◇◇◇

Marissa is waiting for final word of when CC will be returning to Austin. She's grateful that the media's interest in Carissa's case has dwindled. However, she is bracing herself for another round of media questions when the Nassine brothers finally go to trial. According to Tío Hector, it could be at least a year before the district attorney's office is ready to proceed with the case because of the complexity of the charges and the multiple jurisdictions involved. The district attorney is now working with the FBI and the DEA. In the meantime, Tío Hector has maintained his distance from the investigation because of his relationship with Carissa. It's the only way to prevent any accusations of improper conduct on the part of police investigators. Only as a professional courtesy is he briefed on the progress of the case against the Nassines.

Removing herself from covering the criminal proceedings involving the Nassines was difficult for Marissa. The undercover video she and Ken managed to capture left her feeling emotionally raw. Also, it's very likely she'll be called as a witness to testify against the brothers. As rewarding as it was to help snag those two evil men, she knows she should distance herself from what goes on in court. She also knows it will be impossible for her not to let her emotions get the best of her.

She is still anxious to talk to CC about what happened to her in the parking lot that day. During their short visit, she didn't get a chance to tell her about the video of her being slapped by Hadid.

Hadid and Nassour are also being questioned about the disappearance of fellow nightclub owner, Enrique Sanchez. And if murder and kidnapping were not serious enough, the two ruthless men face charges of failing to pay thousands of dollars in taxes related to the operation of their many businesses. Before the start of one of their initial court hearings, about fifty former employees gathered outside the courthouse to let prosecutors and the public know they hadn't been paid for at least six weeks before all of the clubs were raided.

While Marissa is no longer covering the proceedings, she's been following them closely. She wants to see both men serve long sentences for the crimes they committed, especially for the corruption of her sister. Beyond all their recent criminal actions, she must accept the fact the two brothers won't face any charges in connection with the murder of her parents. Unfortunately, there's no concrete evidence connecting them to the brutal crime. The two were merely children themselves at the time her parents were killed.

She has since talked to the University of Texas Professor who reiterated what Hadid had confessed. He explained the slaying of her parents was in retaliation for the downfall and subsequent death of Nassine's father. The professor said that in some cultures, such acts are justified when committed to protect the honor of a respected elder. Marissa could never condone this eye for an eye belief, although she admits to herself that the death of her parents and the abuse of her sister sometime leaves her wishing for lethal revenge of her own. Fortunately, such negative thoughts vanish almost as quickly as they appear. It's impossible to stay angry or resentful now that she is surrounded by good, hardworking, positive people. Dwelling on the negative is such a waste of time.

Of course, the occasional happy hour with friends also provides an opportunity to let off some steam. Having a good-looking, smart, extremely talented and sexy boyfriend is also another bonus in her life. Through all this turmoil, Ken has been a steady presence. He completely supported her decision to walk away from the station. Marissa and Ken agreed it'd be impossible to hold management to any of her recommended changes if they refused to put them in writing.

While Ken appreciated her insistence that he be allowed to return to KATX, he let her know it wasn't part of his future career goals.

Instead, he shared with her his plan for establishing a video service that specializes in offering hard-to-get news video, like the undercover footage they captured with a hidden camera. News outlets can't afford the liability of hiring such daring photographers, but all the stations are anxious to get their hands on it. Which is why streaming dramatic video online is a win-win for the news stations and for Ken! He's already provided a video revealing state workers encouraging disabled students to fight with each other. A relative of one of the students took him into the state facility to see the bloody fights for himself. Ken also took his camera undercover as he joined the ranks of underpaid kitchen workers at a four-star restaurant. He revealed how cheap ingredients were being used instead of expensive ones to feed wealthy patrons. His ideas for other undercover opportunities never ceases to impress Marissa, not only because they're a unique look into otherwise off-limits situations, but because the incidents are of interest to the public.

It's the same sense of accomplishment they first shared back in November when they were celebrating the news that the Regency Dance Studio was dropping its lawsuit and closing its doors.

Marissa had just walked away from her job and Ken was just beginning to set up his freelance operation. They decided to move in together to save money and to collaborate on ideas. They didn't need much of anything else. They managed to live on love and cheap tequila with just a slice of Serrano pepper to add a little kick. Ken encouraged her to fly to Miami to meet with Marcus Feldman and to see exactly what AAN was willing to offer. She remembers calling Ken from the hotel to let him know that the contract was for a full-time anchor position for the network's Spanish language newscast with the opportunity to advance to AAN primetime. It was a fantastic opportunity that more than tripled her previous salary.

Then, just as she was about to accept the AAN offer, she heard about the major housecleaning effort underway at KATX. The new general manager called her to request a private meeting to discuss his plans for the station's future. Their meeting took place in late December. He offered her the main anchor position at six and ten p.m. with the ability to work on investigative pieces at least once a month. All the caveats were in writing, but the best part was the provision allowing her to work with the photographer of her choice. And, that included her choice of a freelance photographer not employed by the station. Ken's newest video will air in tonight's ten o'clock newscast. It shows women using life-sized dummies to fool state authorities into thinking teenagers are being cared for in the group home they operate. There's video of one dummy resting on a futon. One is seated at the kitchen table during mealtime and a third dummy is sitting on a couch watching TV. As a freelance photojournalist, Ken is free to work on the projects of his choice with whomever he chooses—including Marissa.

Partners. Working together side-by side. Making decisions together. Collaborating on meaningful news. It's a rewarding and very rare arrangement that allows Ken and Marissa to enjoy their professional, as well as personal lives.

Marissa feels that returning to KATX is the best decision she's ever made. Mario's addition to the anchor line up is another bonus for her, as well as for the viewers. Together, they are the first male/female Hispanic duo to anchor the main evening newscasts in Austin. It's more than on-air history being made. To her, it's a personal victory that she knows her parents would be so proud of.

Suddenly, her quiet time reflecting on the last three months of her life comes to an abrupt end as the lights of the news studio are turned on and the crew members file in to take their positions behind the cameras. "Hey, Marissa. If you're ready, the director wants to shoot tonight's promos before we all take a dinner break. Is that, okay?" the floor crew leader asks.

"Not a problem. I've updated the script and I'm ready to go. Just give me my cue." Marissa is smiling with genuine enthusiasm. She is doing what she loves best. She is making sure viewers are getting the latest facts in a brief, informative way that's both entertaining and easy-to-understand. No sensationalism. No hype. It's what viewers have come to expect and it's what she plans to deliver from now on.

"Okay, Marissa. Here we go in 3-2-1…"

"Hi, everyone. I'm Marissa Cavelo. Here's what's coming up tonight at ten…"

The End

About the Author

Olga Campos Benz is one of the most honored anchor/reporters ever to grace the Texas airwaves. A University of Texas graduate, Olga spent more than 30 years covering the biggest news stories in Houston, Corpus Christi and Austin, Texas. Following her retirement as a broadcast journalist in 2010, Olga enjoyed a smooth transition into an arena she knows well thanks to her active role as a volunteer and community supporter. She serves on several non-profit boards including The Health Alliance for Austin Musicians (HAAM), the Joe and Teresa Long Center for the Performing Arts, the Austin Film Festival, the Writers' League of Texas and as an Advisory Council member of the University of Texas' Division of Diversity and Community Engagement. In 2013, the Austin Business Journal named her among the "Profiles in Power: Women of Influence." She is a 2014 inductee into the City of Austin Commission for Women Hall of Fame and the 2015 Distinguished Alum of the Greater Austin Hispanic Chamber of Commerce Hispanic Austin Leadership Program. She and her husband, Kevin Benz, live in Austin and have twin daughters, Corazon and Allegra.

48765356R00192

Made in the USA
San Bernardino, CA
04 May 2017